W9-AZZ-876

THE NAKED HEART

by Jacqueline Briskin

THE NAKED HEART

DREAMS ARE NOT ENOUGH

TOO MUCH TOO SOON

EVERYTHING AND MORE

THE ONYX

PALOVERDE

RICH FRIENDS

AFTERLOVE

CALIFORNIA GENERATION

JACQUELINE BRISKIN

THE
NAKED
HEART

**Delacorte
Press**

Published by
Delacorte Press
Bantam Doubleday Dell Publishing Group, Inc.
666 Fifth Avenue
New York, New York 10103

Library of Congress Cataloging in Publication Data
Briskin, Jacqueline.
   The naked heart: a novel/by Jacqueline Briskin.
      p.   cm.
   ISBN 0-385-29707-6
   I. Title.
PS3552.R49N35   1989
813'.54—dc19   88-29937
                                                                          CIP

Manufactured in the United States of America
Published simultaneously in Canada

May 1989

10 9 8 7 6 5 4 3 2 1

BG

This is for Bert
and
for Katie

Then the gallant knight, Guy de Permont, after four long years battling to free the Holy Sepulchre from the infidel Moor, returned home. He learned that his cousin, Arnaud, into whose care the baron had entrusted family and lands, had taken the fiefdom unto himself, thrusting Sir Guy's wife and young son into a far and desolate valley. Ere long the gentle lady had laid down and breathed her last. But the child had survived in the way of an animal, eating the berries and fresh carrion that he found on his lonely way. Baron Guy hearing this tale grew full wrathful, swearing that the vast wrong could not be repaid by Arnaud's death alone. And he joined with his son in a mighty oath to make the dishonorable Arnaud suffer as they had, down all his generations. And thus it was that Arnaud's branch became lowly as the basest born serf while unto this day Guy de Permont and his seed flourish.

From the *récits* of Godefroy d'Angers (1290–1338)

THE
NAKED
HEART

1

That afternoon in October of 1941 when Gilberte de Permont made the mistake of introducing her second cousin, Quent Dejong, to her friend, Ann Blakely, a cold rain punished Paris.

Not that the city needed additional punishment. For more than a year now, since red-and-black swastika flags had been fluttering across the northern half of France, Parisians had subsisted on tight rations of unpalatable food—some called it "the time of the rutabaga." They lacked coal for heat and gas for cooking. They were trussed by innumerable regulations. They were taxed to support the two million French prisoners of war behind barbed wire in the Third Reich, they were taxed to support their conquerors, they were taxed unendurably. The Gestapo cast its net of terror. To add to the general misery, this premature autumnal chill promised a repeat of the previous year's freezing weather—the first winter of the Occupation had been the bitterest Paris had seen in over a century.

The rain had stripped the horse chestnut trees that arched across the rue Daguerre and without the softening foliage, the drab apartment buildings appeared exactly what they were, warrens for petty civil servants, frugal merchants, teachers, unsuccessful *avocats* and doctors. Paper tape was prudently crisscrossed over windows to prevent the glass from being shattered by reverberations from possible future RAF bombing raids. The black-bordered red poster that listed names of hostages executed by military order wept pink-and-gray dye stains down a brown stucco wall. A rain-slick sign on the back of a bench forbade Jews to sit.

Gilberte de Permont, being six inches taller than Ann Blakely, held the large umbrella that protected them from the light but persistent rain. As the two girls wearing lumpy school overcoats and thick black lisle stockings circled a heap of sodden leaves, they appeared to conform to the rue Daguerre's general gloom.

Then Ann laughed. A soft, delightful sound that brightened the morose afternoon. Darting ahead in the drizzle, she skipped along backward, her small feet moving confidently as a dancer's—obviously she had no fear of tripping on her derriere.

Ann, at seventeen, was not beautiful, and some might not even see her as pretty—her high, rounded forehead was not balanced by the delicacy of her chin. She was too thin from the wartime shortages, yet nevertheless an aura of vitality surrounded her and she was charming with her cold-stung red cheeks and the way her full, soft lips flattened over her white teeth in a smile that invited others to share her pleasure. Her eyes were by far her most memorable feature. Thick lashes several shades darker than her auburn hair shadowed the liquid purity of the huge brown eyes, which now showed a mischievously glittering wedge.

"But how do you know they all want that?" she demanded. "I mean, don't some men enjoy normal amatory diversions?"

"Normal?" retorted Gilberte de Permont. "Dear friend, must you always be so naive?"

"Since when has it been naive to challenge the famed de Permont knowledge of the masculine sex?"

"Need I remind you," Gilberte drawled, "that you were in darkest ignorance until I explained the physiology of the male organ."

Ann's face turned the same crimson as her cheeks. Her easy blushes irritated her and she flicked droplets of rain from her shoulders, returning to the shelter of the umbrella. "I was fifteen then. Besides, since neither of us has gone all the way"—she switched to English for the phrase *all the way*—"how are you so positive that no man prefers the act right side up?"

"Who but an American would question *soixante-neuf*?"

"I was born in Paris!"

"Nevertheless you're a direct descendant of Puritans, whereas I, dear friend, am your polar opposite. . . ."

Ann laughed again, but this time with a note of disbelief. She still could not encompass the fact that friendship had bridged the vast chasm between them.

Gilberte, as her name indicated, might have stepped from the pages of Proust. Her family was listed in the Almanach du Gotha; Louise de Permont, one of Marie Antoinette's ladies-in-waiting and confidantes, had knelt at the guillotine a few days after her queen; and the tale of an early ancestor, Guy de Permont, had survived the centuries in a few lines by the medieval trouvère Godefroy d'Angers.

Gilberte was exquisite. She sleeked her shiny black hair back in a long mane to display the perfection of her profile. Her clear, pale topaz eyes were almond-shaped while her black brows tilted upward, a combination that gave her a hint of the exotic. Her luminous ivory skin was the envy of the *classe de première* at Cours Madame Bernard, where most of the girls were either afflicted with adolescent acne or suffered the gray pastiness that came from the Occupation's fat-free diet. Had a male, no matter his age, been on the rue Daguerre he would have turned to look at Gilberte. Not for the face. For the startling body. She was tall, a model's height, and even with the layers of drab clothes it was possible to make out the slender, sensual curves, the fine legs, the opulent, beautifully shaped breasts.

Her beauty and casually proud carriage proclaimed her no native of this enclave of petit bourgeois. And in fact she had lived here only a little over a year. When the de Permonts' four-story mansion on the boulevard Suchet was commandeered for General Count von Hocherer, the family had moved into the flat directly above the Blakelys': Gilberte, like Ann, had enrolled at Cours Madame Bernard, a ten-minute walk away. Her detached smile had not endeared her to either her classmates or her teachers, and neither had her advanced education nor her keen intellect, both of which she flaunted. Yet Ann noticed that her new friend's hands trembled after even minor encounters. It was apparent to Ann that Gilberte's air of sophistication was a cover-up. Why anyone so naturally superior should be vulnerable and lacking in confidence remained a mystery, but Ann, bound by her own characteristic of fierce loyalty, drew away from her erstwhile companions because Gilberte needed protection.

Most of the young men were either shut away in prisoner-of-war camps or doing forced labor in Germany, but occasionally the girls were invited to the cinema by Pierre Dalmais and Charles Main-froy, friends of Ann's who, being only seventeen, attended Lycée Paul Bert. Gilberte spoke in the knowing innuendos of a demimondaine, but she never permitted Charles's ardent fingers to creep on her full, firm breasts, never even granted him a kiss. Ann, filled with inchoate sexual yearnings, sometimes got carried away as she sat with Pierre in the last row of the darkened theater—once during a Jean Marais film she had actually allowed him to clasp her hand on his woolen short trousers so that she could feel the hardness and heat of his erection. She liked Pierre, she pitied him his heavy glasses, but where was love? She had jerked away her hand. The betrayal of her hormones had disturbed her deeply.

"What have you been reading, anyway?" she asked. "Krafft-Ebing?"

Gilberte stepped over a gutter. Her knowing expression faltered, and she looked far younger. "I overheard Madame de Lavadière and Maman."

"Your *mother* was talking about it?" Startled, Ann splashed her shoe in the running gray water. She could not imagine the Baronne de Permont, armored in her invincible chic, considering a variation so messy, much less talking about it.

Gilberte stepped as far away as she could while keeping them both sheltered. Her narrow, lovely lips were pressed tightly together, as if she were suffering some deep internal pain. Ann regretted her blurted remark. Another mystery about Gilberte was the hurt manner with which she shied away from discussing either her parents or the time when she had dwelt in the patrician *seizième arrondissement*.

They crossed the street and Gilberte moved closer again.

"Maman was discussing the supposed preferences of a connection of ours," she said. "Harrison Dejong."

"Harrison Dejong? What kind of French name is that?"

"He's American."

"You have family in America?" Ann could not prevent her voice from rising in a hurt wail. How could Gilberte, her closest friend to whom she told all (even the highly embarrassing Pierre incident) have withheld this?

"Papa's late Tante Mathilde married across the Atlantic and had a daughter whom Harrison married. He's the same age as Papa, but since *cousine* Jessamyn died, he's kept marrying younger and younger girls."

"How many wives has he had?"

"Twenty—or is it thirty?"

Laughing, Ann said, "Gilberte."

"Four actually. The rest were flings."

"He must have hundreds of children."

"A mere three."

"Legitimate?"

"Nothing else counts," Gilberte said, her slim hand tensing on the umbrella handle.

"Male or female?"

"Two little girls, and a son, Quent. He's the oldest, from the first wife, which makes him my second cousin. Twenty-three. Tall, dark and handsome."

"You sound smitten."

"I haven't laid eyes on him since I was fourteen."

"The exact age Juliet fell in love."

"Yes, and recall what happened to her."

"Is he married?"

"No, but he's catching up with his father in the other department. Besides deflowering the obligatory virgins and debutantes, there was talk of him and Lana Turner."

"Lana Turner!"

"Or was it Betty Grable? Or both?"

Ann's expression was dreamy. In a world where the male sex was limited to spotty boys like Pierre or careworn, middle-aged men like her father, the glamorous exploits of Gilberte's second cousin lit flares along her broad streak of romanticism. "What does he do in his spare time?"

"Climbs mountains. Oh, and I believe that since finishing university he's connected to the family bank."

They had reached number 74, their building. Horizontal rows of dun-colored stone alternated with a particularly bloodlike shade of bricks in a manner that some turn-of-the-century builder had considered artistic.

The murky vestibule with its chipped gray, brown and white tiles was dankly cold. The combined coal ration of the tenants was scarcely enough to permit the big basement furnace to be lit on weekends.

As their wartime wooden soles clacked across the tile, Gilberte said, "Come on up."

"Are you sure I won't be in the way?" Ann asked. "It's your turn."

This was Thursday. The de Permonts dined *chez* the Blakelys on Tuesdays, the Blakelys went upstairs to the de Permonts' on Thursdays: the scarcity of gas made collective cooking a necessity. On her days, Dorothy Blakely rose early to concoct dishes from the meager available food and to arrange her late mother-in-law's silver and china on the good cutwork cloth, hiding its darn with a bowl of wax fruit. And during the shared meals, Horace went so far as to whip his worn leather notebook from his vest pocket and pencil down the title of a book, the name of a wine, a historical fact that the baron had let drop. Ann, red-faced at this overt deference, would wonder what the baron and baronne thought of these twice-weekly occasions. She never found out. The baronne always smiled her delightful, faintly malicious smile while the urbane and ugly baron appeared to enjoy himself tremendously. Maybe the Blakely ménage amused them both in much the same way as cavorting pet dwarfs had amused their ancestors.

"Are you fishing for another invitation? You know I don't have anything to do with the preparations," Gilberte said.

"I'll be there as soon as I can get away, then."

Her mother must have been watching out the window. As Ann unlocked the door, Dorothy was waiting in the dim hall of their flat.

"Do take off those wet things, dear," she fussed. "Here, put this on."

She reached to the coatrack for a sweater that she had knitted from brown *fibranne,* the wartime substitute for wool: lacking ration coupons for the full number of skeins, she had unraveled an old maroon muffler to complete the sleeves. Ann, who had an eye for style lacking in her mother, cringed at the garment's ugliness.

Taking off her damp coat, she hung it up. "I'm already so bundled up I can't move."

"We can't have you catching a chill."

Dorothy fretted continuously about the family's health. With good reason. Last winter she herself had come down with a sniffly sore throat that inadequate nutrition, icy rooms and endless queuing in rain and snow had transformed into pneumonia. She had been ill for two months, and during that bitterly cold time had lost twenty pounds as well as that attractive forcefulness which Ann thought of as a peculiarly American quality. Dorothy's stockings were the heavy ribbed kind that farmwives wore and her ancient Persian lamb coat was buttoned to its age-flattened collar. Because they were going to the de Permonts', she had applied lipstick and rouge, thus emphasizing the pallor and dryness of her skin.

She looked so ill and anxious that Ann gave her a bear hug. "You know me, Mother. The original Eskimo. Hot-blooded in all kinds of weather." She spoke in English.

Dorothy smiled at the embrace, then pulled away, the lines between her eyes deepening. "Ann, how many times do I have to tell you? Speak French. Only French."

Before the Occupation, Dorothy and Horace had used their native tongue while Ann had slipped as easily as a dolphin between the two languages. The new laws, however, made it an offense to speak English in public. Dorothy and Horace, overcompensating for their neutral status by adhering rigorously to every regulation, now used French even under the feather coverlet of their sagging double bed.

Ann raised a hand to her eyebrows, peering comically into the tenebrous shadows, saying in French, "Not a *flic* in sight, Mother. You're quite safe." She hugged her mother again, feeling the unfamiliar boniness. "I'm on my way up to Gilberte's."

"But dear, we're going to dinner. You'll wear out your welcome."

"Gilberte's helping me with my Cicero." Ann could feel the heat in her face. She had difficulty with the whitest lie, which this was. Studying never made the agenda on the afternoons that she and Gilberte spent together.

"You never visit your old friends anymore."

"I see them at Madame Bernard's," Ann mumbled. Even though this wasn't a lie, it was sophistry. True, she saw Jeanne, Marthe, Lucie and Emma sitting at their scarred desks, but because of Gilberte's fragility, this was the extent of the contact.

"I must admit I feel safer having you in the building," Dorothy said. "What with those awful cordons."

The SS would barricade several blocks to examine the papers of everyone trapped on the streets—the Parisians called it a barrage. Generally such inspections took place in the Jewish quarter, the Marais. Ann shivered, remembering the time she had been caught in a cordon after visiting Lea Blum. (Lea, with her sparkly green-blue eyes and quick sense of humor, had been Ann's friend before

the conqueror's racial laws had barred Jewish children from attending any but Jewish schools.) Ann had naturally kept these visits
from her worry-prone parents, so her fear as she had waited under
the leveled machine guns of expressionless, black-uniformed men
had been exacerbated by filial guilt: the entire hour she had felt a
degrading urge to urinate. As soon as she had showed her American passport, she had been released. On her next sub rosa visit, the
Blums' door had been answered by an elderly stranger. "Madame
and Monsieur Blum are *métèques,* they weren't born in France,"
explained the old lady. "Refugees like them are being resettled in
the east." Ann's legs had trembled. She had often heard that
phrase, *resettled in the east,* and now was wondering if it was yet
another of the euphemisms that the conquerors doted on. Did
resettlement mean witty Lea was now in a concentration camp?

"You look quite pinched, dear," Dorothy said. "I'll heat you
coffee, and there's some bread."

Ann suspected Dorothy saved her own rations to feed her as
snacks. "No thanks, Mother. If I eat now I won't have any appetite
for dinner."

"Well, put this on." Dorothy draped the cardigan over her
daughter's slender shoulders. "And change your shoes."

In her room, Ann put on dry shoes and stockings, combed her
auburn hair, which the rain had turned into an annoyingly irrepressible mass of curls, then eyed the sweater. Her mother would
be upset to find the hideous thing here, so she picked it up.

Though Ann chafed under the only child's burden of parental
solicitude, she had become protective of Horace and Dorothy.

Since the Occupation, they faded and dwindled each time they
left this flat until it was only their shadows, gray and timid, that
ventured onto the street. Ann's throat ached when she heard her
mother's incisive voice lowered deferentially to the shopkeepers,
she wanted to weep each time she watched her father dash off to
work an hour early because he feared the boulevard Raspail métro
would be yet more jammed than usual and he might be unable to
crowd into a train—as if kindly Dr. Descourset would fire him for
being late!

Poor Mother, she thought, picking up the sweater. *Poor Daddy.*

* * *

Horace Blakely and Dorothy Strahearn both came from Madison, Wisconsin, but did not become "interested" until they entered the University of Wisconsin, whose rolling campus dominated the small city. Then Dorothy noticed that Horace had large, poetic brown eyes. He, in turn, saw the way that her smile lit up her rather fleshy face.

Both were virgins. They kissed endlessly in his old Model T, but never undid any buttons. He would press his face between her generous breasts, she would caress the tendons in back of his neck. During these petting sessions their blood would spin and afterward both felt a primal discontent. During the courtship, each became aware of the other's faults. Because love was involved, however, neither was disillusioned. Horace realized that Dorothy liked calling the shots—which was fine with him. He was a natural follower, and besides, his widowed mother also had a take-charge manner. Dorothy understood that Horace's boastfulness was harmless. He was studying architecture and so it was natural that he would claim acquaintanceship with Frank Lloyd Wright and make numerous pilgrimages to the great architect's home, Taliesin, parking on the country road in the hope of glimpsing the great man. Horace, dear, noncompetitive Horace, needed heroes.

One humid June afternoon in his senior year, the local police, having been informed that an old Model T was often seen below the hilltop estate, took him in for questioning. He was so rattled that he blurted out every minor sin he'd ever committed, including those petting bouts with Dorothy. The *Wisconsin State Journal* reported the incident under the headline U OF W MASHER STALKS WRIGHT. The laughter on campus and in town lasted only a few days, but Horace viewed himself as an object of perpetual scorn. His desire to become an architect dwindled, and only Dorothy's firmest tones prevented him from quitting the university.

A few weeks later, when his mother died suddenly from a cerebral hemorrhage, he blamed it on the shock of his false arrest—and himself. Dorothy came to the brick house on State Street and, forgetting proprieties, comforted him in the age-old way. Taking into account mutual inexperience, the act was more successful than it might have been.

They were married before the will was read. Mrs. Blakely had been far better fixed than her son had suspected. He had inherited $15,357 as well as the house, which, being an easy walk from the domed state capitol building, would fetch a good price, maybe as high as $5,000. Horace, aching to leave the scene of his humiliation, approached the subject that same night.

"What I really want to do is write a novel," he said as he and his bride lay in postcoital contentment. "A true, honest book like *Main Street.*"

"A lot of authors do well," replied Dorothy, who always looked at the practical side.

"What do you think . . . of Paris?"

Dorothy, filled with pity for his new reclusiveness, sharing in the general belief that anyone, given the time, can write and sell a novel, replied, "Dearest, what a wonderful idea! The franc's down to almost nothing. We could live on very little while you get established."

They settled in Montparnasse. Though the rue Daguerre was more middle-class than State Street, many American writers lived in the area. Horace sipped a glass of wine at Closérie des Lilas and at the Dôme, but could think of no way to strike up a conversation with that fat woman from San Francisco, Gertrude Stein, or that stuck-up young nobody, Ernest Hemingway. After a few visits, he told himself that he ought to be at home with Dorothy, who was expecting.

Ann was born after a long, dicey labor: kissing his exhausted wife, Horace vowed *Never again,* and rushed off to register his daughter with the American embassy on the place de la Concorde. She was a lively, healthy baby, but her doting parents brooded over her least cough. They attempted without success to curb her courage and small explorations, her impulsive nature.

Due to Dorothy's frugal housekeeping and the continuing favorable rate of exchange, Horace's inheritance dwindled slowly, but by 1930, when they had tacitly agreed that with two novels rejected by the entire publishing community he would never earn a living as a writer, their bank account was below five hundred dollars. The Great Depression whistled bleakly through the United States and finding a job back home was an impossibility for a man without qualifications, and he shrank from returning to Madison. But how could they stay in Paris?

Typically, it was Dorothy who solved their dilemma. While consulting with Dr. Descourset about a minor vaginal infection, she was told that the previous day his bookkeeper, who also had charge of the ten-bed private clinic, had absconded with the funds. "Doctor," she said, "my husband has decided to give up writing. He's highly trustworthy, a fine administrator and an excellent accountant."

The doctor stroked his graying beard, agreeing to interview this gem.

When she broke the news to Horace at lunch, he dropped his fork in his omelette. "Dorothy, I've never opened a ledger in my life."

"I'll teach you," she said firmly. Back at the University of Wisconsin, she had taken two accounting courses.

That evening, Dr. Descourset gave Horace the job.

Busy with their lives, the Blakelys paid little mind to the lengthening shadow cast by the Third Reich. In 1938, during the Munich crises, their friends from the American Church on the Quai d'Orsay were all booking passage home. But with a third of a nation still out of work, and the Madison laughter still ringing in Horace's mind, the Blakelys numbed their ears to talk of war. It wasn't until September 1, 1939—the day the blitzkrieg against Poland touched off the powder keg of Western Europe—that Horace began bombarding possible employers with resumés. One of the few replies came from a small cheese factory near Milwaukee: *Haven't you folks in gay Paree heard of the Depression. There are no jobs here. None.* Horace attributed the snide tone to knowledge of that yellowing newspaper clipping.

When Wehrmacht divisions goose-stepped down the Champs-Elysées, the Blakelys staunchly informed each other that they were neutrals and in no danger. Dorothy waited in the endless lines and coped with ration cards and increasing shortages, Horace stayed late to grapple with the snarl of bookwork surrounding the new tax regulations. But they were in no danger, no danger whatsoever.

Neither parent had ever hinted to Ann of the financial and psychological concerns that tied them to Paris. She understood without being told and without passing judgment. She herself couldn't decide whether she belonged in that mythic place "home," which she had never seen, or here in Paris. Suspended between two allegiances, she worried whether departing France in its evil hour would constitute an act of disloyalty. Gilberte listened to her ramblings sympathetically.

3

The de Permonts lived on the third, the top floor. Reverberations from a Luftwaffe raid had shattered several panes in the skylight, and the glass had been replaced with plyboard. Climbing the tiled staircase, Ann could hear the rain, coming down vehemently now, pelting against glass and wood like riffs on different drumheads.

Jacques, the baron's man, answered the door. Seeing Ann, his left eyelid drooped and his nostrils flared as if she represented every one of the bourgeois denizens of the rue Daguerre. "Mademoiselle de Permont is expecting you, Mademoiselle," he said. "In the drawing room."

Usually the girls sat in each other's bedrooms for privacy. Sometimes they would discuss men and the mysteries of sex. Sometimes they played Design, a game they both enjoyed with a certain amount of embarrassment because of its resemblance to paper dolls. Ann would sketch an outfit, then Gilberte, with her *seizième arrondissement* knowledge of haute couture, would take a pencil and slash at frills or a false line. Ann would modify, and eventually they would both end up with a complete wardrobe—Design helped mitigate the absence of actual pretty clothes.

"She's in the drawing room?" Ann echoed.

He draped the *fibranne* sweater gingerly over his arm. "If you will be so good as to come this way, Mademoiselle."

She followed him around the eighteenth-century table inlaid with Sèvres porcelain. This flat, directly above hers, was identical. Yet what seemed spacious for the Blakely family appeared excessively inadequate for the de Permont ménage. This was in part due to the scale of the furniture. Horace and Dorothy had purchased highly varnished suites mass-produced for homes like their own, while the de Permonts' eighteenth-century pieces had once graced the rooms and antechambers of a château in Ile de France, then the mansion on the boulevard Suchet. When the baronne had commissioned Hector Guimard to make art nouveau furnishings for the Paris house, the displaced pieces had been stored in the basements. In 1940, when the German military administration had "leased" the property and everything on it, including the baron's crimson Bugatti, the baronne's Daimler, the dust-thick wine bottles in the cellar, the chef and other servants, General von Hocherer, a pewter-haired Prussian aristocrat, had invited the baron to take whatever his family would require in their exile, including Jacques and the baronne's personal maid, Hélène.

Jacques tapped on the living room door, then opened it.

Ann halted on the threshold, a shock traveling through her as if she had accidentally brushed against a live wire.

Gilberte had two men with her.

But Gilberte never had guests! It was invariably Ann who made the introductions, and when Gilberte hid her shyness under proud irony, Ann grew yet more protective.

The rain had drowned out Jacques's discreet knock and her entry. The threesome didn't look up. They sat in front of the *faux* fireplace where glowing artificial logs squandered the household's electricity ration. Gilberte, cigarette extended in a long onyx holder, had her head thrown back as she exhaled blue wisps of smoke through her narrow nostrils. She'd found time to change to a dress Ann had never seen. Crimson jersey clung lightly to her slender curves and voluptuous breasts, crisp white cuffs and collar drew attention to her long, graceful neck and her narrow wrists. *Probably one of the baronne's Chanels,* Ann thought: through Gilberte's tutoring in the Design game she had learned the signature styles of renowned couturiers. Smoothing the damp, heavy wool of her old navy skirt, part of Madame Bernard's uniform, she accepted that the pleats were hopelessly gone.

Though the two visitors faced away from her, she immediately recognized them as American. Their easy, lounging posture with long legs stretched out and their close-cut hair cried out "made in the U.S.A."

As Jacques clicked the door shut, Gilberte looked up. For the briefest instant the clear topaz eyes measured Ann, then she smiled. "Oh, here you are," she said.

The men, turning, rose quickly to their feet.

Both were in their early twenties, both were attractive, yet Ann's first confused thought was: *Complete opposites.*

The dark-haired man was well over six feet and she could tell that the breadth of his shoulders was due only in part to the wide American padding in his finely tailored pin-striped suit. She got a quick impression of strength, command—and gravity.

The blond man was running a hand over his crew cut as he gave her an ingenuous grin. He was tallish, yet beside the solidity and height of his companion, he appeared short and boyishly slight.

"Ann, permit me to introduce Mr. Porter." Gilberte spoke English, her tone mocking her formality as she indicated the fair-haired man with her cigarette. "And Mr. Dejong. My friend, Miss Blakely."

Dejong?

Wasn't that the name Gilberte had used earlier, when she had tossed out the information that she had relations in the States? Ann inspected Mr. Dejong more carefully. Yes, his hair was the same true raven black as Gilberte's, and though the resemblance ceased there, he possessed the same look of good birth. Ann sometimes questioned whether this visibility of class was actual or a figment of her high-blown imagination, but whichever, this man had it. Narrow, high-bridged nose, deep-set eyes and a tan that was a rarity in this land of wintry defeat.

Then questions were jumbling in her mind. If Gilberte had at long last chosen to mention her American family's existence, why hadn't she also mentioned that her cousin—no, her second cousin —was in Paris? Had she known he would be visiting this afternoon?

If so, why hadn't she warned Ann to change to her good dress, rayon stockings and high-heeled pumps?

The questions faded. Mr. Dejong was staring steadily at her.

Flushing, she looked away.

The blond man was saying, "I'm Larry Porter. Call me Larry, okay?" His smile was warmly coercive.

"And I'm Ann."

"What a gaffe," Gilberte said. "I'd quite forgotten the American addiction to first names. Ann, this is my cousin, Quentin, Templar, Pierre, Dejong."

Larry whistled. "Hey, that's a list long enough for a prince of the blood."

"Quent," Quentin said, his gaze still fixed on Ann.

In the gray afternoon, his dark irises were indistinguishable from the pupils. She had never been examined in precisely this way, an assessment presumptive and intensely personal. Okay, so Quent Many-Names was rich and terrific-looking, and had picked his way through debutantes and movie stars. That gave him no right, none whatsoever, to stare at her as if he had *le droit du siegneur*. Then his unsmiling lips parted, as though he were recalling music heard long ago.

She drew a breath to regain her composure and crossed the lovely, faded garlands of the Aubusson rug to the warmth of the electric fire, sitting on the low velvet ottoman. The fake logs cast a rosy glow on her face.

The others sat, too, and there was a silence while rain gusted on the windows. Larry, appearing disturbed by the lack of conversation, leaned toward Ann, tapping a pack of Camels so that the tips poked out. "Smoke?" he offered.

"Thank you, but I don't," she said.

"What about some whiskey?" Gilberte indicated the silver tray set with a bottle of Black & White. "Quent brought us a rarity."

"No thanks," Ann said. From the corner of her eye she saw that Quent was still watching her: to cover her awkwardness, she did her imitation of Groucho Marx. Raising and lowering her eyebrows, she said, "And Mother thinks I'm translating Cicero!"

Larry laughed. "I sure wasn't expecting anyone like you," he said.

"What's Gilberte been telling you about me, anyway?"

"Not one word, I swear," Gilberte said. "They both believe you to be of high virtue and intact reputation."

Quent said, "You're American."

Normally Ann would have gone into the specifics, but his air of total assurance as well as that intense examination popped other words onto her tongue. "I was born in Paris."

"You speak English like an American," he said in French.

"And you speak like a Parisian," she retorted.

"I spent a lot of time with Grand-mère—my grandmother."

"My great-aunt Mathilde," Gilberte added.

"Ann seems authentically Gallic to me," Larry interjected. "But then I'm just a hick from Van Nuys."

"Van Nuys?" Gilberte asked. "Is that a place?"

"More a state of mind. It's in the boondocks of the San Fernando Valley—that's a sort of suburb of Los Angeles."

"Blakely's not a French name," Quent persisted.

"She *was* born here." Gilberte tapped her cigarette holder lightly against her teeth. "And she *is* American." The slight wryness smoothly informed her guests that this conversation had gone beyond the usual male-female sparring badinage.

"Daddy registered me at the embassy," Ann said quietly. "An hour after I made my appearance."

Quent did not take Gilberte's hint, but pressed on. "What're your parents doing here?"

"Breathing, eating, the normal things."

He shook his head slightly, as if shrugging away her rebuttal without rancor. "The Americans are nearly all gone."

"France is our home. My father runs a hospital."

"There's a war on—"

"Quent," Gilberte interrupted, smiling. "Don't you think you've delved into Ann's nationality enough? She sings the 'Marseillaise' three times daily, her name is loyalty."

"But we're about to get into this mess," Quent said.

"Are you a military expert, Quent, as well as a banker?" Gilberte, continuing to protect Ann, took on a yet more challenging insolence.

"Anyway, what's the big deal about being in Paris?" Ann asked. "You and Larry are."

"We're living dangerously," Larry said. "Quent's over for some fiduciary hanky-panky at the Dejong Bank's Paris branch. Me, I'm a dashing foreign correspondent."

Eager to veer the conversation from herself and her family, Ann asked, "Then where's your trench coat?"

"The *Los Angeles Sentinel* has seventy thousand and thirteen readers. With circulation like that, Ann, you can't expect them to come up with the dough for luxuries."

Ann clasped her hands around her knees. "What kind of stories do you send home?"

"Heavily censored ones," Larry said. "Every word goes through Berlin. And we haven't been allowed out of Paris for weeks."

"What do you do, then?"

"Shoot the breeze with the genu-wine trench coats. We Americans are cooped up in a fleabag near the Champs-Elysées, the Hotel Pyramide. Sour wine, no women, no song. Since my buddy Quent checked in, my social horizons have expanded considerably." He grinned at the girls.

Gilberte stubbed out her cigarette, removing the butt from the holder. "You can't know what heaven American cigarettes are."

Quent took out a pack of Tareytons, tossing it to her.

"A million thanks." Gilberte smiled. "Ann, before you interrupted, Quent was ready to impart top secret information about the recent events at Gare de l'Est."

Three days earlier, on Monday, a stretch of tracks in the massive trainyard outside the Gare de l'Est had been dynamited into tangled twists of metal. Windows and dishes in nearby houses had shattered. Black smoke had billowed into the rainy sky, a beacon for every Parisian to see. It was the lunch hour, so the linemen were home eating. The sole fatality was an elderly French guard. Had the explosion occurred five minutes later, however, a train filled with joy-seeking German soldiers on leave would have been destroyed. Rumors sizzled through the city about a Resistance effort that had almost succeeded. Usually following what the *Propagandastaffel* termed terrorism, German soldiers scoured the nearby streets, and innocent people were hauled away to be shot for an act in which they'd taken no part. But this time no hostages were taken. And on the evening news, Radio-Paris and Radio Nationale reported tersely that a railroad worker had been killed in a natural gas explosion. *Paris-Soir* and *Le Matin* and the rest of the press had buried identical information on the fourth page—since newspapers were limited to four pages, this was the back page. The question everyone asked was, why? Why was the *Propagandastaffel* covering up the incident?

Quent lit Gilberte's cigarette and one for himself with a gold lighter. "I was about to say that there are pockets of natural gas under Paris."

Ann held two fingers over her upper lip, simulating a Hitlerian mustache, and raised her free arm in a Nazi salute.

Quent responded with a smile, his first. He looked younger, less formidable, disconcertingly handsome. "That's all the information I have."

"Come off it, Quent," Larry said. "You've been wheeling and dealing with the Jerries all week."

"Getting the runaround, you mean." Quent turned to Ann. "I'm with a bank, and you can imagine how eager the *Bankenaufsichtsamt* is to let me transfer our funds to Switzerland or Sweden."

"Well, do the bank crowd *all* agree it's natural hot air?" Ann asked.

"The guy I'm dealing with is okay, he went to Harvard Business School a few years before me. Privately he told me that the Gestapo are all uneducated pigs and he wouldn't be surprised if they had no idea what the hell had hit them."

Ann said, "Today dynamite—"

Quent finished the phrase, "Tomorrow the world."

Gilberte had been glancing from her cousin to Ann and back. "Enough of serious matters. I'm dying for Dejong trivia. What's Irene doing?"

"She's engaged."

"Never!"

"To a Yale man," he replied.

Gilberte barraged him with questions about her American family-by-marriage. Larry, apparently as ignorant of these people as Ann, smiled amiably and put in an occasional suitable wisecrack.

Ann, feeling the chill of an outsider, leaned closer to the warmth of the fire and remained silent. Gilberte, having defended her from Quent's interrogation, now was issuing a warning that her cousin was off limits.

At a discreet knock everyone turned to the door. "Monsieur Dejong," Jacques said. "Monsieur the baron requests that you join him."

Quent stood. "See you later," he said to Gilberte. Turning to Ann, he said, "You really ought to convince your parents to leave, Ann. It's only a matter of time before this'll be enemy territory."

"Thanks for the advice."

He leveled that odd intent gaze on her, and for the first time she realized that his eyes, which she had assumed were brown, were in actuality a deep shade of blue.

"I'm serious." he said quietly.

Aware she was blushing, she said formally, "It was a pleasure meeting you."

Larry was on his feet. "I better get a wiggle on too," he said. "Gilberte, Ann, let me repeat. You two gals're the bright spot in a dreary autumn."

As the door closed on the two men, Gilberte's chin rose slightly and she stared at the oval portrait of a long-dead de Permont whose painted eyes peered back with equally chilling hauteur.

After nearly a minute's silence, Ann said, "Well, I must begin my battle with the Latin tongue. Are your parents still expecting us for dinner?"

"That's a peculiar question. This is Thursday."

"I thought . . . with your cousin in town . . ."

"Don't worry," Gilberte said. "We're expecting you."

4

Seven-thirty was the dinner hour, but Horace and Dorothy, as usual, insisted that they leave the flat at seven-twenty. As Jacques opened the front door Gilberte appeared, brightening the gloom with that smashing crimson dress.

"Ann, you forgot something. I have it in my room."

Ann, realizing this was an excuse to give them privacy, felt a tension between her shoulder blades relax. She trailed her friend down the short corridor leading to the bedrooms.

The lovely faded silk damask curtains were tightly drawn, the thick royal blue blackout shade pulled down, the exterior shutters closed. Each day the newspapers printed the changing minutes when the blackout would be enforced. After that time sporadically cruising German patrol cars shot out any window where a glint of light showed. (Paris ran on Berlin time, which because of wartime economics had been set back two hours: now, in the autumn, Parisians rose long before dawn.) The power ration was insufficient to light more than one room per household, so a chamberstick's flame was reflected again and again in the glass frames of the watercolors that covered the walls—one of Gilberte's ancestresses had possessed artistic talent.

Gilberte handed Ann the *fibranne* sweater. "You must have been worried," she said gravely.

"Panic-stricken. Imagine losing this treasure."

Their shared laughter further cleared the air. Gilberte sat at the scarred but priceless fruitwood antique that doubled as her dressing table and desk. "Well?" In the shorthand of their friendship, she was inquiring about Ann's opinion of the two men.

"Did you know they'd be here this afternoon?"

"I didn't have a glimmer of Larry Porter's existence until he showed up."

"But what about your cousin?"

Gilberte shrugged.

"Swell of you to warn me," Ann said. "That way I could keep on my chic uniform."

"Oh, stop fishing for compliments. Men don't notice clothes, or even looks when a girl has the kind of glow you have."

Ann perched on the edge of the bed, warmed yet surprised. She and Gilberte both professed disdain for their classmates who used lavish and reciprocal praise to bolster each other's egos. "The original glowworm, that's me," she said.

"It's not my description, it's Maman's. Larry Porter agrees with her."

"He's adorable, isn't he? The all-American boy, grin and all."

"For a minute there I was positive you'd scratch out some eyes."

"I never unleash my claws on so cute a face."

"Stop being coy. Let's hear the Blakely snap judgment on Quent."

Ann hesitated. Intuitive, she either liked or disliked people right off the bat. Her feelings for Quent Dejong, however, kept veering like a broken weather vane. His assuredness irritated her and made her feel dithery. In retrospect every word she'd said to him seemed gauche or naive. His size had also caught her off-balance, making her feel a squat peasant girl. Needless to say, she found him utterly glamorous. He was too far above her for this glamour to have validity. Gilberte wouldn't be joyous to hear the amount of emotional bilge she had dropped overboard. On the other hand, he was Gilberte's relative, so it would be impolitic and impolite not to make a kindly comment. "He certainly knows how to control a situation," she said.

"Why that flat tone? Aren't you the girl who's always saying a man ought to be sure of himself?"

"Hey, that's a good song title. A ma-an ought to-ooo beee—"

"There's another side to him altogether," Gilberte interrupted. "I kept thinking of the last time I'd seen him. It was three summers ago, in August, and we were in the Ile de France place. The weather was unendurable, it never cooled off, and there were so many fat, lazy bees that the entire world seemed to buzz. We would go riding together, loping along because it was too hot to gallop. The heat reminded him of the American Southwest, the desert, and he would wax poetic about the vastness, the thunderheads that raced across a huge sky, the Indians and ruins of their ancient cliff dwellings. When we'd get back, we'd swim in the river to cool off."

"Cool off from what?"

"I was fourteen!"

"The exact age of Juliet."

"You're repeating yourself, Blakely."

"Pardon me. I should've remembered. You never go in for grappling."

"Who could be amorous with the clowns around here? Garlic breath and chilblained hands." Gilberte's disdainful snort flickered the candle flame. "If things were normal, there would be balls, dinners, *thé dansants,* the opera. I'd be a femme fatale, luring all the men to my boudoir."

Ann bit her lip. The same social events still existed, attended by contingents of top-ranking Nazis. As a point of honor, the baron absented himself, keeping his wife and daughter away too. Even so, it seemed odd that no equally patriotic young men had wound their way through the drab streets of Montparnasse to beautiful Gilberte de Permont's chaste boudoir.

Gilberte said, "I told Quent he shouldn't have hammered away at you."

"It's none of his business where we live!"

Gilberte smiled again. "Exactly what I said. But that's how he is, responsible for the world and all Americans therein."

At a tap on the door they both turned. "Dinner is served, Mademoiselle," Jacques called.

* * *

The chandelier was far too massive for the small dining room. Two hundred years earlier it had cast a magnificent light, the myriad rock crystal prisms reflecting a hundred candle flames, throwing diamond rays on the satin clothes of the men and women of the court. Now, however, its bronze arms were twisted, many of the prisms gone and what remained chipped and dingy because there wasn't enough gritty ersatz soap to wash them. Three forlorn candle stubs hung low to the heavy old mahogany table. The reduced light had one advantage: diminishing the contrast between the elegant de Permonts and Dorothy and Horace.

"I don't know how you manage it, Baronne." Horace patted his stomach as he complimented his hostess. He resembled the Michelin tire man in his dinner jacket from college days, which was padded out by a heavy cardigan and several layers of underwear. "This is a prewar banquet."

On the massive sideboard lay the carcass of an undersized hen, a tough little bird with a gamy flavor, with not a scrap of flesh remaining. The rutabagas dressed with a sauce made from the drippings and the liver were gone.

"Our esteemed Monsieur Vallat," said the baronne with her delightful, faintly malicious smile. Like the Blakelys, the de Permont ménage was registered at Vallat's boucherie on the rue Delambre, the only shop where they were legally permitted to buy meat.

"Do you think he deals on the black market, Vallat?" Horace asked anxiously.

" 'Orace, if he did our dinner would have been plumper," said the baron.

At this moment Jacques entered the dining room.

Horace adjusted his wire-rimmed bifocals more firmly on the bridge of his nose. "That was an excellent meal, Jacques."

"Hélène does the preparation, sir." Jacques got sauce on a white glove as he inexpertly balanced the plates on the heavy silver platter. "I have no connection whatsoever to kitchen matters."

After he left the room, the baronne murmured dryly, "That puts us in our place."

The hardships of the Occupation had in no way dimmed

Baronne Vivienne de Permont's luster. With her long, slender, unlined throat, her artful blond upsweep, the pair of diamond clips at the decolletage of her three-year-old Schiaparelli dinner gown, a white fox cape thrown casually over her shoulders as if for effect rather than warmth, she might have been a model—had such a plebeian occupation occurred to her.

Gilberte had inherited her looks from her mother. A genetic blessing. Baron André de Permont was, to put it bluntly, an extremely ugly man.

Seated opposite his wife, he appeared taller than she. His heavy shoulders matched his barrel chest, but unfortunately the legs tucked below the table were extremely short. His brow jutted like a porch over his eyes. All in all, he bore a resemblance to paleontologists' renderings of Neanderthal man. These physical deficiencies were negated by the force of his personality. The small eyes shone with wit and intelligence. His authoritative bearing was precisely counterbalanced by the amused skepticism of his smile. (Gilberte had either inherited or copied the way that the smile pulled down one side of his mouth.) He had near professional knowledge of a variety of fields from geology to international law and finance to Chinese history to musical composition: this erudition, which could have been deadly, was shot through with brilliant veins of humor and enthusiasm. It was possible to see what had lured the exquisite ViVi from a wealthier husband and thrown her into a scandal that for more than a decade and a half had titillated the upper reaches of French society. (Precisely because the scandal was so juicy, it had never been permitted to trickle down to the lesser classes, so the rue Daguerre was not privy to the gossip.) The baron, serving in various prewar cabinet posts, had been an outspoken critic of the Third Reich: *Le Monde* had regularly printed his scathing wit at the expense of the *Übermenschen*. This was why the Kommandant had not "rented" the home of some wealthy Jew for General von Hocherer but had ordered the baron from his mansion on the boulevard Suchet. When Ann had asked why he had risked staying in the occupied zone, Gilberte, who relinquished her role of worldly cynic when it came to her father, had explained with proud terseness: *He wouldn't run away. In our family, we never run.*

Horace leaned toward his host. "Did you listen to the news tonight, Baron?"

"They had BBC so jammed I couldn't make out a word."

"Mmm, yes. Then I turned to Radio-Paris."

Ann flushed, embarrassed by her father's pretense that he had tried to listen to the outlawed British radio band.

Horace went on, "They announced that the Germans have taken six hundred and fifty thousand Russian prisoners in the last three days. I ask you. Who does the *Propagandastaffel* expect to take in with those ridiculous figures?"

"Kluge's Fourth Army is rushing toward Moscow, they have Leningrad encircled, they've cut off the Crimea."

Horace's rabbity jaw quivered. "You're saying you believe the numbers then?"

"One thing I do know," the baron replied with his mordant smile. "The Russians aren't invading Germany."

With a tentative little laugh, Horace said, "At least there'll always be an England."

"Even BBC admits that German subs have been cutting holes in the Atlantic convoys."

Horace looked down at his heavy damask napkin. "Terrible, terrible," he muttered.

The baron's small eyes twinkled. "Myself, I see the war as going excellently."

"But you just said—"

"My dear," the baronne interrupted, then paused. This hesitation, a mannerism of hers, hinted that some delightful drollness would follow, so her slightly husky voice commanded the same attention as her celebrated beauty. "War is a serious matter."

"But I am being serious, my dear." The baron glanced from Horace to Dorothy. "The time has come when your Monsieur Roosevelt must lead the United States into the breach."

Dorothy, a lifelong Republican, pushed at the worn flat cuffs of her ancient Persian lamb coat as if readying herself for the fray. "Baron, believe me, most of our country isn't behind Roosevelt. Not at all. The voters don't share his militarism. The majority has no intention of getting into another European war. Besides, according to our Constitution, only Congress may declare war."

"Then," the baron said, "Roosevelt will slide your Congress into the declaration."

"Where did you hear this?" Horace asked anxiously. Though André de Permont belonged to the losing side and had cut himself off from those former political associates who hobnobbed with the Germans, Horace saw his hero as privy to top secret communiqués.

"It's too obvious, 'Orace."

"I'm not following."

"Monsieur Roosevelt realizes that your country would be exceedingly badly off with Hitler the winner—and believe me, at this minute, the Third Reich is riding hard and fast to the finish line. Your president, being the shrewd politician that he is, will allow an incident to happen, an incident which will goad your Congress"— he gave Dorothy a smiling bow—"into declaring war."

"Quent thinks it'll be soon," Gilberte put in.

"Quent?" Horace asked.

"My young American cousin," the baron replied, explaining with uncharacteristic earnestness. "He's in Paris on banking business."

Horace reached toward his vest pocket for his notebook. "Baron, what information did he pass on about the United States?"

"No facts, only his opinions."

Horace's hand fell. "Much as I admire France, and as essential as my work at the hospital is, I'd never permit Ann and Dorothy to remain if there were the least chance they would be trapped."

"The Germans won't gun down Americans," the baron said dryly. "They'll exchange you for German civilians. No doubt they have as many spies and fifth columnists in your country as they had in ours."

Gilberte was gazing at her father, her lips parted like an adoring small child's. "Papa, Quent told Ann that the Blakelys should leave right away."

"Did he now?" The baron patted her hand, then looked down the dimly lit table to Ann. "Tell me, how did my American cousin strike you?"

"Extremely sure of himself," Ann replied.

"Ann!" Dorothy cried.

The baron's eyes gleamed wickedly. "He does have a good deal of confidence for somebody his age. But that goes for you, too, Ann. Horace, Dorothy, you should be proud your daughter has so much spirit."

The couple didn't look the least proud. They looked chagrined.

Jacques returned with a crystal bowl whose size further dwarfed the three tiny, wrinkled apples cut in half.

While Ann got ready for bed she again went over the idiotic responses she'd made to the Playboy of the Western World, Quent Dejong. Knowing she couldn't sleep, she decided to again look at the fashions in last month's *Pour Elle,* the Occupation's substitute for *Marie Claire:* the magazine was in the living room. Leaving her room, she halted to allow her pupils to adjust to the darkness. At the end of the near-black corridor, a lumpy shadow shifted. Small hairs rose on her arms. The church clock began sounding the hour and it took until the tenth rain-hushed boom before she could make out that the shadow was her father. He stood by the front door, which, from the narrow, lighter line, was ajar.

Masculine footsteps trotted down the tiles of the staircase. The current curfew hour was midnight, so she wasn't surprised that somebody might have a late night errand. But why should her father be watching?

After the steps had faded, she called, "Daddy?"

Horace jumped. "Ann, is that you? Why aren't you in bed? You oughtn't to be roaming around like this." His voice rose.

"I was getting the *Pour Elle.*"

"Oh. Well, I was locking up for the night." Noisily he slid the chain into the bolt.

Though Horace's snooping disturbed Ann, it didn't surprise her. She was reasonably certain that the masculine footsteps had belonged to the baron. And for a while now she'd known the depth of Horace's admiration for their neighbor. On a warm Sunday afternoon the previous June, she had been browsing in the plane tree–shaded bookstalls along the Left Bank. Glancing up, she had noticed the baron crossing the street to go into a brasserie. A few seconds later, she had seen her father skittering hastily along the far side of the quai.

"Daddy," she had called.

A heavy horse-drawn wagon had been rumbling by, so he hadn't heard her. Reaching the brasserie, he'd slowed to a saunter. Doffing his straw hat, he'd gone inside. That evening at the supper table he had talked about the coincidence of bumping into the baron at the Brasserie Wepler, and for many days thereafter had elaborated on the "chance" meeting in the same way that an adolescent might ramble on about glimpsing a celluloid idol in mortal flesh. The incident had in no way diminished Ann's filial love, but had smudged this love with pity.

She returned to her bed without the magazine, blowing out the candle, pulling the goose-down duvet up around her ears. Shivering, she thought, *Poor Daddy . . . president of the André de Permont fan club . . .*

5

By the following afternoon the sky had cleared and there were only a few puffed white clouds: it was one of those blue, seasonless days when Paris blazed with her most delightful flirtatiousness. Men and women of all ages and classes and persuasions forgot the Occupation, smiling about liaisons past, present and future.

Swinging their satchels, Ann and Gilberte sauntered along the rue Daguerre beneath the arch of nearly bare branches. All at once Ann halted.

Gilberte had just flabbergasted and obscurely wounded her with the information that Quent, when aged fifteen, had gotten a girl pregnant.

"Very precocious," she said, attempting sophistication to cover her shock. "A debutante?"

"A stepmother's secretary, I think. I'm not up on the details."

"Did she have the baby?"

"No, a minor operation."

"An abortion? But the baby was *his.*"

"Ever the sentimentalist," Gilberte said dryly, then her tone grew earnest. "Ann, be sensible. Quent was *fifteen.* What could he have done? Marry her?"

Ann sighed. Gilberte was right, and she couldn't quite grasp why the story was so disillusioning—after all, hadn't Gilberte's introductory remarks about her cousin indicated he was a dashingly glamorous wolf? Stepping around a paving block upraised by a tree root, she was silent as they approached number 74.

The brilliance of the autumn sun intensified the shadow falling from the false portico: Madame Jargaux, the concierge, with her black shawl clutched over her shapeless black coat, was invisible to the girls until they reached the building. The old woman's gray head was bent into a handkerchief.

Ann dropped her satchel, darting up the shallow step. "What's wrong, Madame Jargaux?"

"Mademoiselle Ann . . . I've been waiting . . ."

"Is it Léon?" Ann put an arm around the concierge's quaking shoulders. "Has something happened to Léon?" Corporal Léon Jargaux, the widow's only child, had been confined in a prisoner-of-war camp in Silesia since the summer of 1940.

Madame Jargaux shook her head, unable to speak.

Of all the tenants, Mademoiselle Ann was her favorite—even if the girl did rush into the hall with mud on her shoes, necessitating mopping of the tiles. She had a smile that made the concierge feel a conspiratorial, mischievous girl again. Also, she had a sympathetic way of listening to problems rare in one so young.

"Come on inside," Ann said. "Mother'll make you a cup of coffee, and then you'll tell us."

"Madame Dorothy . . ." the old lady managed to get out, then wept harder.

"Mother?" A membrane formed in Ann's throat, and she, too, couldn't speak.

Gilberte, who had retrieved Ann's satchel, asked, "What about Madame Blakely?"

The concierge disliked Mademoiselle de Permont, mostly because the ménage included those two high-and-mighty servants. Yet Gilberte's autocratic tone was the correct antidote for nascent hysteria. Wiping her eyes, Madame Jargaux mumbled, "The *agents de police* . . . they have her."

"The police?" Ann asked, clearing her throat rustily. "Mother?"

"They came soon after you left, it was still dark as the grave. They drove up the rue Daguerre with their whoo-whoo siren, banging and banging on this door like they wanted the dead to wake. They made me lead them upstairs to the flat, even though I explained that in the morning my legs are stiff and that I—"

Gilberte cut in, "What did they want with Madame Blakely?"

"Something about her papers. They needed to examine her papers."

"Papers?" Gilberte asked. "Didn't she show them her American passport?"

The concierge lifted her gnarled, arthritic hands to the bright blue sky, showing her baffled ignorance. "They made her go with them in the police van. I ran right to the *boulangerie* and Monsieur Remigasse helped me telephone the *clinique*. And I spoke to Monsieur 'Orace." She quavered out the last two sentences. There were no telephones in the building: in emergencies, the tenants went to Remigasse's bakery on the corner of the rue Daguerre and the rue Delambre. To Madame Jargaux, the baker's wall instrument was an oracle that spoke only news of the direst nature. "Monsieur 'Orace, he came home immediately, then rushed off to the commissariat de police."

"What did he find out?" Gilberte asked.

"Who can know? He hasn't returned either. Maybe he is arrested too."

Ann made a soft, gasping noise that she stifled by biting deep into her lower lip.

"They're keeping him waiting, Ann," Gilberte reassured. "You know how the police are since the surrender. The Nazis got rid of the good ones."

"Madame Jargaux," Ann whispered hoarsely, "did somebody tell you my father's been arrested?"

"No, never. It just popped into my old head," Madame Jargaux said. "A stupid idea."

"I tell you he's being kept waiting around by some nasty, officious little civil servant."

"Probably," Ann said uncertainly.

"If only Papa were home, he'd find out for you," Gilberte said, sighing. "But he left early this morning and won't be home until just before curfew."

"And your *maman*'s gone too."

Gilberte's lips tensed. As if her frivolously decorative mother would be any help! "If you're worried, Ann," she said, "why not call your embassy?"

Ann briefly shut her eyes. Calling the embassy would be the final ceremonial of disaster. Following the surrender, the Germans had informed the State Department that since the northern half of France was now part of the Third Reich, the United States' Paris embassy was superfluous and the staff of the Berlin embassy could perform all necessary duties and obligations. (There had been no ambassador to Nazi Germany since 1938, when President Roosevelt had recalled his envoy.) The delegation, before departing, had warned United States citizens remaining in the occupied zone that they would have to handle all but the gravest problems on their own.

Gilberte was watching Ann's face. "I know it's a long-distance call," she said. "If you're short on coins or cash, I can float a loan."

"Berlin's too far away, they can't do anything," Ann said, then blurted, "I'll go to the commissariat de police."

"No . . ." wailed Madame Jargaux. "You can't! Mademoiselle Ann, I forbid it." The police throughout occupied Europe were forced to cooperate with the German garrisons, so it followed that the local populace sedulously avoided contact with them.

"She's right," Gilberte said. "Besides, what's the use? Your father's already there."

"There's no other choice," said Ann, who had reached the decision without any thought of alternatives.

Gilberte's eyes were bleak with sympathy. In the same spot she would have done the same thing, yet she continued to argue. "It's a wonderful idea, Blakely, barging off before you know what's happened."

"Mother's in trouble, and Daddy, when he's rattled, he's not very good at explanations."

Gilberte gripped her arm. They seldom touched, so the gesture showed the depth of Gilberte's anxiety. "Ann, please listen to me," she said quietly. "For all you know at this very minute the two of them could be unwinding over a glass of wine in some café. How will it be if you land yourself in prison?"

"Mademoiselle Ann." Madame Jargaux blew her nose. "You're a young girl, a pretty young girl. Madame Dorothy and Monsieur

'Orace would never forgive me if I let you go anywhere near these *boche*-loving scum."

Ann drew a wavery breath.

Gilberte saw her friend's struggle for control. With patrician tact, she ceased arguing. Opening Ann's satchel, she handed her the scuffed black purse. "Here. You'll need your papers."

6

The signs on the dingy buff paint of the commissariat de police waiting room that forbade talking were superfluous. The even dozen people marooned here were too immersed in their own fears to strike up any kind of conversation. Ann heard her stomach rumble—her hunger had intensified until she felt hollow and light-headed. She had been sitting on this comfortless bench since before five, and the hands on the large clock were jumping to seventeen minutes past eight.

Arriving at the commissariat, she had joined the queue in front of the window that dealt with inquiries about those taken into custody. Finally it had been her turn. The corporal with the narrow, pimply face behind the *guichet* looked her up and down in a way that made her recall stories that the German authorities had been recruiting police from among the murderers and rapists in the city's prisons. But he had been all business as he jotted down her information and sent her to wait in here.

Since then Ann's mind had swirled in a miasma of questions. Why had her mother been taken away in a police van? Was checking her papers an excuse to take her into custody? But why would they arrest a neutral housewife? Her father wasn't in this waiting room, so where was he? Was either of them in the local commissariat? Had they already cleared up the matter and left? Or had they been transferred to a terrifying place like the huge commissariat near Notre Dame? Although the air in the waiting room was so frigid that her breath showed, she was clammy with perspiration, and she took off her coat, clasping it in her lap. Her worries kept blundering into thoughts of Quent Dejong.

She jerked erect as the door opened and a guard stationed himself there. After a minute, footsteps sounded in the corridor and a flabby-cheeked man stepped inside. He was shaped like a breastless old woman with narrow shoulders and broad hips, the pockets of his shiny black suit sagged, yet his brisk step and purposeful air as he marched to the table proclaimed him Authority. He pulled the chain of the green-shaded lamp, encircling himself in light.

"Mesdames and messieurs, I am Inspector Dubret," he said in educated accents. "When I call your name, if you would be so kind as to step over here."

He murmured quietly to the supplicants before him. Some smiled and effusively thanked him while others, like the trimly dressed young Jewish-looking woman, went white and left dejectedly. The Algerian was led away. The three men who had come in after Ann were called. When everyone else had left, she clasped her coat and purse, approaching Inspector Dubret.

"I'm Ann Blakely. Do you have any information about my mother?"

"What's her name?"

Ann could see BLAKELY penciled atop the form in front of him. *Bastard,* she thought, forcing herself to take a calming breath. "Dorothy Blakely."

He consulted the paper. "She's here in the commissariat."

"But why? She's an American. A neutral!"

"Mademoiselle, there's no reason to upset yourself. Her passport is being verified."

"What about my father?"

"Your father?" Inspector Dubret peered judiciously down at the thin, grayish wartime paper. "I don't see any request for information about Monsieur Blakely."

"He came to find out about Mother, and didn't return. I don't understand any of this. Why is her passport being checked? We're neutrals. Americans."

"So you said. I pride myself on an ear for accents, and you have none whatsoever. May I see your papers?"

Fumbling, Ann extricated her passport and her *carte d'identité*.

He stared at the identity card with its photograph and official stamps. "A good likeness," he said finally. Opening the passport, he turned the pages slowly. "You'd be surprised at the excellent counterfeits of neutral papers that are floating around Paris. There are new regulations that require us to contact the embassies concerned. We're calling Berlin, as I said, to verify Madame Blakely's identity."

Replacing her papers in her purse, Ann asked in a muted tone, "Is my father here? His name's Horace Blakely."

"I'll see what I can find out." He snapped his fingers at the waiting guard. "If Figeac hasn't left, get him, will you?"

A minute or so later, the pimply corporal trotted in, closing the door after himself.

"Figeac, this is Mademoiselle Blakely. She wishes to know if her father, Monsieur Horace Blakely, made an inquiry today."

"I see strangers from morning to night," Figeac retorted in a schoolboy whine.

"The young lady is quite disturbed. She says her father is an American."

"An American? Ah, now it's coming back to me. The man with the American passport. He was worried about his wife, so I sent him directly to room thirty-four."

"Room thirty-four . . . ?" Ann's voice wavered.

"Our experts on foreign documents work in there," Dubret explained. "Probably your father decided to wait with your mother. Figeac, you were on your way home? Could you spare a minute to show Mademoiselle Blakely the way to room thirty-four?"

Heavy weights were lifting from Ann's shoulders. With a blazing smile, she turned to Figeac. "I'd be so grateful."

"Oh, all right. But hurry it up with the search."

"Search?" Ann gripped her coat above her breasts.

"You can understand, surely, Mademoiselle, that we can't have visitors wandering around with knives, razors, guns," said the inspector. "If you would please give me your purse and coat."

Ann complied with a little sigh of relief. *I've really let this place get under my skin.*

Inspector Dubret meticulously put his hand in each pocket, coming up with lint and a crumpled handkerchief. He unsnapped her bag, setting aside her papers, money purse, unfolding the handkerchief, holding up the band with the faded, stained out clean knitted padding—she was expecting her period. Looking up, he asked, "Why aren't you continuing?"

"What . . . do you mean?"

"Exactly what he said." Figeac's pimples seemed more pronounced. "Show him the rest of your clothes."

"No!"

Inspector Dubret struck a match, lighting his cigarette. "If a weapon got inside the commissariat, I'd be held responsible for not following procedures."

"Isn't there a matron?"

"She went home," Figeac said.

"Would you prefer," asked Dubret, inhaling, "to return in the morning?"

"If they're still here," Figeac added.

The exchange was smooth as lines in a play, and Ann accepted that this was a nasty little charade they had played many times before on young, frantic women. It was no coincidence that she'd been kept until last. *Are they going to rape me?*

"There's no way I'm going to undress," she said in an astonishingly level tone.

"That's not necessary." Figeac reached for her. "We'll do a body search."

She tried to squirm away, but he was twisting her arm behind her so painfully that she worried he'd snap the bone. Sweat showed on his acne-marked forehead, his sour breath surrounded her. Inspector Dubret smoked, watching as benevolently as if they were romping children while Figeac cupped her breasts in turn, squeezing, fondling, then shoving his hand inside her blouse, worming below her underwear and brassiere. As his moist, hot palm touched her bare nipple, an involuntary shudder contorted her body. Attempting to control her nausea, she stared at one of the pair of swastika flags that flanked the table. Her nipple was pinched between rough fingernails. She closed her eyes: the Nazi symbol remained behind her lids.

Figeac was gasping hoarsely. Pulling up her skirt, he passed his hand roughly up and down the ugly, warm knickers that all the girls at Madame Bernard's wore.

"I can't feel anything," he said hoarsely. "But who knows?"

"Mademoiselle, will you place both hands on the table and bend forward."

The reason was only too clear. "No!" she yelled.

Abruptly, Inspector Dubret's hand shot out, grasping the nape of her neck as if she were a puppy. She struggled, squirming and panting, but her head was jammed downward. He leaned his fore-arm across her neck, a heaviness that forced her chin upward, clamping her neck against the table. Her struggles ended in a loud gasping for breath.

Figeac yanked her skirt over her head. Her darned woolen bloomers were tugged down around her ankles, the rayon under-pants following. His panting rang in her ears as he kneaded her buttocks then spread them apart. Her muscles tensed. Pain shot through her as a finger plunged into her anus, moving back and forth like a rat trying to find its way from a narrow maze until she felt as if her bowels might move involuntarily. The stench of burn-ing grasses from Dubret's wartime cigarette filled each struggle for breath. The finger withdrew. The lips of her vagina were parted. She froze, anticipating rape. But again there was an exploratory burrowing, this time with two digits. The fingering became jerky, erratic, intensely painful. Inspector Dubret's arm was shaking, yet the pressure remained constant. Figeac gave a muted howl and his fingers spread her wider. Her whimper came out thinly. Then, suddenly, the fingers departed. Inspector Dubret's arm shifted.

"Mademoiselle Blakely, we are satisfied you aren't concealing a weapon," he said. "Arrange yourself."

Icy air chilled her exposed buttocks. Paralyzed by revulsion and shame, she couldn't force herself to move.

Hands pulled her skirt down, raised her to standing position.

She glimpsed Figeac slowly, lovingly, replace his moist, purplish penis in his long drawers. She had never seen a man's penis before.

"Now Figeac'll take you to your parents." Inspector Dubret's voice was composed, but redness splotched his sagging jowels.

Trembling, she pulled up her underwear, straightening her clothes. She followed Figeac down the dark, empty corridors, attempting to calm herself. She couldn't let her parents see her in this state. Figeac opened a door. She could smell the fresh night air.

"Get on home," he said.

The entire business had been a sham! "You're worse pigs than the Germans," she said thickly.

"Nothing happened," Figeac said in his aggrieved whine. "A little fun, that's all."

7

Filled with panic for her missing parents, her body still quaking from the "search," Ann kept tripping over the curbs of blacked-out streets: on reaching the sanctuary of 74, rue Daguerre, she dropped the apartment house key and had to fumble around on the ground searching for it. When she finally trudged up the tiled stairs, the concierge's frosted glass door opened. "Thank the good lord you're safe!" cried Madame Jargaux. "*Eh bien.* What about Madame Dorothy and Monsieur 'Orace?"

Ann realized that she'd been clinging for dear life to the hope that both parents would welcome her home with hugs. Concentrating on the familiar array of mimeographed German regulations that covered the panes of the concierge's door, she explained about the checking of neutral passports.

"Well, at least you're here safe and sound. Come inside. We'll have some good hot leek soup."

That the kind, garrulous old woman had been waiting to share her rations cut through the fears jumping in Ann's mind. Swallowing, she said, "Thank you, Madame Jargaux, but I'm too tired to eat."

In the silent flat, she gave way to gasped-out sobs, then washed her genitalia, scrubbing with the gritty ersatz soap until the flesh burned. Too weary and distraught to bother with blackout regulations, she felt her way to the living room and slumped on the couch. *Where are they? Where?* The tears began again. *Why didn't Figeac rape me?* In some ways it would have been preferable if both he and Inspector Dubret *had* raped her. At least she wouldn't have been reduced to a "little fun."

The bell buzzed. Joy flooded through her—*They're back. Thank you, God, thank you!*—as she raced to fling open the front door, which she had neglected to bolt.

"Ann, is that you?" asked Gilberte from the blackness beyond the threshold. "Are your parents home?"

"No . . ." Ann slumped against the jamb. "They're checking the passports."

"Still? As soon as my father gets back, he'll find out what the pigs are up to. Now come on up to my place."

"I have to wait here for them."

"Pin a note on the door."

"I *can't* leave."

"Then I'll stay down here, *d'accord?*" After a brief silence, Gilberte said, "Would you rather be alone?"

"Yes . . ."

"If you need anything—or just want another human being with you—come up. Any hour, any time."

Ann returned to the living room sofa. Body limp, tears seeping beneath her closed eyelids, she passed the first sleepless night of her life.

Jacques answered the door. For once the disdainful droop of the servant's eyelid didn't register with Ann.

"Will you please tell Mademoiselle de Permont that I won't be going to school with her today."

"Ann?" the baron's voice called from the shadowed bedroom corridor.

"Baron? You're home?" Ann asked, her voice rising. Listening in the dark for her parents, she'd believed she'd heard every sound on the staircase.

"Since before curfew." He came into the hall, a towel draped around his heavy neck, his maroon bathrobe with the gilt-emboidered crest exposing a short expanse of thin, black-haired legs.

"Gilberte just told me about your parents. Has either of them returned yet?"

Blinking, Ann shook her head.

He took her arm. "Come to my study."

Being on the top floor, this flat had an oddly shaped cubbyhole where the stairwell would be. Ann, perching on one of the pair of Jacobean chairs jammed on either side of the small Louis Quatorze gilt table that the baron used as his desk, blurted out the little she knew about her parents' disappearance. "The inspector told me they've placed a call to our embassy in Berlin," she finished. "To make sure Mother's an authentic American."

The small, quick eyes were filled with concern and sympathy. "Why not you and your father?"

During the long night she had pondered this same question. "Perhaps they only check one passport per family. Perhaps they're still mixed up. It's a new regulation."

"Ah, yes, another vital bit of German jurisprudence." The baron gripped the ends of the towel until the tendons of his hands stood out. "Ann, I'll find out what's going on."

Ann, immensely grateful, felt darts of trepidation on his behalf. Even the highest-ranked Aryan-loving collaborationists avoided making queries about prisoners hauled in by the German-controlled police, and the baron trailed a prewar history of anti-Nazism.

His mordant smile proved he could read her thoughts. "I'll be sticking my neck out a little, but what are necks for? Your parents are my friends and—"

The door opened. Gilberte crowded into the dinky room. Normally impeccable and in command of herself, her jacket was unbuttoned, her black hair tangled. "Jacques said you were here, Ann," she cried breathlessly. "My God, I've been frantic! What's happened?"

Ann sighed. "Exactly nothing."

"I'm looking into the matter," the baron said. "Won't you two be late for school?"

"That's why I came up," Ann said. "To tell Gilberte I'm not going."

"Of course you are," the baron said sharply.

"Papa's right." Gilberte edged around Ann's chair to link her arm in her father's—she was several inches taller than he. In this pose, the incontrovertible lines of affection between the pair showed visibly. "What would you do here? Go crazy?"

Ann went crazy at school.

German and Latin declensions, logarithms, names, dates, slithered from her mind as she visualized Horace and Dorothy being worked over by pettifogging civil servants like Dubret or brutalized by uniformed clods like Figeac. At last it was four o'clock. She pelted away from Madame Bernard's, leaving Gilberte in her wake. As she charged up the stairs past the concierge's loge, Madame Jargaux stuck her head out. "Good news," she bawled. "Wonderful news!"

Ann took the stairs two at a time, leaning on the bell.

Dorothy opened the door. "Why must you always be in such a rush, dear?" she asked. "I can't get here any quicker." Her prosaic remark did not match the moisture gleaming in her eyes.

Flinging herself at her mother, Ann gasped in the odors of camphorated mothballs and cooking combined with the faint salinity of sweat. The prememory odors of comfort. "What happened? When did they let you go? Where's Daddy?"

"One question at a time, I can only answer one question at a time. I came home around ten this morning. And where else would your father be at this hour but the hospital?" Dorothy's eyes remained moist yet she put iron in her voice. "Now I have a bone to pick with you, Miss. Madame Jargaux tells me you took it on yourself to go to the commissariat."

Dorothy always kept her personal woes and crises to herself, just as Ann would conceal what had happened to her at the police station; however, this out-of-place, mundane rebuke was more than Ann could take. "Believe it or not, I was terrified!"

"Madame Jargaux also said that she explained it was a routine formality about my papers."

"A police van came and hauled you away! Will you stop acting like it's the sort of thing that happens every day?"

"Ann, I understand how you must have felt. But I won't have you rushing into things where there's no need."

"You were both kept all night!"

"Daddy stayed with me." Dorothy was leading the way to the kitchen. "And by the time they could reach our embassy, it was nearly curfew. The inspector was very kind. He let us spend the night in his office."

Dorothy, opening a cabinet, had turned her back. Ann peered at the thin, set shoulders, unsure if this was the truth or if her mother was trying to protect her from the truth.

"Did you run into the Baron de Permont?"

Dorothy was taking a cup from its hook. The china slipped in her hand, and with a gasping cry, she rescued it from falling. "The baron? But why would we see him?"

"He was trying to find out where you were."

"You went to the baron?" It was a measure of Dorothy's distress that she lapsed into English. "How could you have . . . bothered him?"

"Gilberte told him, she was nearly as beside herself as me. But Mother, I would've gone to Hitler himself. It so happens I love you and Daddy very much."

"I know, dear, and we love you." Dorothy wiped her eyes and blew her nose. "But you have to understand it's not up to us to interfere when the police carry out the law."

Since when is it legal interference to find out about your family? Ann thought. *Quent Dejong's absolutely right. Paris is no place for an American.*

At dinner, Ann said, "We ought to go home."

Horace glanced across the table at his wife. "We're arranging it," he retorted.

Surprised, Ann dropped her spoon into the watery potato soup that was their dinner. But, of course, it made sense that the past day and night would have put a different perspective on her parents' mysterious yet transparent fears about returning to their native land. They who were such wraiths beyond these walls must have shriveled to near nonexistence in the commissariat.

"As a matter of fact," Horace went on, "I think we'll leave before I relocate."

"Right away?" Ann asked.

"You would ask that, Miss Impatience," Dorothy said with a forced yet fond laugh.

The following week, the Wehrmacht took Odessa, German artillery pounded Moscow, a German sub "inadvertently" torpedoed the USS *Kearny* off the Iceland coast, and in Nantes, as a reprisal for the death of a German officer, fifty innocent French hostages were shot.

Horace and Dorothy stayed up late discussing plans. Their savings would pay for third-class passages home, but would the crossing be safer on a Swedish or Argentine vessel? When and how would Horace inform Dr. Descourset? How should they go about selling the furniture? Their voices remained rational. Yet as they planned their eyes glazed over as if they were gazing into a paralyzingly bright light.

8

Sirens woke Ann that night in mid-November. Practice alerts were inflicted on the population two or three times a week. Horace was already rapping on her door, anxiously urging her to hurry.

In the dank basement babies wailed, small children whined and coughed, neighbors gossiped. The de Permonts weren't there. As usual. The family displayed patrician arrogance toward possible danger and also the *défense passive,* the air raid warden. The two servants, however, had showed up, isolating themselves by the chill behemoth of a furnace. Within a half hour, the all clear sounded.

Ann flipped up the blackout shades, opening the curtains and window to push back the shutters just as the sun burst through a patch in the flocked clouds. Stretching her arms in the lemon light, she glanced at her alarm clock. Five to twelve already? At one-thirty she and Gilberte were going to the Montparnasse Odéon to see Jean Delannoy's *Pontcarral,* a historical film that rumor said was an anti-German statement.

Dressing hurriedly, she went to the kitchen. Dorothy sat frowning over their assortment of ration cards. "They've announced a cut in the bread ration." She sighed.

"Then let us eat cake," Ann said, kissing the top of the graying head. "Mother, soon you won't have to worry about coupons, you'll be making sticky buns and basting turkeys. Has Gilberte come down?"

"Gilberte?" Dorothy's voice was pitched too high. "Were you expecting her?"

Since their night at the commissariat de police, Horace and Dorothy had suffered a mystifying sea change in their attitude toward the de Permonts: the relationship, formerly Dorothy's greatest pleasure and a vital prop in Horace's self-esteem, had somehow become onerous to them. They had canceled a Tuesday and the following week a Thursday dinner with the excuse that Horace had to work late. They did not linger when they were at the de Permonts, and hurried through the meals at home. When Ann said she was going to study with Gilberte, Dorothy would invent household chores for her. The only reason for this abrupt volte-face Ann could come up with was that their pride had been wounded by the subtle overtones of noblesse oblige in the baron's attempt to help. (For all his connections in high circles, he had learned only what the Blakelys already knew: Bearers of neutral passports were being routinely picked up in an effort to extirpate phony papers.)

"We're going to the movies this afternoon. I'll run up to tell her I'm nearly ready."

"You are not leaving this kitchen until you've eaten!" Dorothy said urgently. "You're far too thin!"

Ann soaked the tough, unpalatable gray bread in her watery café au lait without argument. Since her parents' overnight absence her own attitudes had also changed. She had always loved Horace and Dorothy, but where she once had struggled against their endless clucking and fussing she now protected them. She no longer felt obligated to crack their self-delusions even though they drove her half crazy with ditherings over their departure.

In all honesty, she was *glad* they hadn't made any definite plans. She felt a clutch in her throat whenever she thought about leaving the land of her birth in its time of sorrowful defeat. How could she sail away to eat ice cream and thick steaks while everyone she had known in her life was growing thin and pasty on a wartime diet? How could she say good-bye to her schoolmates, teachers, neighbors, to Madame Jargaux? How could she leave Gilberte, who knew her every secret?

Finishing breakfast, she ran upstairs to the de Permonts' flat, attempting to quell her annoyance that Dorothy was puffing after her.

Nobody answered the doorbell. Ann rapped her knuckles sharply on the wood.

"They're out," Dorothy said.

"But that's impossible! Gilberte and I've been talking about the movie all week."

"There's always a reasonable explanation." Dorothy's favorite platitude. "Now come on back down."

"Either Hélène or Jacques is always here." Ann's soft mouth was white and flat, as if her lips were pressed against glass. "I'll go get Madame Jargaux, she'll let me in."

"No!" Dorothy shouted, then, controlling herself with several jerks at her knitted muffler, lapsed into her I'm-the-mother-here tone. "Gilberte forgot. They're out, dear, and that's that."

But Ann was already bolting down the stairs. She blurted to Madame Jargaux that the de Permont flat was empty.

"Impossible!" The concierge shook her head so vehemently that several wisps of white hair escaped her bun. "They haven't left this morning. Not the family. Not those two stuck-up pieces."

"Hélène or Jacques always answers the doorbell. Let me borrow the key?"

Madame Jargaux drew up her shapeless form as if on sentry duty. "Never, never have I let a tenant's key out of my sight." Then, peering into her favorite's worried face, she relented. "But if, as you say, nobody is there, it's my duty to check on the gas."

The old woman halted on every other step to massage her arthritic knees, laboring upward with agonizing slowness. When, finally, she unlocked the door, Ann gave an audible gasp. Her imagination had ransacked the flat. But the huge old escritoire and the Sèvres-inlaid table still presided over the neat hall. The only signs of disorder that she found as she hurried through the other rooms were the rumpled beds and Jacques's cot standing near the kitchen stove.

"I can't understand it," Madame Jargaux said. "Even if the

baron and his family left during the alert, what about the others? *They* were in the cellar with the rest of us. How could five people vanish just like that, poof?"

Ann shivered. There was no magic in Paris: all vanishing acts were performed under the aegis of the police or the Gestapo.

She had to find out what had happened to the de Permont ménage. But how? She wouldn't be idiot enough to go to the police again.

Quent Dejong, she thought. He was constantly in some near or far region of her mind, yet as the idea sank in she accepted that, related to the de Permonts and with connections to important Germans, he was the perfect answer. Was he still in Paris? Gilberte, reverting to that baffling fetish for privacy, had drawn a curtain around her second cousin after the disclosure about the girl, and Ann, afraid of those giveaway blushes, had not inquired about him. What was the name of the hotel where he'd been staying with Larry Porter and the other cooped-up American journalists? Hotel Pyré-nées? Hotel Pyramide? Yes, that was it. Hotel Pyramide near the Champs-Elysées. An area thronged with German soldiers. Dorothy would never let her go to the Hotel Pyramide. Helping Madame Jargaux labor down the steps then returning to the apartment, Ann pondered means of escaping her mother.

"I guess I'll go to the movies by myself," she said.

Dorothy turned to give her a penetrating maternal look. "That doesn't sound like you," she said.

"Why not? For some reason or other Gilberte's stood me up, and you know how crazy I am about Delannoy's films. They say this is his best."

Dorothy's hazel eyes narrowed speculatively. She was guessing that the girls had arranged to meet those two boys from Lycée Paul Bert, and Ann wanted to keep the date. Her belief was fostered by the care with which her daughter dressed, putting on her good blue sweater and checked skirt, tying her green scarf outside her coat.

"I'll walk on over to the cinema with you," she said. "I promised to help Daddy." A far more astute bookkeeper than Horace, she untangled the new German taxes for him.

During a newsreel clip of Messerschmitts swooping in formation at a British convoy, Ann slipped out of the Odéon.

Emerging on the Champs-Elysées, she took a step down back into the warm, stale air of the métro station, unnerved by the huge swastika atop the Arc de Triomphe and the hundreds of smaller crimson and black flags, the absence of any traffic other than German staff cars on the broad boulevard, the twin rivers of German uniforms.

Hitler had designated Paris as a giant pleasure park for troops stationed across Western Europe. *Soldaten* on leave crowded the cabarets, guzzling wine and gaping at nude show girls, they gorged themselves in cafés where the menus were inked in German, they denuded shops to send finery home to wives and sweethearts. The Nazi high command had requisitioned the city's brothels, segregating them in an orderly manner: the exquisite girls of the celebrated establishments around the place Louvois were reserved for the exalted ranks while the less pretentious houses accommodated officers of lower rank and common soldiers lined in boisterous, drunken queues outside wildly busy cribs. The *putains* who patrolled the streets were fair game for all.

A *Matrose* had halted on the step next to Ann. He was not much taller than she and approximately the same age. Removing his sailor's hat, he gave a timid smile, then looked up at the lowering gray sky. "I hope it does not make rain," he said.

She told him in her equally rudimentary German—an obligatory subject at Madame Bernard's, and not one she excelled at—that she, too, hoped it wouldn't rain, adding, "I'm meeting a special person."

Turning crimson, the young sailor stumbled up the last step, rushing in the direction of the *Soldatenkino*, the movie house set aside for members of the German armed forces.

Ann asked an angry-eyed old man roasting chestnuts the way to the Hotel Pyramide. Either purposefully or accidentally, he gave her the wrong directions and she blundered up and down the narrow streets that webbed between the broad boulevards leading to l'Etoile. She passed a dingy hotel where Germans and their thinly clad, shivering whores waited for rooms, she hurried from a pair of drunken Luftwaffe pilots who shouted bawdy compliments at her, she rebuffed a polite, studious-looking young lieutenant. With every wrong turn her fears increased. She was running by the time she turned on the rue la Boëtie and saw the sign with letters missing. HOT-L PY-AM-DE.

In a small lobby fogged with cigarette smoke, American voices boomed. With so much noise and smoke, Ann was surprised to count only five men arguing around the low, bottle-cluttered table.

Neither Larry nor Quent was there.

The desk clerk had looked up from her knitting. The glint in her close-set eyes made Ann decide to avoid her. She moved stiffly to table. The group—were they all journalists?—deferred to her femininity by pushing from their low chairs to assume a crouch halfway between sitting and standing.

"Hey, *bonjour chérie,* hello *bébé,* he-llo," said a balding man with a thick black mustache.

"Could you tell me—do any of you know if a Mr. Quentin Dejong is staying here?" she asked in French.

"He's seeing a man about a dog," the mustache responded.

What was that about *un chien?* Cut off from American films and magazines, had she missed out on the latest slang? Worried it might mean Quent was no longer in Paris, she asked, "What about Mr. Larry Porter?"

"Larry? He's out. Knowing good old Larry, he's rounding up hootch. I never met me a boy with more God-given talent for sniffing out the creature comforts. Sit down and rest your—"

Ann heard no more. Quent came jogging down the stairs. He looked larger than she remembered, stronger, more invincible. Relief spread through her like a powerful elixir as she mentally ceded him a portion of her worry.

He halted, his head tilting in surprise. "Ann."

She had been planning how to prod his memory if he'd forgotten her. "Hello, Quent."

"What brings you here?"

"Either you or Larry," a southern voice guffawed. "The little lady's impartial, she's looking for one or the other of you."

Quent paid no attention to the words or the good-natured, boozy laughter.

Reaching for the handsome tweed overcoat on the rack, he said, "Let's get a cup of coffee."

9

Across from the hotel, a mechanic converting a car to gazogene braced the torpedo-shaped fuel cylinder behind the trunk. Quent glanced at the begrimed blue uniform. Ann understood to say nothing of importance until they were out of earshot.

As they started in the general direction of l'Etoile, Quent's physical presence tugged at her with a force that equaled gravity: to avoid being pulled into his orbit, she shifted on the narrow sidewalk, hurrying along so close to the buildings that her left glove kept grazing shop windows.

"I'm not sure if he's a spy or not, but he or somebody else in the garage is always puttering outside," Quent said as they turned a corner. "The woman at the desk definitely sits on us. You should hear the press guys invent tall tales about new weapons—the latest is a Flash Gordon–type cannon that dissolves matter."

"God, wouldn't you love to see the reports filed to the Gestapo?" she asked, laughing.

"That's more like it," he said. "When I came down the stairs you looked like you'd just heard the sounding of the last trump."

Her laughter ceased abruptly. A few meters ahead of them, a *bonne* was lugging a string bag of dirt-covered carrots. Ann waited until the elderly maidservant had disappeared into a building with boarded-over windows before whispering, "I didn't know who else to turn to. It's the de Permonts—"

"What's wrong?"

"The flat's empty."

He halted, peering down at her. "What do you mean, empty?"

"Nobody's there."

Some of the high color had drained from his face, making visible two small, seed-shaped scars that probably had been left by chicken pox, one near his left eye, one by his mouth. "The servants?" he asked in a flat, hard voice. "What about them?"

"The place is deserted." Ann sighed. "The concierge let me in. No signs of ransacking. The beds were slept in. It's all so weird and terrifying. Madame Jargaux—she's the concierge—didn't hear anyone leave."

"What about the alert last night? They could've slipped out then."

"The baron, the baronne and Gilberte, perhaps. They weren't in the basement. But Jacques and Hélène were." She felt a drop of rain on her face. "And now all five of them have disappeared."

Quent shoved his hands in his pockets. He might have been dismayed, angry, guilty, all she knew was that his expression frightened her. Then his face went blank, as if he had mentally removed himself. He looked unreachable—and intolerably lonely. "It's starting to drizzle," he said.

They began to walk again, their shoes leaving prints until wetness had entirely covered the pavement.

Finally he said, "They don't usually take in whole families unless they're Jewish."

"If they *have* been arrested, then what?"

"Let's hope they're nowhere near a jail."

"But say they are, can't you get them released?"

"How?" he asked levelly. "By making bail?"

Ann felt the blood surge into her face. "I'm not an idiot. But you *do* work with big-shot Germans."

"Bankers," he said, "are the same all over the world. A cautious breed."

Neither of them spoke again until they had passed the empty, rain-slick street where the Luftwaffe pilots had bawled out compliments, then Quent said quietly, "I'll find out what's happened to them."

"I thought bankers were a cautious breed."

"General von Hocherer would help."

"Von Hocherer? Don't you know he's the creep who requisitioned their house?"

"It was requisitioned for him. The point is he likes and respects André."

"He let them take some furniture from the basement. That doesn't constitute a friendship."

"In the twenties the two of them were on a committee to lower the reparations that France was demanding from Germany."

"They worked together?" Ann couldn't keep the shock from her tone. The moat of secrecy that Gilberte had dug around herself and her family was broad and deep.

Quent nodded. "I don't have to tell you how far the committee got. The German economy went kaput, and the vermin crawled out. But Hocherer's old school, a Prussian aristocrat. He lives by a code of honor."

"Don't all the Nazis?" *Why am I bickering and being so damn clever?* The answer was clear: to repay Quent for that coldly spoken crack about making bail.

"He's not a Nazi, he's a soldier." Quent, who wasn't wearing a hat, dashed a hand across his tanned forehead, scattering raindrops. "Ann, hasn't it entered your head that the de Permonts might have sneaked across the border to the unoccupied zone? Right now they could be trying to find their way to Spain or Switzerland. Say I go to one of the people I do business with. The minute he can get away from me he'll call Berlin and Berlin will contact Vichy."

The Vichy-based government of the unoccupied zone danced to whatever music the Germans chose to play. But would the family have fled? Ann could hear, actually hear, Gilberte's light, faintly caustic voice saying, *De Permonts do not run away.*

"They're still here, Quent."

"They might have been forced to leave." His face was drawn into gaunt lines.

He looks guilty, she thought. "So you think he'll help, the general?" she asked quietly.

"If it's bad news, he won't be able to do much—when it comes to what's known as Internal Security of Occupied Territories, the Gestapo outranks the army." Quent walked faster, changing the subject abruptly. "There's a place near here with prewar pastry."

"I'm meant to be at the movies. I have to get back."

"It'll look odd to the resident spy if I head right back home to the Pyramide."

"Good point." Then, surprising herself, she said, "I didn't mean to sound so snotty before."

"You're upset, I'm upset, so let's declare a truce."

Reaching the Champs-Elysées, he turned left. The men, making the best of their leaves in dreary November weather, were window-shopping or taking snapshots of each other from under dripping canvas canopies. The uniforms no longer intimidated Ann. Quent was larger, stronger than any German.

"Here it is," he said.

The *salon de thé* stood on a corner. Tubbed fir bushes surrounded both sides of the glassed-in, crowded terrace. The feminine clientele was young and wore chic, frivolously elaborate hats while the men, a generation older, were either well-tailored civilians or high-ranking officers. A string trio played *Chanson d'Amour,* but French and German drowned out most of the sweetly tender notes.

Their wet coats were taken. Quent, apparently oblivious to the crush waiting to be seated, raised his hand. A sleek, fox-faced man greeted him by name and led them between the packed rows of small tables.

The groups nearby were too absorbed in their own conversations to be listening to anyone else's, but Ann deemed it prudent not to discuss the de Permonts. She found herself teasing Quent, and joking in the attempt to elicit smiles. He didn't smile easily, but when he did his authoritative air lessened, he looked younger and she had the illusion that he, intimate with the world's glamorous women, might actually be enjoying her company. His smile showed teeth that were straight and exceptionally white.

The waiter set down their orders. Her hothouse raspberry tart was made from real cream and real eggs, and she needed to exert her full willpower not to wolf it down.

"That's a nice-looking sweater and blouse," he said.

He was referring to the collar she had trimmed with lace from her old party dress and sewn to the fraying neckline of her powder blue pullover. "Oh, this old rag?" she said.

"The color suits you."

"I made it."

"Is that what you do with your spare time? Sew?"

"Lord, doesn't that sound domestic?"

"Are you?"

"You should hear my mother on that subject."

"Not domestic, then."

"What I'd like to be is a fashion designer." Visualizing her worked-over, erased sketches from the Design game, she sighed.

"Ann, what is it?"

"The one with talent is Gilberte."

His expression hardened subtly, and she again had that sense he was traveling away from her. Was he like Gilberte? Wanting to keep himself and his family on a remote island safe from plebeian invasion?

They had both ordered tea, which in this place was not the flat, ersatz infusion of grasses. Taking a soothing sip, she said, "You don't know what it's like to drink the genuine thing again."

"A demanding clientele here," he said.

"But you get a table right away." She made her tone teasing.

"I've known the owner the longest."

"Do you have a portrait in the attic growing older for you or what?"

"Grand-mère used to bring me here. She had a house in Neuilly."

"How old were you when you started coming?"

"So little I can't remember."

"One? Two?"

"It was a treat to be away from Nanny Greves, that's all I can tell you."

"Nanny Greves—it sounds like a Galsworthy novel."

"You've got the picture."

"What was your favorite dessert?"

"I always ordered the same thing, the *tarte tatin,* because the caramelized sugar on top of the apples was so hard that the waiter had to slap the knife down hard."

"You really are a long-term customer. But then *you'd* probably get a table anywhere."

"Ann?"

"Yes."

"Don't say things like that."

"I meant it as a compliment."

"You meant it as a judgment."

She started to whip back, then, realizing the validity, flushed and looked down at her cup. He reached over, touching her little finger with his own. The voices and clatter faded into the blood drumming against her ears, and she had a peculiar sense of momentum, as if she were bicycling down a hill very fast, a little afraid, but this fear only intensified the excitement. She tried to warn herself that her response was out of all proportion to a light touch on her pinkie. But never in her life had she felt so vulnerable to another human being, not even hammerlocked over the commissariat table. At the memory she shivered, moving her finger.

"I have to get back," she said. It sounded more flatly ungracious than she intended.

He got up. He did not ask for the bill, and the waiter didn't rush after them. The fox-faced man helped her on with her damp, shabby coat, effusively bidding them farewell as she balled the drenched scarf into her pocketbook.

At the George V métro entrance, she fished out centimes—there was a shortage of small coins and one couldn't buy a ticket without the exact change.

"I'll let you know as soon as I find out something," he said.

"Thank you."

"Thank *you.* Ann, I'm grateful that you told me right away."

"Uhh, please don't come to the flat. My parents would be beside themselves if they knew I'd . . . well, been, you know. Tracking down missing people."

"I'll figure out a way to get in touch."

Compelled to protect her parents, she said, "They're worriers."

"Have they decided to go home?"

"Yes, we're leaving soon." She looked up at the poster glued on the white-tiled wall, a ravening British Tommy bayoneting a female depiction of France. "They're deciding which ship would be safest."

"What about the Pan Am Clipper?"

"Fly?" She'd never been on a plane, and neither had Horace or Dorothy—or any of the people she knew. The clipper flew twice a week from Lisbon to New York via the Azores. The fare was outrageous, and she'd heard there was a year-long waiting list.

"I'm fairly sure I can arrange seats," Quent said.

"That's very nice of you."

"Ann, it's time to get out of Europe. Are they serious about leaving, or just talking about it?"

Embarrassed, she mumbled, "I appreciate the offer." And ran down the métro steps.

The cars were crowded. A round-shouldered Luftwaffe sergeant offered his seat, and she shook her head in refusal. Gripping a bar, she jounced through the dark tunnels with a brooding expression. She had gone to get help for the de Permonts. And what had she done? Spent most of her time flirting with a man that Gilberte— her best friend, her absent best friend—was interested in. And what a pointless flirtation! Quent Dejong came from a world of nannies, houses in Neuilly, debutantes and movie stars, a world that the war had not disrupted.

Yet her unruly body kept recapturing the melting sensation invoked by the touch of his little finger.

10

Two icy weeks passed. Ann couldn't cure her compulsion to run upstairs once or twice a day to bang on the never-opening door. Neither could she control her increasing resentment toward Quent Dejong. On that rainy Saturday afternoon she had judged him to be rock-solid sincere. Since then she was becoming more and more suspicious that he'd done zero. Normally her emotions toward others remained constant—she was loyal in the extreme—so her seeping trust in him hurt until she wanted to scream or whimper. The closest she could come to a kindly explanation for his silence was that he might have been genuinely distraught when she'd told him but later had realized he was in Paris to conduct business for a bank with his own patronym and not to search for distant relatives who were probably in bad with the German authorities.

There was another alternative: He might have uncovered the truth, either happy or dire, and forgotten to let her know.

Her parents continued their endless conversation about leaving, cutting off her attempts to talk over the de Permonts' disappearance. The press continued to trumpet Axis victories. The weather continued bleak.

As Ann raised her umbrella on the wet granite step outside Madame Bernard's, she heard her name whispered, then a snicker.

She had become as one with the mosquito swarm of speculation about Gilberte's prolonged absence—the hardiest, most persistent rumor was that Gilberte's aristocratic parents had hidden her shame in the country. Ann's staunch denials were turned inside out as proof of Gilberte's *enceinte* condition.

Biting down on her lower lip to contain her anger, Ann hurried away from school along the rue de la Grand Chaumière, crossing the boulevard du Montparnasse. By the time she reached the lattice of narrow alleys that was her and Gilberte's favored route home, the anger had faded and she was once more sunk into worried gloom.

"Ann! Slow down," called a masculine voice in American accents. "Whoa there, girl."

Larry Porter, waving, dodged around a muddy puddle that had gathered where the cobbles were missing. The collar of his trench coat was turned up, and rain had darkened the shoulders.

He trotted up to her. "You trying out for the four-forty or what?" he asked, switching to English.

"So you do have a trench coat," she said.

"For this weather only," he replied, laughing. Reaching to hold the umbrella, he took her satchel. "Do guys carry girls' books around here?"

"It's not a deeply ingrained custom, no," she said. "Is it in Van Nuys?"

"What a memory!" He laughed again.

"Why are you following me?"

"Following pretty girls *is* a deeply ingrained custom in Van Nuys," he said, grinning. "I'm a messenger with word from a mutual friend."

"Gilberte?" she asked excitedly.

"Quent Dejong. He said to tell you he would've come himself but had to head over to the Vichy zone on some urgent business that, or so I gather, could be conducted only by the upper echelons of finance."

Why should a rich, important man, Ann thought, *take time off to come and tell me in person?* What a grim place this alley was! Broken windows and the paint totally worn from doors and shutters, several of which dangled from their hinges.

"You don't seem very interested in the secret message," Larry said.

"I am. Tell me."

"He said, 'The general thinks he might have a lead.' "

"That's all?"

"That's all. 'The general thinks he might have a lead.' "

"You're sure there wasn't anything else?"

"Nope. And Quent had me repeat it five times. Make any sense to you?"

She nodded. The sentence meant that since her visit to the Hotel Pyramide, Quent Dejong had telephoned General von Hocherer about the de Permonts' absence. And that was all he'd done. *Couldn't he have put himself out a little bit?*

"I don't mind telling you that it's as obscure as hell to my wooden skull." Larry knocked at the side of his head. "He also told me I shouldn't let anybody see me talking to you. Again his exact words. 'Larry, I'll beat the holy shi— the holy hell out of you if you go to her place or anywhere near her school.' So here I am, rushing after you like a trained bloodhound."

"Thank you," she said.

"Can't you whip a little more enthusiasm into that gratitude?"

"I do appreciate it."

"Good," he said. "I'm glad." Handing her back her satchel, he leaned forward and, before she could gauge his intentions, kissed her on the cheek. For a moment he touched his warm tongue to her skin.

She moved away rapidly, irritated by her ardent wish that it was Quent Do-Nothing Dejong who had kissed her.

Later, in dry clothes, huddled under her duvet, she attempted to read tomorrow's literature lesson, an essay of Montaigne's. *L'utilité du vivre n'est pas en l'espace, elle est en l'usage.* . . . The value of life lies not in the length of days, but in the use we make of them. It might have been a satisfying philosophy in Montaigne's era, but in today's Paris, with your best friend possibly being shortchanged on the length of her days, it offered no solace.

Leaning her head back on the bolster, she sighed waveringly. *Gilberte, where are you?*

Gilberte
La Santé Prison, 1941

11

Gilberte lay on the upper bunk, a bent finger resting below her nostrils in a futile attempt to block the odors from the overflowing commode.

Why am I here? she thought. *What's going to happen to me? Where are Papa and Maman? Are they in this sinkhole too? When will I be told why I'm here? Are they still alive?*

There were no answers. The only certainty was that for fifteen days she'd been inside the Santé prison.

When she was seven her governess had pointed out the prison as the chauffeur drove them along the boulevard Arago and Gilberte, deep into *The Count of Monte Cristo*, had shivered pleasurably at the improbably thick, thirty-feet-high stone walls. In those prewar days the Santé had held six hundred prisoners, but since the Occupation the population had multiplied and now hovered around twenty-eight hundred. Gilberte and seven other women were jammed into a cell intended for two. (At night, according to the warden's current regulations, they rotated in pairs, lying on their sides so the narrow bunks could accommodate two each while the other four stretched out on the icy cement floor.) Except for Berthe, the broad-hipped young whore, they were middle-aged, middle-class women who had in some way run afoul of the proliferation of German laws.

At this moment the two shopkeepers were holding forth.

"I never sold as much as a dried pea without a coupon."

"*Moi non plus*, Madame, *moi non plus*. Never even a shoelace under the table."

"Not a centime extra would I take."

Gilberte winced. These often repeated litanies of innocence grated unendurably against her anxieties. *Where are my parents?*

On that Friday night when she had awakened to the air raid siren, her father had called from the corridor, "No need to get up, Gilberte." Despite the threat of stiff fines for not taking shelter, the family avoided the basement bomb shelter.

Curling up in bed, Gilberte had thought about the Delannoy film she and Ann would see the following afternoon. Ann, being Ann, had needed to be dissuaded from including those two dreary boys from Lycée Paul Bert. Charles, Gilberte's "date," was forever attempting to maul her—like most of the masculine sex, he behaved as though she were a mirage whose reality needed tactile proof. Gilberte's thoughts had wandered drowsily. . . .

She was asleep when a fist hammered against her door.

An SS poked his close-cropped scalp inside, shouting at her to get dressed—"*Macht schnell!*" She could hear other bawling German commands, her mother's pretty, faintly malicious voice, her father's irate, gravelly tones.

Gilberte, who was firmly convinced that her father belonged to the Résistance network, could not control her shaking fingers. She fumbled with lingerie buttons and snaps for what seemed decades, putting on her school suit for no better reason than that it hung airing on the armoire door. When she finally emerged, only the shave-head remained. Hurrying her down the stairwell with a flashlight, he'd shoved her into the back of a police van. She'd been alone in the darkness.

The thin, ticked mattress sagged as Mademoiselle Lesdain, the thick-waisted modiste, hauled herself up onto the bunk. Gilberte flinched. She seldom spoke to the others, and felt their physical impingements as a gross personal insult.

They in turn disliked her openly, calling her "*la dauphine*." But she was used to contempt. All of her life people had pointed an actual or hypothetical finger at her.

Her parents were not married.

Their separate marriages, each arranged by family, each long abandoned in the flesh and spirit, remained legally binding. Her father's devout, humorless wife refused to hear talk of a divorce. Tucked away in her big, ugly nineteenth-century house just north of Cáen, she presumably was on her knees praying for a swift German victory and for her husband's soul. ViVi's spouse, Romain Cagny, an amateur anthropologist who spent most of his time on expeditions to remote and primitive places like Torajaland in the Celebes, had signed an ironclad marital settlement that tied up the bulk of his assets. (His father, whose fortune welled abundantly from the manufacture of vitreous china lavatories and bidets, had agreed to the clauses in order to pluck for his son a bride from the great if impoverished de Mascaret family tree.) Oddly enough, when ViVi departed the ostentatious Cagny mansion in Saint-Cloud to live openly in André's tall, gracious town house on the boulevard Suchet, it was not the wronged spouses who showed undue distress—the marital state suited neither Romain Cagny nor Hortense de Permont. However, their friends, whose own marriages were pocked with infidelities, were worldly enough to realize that to keep their circle's comfortable place atop the social order the conventions must be given lip service.

André and ViVi outrode the ostracism by ignoring it, but no parent, not even the raffish or forgetfully tolerant, cared to expose an innocent offspring to the ménage.

So Gilberte was the one who paid the piper.

Her earliest memories were of the servants whispering, "La p'tite bâtarde." In the manner of very young children, she accepted that she was guilty of some mysterious crime. Her inner shame cut so deep that she never questioned her punishment—she was not invited to birthday parties, never played in other nurseries and no little girls visited to share her trove of dolls. In the late afternoon her nurse would dress her in one of her convent-smocked party dresses, brush her black bangs and take her downstairs to the salon with the beaten bronze walls and the sleek modern furniture. Usually there were guests, but the baronne (as ViVi now styled herself, not as cover-up but merely because it made life simpler) was always the most beautiful lady. Gilberte loved looking at her mother.

But it was her father who filled her universe. He smelled of clean shirts, brandy, pipe tobacco and his own unique brand of salty sweat. He and Gilberte explored the countryside in his bullet-shaped Delahaye, which had only two seats. They rode in the nearby Bois de Boulogne, he on his stallion, Bucephalus, she on her pony, Frou-Frou. In August, which was always spent at the rambling de Permont château in Ile de France, he would swim with her in the pond—for the rest of her life she would consider a man emasculate if he lacked abundant body hair. As if to compensate for the circumstances of her birth, he imbued her with the myths and tales of the de Permont family. Gilberte's favorite ancestor was Guy de Permont, whose return from the Crusades was immortalized by the medieval trouvère Godefroy d'Angers. She tingled with a vindicatory thrill each time her father reached the climax of the story, how the Baron Guy had discovered that his evil cousin Arnaud had taken over the fiefdom by kicking out Guy's wife, who had died, and his young son. "Rather than killing Arnaud," her father would say, "Guy repaid him in kind. He reduced that worm to the dirt where he belonged, and saw to it that his family stayed in the mud forever." To Gilberte, the generational punishment outclassed anything in the Bible.

Her first governess, Mademoiselle Gottshalk, sometimes laughed at inappropriate moments and had breath that smelled of violets. One night Gilberte awoke to hear loud snoring. The governess was slumped with her head on the schoolroom table, her carrot-red hair covering her face, an Armagnac bottle in front of her. When Gilberte poked her arm to awaken her, she eased sideways like Olympe, the life-size doll in *Tales of Hoffmann,* sliding onto the carpet. Gilberte fled down the dark corridor to her parents' rooms.

A light shone around her father's door. Weak with gratitude to find him home, she turned the bronze handle.

Maman, stark naked, was bouncing up and down on Papa as if she were trotting on a pony. He stroked and patted her, and then soon they were both galloping fast and making loud gasping noises. Gilberte stared through the narrow slit of open door, knowing she shouldn't watch yet unable to move. She was in the clutches of a bewildering emotion that years later she would identify as a lover's betrayal.

She lived in near total isolation from both sides of her family, the sole exception being Mathilde Dejong, her father's aunt, a wrinkled, imperious septuagenarian with hair dyed a startling black. The widow of an American, Tante Mathilde ceaselessly traveled back and forth across the Atlantic. Whenever her grandson accompanied her entourage, she brought him to visit. Quent, six years older than Gilberte, treated her with absent kindness, permitting her to tag after him: he shared her unqualified admiration of her father. Reaching puberty, she realized that her second cousin was exceptionally handsome. His father's reputation with women leaked over, making him seem yet more dashing, and then, too, there was that scandal of the pregnant girl, about which Gilberte knew only the gauziest details.

Other than Quent's infrequent if memorable visits, Gilberte's life was devoid of contact with young people. Those first days at Madame Bernard's were torment. That her classmates were petit bourgeois gave consolation when she was alone—but none while the girls were sniffing around her like dogs. Then Ann Blakely, the American girl with the large, sparkly brown eyes who lived in the apartment below, suggested they walk to and from school together. Gilberte hid her pleasure beneath sarcasm. Before long, however, Ann's warmth and unstinting esteem relaxed her defensiveness. Although her friend repeatedly proved empathetic, sympathetic, loyal, incapable of betraying a confidence, Gilberte could not confess her deepest shame, her bar sinister. Accordingly, she had drawn a pentagram of secrecy around her parents and her past life.

Metal scratched in the lock of the cell.

Gilberte refused to succumb to the urge to look up. But the other women, abruptly silent, turned toward the door in fear. The Santé followed an unvarying routine. Two hours earlier they had eaten the brownish slops that passed as the midday meal: nobody was due until seven, when the slack-faced idiot would arrive to empty the commode.

The door creaked open.

"Well, if it isn't the tall, dark and handsome stranger my cards promised me." The raucous tone belonged to Berthe, the irreverent whore, who dealt a greasy, dog-eared Tarot deck to foretell the future of anyone interested.

"Which one of you is Gilberte de Permont?" a man boomed in German.

Gilberte propped up her head on her elbow, a seemingly negligent gesture. A dwarfed SS private with burly shoulders stood in the doorway. Though the Santé was under both German and French jurisdiction, thus far Gilberte had seen only French authorities. The black uniform and death's-head insignia jumped in front of her eyes as she asked in German, "Did I hear my name?"

"Captain Knecht wants you."

"Knecht? Knecht? I don't know any Captain Knecht. Oh, well, tell him I'll be there in a few minutes." She slid casually from the bunk. "I have to wash my face and comb my hair."

"Now!" As the dwarf stumped into the cell, the women hastily pulled in their feet so he could yank Gilberte into the corridor.

12

Though Gilberte knew the Santé covered a rough trapezoid of several city blocks, she lacked any idea of the prison's interior geography beyond the route to the sunless, cobbled yard where she and fifty other women walked daily silent ovals for a half hour under the rifles of guards.

The dwarf was leading her in the opposite direction. As they passed a narrow stairwell that led downward, she heard a prolonged, muted howl. The goose bumps were still on her arms when they reached an iron door guarded by two SS privates. Even if she weren't fluent in German, she would have understood the lewd tenor of their jokes about midgets getting all the good jobs. Stepping onto the Gestapo side of the Santé, she found herself in a brightly lit corridor noisy with *Blitzmädchen,* gray-uniformed German women auxiliaries, clattering away at typewriters.

The dwarf opened an office door. Clicking the heels of his boots together, he raised his arm in a smart Nazi salute. "Heil Hitler, Captain Knecht. The prisoner, sir."

Captain Knecht looked up from his cluttered desk. With his plump, lined face and rounded shoulders, he reminded her of the shy, punctilious tutor who'd taught her botany.

"Ah, Mademoiselle. I won't be a minute." He spoke excellent though heavily accented French. "Please take the chair."

She remained on her feet. She was ill with terror and anticipation, but she looked around the office with what she hoped was arrogance, pretending amusement at the messy surroundings: letters were strewn across the desktop, forms were piled across the floor, a patchwork of Paris street maps covered the walls. A radiator hissed. After the freezing temperature of the cell, the warmth felt equatorial and soon she grew dizzy. She sat.

At this Captain Knecht screwed the top on his fountain pen, peering earnestly at her through rimless glasses. "You are beautiful, Mademoiselle. Somewhat like Vivien Leigh."

"Is that my crime, looking like an English film actress?"

As she spoke the door opened, and the little man returned with a coffee tray, holding it one-handed with a dexterity that made her wonder if he'd been a waiter in civilian life. He cleared a place on the desk.

"Thank you, Wissman," the captain said. "That will be all." After Wissman had heiled and saluted his way out, Captain Knecht indicated the platter of small cakes. "My orderly has found an excellent *pâtissier*. May I tempt you, Mademoiselle?"

The odor of fresh baking filled her mouth with saliva. How long since she'd eaten food prepared with real sugar, real butter, white flour?

"Thank you, but eating now would ruin my dinner," she said.

He ignored her irony. "Then you must excuse me." He let his plump fingers hover delicately before swooping down on a pink-iced petit four. He downed three cakes then dabbed his lips with a napkin. "It's regrettable you're here," he said. "Most unfortunate."

"But alas, girls who resemble Vivien Leigh are being rounded up?"

"Perhaps you recall that damage outside the Gare de l'Est a month or so ago?"

"The gas explosion?"

He poured himself another cup of coffee. "Sabotage."

"I thought the *Propagandastaffel* told the truth and nothing but the truth."

"Mademoiselle, this pseudo-cleverness is unworthy. A great many innocent German boys could have been killed."

"I plead not guilty."

He clasped his soft, pale hands on the desk. "Working together, I'm sure we can arrange a release for you and your mother."

"Maman? So she *is* here?" Before the words were out, Gilberte regretted her pleading tone, her childish use of *Maman*.

"She is. And your father too."

"But why?"

"A witness places him in the vicinity of the Gare de l'Est at the time of the terrorist attack."

Hot pride surged through her. She longed to shout that her father, from the de Permont family, which had always served France, could be expected to blow up enemy troop trains. But at the same time her mind was twisting with the image of her father strapped into a torture chair. "Set your mind at rest, Captain Knecht," she said. "My father doesn't go around igniting natural gas deposits."

"I told you we have a witness who saw him just prior to the attack. My problem, and yours, Mademoiselle, is that he refuses to name his accomplices."

"He had no accomplices. He had nothing to do with the explosion."

"Kommandant von Schaumburg has taken a personal interest in this case." Kommandant von Schaumburg, as all France knew, headed the military occupation forces of Paris. "He is convinced that you and your mother were also actively involved. I don't happen to agree, but . . ." Captain Knecht raised his scanty eyebrows to indicate that the Kommandant was his boss. "I could prove you and she are innocent if your father would tell me who *did* work with him."

"Have you discussed this with my father?"

"Naturally. A most congenial man, if uncooperative. Madame Cagny"—as he used the name, Gilberte stiffened—"refused to speak to me at all. She actually refused to speak." Captain Knecht glanced down at his gold wristwatch. "I've arranged for your father to be brought."

"Here?"

"Yes, here. You'll have a half hour alone."

"So that I may weep and grovel and plead with him to invent a few false names?"

"You don't need to bring the matter up."

"But it *is* why you're allowing us to see each other?"

"Of course it is." The captain rose to his feet. "One more thing you ought to know. Kommandant von Schaumburg is no softy when it comes to saboteurs, young or old, male or female."

He walked duckfootedly from the office. Gilberte twined her fingers tensely. *I won't plead with Papa,* she thought. *I'll never, never ask him to betray anyone.*

The little orderly, Wissman, returned for the tray, the radiator gave a series of knocking hisses, the clock on the wall loudly ticked away seven minutes. Why hadn't they brought him? Again she conjured up tortures.

Suddenly the door swung open. Her father stepped inside, casual as if entering his own study. She had never before seen him unshaven, and the beard spreading like heavy grime below his cheekbones came as a mild shock. His eyes were shadowed, his clothing, normally impeccable, rumpled. But he was untortured, unbroken, erect as always.

She ran to him, he embraced her tightly, then pulled back, peering at her. "Gilberte, what are you doing here?" he asked.

"Didn't Captain Knecht tell you? We have a half hour together."

"You never should have come."

His anger made her swallow sharply. "What choice did I have?"

His arms fell from her. "My God," he whispered. "Are you saying you're locked up in this *pissoir*?"

"You didn't know I was arrested when you were?"

"Stupid of me, but I never thought of the possibility. Well, leave it to the Nazis to round up schoolgirls. What about your mother? Is she in the Santé too?"

"Yes. Captain Knecht says he questioned her. She refused to answer, she didn't say a word."

The baron chuckled. "That's my ViVi."

Gilberte felt a stab of dismay. Why hadn't she maintained a patrician silence with the soft, pedantic Gestapo officer? "Papa, I'm so proud of you."

"For being a jailbird?"

"For trying to blow up the troop train."

"I, Gilberte?" Speaking reproachfully, he glanced around, scanning the street maps as if searching for tiny listening holes. "If it *had* been me, the train would have been destroyed."

Gilberte joined the act. "I told Captain Knecht he was crazy."

"If he'd studied my military career, he'd know I'm not a bungler."

"What can one expect of a German? Of the middle rank?"

The baron laughed, then his forehead creased. "Gilberte, I wish with all my heart you weren't here."

"Me too. The chef is absolutely rotten."

His expression grew pleading. *He wants to apologize,* she thought. When had her father ever apologized? He was too proud, too jaunty, too secure about his place in this world to apologize. Gilberte couldn't bear the contrite misery in the small, raisin-dark eyes.

"Papa, I'm fine," she said softly, and touched his hand.

"In here?"

"It's educational. Like being in a boarding school. One of the women in my cell is a *putain* who reads our fortunes. Believe me, I'd do well on an exam about the meaning of Tarot cards."

He managed a smile.

I did not ask him to betray anyone, she thought. *That proves I'm a real de Permont.*

The following afternoon little Wissman again came to the cell for her. This time Captain Knecht wasn't in his office. Instead, her mother sat in his chair with her hands composedly in her lap. The baronne's blond hair was pulled into its chignon, her makeup carefully applied, her outfit, a black prewar Chanel, remarkably free of wrinkles. Evidently she'd been expecting Gilberte, for she rose with swift grace to kiss her daughter on both cheeks.

"*Ma chère,* how good to see you," she said. "But your suit!"

"My coat's even more dubious. It could have gone through the Hundred Years' War—I use it as a blanket."

"A what?"

"Blanket."

The baronne frowned. "In circumstances like this, *ma chère,* one must make every effort to keep oneself neat." She indicated a tray set with a platter of thin-sliced bread that glinted with butter. "They've served us *thé anglais.*"

"You're going to eat their food?"

"Why not?"

"It's *theirs.*"

"I don't understand you, Gilberte. Servants always bring us our meals." The baronne poured two cups of rich, dark tea. "Have you met Captain Knecht?"

"Yesterday."

"I had the pleasure the day before you, then." The baronne extended the platter.

Gilberte took a slice of bread. "Thank you."

"The captain tells me your father is here too. He has an *idée fixe* that Papa with his own hands blew up some railroad or other. Imagine! A colonel in the French army setting dynamite!"

Gilberte looked at her mother. Was she feigning, or was the indignation natural? It was impossible to pierce what lay behind those limpid eyes.

"It's too droll," Gilberte agreed, knowing that she would break down if she mentioned seeing her father, and therefore could not mention yesterday's meeting.

"How are your quarters, *ma chère?*"

"Adequate."

"Mine also." The delicate nostrils flared. "But I must say that the company leaves something to be desired."

"*Je suis d'accord.*"

"I've always said one can forgive anyone but a bore." The baronne paused. "May I offer you more bread and butter?"

Gilberte longed to wolf down the entire platter, but manners had been drilled into her. Never, never take a second serving.

"No, thank you, Maman," she said. *If Captain Knecht is monitoring our conversations,* she thought, *he's learned nothing beyond the mores of French society.*

13

Gilberte's two summons by the diminutive Wissman roused a storm of conversation in the cell. She heard each inquiry as an avid probe. *All they want is grist for their gossip mill,* she would think, withdrawing behind her little smile. *La dauphine*'s persistent refusal to discuss what transpired on the German side increased the general resentment. But how could she let them in on the terrors that ripped her apart?

It was immaterial whether or not her father confessed to mangling a section of railroad yard, she realized: the Nazis were convinced of his guilt. What Captain Knecht was after were his contacts in the Résistance. And André de Permont, lacking the capacity of betrayal, would never give names. Her mind dwelt continuously on stories of Gestapo interrogations—beatings that bared rib bones, teeth extracted, gouged-out eyeballs. Her anxieties touched far more lightly on her mother. Not only was the bond weaker, but to Gilberte the baronne had always appeared invulnerable in her carapace of beauty and stylized manners. Besides, although this was doubtless irrelevant to the Gestapo, her mother, like herself, had taken no part in the incident.

In this state of panic for her father, time became a gluey element to be battled through. Then on the morning of the third day after she had seen her mother, Wissman came for her.

When they reached the narrow stairwell, the diminutive orderly said with a wolfish smirk, "Today you go down."

She could not control her shudders. Yet the prison basement was commonplace enough with its scarred green paint, pipes running along the ceiling and a *gemütlich* recreation area formed by shoving two shabby brown couches against walls affixed with photographs of wives and sweethearts. A half-dozen SS noncoms smoked and excitedly discussed a surprise air attack on a place Gilberte had never heard of, Pearl Harbor. As she passed between the couches, the war talk ceased and the men commented graphically on her extraordinary physical endowments.

She stared straight ahead. Wissman led her around a corner to where a pillow-bosomed *Blitzmädchen* sat at a desk filing her nails. Wissman told her he was escorting the prisoner to Captain Knecht.

Glancing down a list, the auxiliary said, "In room fourteen."

Captain Knecht's black tie had been loosened, making him appear even less martial. On the battered table in front of him lay three manila folders. As Wissman prodded her forward, she read the heavy Germanic script on the flaps. *Baron André de Permont. Vivienne Cagny. Gilberte.* Her mind went blank for an instant. The single name reduced her to the level of a household animal, a dog or cat.

"That'll be all for the time being, Wissman," the captain said.

Knecht had the only chair in the dingy, windowless cubicle: she stood in front of the table, her mouth dry, her armpits wet.

Opening her file, he said, "I need you to verify a few facts and answer some questions. You were born to Vivienne Cagny and Baron André de Permont on October first, nineteen twenty-four?"

"So I've been informed."

Peering down at her dossier, he inquired into minute details of her childhood, the names of her nurse, governesses, tutors, which subjects she had learned, what restaurants and operas she'd been taken to. As she responded, he either checked his reports or wrote down her words with agonizing slowness. She accepted that if this were indeed a softening-up process, it was working. Her spine ached, fear pressed increasingly on her bladder.

It must have been several hours before he reached the family's move to the rue Daguerre. "And you took two servants?"

Responding to his nit-picking inquiries about Jacques and Hélène, she wondered what had happened to them. Were they still
living in the apartment? Or when they had returned from the
basement to find their employers gone, did they bolt into hiding?

He came to Ann—the American girl Blakely, as he called her—
delving into their friendship.

"And your fathers were equally close?" he asked.

"They were mere acquaintances."

Captain Knecht shuffled pages. "Ah, here it is. You said that your
families dined together twice a week."

"To save cooking gas."

"So they were more than acquaintances?"

"Only for convenience. Perhaps you've heard. Gas is rationed."

As Knecht pursued the relationship between her father and the
chinless wonder with exacting thoroughness, Gilberte's attention
kept wandering to her lumbar discomfort and her need to urinate.

"Do you know any other Americans?" he asked.

"None—unless you count my cousin."

"Cousin?" Knecht pushed his rimless spectacles higher on his
nose, peering at her. "You have American relations?"

Furious at herself for the lapse, she said, "Doesn't everyone?"
And succumbed to pressing her hands to the small of her back.

"I must remind you, Mademoiselle, that this is not the time for a
massage. It is an official interview." His voice had altered from a
pedantic drone to a bark. She let her hands drop. "The family
name of your relations?"

"Dejong," she muttered.

"Dejong?" he asked, his pale brows rising. "Of the Dejong
Bank?"

"I have no idea," she lied.

"The owners of the bank, I believe, are connected in some way
to the Templar steel fortune?"

Quent, Jason Templar's grandson, was the sole heir. "We never
discuss business in my home."

The captain wrote several spidery paragraphs on the back of a
page before carefully blotting the ink.

Please, please, please let this be over.

He questioned her another fifteen minutes before returning the dossier to its folder. "Come," he said.

At the first step her right ankle bent inward. She limped painfully along basement corridors, forced to keep up with the two men— Wissman had been waiting outside.

The orderly opened a door and a cloud of tobacco smoke laced with the rankness of sweat burst out. The two SS smoking on sturdy, ladder-back chairs had removed their uniform shirts and their grayish underwear showed dark patches on the chest and under the arms. The younger, he couldn't have been more than seventeen, jerked to attention, saluting the captain with the stiffness of a Hitler Youth in the presence of the Führer. Knecht waved a hand to show informality was in order. The boy retrieved his fallen cigarette butt from a puddle. The large, footed bathtub filled with water was a stark anomaly in the cell.

But how could she be taking in these peripheral details when her senses were sharply honed on her father?

He had not looked up. He remained slumped on the floor with his head resting on his knees. The circle of black hair left to him dripped with water, and his drenched shirt clung to his thick chest to show each labored breath. One hand clutched his forehead: where the index fingernail should be was an ugly, reddish ooze. Gilberte felt a sharp wrench, as if his brutalized nervous system were being hooked up to her own. She took a step toward him.

Captain Knecht gripped her arm, pulling her back. He glanced at the older man. Large, bland-looking, freckled, he shook his head.

"Baron de Permont," the captain said in a lecturing tone. "I've informed you of Kommandant von Schaumburg's orders. Everyone involved must be rounded up and arrested. Personally, I'm beginning to agree with him that you did work with Madame Cagny and your daughter. Nobody would go to these lengths to protect some railroad workers, a few *cheminots.*"

The baron grunted, "Go to hell."

The captain cleared his throat, turning to Gilberte. "I'm giving you a chance to talk some sense into him, Mademoiselle."

The baron lifted his head so slowly that Gilberte wondered if his neck vertebrae had been damaged. His bloodshot eyes met hers. Gilberte attempted a smile, but her mouth refused to cooperate.

"Gilberte," he whispered. "My God, they've actually brought you down here!"

"She'll be released as soon as you prove to my satisfaction that she wasn't with you at the Gare de l'Est." Knecht seated himself in one of the sturdy chairs. "Frankly, Baron, your entire attitude baffles me. You're an intelligent man. Surely you must see that the Führer's goal is to cure this century's awful blight of decadence and immorality. Don't most of the French people want the identical thing? And as for the Bolshevik menace, aren't most of you delighted to have the Third Reich as your buffer?"

Why this sudden shift to political philosophy? Gilberte attempted to move away from Knecht, but the pudgy fingers were deceptively strong.

To prove herself unsubdued, she inquired, "If we're all so delighted, why did we fight?"

"Believe me, Mademoiselle, the war was a mistake. It was engineered by the Communists in your government and, of course, the Jews. The same crowd's busy spreading the lie that we're here to exploit France. Nothing could be further from the truth. We pay for every piece of goods we buy. We try to behave decently." The discursive tone had become pleading. "Why, this month we've been shipping you our own milk supply."

Gilberte thought of those cakes, the bread and butter, the real tea. "You're the saviors of Western civilization and nursing mothers."

"Believe me, rationing's equally bad in Germany, maybe worse. You should read my wife's letters. Last winter, the worst weather in a century, I believe, we did everything in our power to help you."

"Then why doesn't your benevolence extend to schoolgirls?" the baron asked hoarsely.

The captain sighed. "Try to understand the Kommandant's position. Naturally I'm not close to a man of his rank, but I have heard him say several times that his greatest happiness would be to restore Paris to its prewar freedom and spirit. Those aren't words of the propaganda hacks, but from the Kommandant's own lips. In the meanwhile, it's his responsibility to protect the lives of our soldiers as well as your civilian population—it was a French worker who was killed at the trainyard. He's a civilized man, but for the good of all, this terrorism has to be stopped. So unfortunately we're forced to use methods we don't enjoy."

"Like torturing my father?" Gilberte asked.

"Mademoiselle, he understands the situation." Knecht sounded like a put-upon teacher. "He can stop us, as well as get both you and your mother released." He raised his voice. "Baron, you have one final chance before we interrogate your daughter."

The baron shot Gilberte an anguished look. Her terror had become an active partner in her biology, yet she steeled herself to gaze back with no trace of fear. This was her moment of truth.

Now she could prove that, despite being born on the wrong side of the blanket, she was a true de Permont. Conversely, if she didn't behave according to the family code of honor now, then she would have proved herself forever unworthy of the proud and ancient name.

She continued to look at her father steadily. She was making a pact with him. He must not betray his Résistance cadre because of her.

His stubbled jaw lifted infinitesimally.

Agreement.

"Captain Knecht," he said, "neither of us has any knowledge that could help you."

Captain Knecht looked at the two shirtless men. "Our guest needs a more comfortable seat."

The older SS grabbed the baron by his arms while the younger lifted his legs at the knees. The baron gave a stifled grunt, grunting again when they dumped him like a sack of rutabagas on one of the sturdy chairs. They handcuffed his wrists behind the back then used heavy rope to secure his ankles to the chair's legs.

They turned to Gilberte.

14

The older man picked her up, ignoring her kicking struggles as he carried her to the bathtub. The boyish one slammed the side of his hand behind her knees. With a cry, she collapsed in a kneeling position.

Captain Knecht leaned over her father's chair. ". . . who worked with you? You couldn't have . . ."

A hand curved around the base of her skull, forcing her head into the icy water. Despite her violent thrashing, the pressure against her head remained steady. She churned as sonic sounds drummed against her ears and her eyes expanded from the sockets. In her panic, she wet herself. Her struggles weakened. She was released. Through her racking breaths, she heard Captain Knecht's soft, pedagogical voice: ". . . with you at the Gare de l'Est?"

Her father didn't respond.

Her head was thrust back into the tub. This time she told herself: *They don't intend to drown me. If I were dead there'd be no chance of Papa talking, they aren't going to drown me. . . .* She forced herself to exhale slowly. But when the air in her lungs was exhausted, animal instinct took over, and she flailed as madly as a landed fish until she was on the verge of blacking out. Again she was allowed up. Retching feebly, she ached to whimper and plead with her father to end all this horror, to confess anything, anything, to tell every name. Yet a tiny, dark corner of her mind refused to capitulate. And this corner, what earlier generations would have called her soul, feared less what the Gestapo might do to her than being stripped of de Permonthood. During her brief respites of raw, shuddering gasps, she heard Captain Knecht's voice, sometimes raised, sometimes droning, and her father's hoarse invectives. At some point she realized that her older tormentor was called Merck, while the boy's name was Ristelheuber.

Finally she was permitted to collapse retching on the soaked cement. When capable of taking in her surroundings, she saw her father slumped forward in the chair with blood trickling from both ears. *Please don't let him be dead,* she prayed to a God all too obviously both blind and deaf.

"There's no point in continuing for the moment. We'll wait until he is conscious," Captain Knecht said.

Wissman left, returning with coffee and crullers. The captain had finished his snack by the time the baron stirred, coming to. Gilberte's head was shoved back underwater. The next time she was permitted to collapse her father was again unconscious.

"That's enough for today, Merck," Captain Knecht said. "We'll try an alternate method tomorrow."

Gilberte, crouching on all fours, head down like a sick animal, didn't notice the concupiscent smiles of the three noncoms.

Upon her drenched return the women, overlooking her previous aloofness, gathered around solicitously. Apparently everyone in the cell other than Gilberte had known about the water treatment —the *baignoire*. She was helped off with her clothes and Berthe, employing her full professional range of obscenities against the Third Reich, wrung them out. Since there was no space to spread things to dry, the sheep-odored mass was clumped over the foot of the upper bunk, which, ignoring prison regulations, they gave to Gilberte for herself. Huddled naked under her overcoat and the cell's allotment of two thin, filth-encrusted khaki blankets, her chest aching rawly with every breath, she passed the night attempting to steel herself against the coming day.

No sooner had she dipped her sour stale bread in the brownish liquid that passed as coffee than the door opened.

"*Guten Morgen*, Fräulein," Wissman said to her. "Sorry to interrupt breakfast, but you must come with me."

"Let her dress, you little prick," shouted Berthe.

Wissman shrugged, smiling to himself. The whore held up a blanket while Gilberte struggled into sodden clothes.

Merck and Ristelheuber had already handcuffed her father into his chair, but the tub was empty and Knecht absent.

"You're looking for the captain?" Wissman asked. "Don't worry. He'll be here. Later."

"Who's first?" Ristelheuber asked with a boyish snicker.

The veins in the baron's battered forehead stood out. "Leave her alone, you sons of pigs."

Wissman snapped, "I've taken enough shit from you, Jew lover." Massive shoulders bunching, he aimed his fist at the stubbled chin. The baron's body twitched, and his head slumped forward.

"That was too hard," Merck reproved mildly. "It's quite a skill, I can tell you, to gauge a prisoner's strength."

"He'll come to," Wissman retorted.

"It could take as long as an hour," Merck said.

"Mine'll stay up that long. Won't yours?"

"Listen, you dwarf—"

Ristelheuber interrupted the argument. "Any bets if she's a virgin?"

"Sonny," Wissman said, "how often do you have to be told that these Frenchies are deflowered on their tenth birthday?"

Merck fished a ten-sou piece from his pocket. "Who's first?"

Gilberte darted for the door. It was locked. The three men laughed as Merck tossed the coin.

Wissman won.

"French women's looks're highly overrated," Wissman said, moving toward her. "But you, you're the exception. Those breasts, that rump, the legs—ooh la la! Take off those wet rags, let's see you."

Help us, she thought. *Somebody help Papa and me.* As Wissman stepped toward her, she retreated to a corner. "If you touch me, I'll kill you," she panted.

"How, *Liebchen?*" Merck asked.

"With her cunt." Ristelheuber guffawed.

Wissman circled the chair where her father slumped. "You know you're in for a treat, little Frenchie."

She curved her fingers, gouging her nails into his cheek.

"Bitch!" he shouted. Grabbing her wrist, he yanked the arm behind her back, twisting until she shrieked at the pain.

Merck began to slap her face, alternating palms for light but stinging blows. Lunging forward as if she were bobbing for apples, an American custom she'd learned at the Blakelys' on All Hallows Eve, she caught Merck's little finger between her teeth. Yelping, he punched her hard in the stomach. For a moment there was no sensation, but she was crumpling over and would have fallen if Wissman weren't holding her. Then pain radiated through her abdomen.

"See, *Liebchen,*" Merck said. "It's better to be nice to us." He reached for her jacket, forcing the top button through the wet buttonhole, working his way down. Though Wissman held her arms behind her back, she continued to dodge on her feet like a punch-happy prizefighter.

"Get away from my daughter," the baron muttered.

"Oh, so you're awake," Merck said. "Well, you know how to stop us."

"He doesn't have any names to tell!" Gilberte screamed.

The baron struggled to escape his bonds, overturning the chair. "You filthy—"

His voice subsided into a grunt as Wissman bent to shove a grimy handkerchief in his mouth. The heavy chair thumped on the cement floor in the baron's struggle to extricate himself from the ropes and handcuffs.

Gilberte continued to dodge around in an effort to escape, but Ristelheuber held her while Merck peeled off her jacket, her sweater. She had omitted her wet petticoat and brassiere, and as he unbuttoned her blouse, her breasts were revealed. Large, firm, high, with aureoled, deep red nipples.

"God," Ristelheuber whispered in awe. "Did you ever see such perfect titties?"

"Silky, too," Merck said, tracing the delicate vein that surfaced in the left breast. "A blue blood."

Wissman fumbled hastily with the buttons of his fly, releasing his erection.

Merck tugged down her skirt, revealing the translucently wet silk panties, and Wissman pushed her onto the cement floor, yanking on the underwear, scattering small pearl buttons from the side placket. She jammed her knees together. Ristelheuber and Wissman each took an ankle. She shrieked as they yanked her legs apart. Wissman lowered himself on top of her. He rammed into her.

She shrieked again.

"You see, I was right," Ristelheuber chortled. "A virgin."

She was out cold before the boy, who had placed third in the coin tossing, got his first turn.

Gilberte leaned against her father's chair, which had been set upright with him still bound in it. The two SS noncoms had left and Captain Knecht had not yet arrived. Wissman leaned against the door, smoking placidly, apparently a million miles away, in actuality listening for all he was worth. The orderly, who had worked two years in Le Havre as a stevedore, was fluent in French, a well-hidden skill that made him the perfect guard when people reduced to the lowest circle of misery were permitted to communicate.

"Will you make me a promise?" the baron asked, his bruised lips barely moving.

"Anything."

"Never, never be ashamed of what happened to you this morning."

"Someday I'll kill them."

"That will be my pleasure."

"Papa," Gilberte whispered, "*do* the Germans have a witness?"

"To what?" The baron's bruised face contorted as he glanced toward Wissman, who was unconcernedly blowing a smoke ring, and Gilberte understood that there could be no letting down for as long as they remained in the Santé. "Somebody—somebody who knows me well—had a grudge and invented a reason to denounce me."

Since the Occupation, hundreds, maybe thousands of denunciatory letters had arrived at Gestapo headquarters on the avenue Foch. Many of these accusations, as the baron had said, were a means to square a grudge, or to rid oneself of an unwelcome neighbor, a business rival, an unwanted lover. Letters were investigated but in a cursory way. The evidence that convinced the secret police was given in person by one in dire need of a favor—an otherwise unobtainable visa, the release of a loved one from prison or concentration camp, desperately needed cash.

Gilberte shifted to peer up at her father. "You truly believe that? Your name was given to the Gestapo?"

"There's no other explanation. They have too damn many details about my life. Whoever it was, this is my true enemy."

Gilberte glanced at his swollen face, the rope and handcuffs. "Not *them,* the Nazis?"

"Yes, certainly them. But this is on a personal level. To willingly turn in a friend, what could be more despicable?"

"He—or she—ought to suffer as much as you have."

"When I find out who it was, I plan to arrange that."

"And the family, too, they should be in as much pain as yours has been." Their whispered conversation, operatically vengeful, had captured Gilberte's imagination. Momentarily she forgot her psychic demoralization, her physical agony, the chilling weight of her sodden, inaccurately buttoned suit, the blouse wadded between her thighs to receive blood. "It will be like the oath Guy de Permont swore with his son."

"Gilberte—" the baron started hoarsely.

Just then the door opened and Captain Knecht came in, ordering Wissman to return her to her cell.

Gilberte's final words to her father were "For as long as I live, Papa, the betrayer's family will suffer. I promise you that."

15

Gilberte's suit took several more days to dry. She was wearing the shapeless mess for the first time on the next morning that Wissman came for her. As he marched her along the prison corridor, his ultracorrect demeanor denied the rape. The evidence was all on her. Bruises puffed both sides of her jaw, and a torn thigh ligament slowed her walk to a mincing waddle. At least the bleeding had stopped. Berthe had handed her a prescription tube with the name and address of a pharmacist on the rue Blondel, telling her that the girls swore by this salve to heal the damage caused by the rough trade—and also as a preventative measure against the unfortunate contretemps that leads to an abortion.

Awkwardly descending the stairs to the Gestapo netherworld, Gilberte attempted to calm the humming panic within herself with the old chestnut that the worst had happened and she had nothing left to fear. Captain Knecht was waiting. His rounded shoulders were yet more slumped, the black tunic showed liberal traces of dandruff and his pale eyebrows were drawn together in a preoccupied frown. Telling his orderly to wait, he led her through the recreation area, where he responded absently to the salutes.

"Mademoiselle, a great many people in this country, in fact the majority, respect our goals. The French are intelligent enough to agree with the Führer that it's time to move beyond petty national-

ism. They see the advantages of a united Europe—a united world.
Think. There would be no more war. No more of this senseless
bloodletting. The money we now spend on weapons could go for
the good of all. I wish with all my heart that every Frenchman could
accept the benefits of being under one flag. Why can't every single
one of you see the enormous benefits of forgetting antiquated
nationalism? Oh, I'm not denying that for a few years while this is
done we must all put aside our personal ambitions. But is that
asking too much? To relinquish chauvinist dreams for a future
where we can live in decency, rear fine, eugenically healthy children? A future where Bolshevism will be a historical evil?"

Goose bumps had risen all over her body. The captain's earnest,
obviously deeply felt harangue was the Nazi philosophy that he had
expounded prior to her *baignoire* treatment, and she comprehended that once again his sense of morality, which was severely
schizoid, needed to be assuaged. *It's going to be bad, very bad.*

"If only you could have a glimmering of our Führer's vision of
tomorrow's world," he said.

"A paradise on earth."

He sighed. "This would be easier for you, Mademoiselle, if you
could let yourself understand." He pushed open the door with a
large brass *8.*

Number eight, though similar in size to the other cells, had no
furniture, no bathtub. The walls were brown except for where they
had been touched up with thicker paint of a rusty shade. Captain
Knecht nudged her inside.

She let out a breathy whimper.

A man and a woman hung on the near wall.

The links of their handcuffs had been passed through big steel
meathooks set into the ceiling so that their feet dangled well above
the blood-splattered cement. The man's feet were bare, but the
woman was exquisitely shod in handmade black alligator. Both
were naked above the waist. Their chests and backs resembled raw
meat.

Gilberte's shaking increased as if she were being subjected to an
electric charge. The most difficult act she ever performed in her
life—a life that held a morbid amount of vicissitude—was to take
those few steps to look into gray, sagging faces. Her parents' faces.

They were both dead. Her mind jerked and twisted, as out of her control as her corporeal parts had been during the water treatment, flashing with a rapid kaleidoscope of ideas and images. Her mother glittering in a silver lamé evening gown as she bent above her bed to kiss her good night. Her father's affectionate voice saying her name . . . *My Gilberte.* How long and frenziedly had Merck and Ristelheuber swung their whips? Who had denounced her father? She would never in this world see her father again. She was alone. This shambled human flesh sealed her loneliness. She was doomed to drift forever solitary in the world's Arctic currents of tyranny, cruelty and duplicitousness. She was alone, alone in her glacial horror, her grief.

Helium seemed to be pumping into her head until the anguished thoughts floated high above her body. *I won't pass out. The least respect I can pay them is to behave like a de Permont and not some stupid peasant girl.* Clenching her hands against her sides, exerting the full force of her will, she quelled her vertigo.

Turning from the bodies, she said, "I gather that among the personal sacrifices you've made for a united Europe is to torture an innocent man and woman to death."

"Mademoiselle, you know in your heart that your father was guilty."

"Do I?" Gilberte asked shrilly. "And what about my mother?"

"Madame Cagny was at the Gare de l'Est with the baron."

Gilberte's disbelieving snort came involuntarily.

"She confessed," Knecht said.

"With your methods, who wouldn't?"

"She could have helped us with the names of her fellow criminals. She was one of the terrorists."

"My mother in the Résistance? My God, you're ludicrous!"

"She was in as deeply as your father."

"Why can't you admit you've had an innocent woman lashed to death?"

"She handled the *plastique.*"

"Ah yes, now you've jogged my memory. A favorite hobby of my mother's, planting a little dynamite here and there at the couturier's."

"She gave details of other incidents. One, the case of the car

carrying Hauptsturmführer Shmatz, I myself investigated. The
timing device was elaborate, and she knew precisely how it
worked."

Gilberte was ready with another caustic denial, but all at once
she recalled, vividly, her parents on a long ago night, making love
on her father's narrow bed. Her mother, driven by love and turbu-
lent passions, had braved ostracism from the society for which she
was so magnificently suited. The de Mascaret family had been
soldiers since the time of Jeanne d'Arc. Why was it impossible to
believe that she would respond to the bugles of patriotism re-
sounding in her admirably invisible veins?

Gilberte turned to look at the torn body in the blood-soaked
Chanel skirt. How could any physically slight, irreversibly vain
woman have resisted the technology of torture practiced in the
Santé's basement? *Maman, forgive me the jealousy that prevented me from
seeing no deeper than your mannered way and beauty.*

Again worried about passing out, she faced Captain Knecht.

"What about me?" she asked with what she hoped was irony.

"You?"

"When is it my turn on the wall?"

"Kommandant von Schaumburg was here for the interrogation.
He no longer believes you were connected."

"Great are the Kommandant's mercies," she said. "Now what
happens to me?"

"Mademoiselle, we are not monsters. You will be sentenced to
six months, that's all."

"What's my crime?"

"Consorting with terrorists."

"Six months in prison for living at home with my parents? That's
too droll."

Gilberte began to laugh. In cell 8 where her parents had been
tortured to death without naming names, she bent over in hilarity.
The captain summoned Wissman and her peals of laughter skit-
tered through the prison as the tiny orderly led her back to her cell.

The women were shrilling excitedly. During her absence the
French guard had passed on the news that three days after the
United States had declared war on the Japanese for a sneak bomb-
ing attack on their naval base in Hawaii, Germany had honored her

Tripartite Pact with Japan by declaring war against the United States. The news snapped Gilberte's hysteria, and she leaned against the wall. Americans in the war . . . It meant that Ann Blakely would leave France—if she hadn't already sailed. And Quent, he would enlist and fight her enemies.

Then her thoughts faded, as did the high, triumphant women's voices. The horror in the basement returned full force with its attendant rush of grief. She did not weep. She had often heard that tears assuage grief, but wasn't it ridiculous to believe that if liquid should flow from her eyes, those drops could in any way lessen her anguish or this hollowed-out sense of eternal loneliness?

She again saw those two meaty torsos.

Somehow she would kill Wissman, kill Merck and the boyish Ristelheuber, she would kill Captain Knecht. But she understood that they, with their sweat and dandruff, were merely instruments obeying orders.

Her father had named the true enemy.

The person who, acting in free will, had denounced him to the Gestapo.

Though Gilberte was the one who had mentioned Guy de Permont and the ancient tale of vengeance, it now seemed to her that the final words her father had spoken to her had extracted an oath of generational punishment. Promises made to the dead grip like skeletal fingers. She could never shrug off that promise.

The Betrayer is my enemy, she thought. *His posterity is my enemy. For as long as I live I'll pursue them.*

Then tears began oozing down her cheeks. She had been right, weeping cannot alleviate grief. Turning toward the wall, she blocked out the high-pitched fusillade of chatter about the Yanks entering the war and gave herself up to anguish.

Quent and Ann
France, 1941–1942

16

"Roosevelt is guilty of the worst crimes against international law."
Hitler's venomous hatred cut like a diamond drill through radio
static.

Ann pushed deeper into the frieze upholstery of the club chair.
She and her parents were in the living room listening to the dicta-
tor address the Reichstag. Ever since the ominous news that Japanese planes had destroyed the American Pacific fleet at Pearl Harbor, and the following day's congressional retaliatory declaration
of war against Japan but not Germany and Italy, Dorothy had
constantly reiterated that Hitler was smart enough to keep out of
the Pacific, Tripartite Pact or no, he had brains enough not to take
on the United States when he had his hands full with Great Britain
and the Russians, the United States would never declare war on
Germany. She maintained her position with rising shrillness. She
had a feverish cold.

Having risen from her sickbed to listen to the speech, she wore
her ancient Persian lamb buttoned over her flannel bathrobe.

Horace slumped on the couch, his chin resting on his frayed
muffler. As Hitler shrieked out a repetition of Roosevelt's name,
his gaze turned questioningly to Ann. He, like Dorothy, understood only a few words of German.

"He's telling them," Ann translated, "that the meanness of the Jews has encouraged the president."

"More of his usual tune," Dorothy said. "You'll see, it's the same old story. Nothing's changed."

"Shh," Ann said. German was her weakest subject and she was having difficulty keeping up with the rancorous crescendo of words. " 'The President of the United States ought to fully understand,' " she translated, " 'and I say this because of his limited intellect, that we know the aim of his struggle is to destroy one country after another.' "

As a pandemonium of cheering drowned out Hitler's voice, Ann said in a flat tone, "That's it. He just arranged that the embassy's passports be returned to the chargé d'affaires. It means we're at war."

"Did Hitler *say* he's declared war?" Dorothy demanded.

"I couldn't hear, but—"

"Then he hasn't," Dorothy said firmly. "Dear, you're just too old to have such a vivid imagination!"

Ann winced at her mother's last-ditch obfuscation. Quent had been right, they should have left months ago. Briefly, she wondered where Gilberte and her parents were—the last she knew was the cryptic message that Quent had sent through Larry Porter: *General von Hocherer might have a lead.* What had the general learned? Was the de Permont family free someplace, celebrating the news that the Americans were in the fight?

The roiling cheers had become cadenced shouts of *Sieg Heil,* which meant Hitler's oratorical fireworks had ceased. Horace pushed heavily from the couch and turned off the radio. The apartment seemed unnaturally quiet, with only the muted echo of roaring from other radios in 74, rue Daguerre.

"We don't even have a consul in Paris," he said.

Ann recalled the Baron de Permont's remark that in the event of war, the United States and Germany would exchange nationals. "Do you think they'll let us go home?"

"Ann, stop this!" Dorothy snapped. "We are not at war. It's against all of Hitler's best interests to fight us. First of all, he knows what happened when we got into the last war. Secondly, he only invaded Russia six months ago, and the *Propagandastaffel* admits that the Russian winter's very hard on their army. His navy and air force are tied up with Great Britain. It simply makes no sense at all for him to fight us."

Ann took a sharp breath. "You ought to write to him at the Chancellery. Since he's so sanely sensible, I'm sure he'll follow your advice."

Dorothy sank back into her corner of the worn couch. She lacked stamina for a prolonged argument.

Ann murmured, "I'm sorry, Mother."

Horace clasped his mittened hands together in a gesture of supplication. "How in God's name could I have trapped you both here? I should have taken you home no matter what."

Ann, who had always tried to jolt her parents out of their procrastinations and excuses, looked at the naked shame in her father's brown eyes and felt no I-told-you-so vindication, only a mournful, choking pity. Swallowing, she said, "We'll be okay, Daddy."

"I was terrified to go back," Horace mumbled. The disgrace of that long-ago arrest outside Taliesin and the subsequent laughter had burned deep into his psyche, yet he could hardly confess to himself, and certainly not to anyone else, including Dorothy, that this foolish barrier had kept him in Paris. It was easier by far to admit to his fears of facing the Depression. "I'd imagine myself selling apples. Or going on relief. So what have I done? Stuck my family in the middle of a war. I despise myself, no man should be such a weakling." His voice cracked and he turned to the wall.

"Horace, dear, you're being ridiculous. How many men rise to your position in a foreign country? And as for Hitler, Ann's no German scholar." Dorothy turned a baleful, fever-reddened gaze on her daughter.

Ann went to Horace, hugging him. His body was lax, unresponsive. "Daddy, everything's going to be fine." Her voice wavered. Much as she loved him, she accepted that he was an ineffectual dear: with Dorothy ill, she, Ann, must take charge of the family. "The embassy in Berlin'll know what's up. I'll go use Monsieur Remigasse's phone."

"I'll go to Remigasse's and try the embassy in Berlin. They'll know what's happening." Horace spoke as if Ann had not just uttered similar phrases.

"We'll go together," Ann said, linking her arm in his.

The afternoon line of shabby women waiting for their bread ration already stretched from the *boulangerie* to the corner. Angry voices rose as the Blakelys went inside. Monsieur Remigasse came to the door, crossing his thick arms over his enveloping white apron as he boomed to his indignant customers, "Mesdames! They aren't here to buy my bread but to telephone to their embassy. It's the Americans."

A small cheer went up inside and outside the bakery. "*Vive les Américains!*" A brave cry. If a Gestapo snoop were nearby, these women could wind up in court for making inflammatory public speeches.

Horace stumbled into the bakery as though unable to recollect why he'd come. Ann went to the phone.

Telephoning long-distance was at best a lengthy ritual, and this afternoon military messages tied up the lines to Berlin. The two Blakelys were still waiting for the call to go through when the last loaf was gone and Monsieur Remigasse hung out a sign FERMÉ: the housewives still on the pavement sighed dejectedly for tonight their families would go hungry. Telling the Americans to stay as long as necessary, the baker tramped upstairs to his wife. In the dark, empty shop, Ann tried to pull her father into conversation, but he had withdrawn into a silence that resembled shock.

They had been there ten hours—it was almost the midnight curfew hour—when the call came through. At the ring of the phone, Horace jumped, staring at the large black box on the wall while it sounded twice. Ann answered. A French operator then a German operator informed her Berlin was ready.

"American embassy, Willetts speaking," said a hoarse American voice.

Holding the earpiece so her father could hear, Ann said, "Mr. Willets, this is Ann Blakely. My family and I live here in Paris. We heard the speech today and want to know what's happened."

"You're lucky to have gotten through, Miss Blakely. All hell's broken loose. Ribbentrop called in Mr. Morris, he's our chargé, to give him back our passports. It's war. The Reichstag has declared war on us."

Horace whimpered.

Ann had anticipated the news, yet her stomach was plummeting as if the bakery floor had suddenly given way and she were falling into fathomless depths. "Wh-what will happen now?"

"You're absolutely fine, there'll be no problems for you." His voice went dry and businesslike, as if he were slipping into an often repeated speech. "The State Department's right on top of plans to get every American citizen home. In the meantime, we're advising our people to be ultracorrect, no flamboyant speeches, no heroic gestures. Obey all the laws, do everything the German authorities say, follow each regulation. Do you understand?" The line crackled, then he asked, "Your family isn't Jewish, is it?"

"No," Ann said.

"It makes no difference. My advice to all United States nationals is identical. Keep away from trouble and carry on as usual. Miss Blakely, it's a madhouse here so I have to say good-bye." There was a firm click and the French operator came on to ask if the call was complete.

The call was nowhere near complete. How could she not have asked Willetts whom to contact about the evacuation plans?

Horace said his first words in hours. "We better get home. Your mother must be worrying."

The following morning Dorothy's fever was yet higher. Ann said she'd stay home from school to look after her, but Dorothy hoarsely insisted that they follow the embassy's command to carry on as usual.

At Madame Bernard's she was greeted by a young lieutenant in field gray. Clicking his heels and bowing, he informed her in an embarrassed voice that as an enemy alien she could no longer attend this school. Ann cleaned out her desk under the curious gaze of the classmates from whom she had estranged herself. She felt neither sadness nor regret at her expulsion. Without Gilberte, the *classe de première* had become a bleak purgatory.

When she arrived home, her father was sitting on the edge of the bed where Dorothy, fully dressed, lay wheezing heavily.

"They were waiting for me at the hospital," Horace said. "They took my work permit. They took it. Enemy aliens can't work in hospitals, they said."

"We don't have a thing to worry about, Ann, dear. Dr. Descourset's continuing the salary. And there's no other difficulty. All we need to do is get a special *éloignement* from the police."

Ann, Horace and the shivering Dorothy hurried through the bleak December morning. The Blakelys were the only Americans to register at this commissariat. They discovered their *éloignement*—extension of visit—had to be renewed daily. If aliens, enemy or otherwise, were found without the large blue *E* stamped on their papers with a handwritten date, they would be shipped to a concentration camp. The commissariat was about ten blocks north on the boulevard Raspail, a pleasant walk in good weather. But this winter was as cruel as the last, and Dorothy was ill. They would sit anywhere from one to five hours in the same waiting room where Ann had been subjected to the body search—the ugly memory bulged constantly in her mind.

The next Monday, a north wind drove sleet at a sharp angle. Horace and Ann supported Dorothy, but returning home she moved more and more slowly until her legs buckled under her. Horace and Ann managed to drag her through the freezing bluster to the rue Daguerre, where Madame Jargaux helped them carry her up the stairs.

Dr. Descourset, in response to Horace's nearly incoherent phone call, left his busy dispensary. A kindly, overworked man, he wore a Vandyke beard and high, old-fashioned collar. After his examination, he drew his former employee from the room.

"Madame Dorothy has the influenza."

"A bad cold," Horace denied, the blood draining from his face.

"Influenza. And I don't like it one bit. Remember her pneumonia last year, 'Orace. She mustn't leave her bed."

Horace looked more than ever like a rabbit, a poor, dazed rabbit run to ground. "We must report in person every day to the police."

"The lungs are congested, the fever is high. 'Orace, they don't print it in the papers, but believe me, we are in the middle of an influenza epidemic, and the death rate is high—the malnourishment, the cold. This week alone I lost three patients."

Horace clenched his trembling jaw, his expression altering to terror-struck determination.

That afternoon he went out.

He returned just before eight, the curfew for enemy aliens. Sitting on the double bed, he unfolded an *éloignement* that extended Frau Dorothy Blakely's visit until one week hence. Even the watermarks on the paper looked official. When Ann questioned its provenance, Horace remained tight-lipped and mysterious. Ann decided he'd somehow come up with a top-notch forgery—the underside of occupied Paris swarmed with master forgers. But how would her anxious, law-abiding father go about contacting a forger?

Dorothy's fever rose and fell, never going below a hundred and two. On the afternoon before she was again due to visit the commissariat, Dr. Descourset made his visit. Tugging on his gray goatee, he pronounced, "You are in no condition to leave the bed."

After the doctor hurried away on his rounds, Horace told Ann he would have to go out. *He's going to the forger,* she thought. She tied his muffler and kissed his nose.

"Bolt the door after me," he said.

17

After fastening the chain, Ann went to the kitchen to wash the heavy coat of earth from the two small potatoes and three gnarled carrots, their dinner, that she had waited in line the entire morning to buy—the evening meal was five hours away and she was already so ravenous that she could wolf down all the vegetables raw. Taking off her apron, she looked in on Dorothy. She and her father had lugged the big radio into the sickroom, and Radio-Paris was broadcasting a full-length performance of *The Merry Widow,* Dorothy's favorite operetta, but Dorothy was snoring heavily. Deciding to keep watch on the invalid, Ann brought in the summery landscape she was finishing as a Christmas gift for her father. The sheet of paper pinned to her drawing board was flimsy, her pastels down to the nubs, but as always when she drew or painted, she lost track of time. Her mind was filled with the imaginary green farmland, so at first she didn't realize that the buzzing was not part of the Strauss orchestration but the doorbell. Not wanting the invalid to waken, expecting Madame Jargaux—who often came up to visit—Ann tiptoed out, quietly closing the door, dashing down the hall, to yank off the bolt. The rose madder pastel dropped from her fingers.

Quent Dejong stood in the gloomy, tiled hallway.

"I was beginning to think you'd left," he said. "I figured I'd missed you at the station."

His words made no sense, but then neither did his being here. Besides, she wasn't in shape to think. Holding on to the doorknob, she made the first idiot remark that blundered into her mind. "Larry said you weren't in Paris."

"I had some business to finish up."

She nodded, not immediately perceiving that he hadn't explained his presence.

He was asking, "Why aren't you at the Gare d'Austerlitz? I just saw Larry off on the first train. You weren't aboard, so I went along the platform looking for you. All the Americans are sitting on their suitcases waiting until the second one is ready."

"Trains?"

"You don't know about going to Switzerland?"

"Should I?"

"Americans are being evacuated in special sealed trains," he said, explaining rapidly that orders to report to the Gare d'Austerlitz at three-thirty today had been posted at the commissariats.

"There was no sign at ours."

Footsteps sounded on the staircase below them. "We shouldn't be talking out here," he said, stepping by her into the entryway.

Ann led him to the living room. Since moving the radio, she and Horace had not been in here and already the air had taken on the musty heaviness of long-unlived-in places. She sank into the couch, hitting one of the sharp springs.

"There's no time to sit down," he said. "We were told the second train would leave in"—he pulled up a cuff to see his large gold wristwatch—"an hour. I've got a car downstairs."

A car? What miracles money wrought even for an enemy alien. "We can't go."

"Oh, Christ!" he snapped. "Are you still stuck on *that*? Ann, don't you understand? We're in enemy territory!"

"Mother has influenza."

"Then," he said, "she'll need to dress warmly." His calm tone conveyed anger more potently than his outburst.

"She's really ill, Quent."

"I just explained. The only way that an American can leave

occupied France is in this sealed train. We're allowed one suitcase weighing no more than ten kilos. Now go pack. Oh, and take some food. God knows how long we'll be—passenger trains are shunted off the tracks by the military."

"She could never survive it. Dr. Descourset pretty much said it would be fatal for her to leave her room."

"Let me talk to your father."

"That's another reason we can't rush off. He's out." Torn between fear of staying and determination not to take the train, she raised her voice. "I'm not about to desert my father, or risk my mother's life."

"Go pack, I'll bring him home. Where is he?"

"He didn't say. He could be anywhere."

"Then you and your mother'll have to leave without him."

"That's impossible," she said. "But Quent, I do appreciate you coming here."

He stared at her through the waning light. After a few seconds she accepted that silence can be a weapon.

"Larry Porter gave me your message," she said in a muted voice. "Did General von Hocherer discover where the de Permonts are?"

Suddenly Quent looked haggard and beaten. "In the Santé."

"The Santé?" Horror raced through her. "But why?"

"I couldn't discover the charges, and neither could the general. It's a Gestapo case." Quent sighed and shook his head. "It was damn decent of him to make the effort—as a rule, the military steer clear of the SS."

It was unbearable to think of Gilberte in the power of black-clad men who were avoided even by Wehrmacht generals. Ann swallowed sharply and fingered a path on the dusty lamp table, leaving a trail of rosy chalk.

"Ann, will you quit acting like you have a choice? There *are* no choices. Your mother'll be fine. Don't you understand? This train is it!" Quent gripped her arm urgently, pulling her to her feet.

Her heart beat with sudden erratic swiftness, her legs felt boneless and she fought an urge to melt toward him, to blend into the warmth emanating from his nearness, to submit to his strength.

"There's my father," she said.

"He's a man, he'll manage."

There it was, that frigid, patrician voice.

"We're a family," she said.

"Can't you be logical?"

"No, if it means we won't be a family anymore." Somehow her tone came out as cool as his.

The dark blue eyes probed her until she felt stripped of coherency. Dropping his hand, he said, "I better get back to the station."

He didn't say good-bye. Not moving, she listened to his footsteps resound rapidly on the drugget, the thud of the front door closing.

The faraway sound of a waltz beat ended abruptly.

"Ann . . ." Her mother's weak, raspy voice. "Did I hear the door? Is Daddy back?"

"No, I was testing the bolt," Ann said, wondering why she'd lied. Her mother would find out soon enough that they had missed the last train with a safe conduct to carry Americans from occupied France.

18

Ann, basking in the March sunshine that flooded through her open window, lifted her arms above her head, a flamenco dancer's pose, snapping her fingers and smiling up at the sun as she would a partner.

Other than a rare patch of good weather there had been little to smile about in the past few months. Right after Christmas, when Dorothy's fever still remained frighteningly high, the *Bankenaufsichtsamt* had impounded Horace's savings account at the Banque Nationale de Paris and also confiscated his deposit box, which held Dorothy's ruby-chip engagement ring and two twenty-dollar gold pieces knotted in an old sock with some silver dollars. In January an SS lieutenant had called on Dr. Descourset to inform him of the new law that barred French nationals from donating money to enemy aliens. The proceeds from selling the silver flatware had evaporated, and now Ann was trying to sell the big radio. Dorothy, staggering, needed support on the way to and from the police station. There was no news of the de Permonts, unless you counted a German van arriving to take their furniture. Ann found escape from this ubiquitous gloom in a one-sided romance. Her nights were crowded with wildly sensual dreams of Quent. As she shivered amid the interminable lines outside food shops, she retreated into memories of him—by now her actual memories had become as limp and stained as the pages of an often read novel, so she invented new ones.

At a tap on the door, she dropped her arms. Dorothy slipped inside, closing the door. The sunlight showed the papery dryness of her skin.

She whispered, "Dear, do you know a girl called Suzette Pamfou?"

Ann frowned. "Suzette who?"

"Pamfou. She says she's in your class." Dorothy pulled the loose cardigan around herself, proving how many pounds she had lost. "You're not permitted to go to Madame Bernard's so I doubt if you're meant to see your old friends. I'll go tell her you're out."

There was no Suzette Pamfou in the school. Pamfou was a peculiar name anyway, a nickname for a pet, almost. While her mother was talking, Ann stood poised in the streaked sunlight, her mind flashing with explanations. Only one made sense. This was a messenger of some kind. To forestall discussion and maternal arguments, she raced to the front door. A girl approximately her size stood there.

Flinging her arms around the stranger, who smelled faintly of violet cologne, Ann cried, "Suzy! How I've missed you!" She made rapid introductions to Dorothy, who peered uneasily at them, and to Horace, who had emerged from the living room to be part of this rare flurry of excitement. "Come on, Suzy," Ann said. "It's deliciously sunny in my room."

Closing the door, Ann got a good look at her visitor. Freckled, diminutive, with a mop of blond curls, wearing bobby socks over her stockings, Suzette Pamfou could pass muster as a schoolgirl with older people, but any schoolgirl, given this excellent light, would recognize her youth as fraudulent. She was well into her twenties.

"Who are you?" Ann whispered. Horace might be in the hall—when his curiosity was piqued, he sometimes engaged in a little harmless snooping.

"What pretty wallpaper," Suzette retorted in a loud, bouncy tone, then she also whispered, "Be on the boulevard Edgar Quinet near the cemetery gate at three-thirty. You'll see a friend."

"Who? Gilberte? It's her, isn't it?"

In lieu of a response, Suzette opened her purse for a tattered book. "Tell your parents you found my *Cousine Bette* and then pretend to run after me. Now, ask me about school."

An elm-lined bridle path ran down the center of the boulevard Edgar Quinet. Before the war the strip near the rue Delambre had been the site of a bustling market: nowadays a few stalls sold battered household objects. Farther up, the space was given over to a line of benches that faced the stone wall of the Montparnasse Cemetery. The bundled-up old people sunning themselves devoted their full attention to Ann as she paced up and down.

Positive that the mysterious friend was Gilberte, she kept turning to scan the broad street for a tall, slender brunette. It was after four, and by now her natural impatience was well laced with foreboding. The police routinely halted Parisians to check their papers, and a young woman with a prison past on her *carte d'identité* could easily have been taken in. And she herself had aroused interest, always a dangerous mistake. As she passed the cemetery gate, she saw that a man was staring at her while he halted in the shelter of a tall tomb to light a cigarette. Exceptionally tall, he wore a cloth cap, faded corduroy trousers and a heavy-knit, shapeless sweater that stretched across his broad shoulders and hung loose at his narrow hips. Most working-class men of this size, youth and obvious strength were either behind the barbed wire in a prisoner-of-war camp or in the Third Reich as "volunteer" labor.

She inhaled audibly as the book fell from her grasp.

The man was Quent.

In spite of her fanciful crush on him, she had been so certain that she was to meet Gilberte that she had never entertained any other possibility. Besides, Quent had left Paris on that sealed train. Stunned into immobility, she watched him raise the hand with the cigarette and come toward her.

Picking up the battered *Cousine Bette,* he handed it to her. "Sorry I'm late, my little cabbage, but you know how it is. The boss needed me—and the old bag of tripe hasn't finished with me yet." He bent to kiss her cheeks. "I have to get back."

The two light brushes of his lips gave her a pleasure so intense that it approached pain—nothing in those erogenous dreams had prepared her for this fleshly reaction. As he linked his arm in hers, strolling in the direction of the boulevard Raspail, her body took on a life of its own. Her round breasts thrust higher, her hips swung languidly. The old people who had watched her would be convinced that she had been waiting for her sweetheart.

Ann murmured, "Suzette Pamfou—or whoever she is—just said a friend. I assumed she meant Gilberte."

"Gilberte?" His muscles under her arm tensed. "She's out of the Santé?"

"I don't know."

"When did you hear from her? What about ViVi and André?"

"I haven't heard anything."

"But you said—"

"I *assumed* it was her. I *hoped* she'd gotten out." Ann's throat had tightened as if for tears, and her usually low voice was high-pitched. "How come you're in Paris, Quent? Did we make you miss the train?"

"No, I left with the others." He glanced around. "Call me Jacques. My name's Jacques Tinel."

"Jacques Tinel . . ."

He tossed away his Gauloise. "How's your mother?"

"Better, but not exactly herself."

"They're going to intern Americans in the next couple of days."

"We've already packed our suitcases."

"You should go to Switzerland."

"Quent, why bring that up? I couldn't. Her fever was horrendous, Daddy wasn't home—"

He interrupted, "I meant now."

"Now? Why not a trip to the moon?"

Quent was silent as they strolled by an ancient man huddled on a bench. "Do you know what a passer is?" he asked in a low voice.

"Sort of." Madame Jargaux had whispered about escape routes. "Passers" were French people who moved Jewish refugees and downed British airmen across occupied territories to safety. "The trip's pretty rugged, isn't it?" she asked.

"Not as rugged as staying will be."

"My mother's still in terrible shape."

"We'd work out the easiest route," he said.

"If we were caught we'd be shot as spies."

"You'd have papers."

"Phony papers."

"Ann, you're no coward."

"Economics aside, we haven't been treated badly at all."

He halted to light another cigarette, and when they started to walk, she felt bereft that he did not take her arm again.

"Now you're using your parents' arguments," he said.

She was indeed mouthing the objections Horace and Dorothy would raise. "I'm being sensible."

"Sensible? By now you must have realized that the Nazis play hardball. But maybe you haven't heard some of the grim stories circulating about the camps. Starvation, disease, overwork, beatings. An unbelievably high ratio of deaths. The good-looking girls sent to army brothels." As he said this his cheeks went yet redder. Quent Dejong had a sweetly prudish streak, an odd contradiction in a very rich man who had precociously paid for an abortion.

She sensed that she was also blushing. "Are you warning me I might not get picked?"

"I'll be over around eight-thirty. After dark."

After dark. The words brought home to her the danger he courted in coming to the boulevard Edgar Quinet on a sunny afternoon. "You're the one who should be in Switzerland," she murmured. "You could be shot as a spy."

"Me? Jacques Tinel?"

"You don't look like a Jacques Tinel."

"Nobody else has questioned it."

"They will. What Frenchman tosses away two half-smoked cigarettes."

"Christ," he said, shooting her a look of irritation before shaking his head to admit, "you're right."

A hunched old woman with a cane tottered by them, staring. With an ostentatious wink at the crone, Quent stooped to brush kisses against Ann's cheeks. "Until tonight, then, my little cabbage."

Walking home, Ann attempted to grapple with the escape idea as though it had been presented by somebody other than Quent, an asexual being. She brooded over the fates of her two friends, Lea Blum and Gilberte de Permont, she thought of her own little hell at the commissariat, concluding that the dangers of internment outweighed those of an illegal journey.

Her parents reacted predictably.

Horace blanched a grayish white. "This crazy idea of Switzerland's got something to do with that Suzette girl," he cried. "I knew there was something fishy about her visit."

Dorothy told Ann she was too old to be so irresponsibly rash, endangering herself—and them—by meeting an American with false papers. "Why is this Mr. Dejong so interested in our business anyway?" she asked.

"Because he's related to Gilberte, and I'm her friend." The rationale of Ann's brain, not her heart.

The couple retired to their bedroom.

Ann knew the outcome of their conference before it began. Horace would defer to Dorothy, allowing her to make the decision, and Dorothy, punctilious to a T about observing every umlaut of the German laws, would refuse to step out of the building without a legitimately issued *Ausweis*—travel permit—grasped in each of their hands.

When Quent arrived, the interview went even more depressingly than she had anticipated. Her parents, not inviting him into the living room, stood in front of the three packed suitcases as if guarding the proof of their goodwill toward the conquerors.

Horace, as the man of the family, spoke first. "Ann tells us you know some sort of a network that moves refugees, Mr. Dejong."

"Reliable people."

"We're not refugees," Dorothy interjected.

Horace braced his chin in further. "Dr. Descourset, he owns the hospital I administered, made the trip to the unoccupied zone several times to see his mother—she's over ninety. He never stopped talking about what an ordeal it was. At every stop the local police, tough types, came aboard to check everybody's papers. And at the border, the Germans have agents trained to spot illegal travelers. One time he saw an entire family shot outside the train— he thought maybe they were Jews with false papers. Another time an old woman in his carriage was arrested for supposed smuggling. And in the unoccupied zone, he says, the police are more strict than here. If your *sauf-conduit* isn't in apple-pie order, it's off to prison."

Ann felt smothered by their excuses, yet at the same time a family loyalty forced her a step closer to them.

"Do you know about Drancy?" Quent asked in that deceptively calm tone. Drancy was just outside Paris, a half-finished working-class housing project that the Germans had turned into a holding place for "undesirables." "And the concentration camps?"

"Atrocity rumors," Dorothy dismissed with a white-lipped smile. "Mr. Dejong, you aren't old enough to remember the last war, but the same type of stories were circulating, Germans cutting off babies' hands and bayoneting nuns."

"And anyway," Horace said, "Drancy and those other places are for unfortunate people, Jews, Communists, the só-called Résistance. We're being interned in a hotel."

"Maybe at first," Quent said. "Not for long."

"We realize you have the best of intentions, Mr. Dejong," Dorothy said. "But what you have in mind is too harebrained to even consider. Crossing France without proper papers, sneaking through borders, giving ourselves over to God knows who. What could be more risky for Ann?"

"Yes," Horace said. "How can we endanger her?"

Ann felt a surge of outrage that now they were serving her up to excuse their timidity—good-bye "duty to the hospital" and loyalty to their adopted city, hello Ann.

"And if I stay, I could be shipped off to a brothel," she said. "Or to one of their breeding farms." At Madame Bernard's there had been much whispered and titillating speculation about the master race's plans for nubile young Frenchwomen. "I've heard that Danish and Dutch girls classified as full-blooded Aryans are sent to Germany. I'm full-blooded, aren't I?"

"Ann!" Horace cried.

"You know as well as I do," snapped Dorothy, "that the Germans have behaved like perfect gentlemen toward you!"

"If there were the least truth in those ridiculous rumors," Horace added, "we'd take Mr. Dejong up on his offer."

"You always rush into things with your eyes shut," Dorothy said. "But we're not about to permit you to put yourself in the worst kind of danger because of a few creaking rumors."

"Protecting you has been our only consideration," Horace added in a trembling voice.

Ann's anger faded. She had never loved them more than in this, their moment of greatest self-duplicity. With Quent's height and strength dominating the dim hall, they looked heartrendingly vulnerable.

Ann turned to tell Quent she would remain with her parents, who needed her, yet looking through the gloom into those slightly narrowed, intent eyes, she heard herself say, "I'm going."

"You'll do no such thing!" Dorothy cried. "You're only a child."

"We'll be in a hotel," Horace coaxed. "The food'll be far better than we've been getting."

"Germans are civilized people."

As they alternated their arguments, Dorothy took Horace's hand. They looked so small, so helpless. Ann moved a protective step closer.

Quent yanked her coat from the rack and peered at the three suitcases. "Which is yours?" he asked.

"You're leaving tonight?" Horace cried.

"What if there's a raid? You couldn't use a shelter—"

"The one with the strap," Ann said. Going to her parents, she put an arm around each of them. "Terrible things *are* happening. Suppose the Nazi in charge of internees hates Americans—say his son is killed by us. How civilized do you think he'll be?"

"You're staying right here, Miss," Dorothy said.

"What about tomorrow?" Horace cried. "You'll have no *éloignement.*"

"Mother, Daddy, those are such dumb reasons. Please come."

But she knew her arguments were useless. She and her parents were shouting across an abyss, and neither could hear the words coming from the other side. She kissed them both, murmuring that she loved them. Dorothy grudged a return kiss, Horace hugged her.

Quent pulled her weeping through the front door.

19

The bright, nearly full moon, a bomber's moon, cast thin silver on the rue Daguerre. At the corner, Ann turned, looking back to number 74. There behind those closed shutters she had been conceived, there she had been brought home as a cherished infant, and there, discounting a few summer holidays in a Dieppe *pension*, she had slept every night of her life. There her parents must be comforting each other. She thought of her final glimpse of them, Horace extending a pudgy, shaking hand toward her, Dorothy's pared-down face twisted with grief. Struggling against another freshet of tears, she trotted to keep up with Quent.

"Sorry, Ann, but we need to get a move on," he said, keeping up his pace. "We have to be in Bagneux before midnight curfew." Bagneux was part of the ring of drab manufacturing suburbs that surrounded Paris—the factories had recently become the target of RAF incendiary bombs.

"It's only about an hour's walk."

"We'll be taking a roundabout way to avoid the antiaircraft embankments."

Did he always have to be infallible? Unreasoningly, she hated him. It was *his* fault she had deserted her parents. "I'm not meant to be on the streets," she said. "It's after curfew now for me."

He halted. Setting down her suitcase, fishing under his heavy sweater, he took out a sheaf of papers. Holding them up to the moonlight, he shuffled through them. "Here's your new *carte d'identité.*"

Narrowing her eyes, she peered to find fault.

A seven-franc stamp and a six-franc stamp and over them, the seal of Paris. Even the photograph, full front of a girl with large dark eyes and a curly bob, was a fairly good likeness. By moonlight, her new identity card looked as masterfully authentic as her mother's *éloignement.* She could make out the black block letters at the top. Her false surname.

"Tinel," she read aloud. An accusation.

"I had no idea it'd be the two of us. It made the most sense for us to be traveling as a family. Ann and Jacques, with her parents."

His clipped tone—that reminder of his innate superiority—increased her irrational fury while decreasing her confidence.

When they came to a sewer grating, he stopped again. "I need your old papers," he said.

As the scraps of her *éloignement,* her *carte d'identité,* her passport and the phony papers he'd arranged for her parents' use fluttered into the sewer system of Paris, her anger vanished as rapidly as it had come. She sighed, her breath showing in the cold, malodorous air. All that remained of Ann Blakely was the weight of grief and guilt in her chest.

Quent picked up her suitcase. "Ann, I don't think we'll be stopped, but if we are, let me do the talking."

She nodded.

After this, he spoke only to guide her. In the beginning she knew all of the alleys and back paths, but soon she felt lost in the maze. They saw nobody, and if it weren't for the occasional muffled voices or muted radio music from the blacked-out buildings, they might have been traversing a city as lost and deserted as Atlantis. The RAF raids were keeping home even those few Montparnasse inhabitants who ventured out at night. As they crossed a broad, empty boulevard unfamiliar to her, a small, open scout car drove by so close that the moonlight showed the thinned lips of the Luftwaffe sergeant who held the machine gun on his lap. *I ought to be frightened,* Ann thought. Yet, inhaling the fumes of charcoal gazogene that trailed the car, she decided that she wasn't.

Quent moved protectively closer.

"What if they'd stopped?" she asked.

"I'd have told them we'd had a fight and you'd run off to your parents'. I'd come to take you back home with me. You know how they delight in seeing the French as hot-blooded idiots."

By now her old, strapped suitcase filled with winter clothing, sketch pad and books must feel as if it weighed fifty kilos, yet he kept up his rapid, effortless pace. Ann's legs were trembling, and her feet numb with cold long before they reached Bagneux.

They passed small houses—several were eerie, roofless ruins— avoiding the rubble of a factory wall. Coming to a square with an antiaircraft gun, Quent tucked her into the shadows, and they edged along listening to jovial German remarks about having scared off the Limey bastards tonight. There was the sharp retort of DCA—the English called it ack-ack—from a distant antiaircraft emplacement, but no sound of planes overhead. Quent nudged her into a narrow, urine-odored footpath that ran between tall apartment blocks.

"We're here," he whispered.

Inside, the blackness was unalleviated. Ann, emotionally drained, physically exhausted, ascended two steep flights conscious only of the warm, enveloping grasp of his guiding hand and a sense of shame that she should be accessible to pleasure after leaving her parents in the lurch. Their footsteps creaked down a hallway. He tapped lightly.

"Who is it?" asked a woman's voice.

"Me, Jacques."

The door opened, and Suzette Pamfou stood holding a candlestick.

"You're so late," she said.

"I heard they'd be checking the métro tonight so we walked."

"Thank God the British stayed on their side of the Channel," Suzette said, resting a hand on Quent's sleeve.

One room with a slept-in bed and Suzette in her bathrobe holding on to Quent's arm—what could reveal more intimacy than this candlelit vignette? Ann pulled back into the corridor.

Suzette peered at her. "Come in," she said warmly, and held her candle into the mephitic darkness. "But where are your parents?"

Quent replied for her. "Mr. and Mrs. Blakely decided the plan was too dangerous."

"I thought they might," Suzette said. Then, noticing the moisture in Ann's huge, dark eyes, she smiled and put an arm over her shoulder. "*Eh bien,* my school chum."

Quent was depositing the suitcase near the bed. "Be back as quick as I can," he said.

"You're leaving?" Ann was too tired to suppress her wail.

The flame glinted on his reassuring smile. "Suzette'll keep you busy."

Chaining the door after him, Suzette took out a camera, enlisting Ann to help her set a half-dozen flashlights around it. "I was hoping you'd get here before the electricity went off," she said.

"Where did the picture on my ID come from?"

"Quent gave it to me." She flipped Ann's hair, then went to the camera. "Pretend I'm a green bean." Because of the greenish hue of their field-gray uniforms, the Wehrmacht had been nicknamed green beans by Parisians. "Look somber."

The camera clicked.

"Does Quent bring people here often?"

Suzette's shoulders raised in a noncommittal shrug. "You can trust him absolutely," she said. "Have you ever known anyone more calm and in control? Another good glower, Ann. I don't have any extra film."

After a third shot, Suzette switched off the flashlights. "While I develop these, stretch out on the bed."

Ann took off her shoes, covering herself with her coat. The pillow smelled of the violet cologne, and she pushed it away. *Quent sleeps in this bed with Suzette . . .* was her final thought before sleep.

She jerked awake.

Suzette stood over her. Dressed to go out in a black coat with some sort of fake fur at the collar and a hat whose scarlet celluloid cherries dangled over her made-up face, she looked like a cheaply smart shopgirl. Her true identity or another chameleon change? "I have to get to work, but I couldn't leave without wishing you *bonne chance.*"

"Thank you." Forgetting her jealousy, Ann thought only of the perils Suzette had undertaken on her behalf. She rose to hug her. "Suzette . . . I'll never forget all you've done for me."

Suzette and Quent murmured together at the door—Ann couldn't hear what they said. Feeling an intruder, she went to the table and saw her grim-faced picture on Ann Tinel's new *Ausweis* and old-looking *carte d'identité* with the thin worn folds. Her ration card, stained from thumbing, had several coupons jaggedly cut from it.

Locking the door, Quent took out a pen. "Ready to sign your ID, Madame Tinel?"

The ink was a rusty shade. "They're so *genuine*," she said.

"Suzette's topnotch." He handed her a new bottle of ink for the *Ausweis*, then pressed her fingerprints on the identity card. "These'll be registered."

Starting to ask how, Ann stopped herself.

"Those're for you," he said, pointing to a maroon dress and black coat hanging on the door of the cheap pine armoire. "The hat's on the shelf."

"What's wrong with my own things?"

"Madame Tinel wouldn't be caught dead in schoolgirl clothes."

Ann changed in the tiny bathroom/kitchen. The maroon wool exuded the odors of cheap cologne and perspiration, the fraying collar of the black coat had turned brown. She had never worn anyone else's clothing and to be surrounded by the bodily secretions of Quent's mistress raised goose bumps on her flesh. There was a nub of dried-out lipstick in the coat pocket. She wiped it off before rubbing a little of the dry, wartime purple on her soft, full mouth. Cocking the blue pillbox over her left eye, she looked into the cracked mirror. Madame Jacques Tinel, a reasonable facsimile of a cheaply smart redhead, stared back.

Quent had emptied her battered suitcase on the bed and was sorting into two piles the shabby clothes that Dorothy had lovingly mended. Her sketch pad and books lay on the rug.

"Nothing like asking," she hissed in English.

"I need space to stow my things."

Ann couldn't meet his gaze. "Madame Tinel has a mean, sharp tongue, doesn't she?"

"She looks sharp, too," he said, whistling softly.

Ann colored. "I thought you'd never notice. Want me to finish the packing?"

"Sold," he said. Closing himself into the kitchen/bathroom for a few minutes, he emerged shaved and carrying two cups of "coffee."

"Ann, before we go any further you might as well know the worst. Last night I found out that our first passer had been arrested. It's possible he talked, so it's not safe to use any others in the chain. I've done parts of the route before."

She felt a hot rush of excitement. They were going to be alone together. The euphoria refused to fade even as it occurred to her that her parents' timidity might prove to be wisdom regarding this particular journey.

"So you're it?" she asked.

"I'm it," he said. "Come on, we've got a train to catch."

20

Wedged against a blacked-out window of the crowded third-class compartment, Ann stared at a copy of *Signal* without having any idea of what illustrations or words were on the page of the magazine. Quent had chosen reading material suitable for the Tinels at the station kiosk so they wouldn't need to make conversation with the other passengers, a precaution that at the time Ann had thought unnecessary. She had set out charged with excited energy. The *agent de police* boarded at every stop for a security check and pretty little Madame Tinel had flirted with them demurely, as befitted a young wife under the blue gaze of her dour though undeniably handsome husband. No questions had arisen over the couple's papers.

However, they had been shunted onto sidings three times, waiting until military trains passed: with each delay Ann had become more anxious until now, with the wheels slowing for Chalans, a border town between occupied and unoccupied France, her breathing had become so difficult that she was reduced to making lugubrious sighs in order to fill her lungs. Hopefully, Quent and the others believed this a normal reaction to the foul air. The windows had been closed all day because of snow flurries, and the compartment was heavy with smoke, fetid with the sweat of the passengers, none of whom from their ripe odors had bathed or changed their underwear in the past year.

She glanced across the aisle at Quent. He was intent on that rotten, antisemitic daily rag, *Au Pilori.*

The train was hissing to a halt.

Chalans, the *zone interdite* between divided France.

The four Wehrmacht noncoms gathered their packages and duffel bags, grousing good-naturedly about the brevity of their passes. With a final lurch, the train stopped, and the soldiers got off. The tension filling the compartment was palpable. Not even Quent's calm, steady gaze over the top of his newspaper could ease Ann's loud, sucking breaths.

After about five minutes the door opened and two SS with bored, tired faces came into the compartment. One had graying stubble and narrow shoulders, the other's blouse bulged over his belly. Who could be less harrowing than these weary, middle-aged sergeants?

Yet Ann froze.

Literally. Solidified blood locked her flesh and muscles. She stared down without seeing her magazine as the Germans rustled passes and identity cards.

"Your papers, Madame?" asked a bored, heavily accented voice above her bent head.

The documents were in her purse, which rested on her lap.

"Your papers?" the voice repeated.

She couldn't move.

"Ann?" Quent tapped her knee. "Is it *that* again?" He gave a little guffaw. "It's close in here, officer, and she's having problems with the nausea. You get my meaning?"

In her stiffened limbo, Ann knew she was blushing.

"*Ach, so?* The first?"

"Started it on our wedding night," Quent responded with loutish pride.

"I have three, all boys. Well, Madame, take my advice, chew bread slowly. That's what my wife did and she never once had to make a dash to the lavatory."

"You hear, Ann? Didn't I tell you to eat a bit more?" He reached for her purse.

The German rustled her *Ausweis.* "You're going to Lyon, eh?"

Quent replied for her. "My *belle-mère* lives there, just off the place Bellecour." Another guffaw. "My job's done. Now it's up to the women. Wish me your luck with sons."

The German returned the papers to Quent then fished in his tunic pocket. "Sometimes peppermint helps, Madame." He dropped a green candy into her lap.

"*Danke schön,*" she whispered.

When the French police came through, the old farm woman with the white whiskers announced that the pretty little madame was *enceinte* and trying not to vomit, so no more of this nonsense with the papers.

Sixteen hours after the train left Paris, they pulled into the Gare de Perrache in Lyon. There was no blackout in Vichy France and the occasional dim light seemed brilliant to Ann as she moved stiffly at Quent's side down the snow-covered station square. They passed through a dark tunnel, a train rumbling above them, and turned up an alley toward a faded, creaking sign, LA RÉSIDENCE DE LYON. In the must-odored warmth of the lobby, Ann slumped in a chair, barely hearing the masculine voices as Quent and the walrus-mustached proprietor filled in extensive registration forms.

Their room was on the ground floor. Quent used the huge key, peering inside. The high, lumpy brass bed left only a sliver of space, this jammed by the washstand and the chipped enamel bidet resting on a stool.

"I'm sorry," he mumbled. "I figured there'd be room for me to sack out on the floor."

After his oafish cover-up on the train, his dismay seemed both absurd and innocent.

"No need to worry." Kicking off her shoes, Ann dropped fully dressed on the bed, pulling the slick duvet over herself. "I'm too beat to make a pass at you."

But her galling failure of nerve at Chalans and her filial culpability refused to release her. Keeping herself wrenched away from the central sag of the mattress, listening to the intermittent rush of trains and boom of church bells far and near, she mentally flitted back and forth between her deserted parents and her cowardice.

"Sleeping?" Quent asked in a low voice.

"Aren't you?" she whispered back. "I'm so ashamed."

"You mean that business at the border? The rest of the trip, you stalled off a lot of questions, so big deal, I fielded one." The mattress shifted. "A rotten way to do it, but I couldn't come up with anything else."

"Oh, Quent, loosen up. You were the perfect oaf. But I could've gotten us both killed—if we were lucky enough to *be* killed."

"You had one bad moment." He reached out to pat her shoulder. Her head was resting on the tough bolster so she was higher in the bed than he. His fingertips grazed her breast. His hand withdrew immediately but her flesh continued to feel the touch. He was silent for nearly a minute.

"It's your parents, too, isn't it?" he said.

She sighed. "I still can't believe that I left them. They depend on me."

"Ann, they trapped you here."

"Oh, you don't understand them!"

"That's true," he retorted in his most clipped politeness. "So perhaps you can answer a question that's been bothering me. Did staying mired in Paris have any connection to your father not lining up a job at home?"

She swallowed, not quite certain whether she was on the verge of tears because Quent had seen through to her parents' sad motivations, or because he had retreated into that impenetrable world of the moneyed class.

After a minute he said apologetically, "That remark was way out of line." He paused. "I get like that when things've been rugged. A real sweet guy."

21

Brightness shone on her closed lids as she woke up. Sunlight was streaming through grubby windowpanes into the cubicle of a hotel room. Rolling over, she saw that the covers were thrown back on the other side of the bed. Quent—where was he? The church clocks began their antiphonal bonging. A single stroke. One o'clock! How long had he been gone? Ann had no illusions that Lyon presented fewer risks for Quent than Paris. Although unoccupied France was not at war with the United States, indeed still received generous aid from Washington, the government, housed in the spa town of Vichy, hopped like a puppet to strings jerked in Berlin: if the fraudulence of Quent's papers were uncovered, the local authorities would be obligated to deliver him to the border where any American would, ipso facto, be judged a spy.

Maybe he's in the toilet.

She raced down the corridor. The WC door, ajar, displayed the vacant, antiquated wooden throne. Charging in the opposite direction, she jangled through a beaded curtain to the lobby.

Quent, leaning on the desk, turned to her. The proprietor halted in midsentence, his mouth gaping beneath the swooping gray mustache. Ann realized how she must look, shoeless, her curly hair wild, Suzette's maroon frock rumpled and pulled awry.

"I was worried about you, Jacques," she said irately. "You might have told me you were leaving."

Quent bristled back. "You don't even bother undressing, you sleep until all hours, and I'm at fault?"

The proprietor gave the uneasy, conciliatory chuckle of an outsider exposed to a marital argument. "Madame, I was recommending the Café Camille a short walk from here, on the quai de Perrache facing the Rhone. Fair prices—and even nowadays Mere Camille manages good, hearty Lyonnais food."

"I'm starving!" Quent barked. "Come and make yourself decent!"

Meekly, she followed him down the hall. Inside the bedroom, she took out her comb. "I'm about as unobtrusive as an exploding torpedo, aren't I?"

"He's safe."

"How safe?"

"He's not in the Résistance, if that's what you're asking. But he suspects something's not quite right about us, so he doesn't ask many questions. This is his way of proving he's a patriot—you know how proud the French are. Also, he's given us this room. If there's a police sweep, we can leave through here." He tapped the grimy window.

She peered out. A narrow path led to a street with a thirty-foot-high stone wall topped with a square lookout tower. "Quent, what's that building?"

"St. Paul's prison."

"A prison . . . you're joking."

"It makes the place less obvious."

"Less obvious!" As she stared at the huge stones blackened by railroad soot, a duo of police holding rifles paced into view. She pulled back as if they could see her. Quent had told her they would be in Lyon one night, then take the train to Annecy. "Well, at least we're leaving," she said.

"About that. This morning I went to the contact who makes the *sauf-conduits*. He says with this heavy snow, the Annecy market day's been changed to Friday. So we're stuck here."

"Three whole days? Next to a *prison*? Why do we have to wait for market day?"

"Annecy's close to the Swiss border so the security's tight," Quent explained. "If there's a crowd they can't check so carefully."

"I guess it's worth waiting for, then." She sighed, sounding more dubious than she felt. The extra days with Quent preempted her fears (Dorothy always had bewailed what she called her daughter's reckless streak) and she hummed as she poured icy water from the ewer into the bowl, washing her face. She applied Suzette Pamfou's lipstick, fussing with the little blue hat.

"You look terrific," Quent said. "Ann, I really meant it, I'm starving."

"You don't tell much about yourself," she said.

It was a remark she did not summon the nerve to make until the following evening. Quent had encouraged her to talk and she had unzipped herself completely with no attempt at self-protection or devious notes of self-enhancement. She had confessed the ambivalences of being a citizen of a country where she had never set foot and her loyalty to the land of her birth. She had stumblingly explained her protectiveness of her parents. She had told him about her boyfriends from Lycée Paul Bert and even exposed her necking activities. Somewhere on the floor above, a gramophone continuously played Caruso records.

"I've done nothing but talk," he said.

"You know what I mean."

He took her hand, playing with her small fingers. "You're a very open person. But I . . . the only way to explain it is to say my life has certain rooms where I've always gone by myself."

"That sounds lonely."

"Exactly." Caruso sang of Aida's celestial charms, Ann waited and finally Quent said, "You never asked about the photo on your original *carte d'identité*."

"Suzette said you gave it to her."

"It's an old snapshot of my mother."

"But she looks like me. . . ." Ann's voice trailed away as she recalled the peculiar intensity of Quent's eyes when she'd met him that rainy afternoon in the de Permont flat.

"What do you think Dr. Freud would make of *that*?"

She tugged on an imaginary beard. "Hmm, very interesting."

Pausing, she said quietly, "Gilberte told me she's dead, your mother."

"She died when I was born."

"Oh. . . ."

"But from what I've heard I imagine she was very much like you. Warm and outgoing. Everyone liked her—Grand-mère said she brought the gift of happiness. People were happy when they were with her." He drew a long breath. "Gilberte didn't tell you any more about her?"

"No, nothing."

"Her maiden name was Templar. Jessamyn Templar. Jason Templar's daughter."

Ann blinked, her lips parting as if he'd stabbed her between the shoulder blades.

She had known that Quent's family, as owners of the Dejong Bank, were rich, very rich. Jason Templar, though, went beyond rich. Andrew Carnegie's rival in gathering together the American steel industry, Jason Templar, or so historians said, had been the more financially successful of the pair. Ann knew all about Jason Templar from *The Tremendous Templar*, a muckraking American best seller that Dorothy had rented from W. H. Smith's bookshop on the rue de Rivoli. Aged twelve, Ann had sneaked the book into her room, in one night devouring the biography's sensational aspects. The representatives and senators who passed laws favorable to Jason Templar alone, his women "friends," the famous diamonds and knee-length ropes of pearls he gave his French wife (abruptly being recatalogued by Ann as Quent's *grand-mère*, Gilberte's great-aunt, Mathilde de Permont), the Templar mansion that sprawled across an entire block of Fifth Avenue, the eleven other homes and estates, the railroad car with solid gold bathroom fixtures, the yacht *Knight Templar* with built-in humidors for his massive cigars, the derby-winning Thoroughbreds, the friendships with royalty. Jason Templar was the son of a prosperous but thrifty Liverpool cabinetmaker. Traveling to the new world to scoop up an immense fortune, he had left thrift far behind: his formidable opulence became a field manual of conspicuous consumption for American millionaires.

It was one thing to read about a famous robber baron, however, and quite another to be sitting on a lumpy bed with his grandson. Ann felt her identity crumble and slip as if a land mine had detonated deep within her. She tried to recall if there had been any mention in the rental library book about the Templar heirs.

Quent was staring intently at her. "In case you're wondering," he said, a muscle jumping near his mouth, "she was his only child, and I'm *her* only child."

The cool, distancing tone finished her off, and she felt obligated to show Quent that she wasn't as lilliputian as she felt. "I told you all about me," she snapped. "How come you held out?"

"Have I missed something? Is there an Aristotelian principle at stake here?"

"The world's never going to crash into your private rooms, is it? You emerge to sleep with an occasional serf, and if anything comes of it, well, what are abortionists for?"

He rose slowly from the bed, staring down at her with blue eyes that glittered in his suddenly white face.

How could she have hit below the belt like this? Unfair, oh, unfair. *Apologize,* she ordered herself. But her lips were numb, her throat locked.

"Just to set family gossip straight her name was Doris Welch," he said levelly. "She called herself Dori and—"

He stopped abruptly. Grabbing the string to douse the light, he pulled back the cretonne curtain.

An instant later she heard footsteps racing from the direction of the prison. Then shouts of "Halt!"

She jerked to a kneeling position on the bed, staring over Quent's shoulder. A window on the other side lit the narrow stretch of dirty snow, then a man, crouched over with knees pounding up toward his chest like pistons, zigzagged into sight. As he reached the window, there was a dry, continuous crackling, and savage streaks of light were clearly visible. He gave a shrill cry, staggering from their range of vision. Three other men raced into view. They also wore civilian clothes, but the one carrying a Schmeisser knelt with military precision, aiming. After another brief, hard rattling, his companions jogged forward while he followed at a leisurely pace, his weapon lovingly cradled in his arms.

Quent dropped the curtain, but remained poised by the window.

Ann, trembling, her throat dry, stayed in place, too. A car screeched to a halt, then there were more footsteps.

An angered shout in German, "French idiots! They got the wrong man!"

"How can you tell? His head's splattered."

"Are you blind? He's not in a prison uniform."

"What are you so excited about anyway? He wouldn't have made a run for it if he weren't guilty of something. Probably an illegal yid or a saboteur."

The steps and voices faded into the chirp of awakened birds.

Neither Ann nor Quent spoke for a long time.

". . . She went to Dad first. It hurt that she told him before me, God how it hurt," Quent said. An hour later, they were lying side by side, holding hands. Neither of them had yet been able to mention the horror beyond the window. Instead, he had told her about his fifteenth summer, the only summer of his life that he'd spent in its entirety with his father, the summer he had been in thrall to Dori Welch, his then current stepmother's secretary. "I told Dori I *wanted* the baby, wanted to marry her. She smiled—she had beautiful teeth, large and white and gleaming. And retorted that Dad had warned her he'd cut me off if we entertained any thought of marriage. She already knew I didn't have access to any of the trusts until I was twenty-one. She wasn't, she said, about to embark on six years of poverty. And furthermore, she sure wasn't ready for a kid. The money my father was giving her would support her in Hollywood until she got her big break. Dori's goal in life, it seemed, was to fill the silver screen. God, it was so banal! And me, I was the most banal of all. I kept persisting that things would work out. I made big plans for the baby."

"It was yours, too."

"That's a moot point. She finally told me that it might be a half brother or sister—'Mr. Dejong also slipped it to me,' she said. Ann, after all these years I can remember her exact tone of voice as she said, 'Mr. Dejong also slipped it to me.' "

"What a bitch!" Ann gripped his hand fiercely.

"I don't think she realized how much she was hurting me. A lot of people honestly believe that money acts like steel-plate armor on a tank."

Flushing in the darkness, Ann swore to herself she'd never be in that group again and was grateful that he changed the subject to their route to Switzerland.

22

Her labored breathing and the crunch of snow under their second-hand mountain boots filled the moving hollow that she and Quent were carving in the fog. Up, up, up the Salève mountain she struggled. Two hours earlier, when Quent had nudged her from the rickety, crowded bus, she had not realized how many kilometers they had to go on foot—or how ungiving a mountain could be.

This was her first time in the Alps. On the train from Lyon to Annecy, she had been unable to stop gazing out the window, she couldn't get enough of the white majesty carved against the blue sky, the purple creases, the faraway, toylike villages. Today, when she longed for the view to distract her from the painful exertion of the climb, a dense cloud squatted over the Salève.

Since boarding the bus at Annecy, Quent had spoken no more than a dozen sentences. She wished he would talk, but his silence didn't desolate her as it would have earlier: she had accepted that tension increased his natural reticence. She concentrated on his back, admiring—and envying—the graceful masculine strength of his stride. Despite being burdened by her valise and the used rucksack that held their purchases, he swung uphill effortlessly.

Yesterday, Friday, they had arrived at the Annecy railroad station in late afternoon, hurrying through what, from the twilit vistas, appeared to be a fairy-tale town. At the bookshop that faced the

Thiou canal, Quent had introduced her to Monsieur Duhay, the tanned, wrinkled proprietor. Duhay had climbed with Quent: over smoky Morteau sausages with a pitcher of *vin de Savoie,* the two men had reminisced about their adventures on perpendicular mountain faces. Ann had listened, knowing that climbing hairy cliffs had endangered Duhay less than sharing this convivial meal with them. She and Quent had slept behind the counter of the bookshop, leaving before dawn. Obtaining food in the country presented far fewer difficulties than in big cities, and at the rue Sainte-Claire market, Quent had bought a nutty tasting slab of Beaufort cheese and a great round loaf of bread. Also two matted, grubby loden coats and their shabby mountain boots. Hers, the smallest in the stall, were too big. She had blisters on both heels.

Something thumped softly behind them. Quent halted, holding up his hand to still her. Cocking his head, he listened intently. There was only the sough of the wind.

"Snow falling from a branch," he said.

"Is it much farther?"

"The altitude bothering you?"

"Not in the least."

"Liar," he said, putting his free arm around her.

She relaxed against his warm side. When they started upward again, she softly hummed *Chanson d'Amour,* a reminder of the *salon de thé* in Paris, and Quent joined in for a few off-key bars—he couldn't carry a tune, a fallibility she found totally endearing. She didn't hum long either. As the fog around them darkened, the temperature plummeted and the thin, frozen air burned her lungs.

A dog barked. Several other dogs joined in. Quent halted. Gripping her arm, he whispered, "Be very quiet. Sound travels weirdly in the mountains and there's a German post over the ridge."

"Germans?" she breathed.

"They patrol the borders in the unoccupied zone," he whispered. "This fog's a lucky break. Duhay heard rumors that the precautions had been beefed up."

The yapping increased. She should have been panicked, yet testing her fears in much the same way she was rubbing her boot up and down to test the cold numbed pain of her broken blisters, she found herself remarkably calm. Why not? Quent—strong, calmly competent, knowledgeable about the Salève—was her guide.

The barking quieted as suddenly as it had begun.

"We'll leave the path," Quent whispered. "There's a trail."

The trail was cruelly steep with drifts up to her knees. Panting, sweating despite the cold, hauled in places by Quent's free hand, she floundered upward between the firs and spruces. Within twenty minutes they were moving downward across broad treeless pastureland.

Here, on the brow of the Salève mountain, a wind tattered the fog. In the twilit gloom, she caught a glimpse of a panorama far below. She gasped, blinking. A necklace of glittery lights curved at the throat of an oil-black lake.

"Geneva," Quent whispered.

"It's so bright . . . it's beautiful."

"The Swiss always light up like a Christmas tree, that's how they show their neutrality to bombardiers on both sides. The border's a few miles from Geneva—"

"Achtung!"

The shout seemed to echo from ahead of them, but she saw nobody. The mountains did play odd tricks with sound. As she wheeled around she saw that a half mile or so behind them SS were jumping from a green truck, two of them already standing to one side holding a group of Alsatians straining on leashes that were invisible at this distance.

"Achtung!" An officer in a long black leather coat was holding a megaphone in their direction.

"Oh Christ!" Quent was no longer whispering. "They've never used that road before. We'll have to give ourselves up."

He'll be shot as a spy. "No!"

"What choice is there?"

If I weren't here he'd make a run for it.

There was a loud retort and the air roared.

Quent dropped the suitcase, encircling her waist, propelling her downhill. She heard more gunfire and a whistling near her head. The hard strength of the arm swerved her toward a stand of trees. A root beneath the snow tripped her. The arm held her upright. As they emerged from the copse, the fog again covered them.

"Speidel, take your men and cover that direction." The shouts seemed closer. "We'll go around the left."

The dogs yapped and snarled.

Quent jerked her to a halt so swiftly that she flung out her arms to maintain balance. She saw they had reached what appeared to be a sheer drop into the fog. Quent kicked a piece of shale. It clattered noisily downward, then the sound stopped.

"Follow me," he whispered. "Do exactly what I do."

He turned, getting to his knees to clamber down. "Come on," he ordered. "I'll hold you."

Not permitting herself the luxury of thought, she dropped on all fours, scrambling backward after him.

They inched down the limestone and granite cliff, his arms around her, his body behind hers. She copied his movements. Her gloves tore and sharp rocks abraded her bare palms. She felt the icy, rough stone through her layers of clothing. A rock fell under her foot, echoing into infinity.

"Be careful!" Quent whispered. It was a command.

He and Duhay had talked about pitons, ropes, carbiners. They had no equipment. Duhay had dwelled on the increased test of climbing in winter. It was icy cold. *Don't think,* she ordered herself. *Just follow Quent.* She reached for outcroppings, hand, foot, hand, foot. After about a hundred feet of near-perpendicular edging downward, he stopped. Their hoarse breathing seemed to roar over the wind and the voices.

"Where'd they disappear?"

"Where do you think, *Dummkopf?* Down the mountain!"

Bullets struck lightning on a nearby rock. Ann fought an overwhelming urge to shout, to scream, to give herself away.

"A bit farther." Quent's whisper warmed her ear.

They descended in tandem.

"This is it," he whispered. "Don't move, *do not move.*"

She embraced the rough face of the Salève mountain. Quent braced his legs and arms around her, enfolding her like a wrap.

The men and barking dogs were directly above. By now it was completely dark, and the temperature was falling rapidly. Her sweat froze on her. Her teeth chattered, and her body shook.

Quent, on the outside, was far more vulnerable to the snap of the icy wind. How long could he hold on?

A rifle snapped methodically, the bullets thwacking on the rock above them.

"My balls are freezing. What's the damn use wasting bullets?" a querulous voice asked. "They fell long ago."

"I saw the girl fall. But the man's still down there. Keep firing!"

Quent began wriggling and shrugging with slow, cautious movements. He was, she realized, unbuckling his rucksack. The silent effort traveled along her own muscles and nerve endings. The rucksack slipped, thumping out of earshot until there was only the sound of the wind.

"There he goes." Cheerful.

Another burst of fire in celebration of death, then triumphant laughter.

The voices and barking faded.

Quent began flexing his quivering arms, then his thighs. "Okay?" he asked, still whispering.

"Fine."

They retraced their footholds up the mountain face, she first, fumbling endlessly for each crevice and outcropping. And always there was the empty wind, waiting to receive them. Finally her hands found level rock, and she pulled herself up, collapsing, rolling inward onto the snow and shale.

Her pupils had become accustomed to the blackness, and she saw the fog-blurred outline crawl up, lumbering away from the edge in a crouch. She heard the sounds of retching, then the crunching of snow, spitting noises.

"Ann?" Quent called.

"Over here."

His heavy footsteps vibrated through her. "Come on."

"One more minute."

"We'll rest at the farmhouse."

"I can't move."

"If you stay here any longer you'll freeze."

When she didn't stir, he grabbed her arms, hauling her to her feet. Her knees were locked and she had to swing her legs, which were numb as logs, from the hip socket as she stumbled along at his side. They regained the footpath.

There was barking ahead of them. A dog so near that there could be no distortion of sound. *Oh, God, the killer Alsatians!* she thought. After being strung out on the cruel face of the Salève mountain, it seemed the grossest unfairness to get caught now.

23

"Here Riffi, here." Quent whistled. "No, boy. Down, down." The dog continued jumping up to lick his face.

A playful pet! With a high laugh, Ann swayed dizzily, clutching Quent's arm.

A door opened. The thin little man in outsize rubber boots who stood there would have been a cartoon of a farmer if it weren't for the backlit halo of white hair that made him resemble Einstein. He clasped Quent's upper arms in a masculine embrace, and the two exchanged a few sentences in the patois of the Haute-Savoie before Quent introduced him as Monsieur Laas. Leading the way to a stone barn, Monsieur Laas explained apologetically to Ann that they would be safer here than in the house. He lit a lantern, indicating the ladder to the loft, following them up with thick blankets and a bucket of milk warm from one of his brown-and-white Montbéliard cows. Gulping milk, Ann wrapped the itchy hairiness of a blanket around herself. Quent said something about being under way in a few hours, but she was too weary to pay attention. . . .

Awakening, she inhaled the heavy sweetness of hay, the warm smell of cattle, the lactic aroma of milk, and heard whimpering groans. Having shared a bed with Quent for three nights in La Résidence de Lyon and having spent a fourth night with him behind Duhay's counter, she knew for a fact that he was a quiet sleeper.

"Quent, you're having a nightmare," she called softly.

The groans persisted. "Quent!" The mournful sounds continued. Standing, she cracked her head against the sharply pitched roof. She crouched, groping her way. As she touched him, the crying stopped. At the same instant her wrist was gripped so tightly that she was immobilized.

"It's me," she whispered.

He released her. "Sorry, Ann."

"Quick reflexes there." She rubbed her wrist. "You were making funny noises. Bad dream?"

"I was back in the crevasse."

"A lulu of a bad dream," she said.

"You don't know the half of it. The entire time we were down there, I couldn't stop thinking about René, he was Monsieur Laas's nephew. René was the most experienced climber in this area, he taught me most of what I know. Last September he fell from that same crevasse. In full daylight. The next day a search party found him with a crushed skull, still gripping a hunk of limestone."

Ann's lungs tightened with retroactive panic. Their skulls could have been crushed, their dead fingers could be gripping broken-off rock.

"Ann, the way you followed me without hesitation—I never saw anyone so brave."

"Brave? Idiotic. But what choice was there?"

"Most people," he said, "would have taken their chances with the Jerries."

"Quent, what if my parents had been with us?"

"I've thought about that," he muttered dejectedly. "They were right not to come. They'd be in prison—or dead."

"We're alive, Quent."

"Yes, alive," he responded in a tone that said the point could still be moot.

Sinking down on the mounded hay, she wrapped her arms around him. In response, he pulled her under his blanket, kissing her with an urgent purpose. She arched against him, her muscles complaining in an irrelevant way. She caressed the firm, warmly living flesh of his back and shoulders with rivaling urgency. Quent smelled of masculine sweat—O aphrodisiac perfume. She pushed yet closer, shaking and needful of the only act on this planet that can cancel the incontrovertible fact of death. He pushed up her loden coat, shoving aside her other clothes to bruise her naked breasts with hot, moist kisses.

Shaking uncontrollably, she pushed down the ugly woolen bloomers that her mother had insisted she pack for internment and her rayon underpants, gasping when he touched that aching, yearning part of her, briefly embarrassed that he found her so wet. She fumbled with his corduroy trousers and he whispered something incoherently as she encircled the pulsing, silky hardness of his penis, bringing it against the epithelial skin where his finger had rubbed. In the hot darkness there was no question of stopping, no questioning of morality or the future and past, only caresses and loud, tremulous breath. When he moved on top of her, she thrust her thighs apart as far as she could. But as he pressed partway into her, she flinched involuntarily, giving a little cry. He stopped.

"Quent . . . please . . . ?"

He tightened his arms around her, as if to bind them together for the eternity in which they might have been joined a few hours earlier. For nearly a minute they kissed, then he pressed again, and something within her tore, her virginity, her maidenhead, the barrier between them. He began to move, hurting her each time, but the pain turned into an adjunct to her desire and then was replaced by sensations so intense that she seemed cut adrift in the roiling currents of love and pleasure.

"Ann, all my life . . ." he said in her ear. "I've been looking for you all my life."

As he spoke, volts of electricity shot through her blood, and her body was no longer in her control. Her hoarse gasps were as involuntary as the violent surges of the flesh that surrounded him. Somewhere far away a voice cried his name, and he rose and fell more swiftly.

They collapsed under the blanket, she gasping more loudly than he.

After a long time, she heard a cow chewing its cud and a faint, ticking sound of a mouse scampering across the loft.

"Sweet?"

"What?"

"I meant what I said."

"Said what?"

"I've been looking for you all my life."

She kissed his wet throat. "I love you."

"I belong with you." His voice resonated against her ear with awkward sincerity.

"Always . . ."

"Always," he said.

An owl hooted. The sound recalled Quent to the world that existed beyond the enclosure of their arms. He raised his wrist to see the phosphorescence of his cheap steel watch. "Almost time for Monsieur Laas to wake us."

The fog had evaporated, and a nearly full moon blazed so brightly that the spangles it cast on the snow shone more brilliantly than the stars. There was no path. They had been crunching downhill on the soft snow for what seemed like hours, moving in and out of the blackness cast by trees.

"Careful," Quent whispered. They had reached a bare outcropping of rock. Reminded of the cliff to which they had clung earlier, Ann took tiny, mincing steps until they reached snow again. They were at the top of a steep embankment. A fallen tree trunk pointed like a finger at the black curve of cleared road.

"The border's on the other side," Quent whispered.

"How far—"

Abruptly he dragged her down. A few seconds later an octet of SS noncoms paced two by two around the curve. Their buttons and the rifles slung over their shoulders glinted in the moonlight.

She held her breath. As they disappeared, the hill cut off the rhythmic beat of their boots.

Quent jumped up, grasping her hand to yank her to her feet. "Move!" he whispered hoarsely.

She raced with him down the embankment, pounding across the cleared road, stumbling down a snowy slope.

All trees had been cleared, and there was no cover of any sort between the road and the thick hedge of barbed wire half buried by snow.

"On the other side," he whispered, "run like hell."

"What about you? Quent, they'll see our tracks—"

He was grasping strands of barbed wire, pressing a boot on the bottom wires. "Get through!"

Galvanized, she crawled through what seemed like twenty strands, unaware of the barbs that tore into her legs and her already ripped gloves. Jumping to her feet, she ran pell-mell downhill, gasping, terrified that Quent might be entangled in the wire, her ears primed for shots. All at once she pitched forward, rolling over and over down the incline.

He caught up with her. "Ann, Jesus, Ann!" He knelt next to her. "Are you okay?"

"Don't stop!" she shouted.

"We're safe. This is Switzerland."

He was bandaging her bleeding palms with strips of his shirt when the Swiss border patrol found them.

The rain was letting up. Ann leaned against the pillows eating a hothouse peach while watching the drops slide in slow dignity down double-paned windows.

She was in the Hallorans' house on Jubilaumstrasse in Bern—Timothy Halloran worked at the American legation. He and his wife, Wilma, were fiftyish with similar round, cheerful faces. When the doctor, after examining Ann for broken bones—she had none—and tending to her bruises and cuts, had pronounced that she needed two weeks of complete bed rest, both Hallorans insisted that rather than stay in the Geneva clinic, she come to their house.

After seeing her settled, Quent had gone to Zurich. He did not explain why, and she didn't ask, guessing he had to do some business for the Dejong Bank. He had sent packages of warm, peacetime clothes—a bathrobe, two dresses, a skirt and sweater, two blouses, an inner-lined coat in a perfect shade of bronze. As each item arrived she had disobeyed the doctor's orders to try it on. Her new wardrobe had been selected with thoughtful care for fit and color, the fabrics were beautiful and, of course, each garment cost more than anything she'd ever owned, yet undeniably Swiss designers lacked the lightness, the chic, of their Paris counterparts. Ann, feeling petty for entertaining such fashion-conscious thoughts about her gifts, let her fingers caress the handsome cloth.

The Hallorans had not known Quent before: Ann had overheard them discussing his connection to Jason Templar in tones normally reserved for anointed royalty.

She finished gnawing the peach to the pit and began to lick sweetness from her fingers. The gauze bandaging across her palms was stained with the juice.

The doorbell rang. Quent had told her when he left that he'd be back soon, but couldn't pinpoint the day. She held her breath, hoping.

Yes. His voice. Her bandaged hands shook and she had difficulty with the sash of his earliest gift, the powder blue bathrobe piped with the same shade of satin. Still struggling with the knot, she started down the stairs.

Rosa, the grumpy maid from Chur, was hanging up a rain-darkened khaki topcoat.

Ann halted near the top, staring down. Quent wore an army uniform with the single silver bars of a first lieutenant on the shoulders.

Gripping the banister rail, she said, "Does the United States have a recruiting office in Zurich or what?"

He glanced at Rosa, who spoke no English, waiting until she had stomped back through the swinging green baize door. "I enlisted over a year ago," he said.

"Why didn't you tell me?"

"The less you knew in France, the safer."

"What about when we got here?"

"It didn't seem germane."

This was hardly the reunion she had been fantasizing for them, she with peach juice on her face, her hair wild, carping down at a tall, overcourteous officer wearing what appeared to be a Savile Row–tailored uniform.

She descended a few more steps. Her thighs and calves remained stiff from the climbing, her broken blisters still hurt: she brought her feet together on each rung, aware that she moved without any of her usual eager bounciness. "Thank you for all the clothes," she said in a subdued tone.

"I lost your suitcase," he said. "The least I could do was replace your stuff."

"It was very thoughtful." A car passed down the rain-hushed street, and she gave him a faint smile. "Is being in the army another one of your closed rooms?"

"Let's hope the door's locked tight," he said, his expression marginally less wary. "I'm in a very hush-hush outfit."

"What about your trips to Paris? Did you get time off for business?"

Now he smiled. "You don't know much about being in the service, do you, Ann? The army doesn't give time off for business. But the bank sure made a perfect cover for my work there. I'm with Colonel Donovan's outfit. He reports directly to the president."

"Donovan?"

"Colonel William Donovan. Sometimes known as Wild Bill Donovan. He's a specialist in behind-the-lines activities."

Two ideas melded together. "Behind the lines?" she cried. "You mean you're going back?"

He glanced around. "Ann, you shouldn't know this much."

Reaching the bottom step, she gripped the ornate newel post. "When are you leaving?"

"Ann, come on, cut it out," he said. "Look, the bank has a correspondent in Zurich and I've pulled strings to get you to Lisbon and on a flight home."

The faraway home that was not her home. She had already determined not to be separated by an ocean from her parents—and now, it seemed, from him. "Mr. Halloran's arranging a job for me."

"Here in Bern?"

"London."

"The Luftwaffe doesn't make life too safe there."

"Hey, what're you trying to do, put our sordid past behind you? I'm going to be a driver." Horace's one prewar extravagance had been typically American, a 1929 Chevrolet that he'd sold at the outbreak of war: Ann had persisted in her desire to take the wheel until he'd given in and taught her. Young as she'd been, she was a far better driver than he. "The army's going to use some civilians."

"If that's what you've decided," he said politely, but his eyelids wavered. She understood then that she'd wounded him by refusing his gift of the near-impossible-to-obtain ticket on the Pan Am Clipper.

Dishes clattered in the dining room. She moved a step toward him. As she did, she perceived without quite formulating the idea that it would always be up to her to take the first step, sensing, too, that he would always intimidate her into nearly not making the crucial move.

They met in the center of the hall under the chandelier.

Hugging him, she murmured, "I missed you so much."

"Me, you."

"Even if we do fight a lot?"

"That's because I'm so screwy about you that I can't see straight." He brushed her lips with a kiss. "Sweet, if anyone puts the past behind us, it won't be me."

Gilberte
Paris, 1943–1944

24

As Gilberte returned to the box along the Paris Opera House's rococo, gilt-columned main gallery, she created a ripple of murmurs and a stir of the men craning their necks after her.

Her black satin evening gown was severely sculpted to her body so that her full, camellia-white breasts rose with dazzling sensuality from the strapless decolletage. Other than the obligatory crimson on her thin, perfect lips, she used no distracting makeup. Her upswept coiffure accentuated the arrogant tilt of her head as she responded with brusque nods to the greetings of the two senior staff officers who darted envious, awed glances at her while exchanging a few words with her companion, Field Marshal Count Bernd von Hocherer.

Walking ahead of him, she passed the marble and onyx *grand escalier*. The attendant unlocked the box.

"Gilberte," the field marshal said, bringing his heels together in an old-fashioned Prussian bow.

"Hocherer," she replied, sweeping inside.

Sitting on the red velvet chair, she folded her bare arms on the prickly crimson plush in front of her. From here she had a view of the entire stage as well as the orchestra pit, where the white-haired conductor was taking his bows.

Tonight they were doing *Otello*. Even before her sojourn in the

Santé, Verdi had been too emotional for her taste, and now the lush, pulsating chords spoke too easily of pain, of loss, of rusty stains beneath the dangling corpses of a man and a woman. To block the second act overture, she gazed around the dimly lit opera house. Before the war, she had often attended with her parents—this was their box. Elderly, high-ranking German officers accompanied most of the chic young Parisiennes displaying their jewels in the surrounding boxes.

Her glance rested on the man at her side. Bernd von Hocherer's ramrod posture, the dueling scar that ran jaggedly down his right cheek, his thin, steely gray hair fit every stereotype of a Prussian officer. But on closer inspection, the short-fingered, delicate hands and the gentle brown eyes were subtly wrong.

The field marshal's preference would have been to devote his life to a gentlemanly study of Greek history, but he came from a distinguished Junker family and accordingly had forgone the classics. In his mind Hitler was a despicable bully who had attained power by appealing to the basest elements of the German people, yet when the Nazi regime rose to power he had retained his commission. Gilberte understood the reason. Count Bernd von Hocherer represented a class, a tradition that went beyond transitory governments; he could no more escape his role than Baron André de Permont could have escaped his. She bore Hocherer no particular ill will for being the conqueror and, conversely, felt no particular gratitude toward him for arranging her early release from prison.

When she had emerged blinking through the gate in the thick walls of the Santé, a polite young aide had hurried up to her, escorting her to the long black Mercedes with the two small swastika flags blowing from the front of the hood. She had been too befuddled to take in his explanations. Not until they had reached the boulevard Suchet and pulled up at the house where she had grown up did Gilberte comprehend that her benefactor was General von Hocherer. Gazing dully at the familiar shell-shaped copper cupola over the front door, she accepted that it made sense for the general to obtain an early release for her and to offer her a home. Following the Great War, he had been a comrade of her father's on a binational, ultimately ill-fated committee to lower the immense reparations that Germany must pay France: like her father, the general honored old obligations.

Upstairs she found a personal maid, a Breton with the top-heavy figure of a pouter pigeon, drawing hot, scented water in the bathroom that had been her mother's. Gilberte threw off the ruined suit, stepping into a bath for the first time in four months. Her pelvic bones jutted out, her ribs pressed against her skin. She scrubbed herself with real, prewar, scented Guerlain soap and a loofah until her thin body was crimson, then she splashed on Chanel No. 5. She could still smell the sweat and semen of endless gang rapes.

A day of her imprisonment had seldom passed without Wissman marching her to a basement room. She'd observed him pocketing money from the others who shared use of her: from his whispered abjurations to keep this private, she knew that Captain Knecht was unaware of his diminutive orderly's pimping. The money and secrecy meant nothing to her. Gang rape was gang rape.

Within a couple of months from her release she was able to cut down to two baths a day. She no longer shuddered uncontrollably at an inadvertent touch. Her flesh began curving in its former felicitous symmetry. Except for her maid, the servants had been requisitioned with the house. Slowly emerging from her benumbed state, she realized that they were making book on how long it would be before *la bâtarde* allowed the *boche* in her bed.

Hocherer, widowed once, with a second wife in Germany, father of seven, sixty-three years of age, was, for the first time, in love. Transparently and obsessively in love. He could not keep his gaze from Gilberte, his hands trembled when he poured her wine, he opened accounts in her name up and down the rue de la Paix and the rue Saint-Honoré.

In April of 1943, Hitler ordered Hocherer to Berlin, personally handing him a field marshal's baton. An unequivocal irony. Hocherer had taken part in two of the assassination attempts against the Führer. His promotion marked the low-water point of Count Bernd von Hocherer's life. The night that he returned to Paris, he opened the connecting door to Gilberte's room. She instantly comprehended the decision was hers, although his hopes were made clear by a bathrobe. The high-collared tunic had hid-

den a puckered and scrawny neck as well as a definite paunch. With
his brilliantined gray hair and soft, pleading brown eyes, he looked
oddly defenseless. She gave the matter composed thought, deciding that after being brutalized so often and by so many men, what
could be less important than whether one more stick of flesh was
shoved into her? He had been patient for over a year. With deliber-
ate slowness, she marked her place in the book, rising to stand on
the linen towel beside the bed. She pushed the narrow silk straps
from her shoulders and the silk chiffon nightgown fell in a midnight blue pool. Hocherer remained at the door, staring. While the
minute stretched into two, then three, she began to wonder if he
were a voyeur—did he merely desire to see her naked breasts and
the explicit black triangle?

Then he shook his head bemusedly. "Aphrodite, Venus," he
muttered as if to himself. "There's no mortal woman this perfect."
Crossing the room, he reverently touched her breasts and ran his
small, quivering hands down her hips. In the baronne's art deco
bed, he traced her body with his lips repeatedly before entering
her. She felt neither revulsion nor the least hint of pleasure, she
felt less physically than when she stepped into the tepid water of
her bath: this banishment of sensation was the one method by
which she could have survived the repeated rapes without turning
the corner to insanity. The thought of Quent had flitted across her
mind—would this act be equally desensitized with him?

Hocherer, aware of her indifference, had wooed yet more tenderly, buying her jewelry from Cartier and procuring a whipped-
cream lynx coat from captured Russian supplies.

Glancing at the rigid-backed figure in the gray uniform next to
her—that historical butt of jokes, the elderly besotted lover—her
thoughts remained in a logical monotone.

Then the Iago, a thin Italian with a deep, powerful voice, moved
downstage to sing the famous "Credo." The torrential aria sent
waves of heat traveling through Gilberte's chest. Like Iago, she
believed in a cruel God. A vengeful God. Oh, how she yearned for
revenge! As a rosebush is pruned to produce one magnificent
blossom, so her other emotions had been cut away by this single-
minded desire for vengeance. Destroying Captain Knecht and
Wissman as well as the energetic torturers Merck and Ristelheuber

had been simple. She had told Hocherer of the torture, of the repetitive rapes, and the following morning they were en route to Stalingrad, where they had starved and frozen, four casualties among the three hundred thousand Germans who had died when the Russians retook the city.

But all of them, even the morally schizoid Knecht, were small potatoes. Her father had been right. Their true enemy was the person who had informed on him.

She had asked Hocherer to find out who it was. After repeated attempts, he had told her that he could not gain access to secret Gestapo files. She still had no clue as to the creature's identity. Her suspicions had fallen on the two servants. Accordingly, she had visited 74, rue Daguerre. The old concierge, Madame Jargaux, had blathered on about the sadness of Madame and Monsieur Blakely's internment, and her initial joy that dear Mademoiselle Ann had escaped to the unoccupied zone, which by this time, alas, had also been taken over by the *boche,* so maybe she was interned too. Gilberte, wincing at the thought of warm, impulsive Ann trapped in a camp, had led Madame Jargaux back to the question of the servants. No, neither Jacques nor Hélène had been seen since the night of the raid. Gilberte's subsequent lack of success at locating either of them made her less positive of their culpability. If they were in tight with the Gestapo for turning in Résistance members, why would they be in hiding?

Someday I'll find who informed on you, Papa, she thought, articulating the unspoken words to the thundering chords of the baritone. *The punishment will be terrible, will last through the generations.*

A prickling on her skin told her that Hocherer was watching her. Thinking of her vengeance, she turned, her lips parting in a hot, passionate smile.

At home on the boulevard Suchet, as Hocherer helped her off with the lynx coat, his hands lingered on her shoulders coaxingly.

Adoration endowed him with remarkable endurance, and as he bucked and plunged above her the sweat poured from him, the mousy-odored sweat of old men heavily tinged with camphorated muscle salve. After about thirty minutes, with a shuddering cry he finished his business. Normally he went in the other room to work and then sleep on her father's Napoleonic campaign bed. Tonight, though, he didn't move.

"Gilberte," he asked in a low, tender voice. "Isn't it time you told me?"

"Told you what, Hocherer?" she replied mockingly.

"The child."

"Child?"

"I'm delighted."

"Hocherer, do stop being oblique."

"It's been over six weeks since your flow."

Jerking from his embrace, she darted into the bathroom.

With mirrored ceiling, green marble fixtures and celadon peau de soie walls, the bathroom resembled an underwater grotto. Gilberte stared at herself, a haunted naiad with narrowed eyes and tangled black hair streaming down her back. When was the last time? The end of October? Yes, it had begun October 30, during the reception for that fat, made-up, posturing ass Göring. And now it was the fifteenth of December.

There was a light tap on the door. "Gilberte? Are you all right?"

She picked up one of the Lalique scent bottles as if to hurl the crystal at the door, yet spoke in a dryly bored tone. "I'm using the bidet."

After the slow retreat of his footsteps, she banged down the bottle. The moon could follow her, she was that regular.

Over six weeks?

How could it be? She'd always pushed in her Dutch cap when Hocherer gave off signs of randiness. He was too old to sire a child, wasn't he? She hadn't become pregnant in the Santé although Berthe's miraculous salve had given out long before her release. Impossible, it was impossible for her to be *enceinte*! She squatted on the bidet frantically scrubbing at the field marshal's semen.

25

In the morning her mind had cleared and she considered the damning physiological points. Her breasts had been sore lately. She sometimes experienced a faint queasiness. She was more than two weeks late.

Of course I'm pregnant, she thought.

It was equally obvious that one course alone was open to her. An abortion.

Her decision had nothing to do with Hocherer: after living openly with a German for nearly two years, after sleeping with him for many months, to feel the least twinge of patriotic shame at bearing his child would be hypocritical to the point of humor.

She rang for her breakfast. Sipping hot, foamy cream mixed with a barley brew (genuine coffee was no longer available, even for field marshals), she skewered her mind to her problem. The logical person to solve it was Dr. Behn, the physician who had fitted her Dutch cap, but Behn, a Silesian in awe of Hocherer's birth and rank, would doubtless confer with the superannuated prospective father, who was delighted. Once she'd overheard three chic young mistresses of high-ranking Germans whispering about their experiences with "the little operation"—however, she didn't know any of them well enough to inquire how one obtained an abortion.

Incroyable! she thought. *The entire population of this planet intent on destroying each other and I can't stop a single embryo.*

Flakes scattered as she buttered her croissant. She yearned for a friend. Ann, yes, loyal and sympathetic Ann. The only friend she'd ever had. Not that Ann, virgin daughter of puritanical Americans, would know the first thing about terminating a pregnancy, but she would make a nonjudgmental sounding board. Gilberte's thoughts moved to Horace Blakely, that dreary bore who had taken inordinate pride in keeping the books of a small working-class clinic. Gilberte bit thoughtfully into the croissant. What was the name of the doctor who had employed him?

"Descourset," she said aloud.

When Hocherer arrived home at one, she was wearing her black-and-gold ensemble with a new, large-brimmed felt hat: they were to lunch at Tour d'Argent with Otto Abetz, the German ambassador, and his French wife. As the car slid along the boulevard Suchet, Gilberte murmured, "About that little idea you mentioned last night—when I woke up, I saw it was settled."

"A trifle late?" he asked, his soft brown eyes showing his disappointment. "Ah well."

Early the following morning, she went down to the basement room where her mother's clothes were stored, searching through armoires until she found a ten-year-old Chanel suit with unfashionably rounded shoulders and an out-of-date midcalf skirt. Hocherer's Mercedes was available to her whenever she wished, but anonymity would be a joke in a car affixed with swastikas: she took the métro to the clinic. Amid the pinch-faced, dowdy patients who crowded the waiting room, Gilberte, in her elegant if dated clothes, stood out like an extraterrestrial being. When it was her turn in the dispensary, Dr. Descourset looked up with an expression of puzzlement. "I'm a friend of Ann Blakely's," she explained hastily. "Gilberte de Permont."

"Ah, yes. Your family moved into their building." His voice lowered sympathetically. "I read a notice of your parents' passing. Typhoid, wasn't it?"

The cause of death given by the Gestapo. Gilberte knew the

doctor could be blackmailed emotionally with the truth, yet her pride and obdurate grief refused to permit any capitalization on their deaths. "Yes," she said without inflection. "Typhoid."

"It's a great loss to me that I never met them. 'Orace was forever telling me about his great friendship with your father."

"They were never friends."

"Ah, well, poor 'Orace was like that, always building things up. In all events, he idolized your father." The doctor tugged at his white goatee. "Well, Mademoiselle de Permont, what is ailing you?"

"It's not me, doctor, but my Claudine, my maid. I promised to visit you on her behalf. Her husband is a prisoner of war in Germany, and she finds herself with expectations of a child. Naturally she is desperate."

"Tell your maid an abortion is far too dangerous." The warmth had vanished from his voice. "The Nazis believe that all French-women of racial purity have an obligation to help populate the Third Reich—and from the news coming out of Russia and Italy, it certainly needs replenishment. The penalty for both her and the doctor is a seven-year prison term. That means a concentration camp."

"If they're caught."

"Mademoiselle, maybe your *maid* is willing to risk it. But this isn't a wealthy neighborhood, the people have no other hospital, and no other doctor."

She felt tears welling. What had happened to her renowned calm?

After a moment, Descourset sighed. "It's for you, isn't it?"

She nodded.

"I know a Jew. Poor devil, before the Occupation he was a highly respected gynecologist, but they took away his license and now he's forced into this kind of thing to survive." Descourset's voice deepened. "By God, someday the Nazis and their rotten collaborators will pay."

The Jewish doctor lived just off the avenue Parmentier. Many of the shops were boarded up, while others were affixed with black-and-yellow posters announcing JEWISH BUSINESS. The sidewalks were crowded. Thin, pale men and women sat with ragged clothes or broken household goods spread carefully in front of them— quite a few of these vendors wore the yellow star centered with the word *juif.*

Gilberte climbed the rickety staircase anticipating a wizened ancient with palsied hands. The man who opened the door was maybe forty, with clean, steady hands and blue, angry eyes.

She explained without adornment or subterfuge what she required. With similar terseness, he named his fee, half of which was payable in advance. She handed over the requisite number of *Reichskredit* bills. He would, he told her, perform the procedure at ten the following morning. "Bring clean towels, pads," he said. "You'll need to rest for a few days. Nothing to eat or drink after midnight. Oh, and have a vehicle waiting. You won't find anything around here."

The following morning, Gilberte flushed her breakfast down the toilet. The street merchants on the avenue Parmentier were already out in force with their pitiful displays when she arrived in a horse-drawn wagonette: three other hippomobile taxis had turned her down after she told them her destination, and she'd had to offer nearly double the doctor's fee before this sour-mouthed driver had agreed to bring her and wait. "One risks being trapped in a roundup there," he had explained defensively.

Carrying a Vuitton hatbox, Gilberte started up the staircase. As she climbed through the odors of rotted vegetables and poverty, a tow-haired little girl wearing a star rushed from the first-floor landing, giving Gilberte a mischievous grin. Gilberte halted to watch the child skim down the stairs.

I can't do it, she thought.

Why not?

The group of cells multiplying within her had no greater significance to her than an abscess. She would have an abscess lanced, wouldn't she?

I can't do it. The irrational voice within her was adamant.

She continued up the staircase. Counting bills into the clean, competent hand, she said, "I've changed my mind."

"Why pay me, then?"

"I keep my promises."

* * *

Hocherer beamed when he heard that the "bleeding" had stopped. A few days later, when Dr. Behn pronounced her with child, Hocherer opened a bottle of Taittinger, toasting, "To our son."

The word *son* caught her unawares, and she felt nausea rising from where the embryo curled in the pit of her stomach. "Hocherer, you're too old to be a clown."

"And you, magnificent Gilberte, are cruel in your beauty and youth."

Gilberte's pregnancy had two peculiar and unrelated side effects. She could not force herself beyond the walls and fences of her father's property. And she embarked on a crazy love affair with the war. Before this, giving no credence to the reports put out by the *Propagandastaffel,* she had ignored the news. Now she immersed herself in *Le Matin, Les Nouveaux Temps, Aujourd'hui,* she kept her bedside radio tuned so as not to miss a special bulletin.

She swelled with happiness whenever the reports were bad for the German forces—*strategic retreats* was a term often used in conjunction with the Russian front, *magnificent defense* with Italy, while *dastardly attacks on the innocent* meant the Fatherland had been bombed.

The servants watched her with eyes yet more hostile. Well fed, well paid and well treated by a German field marshal, they felt shame: it was human nature that they should point figurative fingers at Gilberte, whose greater collaborationism was becoming more obvious with each day. Her bedeviling code of honor prevented her from mentioning their sneers to Hocherer, who had he known would have consigned them all, even the septuagenarian chef and octogenerian gardener, to those lethal labor battalions in the Third Reich.

The high-ranking officers who visited her protector remained cautiously optimistic—the popular prediction was for an Axis victory no later than 1946. When Hocherer was alone with her, however, he would bewail the fact that the Führer, who had appointed himself supreme military commander in 1941, made increasingly suicidal decisions: if any general or field marshal raised objections, the nay-sayer was shot or strangled. Hocherer's pessimism, although based on actuality, was greatly enhanced by his ineluctable personal losses. All three sons of his first marriage had been killed in action, and he brooded that the youngest boy, a sixteen-year-old with a heart murmur, would soon be called.

At the end of February, the field marshal received a summons to Berchtesgaden. He stayed at Hitler's Alpine aerie far longer than he anticipated, writing stiffly phrased love letters that included his hopes for their child. He returned unannounced on a wet night in early March.

Gilberte, in bed, was listening to the late news. She did not turn off the radio.

"How went your conferences with the glorious leader?" she inquired.

Hocherer sat heavily in the armchair. "It's over," he said.

"The meetings?"

"We've lost the war."

"But. . . ." She glanced at the radio. ". . . disastrously heavy American losses at Casino . . . death knell to Allied hopes . . ."

"The fighting's not over. But we're defeated." His bony shoulders were bowed. "When I think of the lost opportunities! That maniac! If our strategy had been different in Russia. If we'd invaded England after Dunkirk." He got to his feet, cutting off an announcement of a large-scale American defeat in the Kwajalein Islands. "Why listen to that bilge? It's all lies. I saw my country. The Americans and British are pulverizing our cities and factories twenty-four hours a day. There's no way we can replace the industry. The Americans have inexhaustible supplies."

"Ah yes, the Americans." Briefly she wondered about Quent. What battles had he fought? What dangers had he survived? He was her sole tie to her previous life, so she refused to consider that he might have been killed.

"This month they dropped supplies to the Maquis."

"They did?" She sat up with a lunatic smile. "Where?"

"Plateau des Glières in the Haute-Savoie," he said. "It's a prelude. Eisenhower's getting ready for the invasion."

"Hocherer, that invasion rumor's got white whiskers."

"Our agents are sending messages that they're working on the plans night and day. The code name is Overlord."

Her heart was beating so rapidly that she thought she might faint. "When will Overlord be?"

"We don't know. Probably this summer. Gilberte, you mustn't worry. I'll arrange it so that you and the child aren't harmed. I'll send you to Switzerland—"

"De Permonts," she interrupted, "do not run away."

"You're having a child."

"What about you? Will you sneak off to Zurich?"

"We don't run away either."

She felt a peculiar comradeship with this gray-haired Prussian, her enemy, the father of the child who at this instant was kicking within her. She touched his liver-spotted hand, a trailing, tentative movement, the first caress she had ever given him.

26

That spring of 1944, several crucial blunders were made by Hitler and his Western Command. Anticipating the Allied landing at the narrowest point of the English Channel, the Germans concentrated panzer and infantry divisions behind the beaches of the Pas-de-Calais area. Then in early June, when meteorologists advised that because of the bad weather there could be no invasion for several weeks, they relaxed the standing alert all along the coastal defenses—which the Führer trumpeted as his impregnable Atlantic Wall.

On June 6 an armada greater than the world had ever seen set out from ports along the south coast of England. The ships battled through heavy seas, heading not toward Pas-de-Calais, but toward Normandy. The Führer, in Berchtesgaden, slept until afternoon: on hearing of the Normandy beachhead, he announced that this was a diversionary tactic to throw his forces off-balance. No reinforcements were rushed to the beleaguered German pillboxes.

Gilberte awoke to see Hocherer standing over her. She blinked up at him in surprise—only when he desired to have sex, which had been banned by Dr. Behn since her seventh month, did he violate her privacy in this spacious bedroom. He wore his black leather trench coat and held his peaked cap.

"Hocherer, what time is it?"

"Ten past six. I'm flying to Normandy."

"Flying?" Hitler did not permit his field marshals to risk their lives in planes. "To Normandy?"

"It's happened. Overlord."

"The invasion. When?"

"Sometime in the middle of the night. Thousands of ships spilling out men and equipment, waves of aircraft bombing our defenses, battalions of parachutists dropping behind our lines—and the lunatic is still convinced this is a small-scale operation."

For this day my parents laid down their lives. Wide awake now, Gilberte sat up, the enlarged nipples of her swollen breasts pressing against her sheer nightgown as she cried, *"Vive la France!"*

"Gilberte, it would be best for you if we won."

"This validates my father and mother, Hocherer."

He gave her a gentle, understanding look and bent over to kiss her mouth. "I swear to be here with you when the child is due."

There was something repellent about his infinite tenderness. She turned her head. "Give my regards to the Yanks, the Limeys and General de Gaulle," she said.

This was the personal maid's day off. The plump little woman raced up, delighted at this unprecedentedly early ring for the breakfast tray. Thus she was able to leave the house before eight.

The lethargy that had afflicted Gilberte the past few weeks had vanished, and she glowed with hitherto unsuspected patriotic fervor. Soon the defacing swastikas would be hauled down, soon the *drapeau tricolore* would flutter again.

While she dressed in the green-and-white maternity smock especially designed for her by Patou, she kept turning the radio dial. German-controlled radio stations did not mention the landing and BBC was being so heavily jammed that she couldn't make out a word. Unable to contain her energy, she decided to walk in the garden. Leaving her bedroom, she heard the static-laden BBC blaring full volume from the big radio in Hocherer's room. A servant must have tuned it for her to hear. In a sudden moment of clarity, a flat-voiced American announced that he was the commander in chief of the Allied forces. *The Yank with a German name, Eisenhower.*

"Citizens of France!" proclaimed General Eisenhower in English. "Because the initial landing has been made on the soil of your country, I repeat with even greater emphasis my message to the peoples of other occupied countries of Western Europe. Follow the instructions of . . . leaders . . . private uprising of Frenchmen may prevent . . ." Crackling drowned him out.

Downstairs, more radios blared. "This landing is but the opening phase of . . . campaign . . . battles lie ahead. . . ."

Gilberte went into the garden with her exhilaration shattered. The tuned radios had reminded her that she was alone with servants who had always despised her and now condemned her—servants who were assuredly watching her to spot any reactions. She held her head stiffly high as she promenaded along the raked path. The two magnificent beeches had been chopped down for firewood, the oval lawn, site of her mother's garden parties, had been replaced by peas vining up strings and rows of lettuce.

At the roar of engines she raised her hand to peer at the cloudy sky. A formation of Messerschmitts on their way to Normandy. Hocherer was right, of course. Because she was his mistress, a German defeat would winnow her out and she should whisper godspeed and success to the planes. She wished each a swift and fiery end. The sound of aircraft faded and she heard the clip-clip of the shears. The ancient gardener was pruning the box hedge, his rheumy gaze fixed on her. Pretending to ignore him, she resumed her walk, keeping up her pace despite a dull heaviness that briefly engulfed her stomach.

What was that? she wondered as the tautness passed. *It can't be a labor pain. My due date's not until the twenty-fourth of June.*

She had very little curiosity about her condition, and the prim-faced Silesian doctor had not been forthcoming. But after ten minutes the heavy sensation occurred again. The old gardener showed a false-toothed grin as she waddled inside.

By noon the pressure recurred regularly and she could no longer ignore what it was, labor pain. She rang her bell. Usually when the little Breton maid was gone, Madame Bolée, the housekeeper, responded herself. Today, nobody came. A downstairs radio blared on. Again that flat American voice—it must be a record. She picked up the telephone. The lines were swamped, and it took over an hour to get through to Dr. Behn's office. A Frenchwoman told her he was on his way to Normandy. Gilberte explained her plight.

"Our doctors are competent, too, Mademoiselle de Permont, they also deliver babies," the woman said loudly, and the phone clicked dead.

The pains intensified and grew closer. She dug her fingernails into her palms to keep from crying out. By five o'clock, her palms were bleeding. She considered going downstairs to the servants' hall and browbeating them into helping her—after all, no matter what was occurring in Normandy, the Germans ruled Paris. But neither her full-blown terror nor the agony of childbirth could untangle the past. Since earliest memory they had despised her, and since earliest memory she had refused to let them—or anyone else—see her vast reservoir of weakness.

She looked in the Paris telephone book for Dr. Descourset's number. The lines remained clogged. It was after eight, twilight, when she reached him.

She explained that she was in labor, and that her doctor, unfortunately, was out of town.

Dr. Descourset remained silent. Possibly since her visit he had seen her picture in a back copy of *L'Illustration*: she'd been photographed attending the first day of racing at Longchamps, and, as *le tout Paris* knew, such highly fashionable, highly visible girls as she belonged either to a German or to a well-connected French collaborator.

"So I find myself in need of a doctor," she said acidly, then held a hand over the speaker to muffle a groan.

"It's a shock to me that you're having the child," he said.

"I decided to let nature take its course and—" She broke off, unable to continue. This pain was harder, more protracted than the others and sweat poured from her. When it released her, she managed to ask in an assured tone, "How long will you take to get here?"

After a lengthy pause, the doctor said, "I'll have to take the métro."

"A bientôt," she said.

She changed into her nightgown, alternately standing and lying in bed with the pains. Nothing helped. She could no longer stifle her screams—the servants assuredly heard her. She shrieked for her father to help her, for Quent to rescue her—but never for Hocherer. She thrashed until her dead mother's convent-embroidered linen sheets were drenched with sweat and urine. It was not quite midnight when she suddenly was torn apart at the rectum.

"I'm dying!" she screamed. "Dyyyinnngg . . ."

In the midst of this horror and fright, she smelled feces. Her bowels had moved. Pressing down involuntarily, she fainted.

When she came to, she heard a mewling like a kitten. Wondering how a cat had come into her room, she shifted her head feebly. Between her thighs a red and bloody creature squirmed, kicking woefully thin legs. She reached out, attempting to shift the infant from the filth, but could reach no farther than to touch the slippery, pulsing forehead.

Then the door opened. *"Mon dieu!"* Dr. Descourset muttered, and hurried to the bed.

"Is . . . is it all right?" she whispered.

"Mademoiselle de Permont, you have a son." He opened his bag, snipping the umbilical cord. The mewling grew louder. "I'd have been here sooner, but Germans barraged my street. They went over everybody's papers with a fine-tooth comb. Doubtless worried about the invasion."

"Is he healthy?"

"Healthier and larger than any I have delivered recently. Listen to those lungs." The doctor pressed the bell. "Mademoiselle, there's a staff here. Why didn't you call one of the women?"

She didn't reply.

"You have a foul lot of servants," he said. There was a discreet tap on the door. "Come in," the doctor snapped. "Bring me a large bowl of tepid water! Soap! Clean bedding!"

She closed her eyes, too weak to move, ashamed of lying in her own foulness.

When the footsteps faded, she heard the doctor cry, "My God, you're hemorrhaging!"

As his fingers reached inside her, she screamed, a long, endless howl, and fainted again.

She didn't come to for a long time.

The plump little maid had returned and was changing the bed while the doctor repacked his bag.

"Mademoiselle, those repairs should have been done in the operating room," he said.

"Thank you," she whispered through chapped lips.

"At least I stopped the bleeding."

After he left, the maid sponge-bathed Gilberte, waving lighted matches to cancel the odors.

Not until then did she deposit the baby, wrapped in a clean flannel towel, in its mother's arms.

The tiny clenched fists flailed, the red, squashed-looking face contorted in an adult yawn. As the unfocusing eyes looked up at Gilberte, she felt an odd sensation twist through her bruised and aching torso, almost as if a blood knot were tying itself.

Ann and Larry
London and Paris, 1944

27

On August 26, 1944, Second Lieutenant Larry Porter was casting a weather eye on the crowd in the Dorchester suite. Larry, assigned to the public relations department of the Office of War Information, had planned the shindig. Its purpose of allowing correspondents to jaw with American top brass about the previous day's liberation of Paris was being expedited at top decibel. Behind a cloth-draped table three corporals were rapidly dispensing Johnnie Walker, I. W. Harper and champagne while a second table bore the remnants of Scotch smoked salmon and Yorkshire ham—Larry had overpaid the black marketeer, but regardless, procuring these items was quite a coup on his part. He also gave himself points for the sprinkling of young females wearing either trim WAC uniforms or soft, pastel summer clothes. A recent arrival, auburn hair curling above yellow dress, stood with her back to him. A shorty, but what he could see was prime. Surrounding her were a barrel-chested chicken colonel wearing the red tabs of the General Staff; Edward R. Murrow, the top CBS commentator; a stoop-shouldered man from the Manchester *Guardian*; and a gray-haired one-star general in the Quartermaster Corps by the name of Harold Mannix. The girl appeared to be telling a story. From the rapt attention being paid her, Larry bet himself that the face matched the shape. Did she belong to one of them? London was filled with

desirable girls but, alas, a goodly percentage were shacked up with
high-ranking old farts like these. She raised one arm, slashing it
down, obviously telling the punch line of her story. Her listeners
burst into laughter.

As the trio of noncoms segued into "A Nightingale Sang in
Berkeley Square," she turned. He wouldn't rate her A-plus, but
then again he wouldn't kick her out of bed for eating crackers
either. Nice boobs. Big dark eyes and soft, sensual mouth.

She stared perplexedly across the room at him, and he gave her
the half grin that got 'em. She smiled back, a glowingly warm smile.
Saying something to her august coterie, she edged around boozy
groups toward him as if to greet an old friend.

Was she an English girl he'd linked up with at some bash? Could
he have been stinko enough to forget *her*?

"It is Larry Porter, isn't it?" she asked.

He leaned forward to hear her. She was American, but with
intonations pitched more softly and agreeably than usual. "Don't
tell me," he said, snapping his fingers. "The Netherlands reception for Queen Wilhelmina two weeks ago."

"Paris. During your days as a trench coat."

"Christ! Ann! Ann Blade, wasn't it?"

"Blakely."

"Blakely, Blakely, Blakely. Never will I forget it again. Baby,
you've grown up. What're you doing in England?"

"I'm General Mannix's driver."

"You're out of uniform."

"I'm a civilian," she explained. "Only wear one when I drive."

"Tell me all about it over dinner. I'm in charge here, so I have to
stick around. You aren't booked up, are you?"

She hesitated before she said, "Nothing that can't be broken."

"Is the date with one of them?" He glanced in the direction of
her superannuated admirers.

"Sort of. But General Mannix is an old sweetie. He'll understand."

"Better embellish. Tell him I'm your long-lost cousin." Larry
leaned down to plant a cousinly kiss on her forehead. Her hair,
which smelled as if she'd just washed it, was a true auburn, a rich
mingling of brown, red and gold.

* * *

An hour later they were being led through the Hotel Connaught's crowded restaurant to a small corner table—Mannix had surrendered his reservation to Ann's "cousin." Second looies rarely got inside places like this, and Larry looked around appreciatively. The men wore a multinational spectrum of beribboned uniforms affixed with high-ranking insignia. The women, on the other hand, had chosen to be festive nymphs in bright, soft prewar dresses and upswept hair. Excited voices were recounting news about the liberation.

An ancient waiter stood over them.

Larry inquired, "Ann, what's your pleasure?"

"That party of yours still has me floating," she said. "Nothing, thank you."

"How're you going to toast Paris, then? A sloe gin for the lady. A whiskey with ice for me."

As the waiter scuttled away, Larry asked, "Are your parents back home in—where was it? Kansas?"

"Wisconsin." The smile faded. "No. They're stuck in German territory. When the evacuation train left, my mother had influenza and was too sick to travel."

"Hey," he mumbled. "I barged right in, didn't I?"

She rubbed her knuckles over her eyes, like a child. "I've had an International Red Cross card from them. They had no idea where I was, either, so they sent it to Mother's cousin in Racine, and she forwarded it. They wrote that they were fine. But their address had been blacked out. Larry, the Germans promised we'd be interned in a hotel. If that was true, why censor the address?"

"Some dumb Fritz officer bollixed up," he said with loud heartiness.

"It came over a year ago. I've mailed them hundreds of letters through the Red Cross. All've come back—Address Unknown."

The drinks arrived, giving him the opportunity to elevate the mood. "To the City of Light," he toasted. "Liberated at last." He clicked her glass. "So you were going to tell me how you ended up here in Blighty."

Lashes veiled the huge brown eyes. "Quent Dejong had an escape network—"

Larry interrupted, "The Quent Dejong I know?"

"Yes, he got me out."

"Well dog my cats. Quent?"

"He worked with the French Resistance, he was in Bill Donovan's outfit."

"Hair-raising deeds of derring-do in the OSS?"

"He was in even before it became OSS." She leaned across the table. "So you haven't heard from him either?"

"Not a word, Ann, but I'll level with you. We only got to be buddies at the Hotel Pyramide. We don't move in the same social circle, he being who he is, and my dad being but a humble Onyx dealer."

In actuality, Hal Porter was a salesman on commission at the Van Nuys Onyx dealership's secondhand lot: during the Depression he had scraped out a precarious living selling an occasional jalopy. Larry in early boyhood had determined to switch from penury to the moneyed class. Accordingly, he had studied the ways of the rich at the movies, learning that they dined in tuxes, they broke speeding laws in flashy convertibles, they got swacko elegantly and never became abusive like his dad, they mowed down acres of improbably beautiful women. Meeting Quent Dejong had been a disillusionment. Oh, he was an okay person, if a bit standoffish, but far squarer than Larry when it came to partaking of the high life for which Paris is famed.

"You seemed good friends," Ann said.

"That's me, everybody's A-hole—pardon my French. Everybody's buddy." Larry fell silent as the waiter's liver-spotted hands set down the pâté du chef, hopefully not a Spam derivative. "You haven't heard from him either?"

She toyed with outsize English cutlery. "Not for a while."

"Enough about the past. Let's get down to current statistics," Larry said. "I see by the ring finger that you haven't gone and gotten engaged or married on me, but are you otherwise bespoken?"

She slowly cut a sliver of pâté and he found himself holding his breath until she murmured, "No. . . ."

"Another coincidence." Grinning, he signaled for another drink. "I'm also footloose and fancy-free."

* * *

He walked her home through Hyde Park, where couples sprawled in the warm darkness. They had just passed an antiaircraft emplacement when the earth shuddered beneath them, and an explosion erupted from the direction of Kensington Gardens. Yet another jet-propelled, unmanned V-1 bomb—a doodlebug, Hitler's new miracle weapon—had gotten by the coastal defenses to wreak its mindless damage. Within a couple of minutes they saw the fires. Rescue workers would be digging corpses and survivors out of the rubble, but from here the blaze gave off a rosy light that Larry associated with beach parties and roasting hot dogs, chugalugging beer, feeling up girls. Ann, who during the second half of dinner had snapped out of her blues about her parents to recount tall tales of her adventures as General Mannix's driver, stared at the glow, turning pensive again.

She lived near the Albert Hall, on Polkington Place. At the beginning of her block yawned a crater, while barriers and fresh rubble surrounded a gutted building across from her place.

They climbed the sandbagged steps and Larry locked his hands behind her waist. "Do I come upstairs?"

She shook her head, murmuring, "I'm sorry."

A jeep was driving down the street. With the advent of the unmanned V-1's, blackout regulations had been relaxed to permit minimal headlights. The blue shadows moving across Ann's face showed an expression of sadness that made Larry feel protective rather than rebuffed.

"Mark well August the twenty-sixth," he said, touching his lips to her forehead. "It's the day Lawrence J. Porter, an officer and a gentleman, fell for you."

Ann shared a large room with two USO coordinators, both married to Marine officers in the Pacific theater of operations, both apparently dedicated to screwing their way through the upper echelons in the European theater. They dashed in and out to change their clothes and pick up their mail. Tonight, as usual, Ann had the place to herself.

In bed, she hugged her arms around herself, thinking of Quent.

He had filled her mind even more than usual because of the constant mention of France.

She hadn't heard from him since Christmas.

He was alive, he wasn't a prisoner. This she knew for certain because General Mannix had checked, and guarded word had come back from the OSS that Captain Dejong was still broadcasting messages. Bumping into Larry Porter at the OWI party had roused her hopes of learning more. For this reason alone she had accepted his dinner invitation—and afterward felt sneaky and devious.

She sighed into the darkness, picturing Larry. Teasing grin, strands of fair hair falling over his high forehead. It required no effort whatsoever to wend her way through conversational gambits with him while she brooded about her parents and Quent.

She rolled over in the narrow bed.

Quent . . .

Why hadn't he written?

Was it impossible for him to get personal messages out? Or was he ending a wartime interlude in the time-honored way, by disappearing from her life? Though Ann wasn't insecure about her relationships, Jason Templar's wealth was as uncrossable as the void between the stars, so she more and more often favored the second reason. Quent was through with her. She could no longer reassure herself by conjuring up his avowals of love. By now she had run through them so frequently that they were all faded, even the ones he'd made at Greatleigh in Sussex. Greatleigh . . .

28

On that damp October evening ten months earlier, she had been washing her rayon stockings when the charlady had bawled, "Miss Blakely, luv, telephone!" Positive it was a message that General Mannix needed her—Quartermaster Corps snafus invariably seemed to come to a boil at night—she grabbed a scratch pad to jot down addresses, running downstairs.

"Ann?" Quent said. "It's me, Quent."

The note pad fell. Her heart expanded and contracted. She hadn't heard his voice in more than a year and a half, since that rainy afternoon in Bern. (His large, firm handwriting, though, was transposed onto her brain from the thin blue V-mail that arrived in clumps: as the intervals between the letters lengthened, the barometer of her fears for him—and by some psychological trigger, her worries about her parents—would rise until it was a battle to maintain a cheerful front.)

"Ann?"

"I'm here." Her voice sounded squeezed from her throat. "Where are you?"

"London," he said. "I'm being debriefed tonight, and after that I have a ninety-six-hour pass. There's a cottage down in Sussex. Can you make it?"

"Yes . . . wonderful."

"Will it be okay with your general?" He knew about Mannix from her letters.

"He'll understand."

Mannix, who often ragged her about breaking the collective hearts of his staff by steadfastly refusing dates, chuckled when she called to tell him that her boyfriend was in London. "Don't worry about a thing, Ann, honey," he said. "He must be quite a guy."

A wiry old man met them at the village station, steering the bargelike 1926 Rolls-Royce along country lanes to a walled estate, turning in at the impressively crenellated gatehouse. Quent had told her they'd be staying at a cottage. She turned questioningly to him.

He was staring out at the magnificent autumnal trees. New captain's bars gleamed on the shoulders of his dress pinks, which hung too loosely on him. With his face averted this way, the small lines—also new—at the corner of his eye were more pronounced. It was sinking into Ann's consciousness that he was being unusually laconic even for him. She hadn't noticed until now because on the train there had been no seats, so they'd stood in the icy, crowded corridor amid a group of drunken American flyers who kept winking at her and singing, "Bless 'em all, the long and the short and the tall." Now, though, she accepted that something was very wrong. And, being human, saw his mood as rejection.

They reached the crest of the hill. Below them lay an immense fantasia of Victorian Gothic—turrets, towers, battlements—that huge copper beeches and decades of ivy growth had tamed to a magical charm. As Ann stared, a flock of doves burst upward from a parapet, a living scarf tossed in welcome.

"How wonderful!" she exclaimed. "But didn't you say we're staying in a cottage?"

"We are. That's a school."

As he spoke the Rolls swept sedately around a curve and she saw small boys racing across a rugby field. The car descended the slope and circled the mansion, which up close appeared yet more excessively, dauntingly immense. After a mile or so they came to a small, thatch-roofed house.

"We trust you find everything to your liking, Captain Dejong," the chauffeur said, oozing to a halt. "Oh, and I do believe Mrs. Caldwell has left tea, sir."

The front door opened into a long, low-beamed room. Logs blazed in the fireplace, faded chintz of a pretty pattern slipcovered the sagging upholstery, chrysanthemums were artlessly arranged in a big Wedgwood bowl. Old and new books were jammed every which way into the shelves that lined the room, more books had been piled on the tables, and one, printed in Greek, was splayed on the sofa arm, as if the reader had forgotten it.

Ann did the honors at the tea tray, her Greer Garson Mrs. Miniver takeoff ringing overcute in the bookish room. Though she'd missed breakfast and lunch, her twitchy stomach was in no shape to receive the thin cress sandwiches and madeira cake. Quent, too, barely ate.

Her conversational efforts finally stuck in her throat. "Quent, I'm sorry."

He had been gazing into the flames. Looking up, he asked, "For what?"

"Babbling on and on. I can catch the evening train to London."

"Is that what you want?"

"No. But, well . . ." She shrugged.

"I'm not very scintillating company right now, am I?"

"It's not me?"

"God, you took it personally?"

In her joyous reprieve, she laughed. "Idiot! Of course I took it personally."

"It's me. The only problem is, I'm not exactly sure who me is anymore."

"Has it been very rough?"

A muscle jumped near his eye. "On the others."

"Want to talk about it?"

His hands clenched, and he shook his head. "One debriefing threw me enough."

"Show me the house, then?" A blush rose from the lemon yellow sweater that he'd chosen for her in Switzerland to suffuse her face. "Let's go upstairs."

"Now there's the best idea of the day."

Dusk was falling and the slit of lead-glass window on the landing did little to dispel the shadows on the uneven, creaking staircase. Near the top, she stumbled. Quent, behind her, held her waist to steady her. She trembled, then held her breath as his hands moved down to her hips and turned her to face him. She had never been more aware of him. The unique smells of him, the pattern of warmth emanating from his large body, his outline, the gleam of moisture in his eyes, which were on a level with her own.

"Ann . . . I've thought of seeing you again a few times too often."

She understood that this was both an apology and a supplication: he was seeking pardon for what the war had done to him, begging her to accept him as he was.

"I never stop thinking about you," she whispered shakenly. "Quent, I've been crazy."

The bedroom windows were closed against the autumnal chill, but a draft stirred the flowered curtains. The pine bed, high and old, had been turned down and a scent of potpourri came from the sheets. For a moment she recaptured the sweetish hay and cow odor in the loft. *The Salève mountain, we almost died,* she thought. *How many more times has Quent been in the immediate vicinity of death?* He took her hand, holding it to his chest, and she felt the heavy reverberation of his living heart against her palm.

She stepped away, raising the soft yellow wool over her head, revealing her carefully ironed rayon slip. From far away she heard the sweet sound of children singing, but couldn't make out the song. Peering at her, Quent tilted his head gravely, then began unbuttoning his khaki jacket. They undressed swiftly, dropping clothes on the rug and planked floor. Naked in the chill air, she moved to the bed. "Wait," he said, staring at her. Embarrassed to look directly at him, she glanced over his shoulder. In the wavery silver of the old mirror she saw the shadowed reflection of a tall, thin but magnificently built man facing a short curly-headed female who, to Ann's eyes, was ordinary beyond measuring and far too big in the hips.

"You're beautiful."

"Goose bumps and all?"

He lifted her onto the bed, pulling the blankets high around them. She forgot her shyness as they kissed, pressing closer, caressing: her body grew moist in various places.

"One second, sweet." He shifted, reaching for something that he'd set on the bedside table, and she, knowledgeable from the conversations of her roommates, understood he was putting on a GI condom. She hated the thin layer of rubber, it would come between them, but as soon as he entered her she forgot everything except the exquisite sensations he was arousing.

"Ann," he said. "Look at me."

His eyes covered her field of vision, and in the twilight it was impossible to see the boundary between the swollen black pupils and the dark blue irises.

"I love you," he said. "Never, never ever doubt that."

"I won't."

"You're everything to me."

As he said the words, her eyes squeezed shut and those involuntary spasms engulfed her.

He stroked the moist hair from her face until she stopped gasping, then he began to move, tenderly at first, his thrusts becoming more imperious. She arched up to meet him until she was swept into another, yet more intense orgasm.

Afterward they lay entwined, not speaking for a long time. He moved away, reaching for his cigarettes. It was dark now, and she blinked in the bright flare of his lighter.

Inhaling, he said, "This is where my parents spent their honeymoon. The cottage is the only really old part of the estate."

"Does it belong to you, the castle?"

"My grandfather built the dreams of his impoverished Liverpool youth."

"I've read about him—but Quent, wasn't his father a prosperous cabinetmaker?"

"He had no father—at least not one he knew. His mother was a dockside trollop who deserted him. He was as poor as it's possible to be and survive. Always hungry, always cold. Aged seven he was scrubbing privies at a foundry. And here's another unpublished fact. Aged eleven, he picked pockets for the steerage money to New York." There was no condemnation in Quent's tone, only wry admiration. "I never knew the old pirate, but after a beginning like that, it goes without saying that nothing could ever be opulent enough for him. Even Grand-mère couldn't tone him down. He built other enormous, garish homes and vacation places that're white elephants now. But Greatleigh, that's what this is called, meant the most to him. Edward the Seventh spent a weekend at Greatleigh. Imagine! He'd been Queen Victoria's meagerest subject, and here he was entertaining the old queen's son."

"So it does belong to you?"

"Not exactly. Grandfather intended to rule his descendants from the great beyond, so he tied everything up in knots. I can't sell Greatleigh. But I have endowed it as a school for slum kids, with the stipulation that I be allowed to use this cottage."

"But somebody lives here."

"The headmaster, Caldwell, and Mrs. Caldwell."

"Do you displace them often?"

"This is the only time."

The following morning was clear with a cold wintry nip to the air. They hiked in what had been the game preserve. Damp mulch muffled their footsteps, gold and russet leaves drifted down, a small, unseen animal rustled in a nearby thicket, and Quent pointed out tracks belonging to a fox. Then a humming invaded the peaceful woods, rising to a deafening roar as a formation of B-17's passed overhead. Quent halted, his hands clenching and unclenching until the sounds faded.

"Come on," he said. "Let's head back."

As they neared the cottage she realized that his eyes were fixed on her. Though he did not touch her, she was drawn into an unequivocal, feverish urgency to be joined to him.

Still not touching her, he asked in a low rumble, "Yes?"

"Yes."

"They're all dead," he said later in the afternoon, when the light was already fading. They sat on the carpet in front of the fire. "All the people I worked with."

"Suzette?"

"Suzette." Nodding, he sighed. Flames reflected redly in his eyes. "Jacques in Lyon, Duhay in Annecy. Laas. All dead. ViVi and André—"

"You mean the Baron and Baronne de Permont? *They* were passers?"

"No—they didn't even know I was involved in that phase. But yes, they're dead."

A sound of grief came from deep in her throat. A log dropped and sparks flew upward. "Quent, are you positive?"

"The Gestapo killed them in the Santé."

"But why? Why?"

"They blew up railroad tracks."

"The Gare de l'Est?"

"Among others." He was clenching and unclenching his hands again. "I got them the *plastique* for that particular job."

"The baronne . . . ? Quent, not *her*?"

"She was a miracle with explosives."

"She's the last person I'd think of in the Résistance."

"Exactly what made her perfect. What nerve she had, ViVi. What superhuman nerve. She never went around the back door. She'd give that knowing, bitchy little laugh and then would plan something incredibly dangerous. I'm reasonably positive that I somehow led the Gestapo to them."

"I'm sure you didn't," Ann said.

"Ann, everybody I've been connected with is dead."

"But that doesn't mean—"

"Dead," he repeated.

"Is Gilberte . . . is she dead?"

"I've never been sent back to Paris, so there's no way I could find out." His shoulders were hunched, and his face forlorn.

I won't ask any more questions, Ann thought. *Oh, Gilberte, Gilberte. Later, deal with it later, when his pass is over.*

After that they kept the war at bay.

Returning to London, they found seats in a compartment and held hands silently, oblivious to the passengers surging in and out each time the train halted.

At her door, Quent clutched her tight, not kissing her, not saying anything, even good-bye. She watched his taxi disappear around the corner of the gray, bombed-out street before she began to cry. Her first tears were for the parting, but soon her grief encompassed the dangers that Quent would soon face. Then she wept for the ugly, brave baron and his arrogantly beautiful wife, she wept for cologne-scented Suzette, for Monsieur Duhay torn from his Annecy bookshop, for Monsieur Laas with his stout cows and Einstein hair. She wept for Gilberte who might or might not be alive. She sat weeping on the sandbagged steps until the cockney charlady came to draw her up to her room.

That November, Quent had sent her three hastily scrawled notes, the last wishing her a happy Thanksgiving. After that, nothing. *Rien, rien, rien* . . .

29

As Ann brooded about Quent, she stirred restlessly. The toasts she had drunk to the liberation of Paris at the OWI party and at dinner were catching up with her, and her incipient nausea wasn't helped any by the stagnant air in her bedroom. The V-1 bomb that had gutted the house across the street last month had also shattered most of the tape-crossed panes on Polkington Place, and now plyboard covered her windows, entrapping the sultry August heat. She threw off the covers but still couldn't sleep.

Paris, she thought. *I'll find them as soon as I get to Paris.*

This had become an *idée fixe* during her years in England: If she could only return to Paris, she'd find her parents and Gilberte. Childish hocus-pocus, she knew, but war is a great fertilizer of primitive superstition.

In Paris, talismanic city, she would also learn exactly what (or more realistically, who) had come between her and Quent. His radio transmissions proved him alive, uncaptured, but if in all these months he hadn't managed to send some kind of message to her, shouldn't she *chercher la femme?*

Finally she got up to sit in the armchair, purposefully removing her mind from the bleak fog of questions that surrounded her parents and Quent, thinking of Larry Porter.

Larry had the freckles and ingenuous smile of the second lead in

Hollywood war movies: at the OWI party he had treated those who outranked him with the same classical though not obsequious deference as the supporting actor shows the star. He made flippantly easy wisecracks and complimented her often. All in all, his lightheartedness was a morale booster. If she hadn't thoroughly enjoyed the evening, she could only blame some flaw in herself, a dark obduracy of the heart. *I've immunized myself against pleasure,* she thought, resting her head back on the antimacassar. Wasn't it about time for a few simple, uninvolved dates? Some fun? Larry had a similar goal in mind. When he called—and she knew without conceit that he would call—why not go out with him?

She fell asleep in the chair.

"What happened to the friend you were all steamed up about in Paris?" Larry asked.

"Gilberte de Permont," Ann said.

She slowed, staring at the silver-gray wavelets of the Serpentine. This, their fifth date, marked their first opportunity for a real conversation. In the past fortnight Larry had taken her to two rowdy drunken bashes at fellow officers' flats, to the Palladium to see a musical revue called *Apple-Sauce!* and last night to a wild party at the Mayfair house of a titled Englishwoman. Today, a bright Sunday, they were nursing Larry's hangover in Hyde Park. Uniformed men rowed girls across the artificial lake, wartime-shabby Londoners sat in rented deck chairs with their faces raised to the sun, boys in darned flannel short trousers pushed sailboats along the cement shorelines, and a nonevacuated baby sat regally in a perambulator wheeled by a bent old nanny. Ahead of them, American noncoms on a makeshift baseball diamond shouted good-natured obscenities at each other.

"As I recall, a real dish, a ringer for Vivien Leigh," Larry said. "Her father's a count."

"Baron." Ann coughed to clear her throat, incapable of adding that the baron and baronne were both dead. "The last thing I know is what you told me. She was in prison."

"The first rule of warfare, don't ask questions," Larry muttered. He vigilantly avoided war's morbid side.

"I'll find out where she is when I get to Paris."

"Not if, but when? That sounds like old Mannix is ready to cross the Channel."

Though nobody was within twenty yards, Ann visualized one of the ubiquitous posters warning about Nazi spies. "He told me," she whispered under her breath, "to get my things together."

"Hmm," Larry said. "Doubtless there's need for a man of my talents in Paree."

"Now that the fighting's over?"

"Don't laugh. Somebody has to bring up the gallant rear—" Larry broke off as a baseball hurtled toward them. Leaping up, he fielded it and in the same motion hurled the ball to a skinny, puffing staff sergeant.

"Hey, sir, frigging nice play! After the duration, you'll be on the Cards lineup with Musial."

Larry raised his hand in a good-natured salute, then turned back to Ann. "Impressive, hey? Well, what do you think of my idea?"

"Haven't you heard, Larry? There's a war on. You don't just pick up and book passage to Paris."

"You're looking at an all-star wheeler-dealer, shorty. Well?"

"It'd be handy," Ann said, "to have a man so well qualified around."

Before she realized his intention, he gripped her upper arms, bending to kiss her on the lips. She had carefully refrained from leading him on, as she categorized necking. They were just friends. But here he was kissing her in Hyde Park on a sunlit afternoon. As she struggled to avoid his insinuating tongue, wolf whistles screeched from the baseball diamond, and somebody with a Brooklyn accent bawled, "Go to it, sir!"

Exactly one month after the liberation of Paris, before eight on the morning of September 25, Ann Blakely drove General Mannix into the city.

They had landed ten days earlier in Normandy at one of the busy artificial ports called Mulberries, and ever since she had been crazed with impatience. Foot heavy on the accelerator, she'd bounced around bomb craters, swerving to avoid the burned wreckage of German and Allied vehicles as well as the bloated, fly-buzzing corpses of horses and cows. Whenever General Mannix had halted at a supply depot to expedite foul-ups, she'd scratched at her shoulders until the flesh between the blades was raw. They'd been strafed by Stukas outside Arromanches and then again near Chartres: sprawling in muddy ditches with bullets thudding around, she had seen the aerial attacks as yet a more surreal method of delaying her arrival.

Even in her fervid haste, however, she had been aware of the duality within herself. An American driver dressed in an American uniform, eating and living amid Americans, talking the same slang, yet at the same time Frenchborn and continuously holding back tears for the war-raped, unharvested farms of her native land.

She pulled up at the Hotel Raphael, whose entry fluttered with the Stars and Stripes. (The Raphael, which a month earlier had housed the German military governor and his staff, was given over to high-ranking American officers.) General Mannix climbed stiffly from the jeep and gave her a fatherly buss. "Take the rest of the day off, Ann, honey," he said. "Go find the old homestead."

On the Champs-Elysées, *drapeaux tricolores* had replaced black-and-red swastikas, the streams of men wore khaki uniforms rather than field gray, the staff cars were of American or British make, but the military bustle remained intrinsically unchanged. Ann braked as a GI darted across the wide boulevard to a thin redhead in a tight, short skirt who could, conceivably, be one of the *putains* she had seen waiting with a German noncom outside a dingy hotel.

On the *rive gauche* Ann's jeep was the only motorized vehicle on the street. She sped past bicycles, hand-hauled carts and wagons drawn by plodding, scrawny horses. Careworn women with their pinched, listless toddlers lined outside the shops. Rations had been drastically cut before General von Choltitz had signed the surrender: since then, with yet more farms destroyed and distribution totally severed, supplies were impossible to come by. In liberated Paris food allocations were at an all-time low.

Ann drove more slowly. She was in Montparnasse, and every meter flooded her with memories. Here, when she was five, Horace had held on to the back of her bicycle seat as she peddled waveringly along. Here, when she was eleven, Dorothy had whispered that soon she would be a woman, primly avoiding mention of the physical symptom of the menarche. Here, she had dented the fender of Horace's old car, here she and Gilberte had practiced flirting techniques on a pair of boys whose acne she could recall, but not their names. Ann slowly paralleled the wall of the Montparnasse Cemetery, where Jacques Tinel, tall, black-haired, chain-smoking, had convinced a lovesick girl in shabby clothes to flee France with him.

Ann turned on the rue Daguerre, pulling up at number 74. Staring at the familiar stone-and-brick building, she was unable to convince herself that time had passed: on the second floor Horace and Dorothy would be somberly discussing some new German regulation: directly above them, the Baron and Baronne de Permont would be wittily dissecting the overblown war communiqués put out by the *Propagandastaffel,* while Gilberte, in the smaller of the rear bedrooms, would be correcting one of her, Ann's, sketches for a ball gown.

A passerby halted to look at the uniformed woman hunched over in the jeep. What did an American have to cry about?

Eventually Ann controlled herself.

A new concierge, red-faced with teeth missing, answered her ring. In a spiteful hiss, she said she had no idea what had happened to that old crow, Madame Jargaux.

"Who lives in 2B and 3B?" Ann asked.

The concierge said that the third-floor flat was rented by a slovenly widow with a lazy crippled son, the one below by a demanding bitch with two squalling brats.

"Have you heard any news of the Blakelys or Mademoiselle de Permont?"

"Who?"

"The Blakelys are my parents, Americans. They used to live in 2B. Mademoiselle de Permont lived in 3B."

"My hands are full enough without worrying about tenants long gone. Mademoiselle, do you have any sardines or powdered eggs with you? They taste foul, but the starving can't be fussy."

"I'm sorry, but I didn't think to bring anything."

"But you *did* think that I had time to stand here all day answering questions? Americans!" The door slammed.

Bleak-faced, Ann drove down the boulevard Raspail in the direction of the *clinique.*

As soon as Dr. Descourset heard she was in the crowded waiting room, he hurried out. In the two and a half years since she'd last seen him, he had aged a decade. His hair and pointed beard were entirely white, his neck wrinkled and shrunken.

"Ann!" He kissed her cheeks, enveloping her in the harsh aroma of lye disinfectant. "What a charming young lady you've become. Let us talk a minute." Since there was a patient inside his dispensary, he led her to the glass-encased office where Horace had struggled with the ledgers.

In a small, high voice, Ann inquired whether he had been contacted by her parents.

"Not since 'Orace came to tell me that you'd left the occupied zone." He sighed. "Ann, I'm sorry, but that's the last I saw of them."

She had been steeling herself for this response. "Doctor, do you remember the people who lived upstairs, the de Permonts?"

"Ah, yes. I heard they were dead. Typhoid."

She leaned toward him. "The daughter too? Gilberte?"

Dr. Descourset's gaunt cheeks drew in until his face resembled a skull. "That young lady is very much alive. No need to concern yourself about her. She is well, quite well. Except for a bald head."

Throughout the liberated areas of France, women who had slept with Germans were being paraded naked through the streets to have their heads shaved.

"Gilberte? Doctor, you must be mistaken. She's no collaborator. Her parents were in the Résistance—they died in the Santé. And I'm positive not of typhoid. Maybe the Gestapo killed her too."

"Ann, I tell you she's alive." The doctor leaned forward on the accountant's stool, in rapid, staccato bursts informing her of Gilberte's request for an abortion, and his subsequent summons to the boulevard Suchet, to the parental home that she had dishonored. "I arrived too late to deliver Field Marshal von Hocherer's bastard—a boy—but I patched her up."

"I . . . I can't believe it. Did Gilberte *tell* you the baby was his?"

"There was no need. She wore beautiful clothes, she was in a magnificent bedroom. Besides, the servant who let me in mumbled that the woman was the field marshal's whore. Ann, she's not the sort you should associate with."

Two spots of redness showed on Ann's cheeks. "Gilberte's my friend. And from what you've told me, she must need help now."

"Loyalty has its limits. If—*when* your dear father and Madame Dorothy come home, they'll tell you the same."

Her parents. Ann remembered seeing them in this glassed cubicle, Dorothy's out-of-date cloche hat bent over the ledger while Horace clasped his hands, humbly waiting for her to find an error in his arithmetic. Ann could no longer hold back her tears.

Dr. Descourset patted her shoulder. "Now, now, child. One thing about the *boches,* they treated Americans in a civilized manner. You'll see. Madame Dorothy and 'Orace will be home any day now."

30

"What's the word on your folks?" Larry asked.

"Working on it, still working on it," Ann said, battling to sound upbeat.

She had been in Paris ten days, ten days of waiting for General Mannix outside buildings while high-level ordnance meetings dragged on interminably, ten days of increasingly dispiriting dead ends in her efforts to find her parents and Gilberte.

"Isn't there one of those alphabet relief organizations who find missing families?"

"Yes, STEFMP. It's for military personnel, but my boss set up an appointment for me."

"To one-star generals," Larry said, raising his glass of Bordeaux. Arriving in Paris this afternoon, he had reserved a table at this narrow bistro near Les Halles. The twin rows of banquettes were filled with uniformed men and a few women, a crowd who chatted in a dozen languages while dining on rare *bifteck* and buttery trout. When most Paris eateries were struggling to serve even truly dreadful food, for Larry to have discovered this place after less than two hours in the city was a mind-boggling feat—but then, as Ann had noticed, he had a dedicated affinity to the high life.

"Any better luck with your friend?"

"She has a baby, a boy, she had him on D day." Leaning across the *crudités*, Ann put the most empathetic light on Gilberte's situation.

Larry whistled. "Straight from the hoosegow to arms of top Nazi brass."

"Who are you to say that?"

"Calm down, shorty. You know my views. The world wouldn't be in this foul-up if everybody on both sides had been getting laid regularly." He grimaced wryly. "I should request an hour or two with the company psychiatrist—me, falling for the last virgin extant on two continents."

Ann nibbled a *pomme frite*. She had never so much as hinted to Larry that she was a virgin. He, however, had taken her purity as his credo. She could perceive no method of breaking his illusion without shattering his ego—or going to bed with him. Both were impossible—she liked Larry too much to hurt him, she loved Quent too much to sleep with anyone else.

Larry was asking, "Think she's still in Paris?"

"I don't know. The WAC sergeant who's helping me about my parents at STEFMP said she'd try to find out, but in a snippy, judgmental way."

"The OWI is not without intelligence sources. And I have friends in Paris."

"You mean that? You'll help me?"

"Your folks are in Kraut hands, so I doubt whether our bloodhounds can dig up any news. But possibly I can discover what cooks with Gilberte."

"Oh, Larry . . ."

He held up a hand, leering. "Save the appreciation for later tonight."

That weekend, winds swept down from the Arctic. Three mornings after Larry's arrival, Ann delivered Mannix to a conference in the Marais then, with two other American drivers, retired to a nearby bar, where they lingered over small cups of *café noir* (American instant) to stay out of the marrow-freezing gusts. At a tap on the window, the trio turned. Larry, fair hair whipping across his high forehead, grinned at Ann. While he went around the corner to the entry, her two companions inquired who was the adorable

looie, and when she replied, "Just a friend," both made simultane-
ous catcalls of disbelief.

After the introductions, Ann asked, "How did you find me?"

He pulled a sad face. "Ladies, you have no idea how she under-
estimates me." Then he touched her shoulder. "Ann, can you
break away from these stunning chicks a minute? I have a little
something for you."

Outside, the wind tugged at her khaki skirt.

"Sorry to drag you out in gale force," he said. "But this is top-
level theft. An old buddy from my press corps days went out on a
limb for me." He slid a folded sheet from a new copy of *Yank*
magazine. "The last name's wrong, but the rest fits."

Ann turned from the wind, unfolding the slick paper. " 'Gilberte
Cagny,' " she read aloud. "I think that was the name of the baronne's first husband." Silently she scanned the remainder of the
blurry mimeographing. *Gilberte Cagny. November, 1941, imprisoned
with parents in the Santé. Father, Baron André de Permont, and mother,
Vivienne Cagny, in Résistance.* The question why the baronne had
used her previous name flicked, but Ann forgot it as she read on.
*Both parents tortured and murdered during Gestapo interrogation. Subject
released March, 1942. Domiciled with Field Marshal Count Bernd von
Hocherer, Nazi criminal. Bore him son on June 6, 1944. Judged by tribunal
to be guilty of collaboration. Dealt minimum punishment. Current address,
12, rue André-Antoine, Montmartre.*

"My buddy's high up in the FFI," Larry said. "Ann, he told me
the Gestapo were hot after names and the de Permonts got the full
treatment. They never talked."

Ann made an incoherent sound and her eyes squeezed shut. She
was not trying to feign ignorance of the baron and baronne's
death, her grief and horror were too tumultuously real to attempt
subterfuge. The refined art of Gestapo torture was being exposed
daily in the newspapers.

"Hey, I should never have showed you that crappy report. I
forgot how close you were to the family."

Knowing how overt signs of unhappiness embarrassed Larry,
Ann blinked away her tears. "It's the wind," she said.

"The poor kid must have gone through a rough time."

"Yes, she idolized her father," Ann said, handing back the mimeographed sheet. "Larry, you've been terrific. I never would have gotten the address without you."

The following morning General Mannix attended a conference on the avenue Foch. Since he was close to his hotel, he gave Ann the day off.

The rue André-Antoine was not a street but a broad, stepped alley that twisted up *la Butte.* Parking on the rue des Abbesses, removing the jeep's rotor, an army regulation to prevent theft, Ann began to climb. In the final week before liberation, the rue André-Antoine had seen battles between Parisians and the remnants of the German garrison. Windows were shattered, doors missing, and a front wall had been blown away so that the house with its exposed rooms resembled a giant dollhouse. The depredations on Gilberte's address, however, had been inflicted not by warfare but by time and neglect. Stucco ornamental pediments had crumbled, paint on shutters and door had worn away. Ann drummed her knuckles against the weathered wood, rapping again, then again.

After several minutes, an asexual voice snarled, "What's all the racket about?"

"I'd like to see Gilberte de Permont—Gilberte Cagny."

"Who knows names?"

"She has a baby."

"Oh, that stuck-up bitch." The door was opened by a frizzy-haired woman in a filthy dressing gown. "Her highness holds court in the cellar."

Ann felt her way down dark, narrow steps to a coal chute. Though there was no coal, a sharp memory of carbon dust permeated the dank basement.

"Gilberte, it's me, Ann," she called. "Ann Blakely."

Getting no response, Ann edged down the dim corridor to the only door. As she tapped, it creaked ajar.

A filthy dormer window below street level cast a murky light that seemed filtered through layers of brown cloth. One wall bulged out, the natural rock of *la Butte,* the others were crudely mortared brick. The high porcelain sink indicated that in the house's heyday this basement-cavern had served as a laundry. Near a packing crate imprinted PROPERTY OF US ARMY was a neatly folded khaki blanket with the same imprimatur. A small teddy bear and a hot plate on a ripped Vuitton suitcase completed the furnishings.

And I used to think the rue Daguerre too mean for the de Permonts! Blowing on her hands, Ann paced up and down in a vain attempt to keep warm. After about a half hour, footsteps sounded in the corridor.

Silhouetted in the open jamb stood a tall feminine figure. The large baby and lumpy, shapeless black coat made the scarfed head appear preternaturally small.

Ann, suddenly a trespasser, murmured, "Gilberte?"

Gilberte jumped. "Who's there?"

"Me. Ann."

Gilberte stepped inside, approaching Ann with that well-remembered expression of cool, derisive amusement, but the baby let out an indignant howl as if he were being clutched too tightly.

"One of our noble liberators," she said. "Are you sightseeing in picturesque Montmartre? Making a tour of the cellars?"

"It was open, so I came in."

31

Pushing open her door, Gilberte had glimpsed a uniformed woman. Her mouth filled with the rusty taste of fear. Once she had diligently exorcised every trace of personal cowardice, but now, with Michel dependent on her, fear licked at her constantly, a faithful, cringing mongrel dog. Collaborators disappeared, some of them doubtless to the next world, many others were being arrested. What did it matter, imprisonment or a bullet? Both would mean the same to Michel: a death sentence. Who in a city of starving children would take in a German by-blow?

When the intruder spoke in Ann Blakely's soft voice, relief swelled through Gilberte. Almost simultaneously, she was trapped by shame. That Ann should find her in a brothel's cellar! A scarecrow in servants' cast-offs! Forming a taut smile, gripping Michel, she went toward her visitor. Diminutively trim in her khaki overcoat, Ann had lost her adolescent gawkiness and had allowed her russet hair its natural buoyant tendencies. She was far prettier.

"Is that your baby?" Ann asked.

"Dear friend, does this look like a crèche for foundlings?"

"What's he called?"

"Michel. Do any of his other vital statistics interest you?" Gilberte whipped off her scarf. Her cropped black hair stood in a thick brush like an American crew cut. "He's Hocherer's. He's the son of Field Marshal Count Bernd von Hocherer."

Ann had anticipated the obvious, Gilberte's shaved head and shabby clothes. Not the new hard look that went beyond the weight loss paring her features to a sharp, cold perfection. Not the expression in the tilted golden eyes, eyes that no longer glinted with teasing but now were like a cornered cat's eyes, filled with desperate calculations. *Oh, Gilberte, what happened to you in the Santé? What did those monsters do to you?* Ann turned to the baby. He was examining her with an unfrightened gravity so adult that she chuckled.

"Hello, Michel, you cutie pie, you," she said in English.

"Did you use bloodhounds to track us down?"

"Larry Porter helped me. So you're using your mother's name?"

My true name, Gilberte thought. *My bastard name.* "And who, pray tell, is Larry Porter?"

"Your cousin Quent Dejong brought him to your flat." As Ann said Quent's name, she ducked her head.

I'd forgotten her little infatuations with film stars, Gilberte thought. *She must have had a crush on Quent. Well, why not? A handsome millionaire.* It never occurred to Gilberte that there was some altered mechanism in her own thought processes. On the rue Daguerre she had never felt superior because of Ann's penchant for adolescent fantasy: now she needed the judgment to boost her ego. "Since you mention it," she said in less metallic intonations, "I do remember that Quent had another American in tow. A fair-haired, Tom Sawyer type."

"Larry. He was a foreign correspondent then. Now he's in the army."

Michel was squirming. He wanted to be put down. Gilberte could not force herself to deposit him in his packing crate, though Ann assuredly guessed its purpose.

Ann sang, "Michel, peekaboo." She held her brimmed khaki cap over her face, whisking it away. "Peekaboo!"

The baby stopped wriggling, tilting his head soberly. After several repetitions of Ann's performance, he responded in a rare smile.

"You darling! Gilberte, let me hold him?"

Gilberte gripped Michel tighter. In his lifetime, she had rarely let anyone else hold him. Even the month when she'd recuperated from her unassisted labor and subsequent hemorrhage, a month when her legs were wobbly, she had refused to either hire a baby nurse or permit the Breton maid to care for him. She'd crept around changing him, bathing him, dressing him, nursing him. Since the liberation, she'd lugged him everywhere with her, even to the foul-odored, unreliably flushing WC on the second floor. It was not her style to play little maternal kitchy-koo games with her son or to sing him lullabies, yet she knew as an unarguable axiom that she would lay down her life for him.

"What about chocolate?" Ann asked, opening her large, shoulder-strap purse. "May I give him a piece?"

Michel had never taken any nourishment other than Gilberte's milk. From the determination of his chewing on her sore nipples, she knew that, at four months, he was ready for solid food. This trapped her. She didn't have enough to eat herself, and if she gave him part of her meager ration, her milk would dry up. That Ann could casually give him treats reactivated Gilberte's full defensiveness.

"How very American," she drawled. "Distributing chocolate bars to unweaned infants."

Ann flushed. "I should have tried to buy graham crackers at the PX."

"And what, pray tell, are 'graham crackers'?"

For a moment Ann's soft, full mouth trembled, then she snapped in English, "I'm getting pretty sick of being treated like, like a— a—"

"Uninvited guest?" Gilberte put in.

Drawing a sharp breath, Ann glanced toward the wall of bulging raw rock. (This cave was the best accommodation Gilberte could afford or procure—shave-heads were not given good rates at pawnshops, landlords welcomed them not.) "You're right," she said quietly. "I shouldn't have barged in. But I've been lonely, Gilberte, so lonely. My parents stayed in Paris and the Germans interned them. I have no idea where they are." Her voice dropped to near inaudibility. "There was a man I cared about. He's stopped writing."

The misery glowing in the enormous dark brown eyes told

Gilberte that this had been no crush on some impossibly out-of-reach idol like Sacha Guitry, Robert Taylor or Quent, but a full-blown love affair. "What about Larry Porter? Isn't he filling that particular gap?"

"He's dear and fun, but it's not serious at all."

Something slithered near the sink.

Gilberte hoisted Michel against her shoulder. "Let's go for a walk."

As they emerged, the ponderous campanile of Sacré-Coeur and the simpler bells of Saint-Pierre began their discursive chiming.

While the bells boomed, Ann summoned up her courage. When the ringing stopped, she asked quietly, "Gilberte, would you like to talk about the Santé? Or about Field Marshal von Hocherer? Or how things went during the liberation?"

Gilberte ached to confide in Ann. Yet even in the old days she had held back her deepest secrets. And now, how could she reveal the shame of gang rape or trivialize the horror of her parents' deaths with words or disclose her omnipresent cowardice?

Shifting Michel in her arms, Gilberte swallowed hard. "What is there to say?" she asked flippantly. "The Santé was over-Krauted. Hocherer, he was what you Americans call my sugar daddy. And as for my current life, surely you don't need diagrams."

The rebuff silenced Ann.

But her offer to be a listening post had filled Gilberte's mind with unwanted memories of the final days that the Third Reich had ruled Paris.

Six weeks earlier, on August 22, Gilberte had awakened to the rumble of distant artillery and the clatter of nearby rifle fire. For quite a few days, men and women wearing armbands of the FFI—the Résistance army—had been making war on the rearguard of the German garrison. Armed with antique hunting guns, M-1 rifles dropped by American planes and weapons taken from German corpses, they set up barricades of sandbags and furniture, hurling homemade Molotov cocktails at tanks. The sounds of the uprising exhilarated Gilberte yet at the same time strung terror through her nerve endings. She was not in the least sanguine about the treatment that the FFI would dole out to her, and ipso facto to Michel.

The shooting had never been this close. Jumping from her bed, she ran barefoot to peer through the space between the shutters. From her limited vantage point, the broad thoroughfare lined with pruned, dusty-leafed trees appeared empty. Then she saw a private in dirt-covered field gray swerve his motorcycle from the direction of the Bois de Boulogne. Another shot came from the house opposite, which had been vacant for five weeks, since the collaborationist owner had moved his household to Alsace. A head moved at one of the round windows set into the mansard roof, and a rifle jumped as it was fired. Abruptly the German toppled sideways, falling several meters from his motorcycle, which crashed into the gutter and lay there, wheels spinning.

An armored staff car swerved into her restricted line of vision. Before it came to a halt, the field marshal, wearing a rumpled, dirt-encrusted uniform, had jumped out. He was followed by two soldiers, both holding machine guns, who crouched behind the car returning the fire. Less than a minute after she'd first seen the car, Hocherer was flinging open her bedroom door.

He halted at the cradle, his brown eyes gentle at this, his first glimpse of his only remaining son. (The ailing boy, drafted with other fifteen- and sixteen-year-olds, had been killed during a bombing raid on the training camp.) Hocherer straightened, turning to her.

"Get ready!" he commanded in a tone he'd never before used with her. "Dress yourself and the child. One small bag for each of you. *Macht schnell!*" He strode into his room.

She went to the connecting doorway, watching him unlock a strongbox and rapidly transfer papers with the Reichstag's eagle seal to the fireplace. As he struck a match, the Schmeissers on the street below set up their distinctive rippling rhythm. Again Gilberte ran to see. Every pane in the collaborator's house had been shot out, and a boy sprawled out of the attic window, blood oozing down his FFI armband. The soldiers firing were boys no older than the frail corpse that jumped and shivered with their fusillade.

"Do as I say!" Hocherer snapped. "They're only a few miles from Paris. Von Choltitz is at work composing his surrender paper."

"Michel and I aren't leaving."

"Gilberte, much as I admire courage, at this time it's not a useful commodity."

Courage? Now that the shooting had stopped, couldn't he hear the thudding of her terrified heart? "Germany," she said. "The perfect holiday spa for a Frenchwoman and her child."

Shoving a last batch of papers in the blaze, Hocherer stood. He rubbed the knuckles of his small hands thoughtfully. "Maybe you're making the right choice," he said after a few moments. "The Russians are racing toward our borders and if they get to Germany before the Americans and the British, nothing much will be left. The *Götterdämmerung* . . . And as for me—after three misbegotten conspiracies to kill Hitler, it's a miracle I'm still alive. But the SS will track me down soon enough. Thousands of people are being tortured to confess who was in on the last assassination attempt— the films of my comrades being slowly strangled with piano wires are delivered daily to Berchtesgaden."

"Delightful man, your Leader."

Hocherer stirred the blackened papers with a poker and the unconsumed fragment of a letter caught fire, blazing orange. "I wouldn't be able to protect you and my child from the lunatic."

"We're not staying because we're cowards, but because de Permonts never run."

"Gilberte, my hard and beautiful love, you're too young to un- derstand how I worship you." Picking up his field marshal's baton, he bent to kiss his son's cheek. "Try not to raise the boy to despise his father's people."

On the morning of August 25, the boulevard Suchet trembled under trucks, jeeps and tanks bearing dirty, jubilant French soldiers. General Leclerc was leading his 2nd Armored Division into Paris. The crowd screamed, wept, waved tiny *tricolores,* threw summer flowers. Women of all ages dashed into the street to em- brace their returned countrymen. Gilberte watched the liberation from her window, her throat clogged with joy, her mind on the rim of panic.

There was a sound like distant thunder when Paris went glory mad: General Charles de Gaulle was striding down the Champs- Elysées. Fatigued but jubilant American, British and Canadian troops were welcomed with more flowers, more tears and an interminable roar of happiness.

On the dawn of the twenty-seventh, one of her mother's sheets was hung as a white flag from an upstairs window: the neighborhood servants and tradespeople began gathering in the front garden. Gilberte couldn't help reflecting that the holiday crowd jostling on the mowed grass and gravel paths below her were direct lineal descendants of the mob who had cheered as her ancestress, Louise de Permont, had mounted the guillotine. She fed Michel a demitasse spoon of the red soporific Dr. Behn had prescribed for her during her convalescence, then laid the sleeping infant in a large suitcase into whose leather she had already cut air slits, sliding the valise back on the shelf. Dressing carefully, she coiled her jet hair in an elaborate knot.

The chef and housekeeper led her down the steps and out the front door. Beneath the shell-shaped copper canopy stood the tribunal of servants who had already sentenced her. The old gardener, as one of the three, quaveringly denounced collaborationists, the sallow-faced butler shaved her head with a straight razor. The "Marseillaise" was roared. Cheers and ribald encouragement as her plump little Breton personal maid stepped forward, then a peculiar, tense silence as Gilberte's new summer frock and convent-made underwear were cut from her. Naked, holding her shoulders straight so that her milk-filled breasts jutted forward, Gilberte flared her nostrils in what she hoped was icy hauteur. She maintained her expression and her erect posture and made no attempt to shield her breasts and pubic hair as they paraded her down the boulevard Suchet. Though General von Choltitz had officially surrendered the city, suicide squads of Germans still remained. Near the avenue Foch, a few meters beyond one of the newly set up medical centers, an SS trooper reared up on a rooftop to fire down at them. The triumphant crowd shattered into a hundred terror-struck individuals. Gilberte darted into the entry of a rococo apartment building. The Breton maid, already there, removed her shabby black coat, draping it over Gilberte's shoulders, which she herself had bared less than twenty minutes earlier. Ignoring the spray of bullets from the sniper, Gilberte galloped back to the house. Grabbing the comatose baby from his hiding place, she raced upstairs to steal the pantry maid's clothes. Packing these with a few of Michel's things in the valise he'd just vacated, she had shoved the diamond earrings and heavy gold bangles that Hocherer had given her into her purse and—

Gilberte was summoned from her memories by a touch on her arm.

"This place is open," Ann said. "What do you think?"

They had reached the rue des Abbesses and though it was scarcely noon, too early for lunch, the door of a café stood ajar.

Gilberte's spine ached from carrying Michel, hunger prowled her stomach, but she summoned up a tone of indifference to say, "It's all the same with me."

The proprietor emerged from the kitchen. Staring with maleficent intensity at Gilberte's kerchiefed head, he shifted his gaze to Ann's uniform. His mustachioed face became an equinox poised between outrage and speculative hope—like all other Parisians, he yearned for solid currency. He could, he informed Ann, arrange a fine early lunch for two, a good wine and real coffee included, for one dollar, American.

Michel, lulled by the walk, began whimpering as Gilberte undid his knitted jacket. Ann played peekaboo again, and a smile pierced his tears.

"Come on, big boy," she said, reaching for him.

This time Gilberte relinquished her son. He nestled contentedly in Ann's lap.

They were served a terrine of an unspecified meat—whatever its provenance, the terrine was deliciously fatty. The omelette aux fines herbes, concocted from powdered eggs and canned butter (doubtless black market, plundered from some American supply depot) was equally ambrosial. Since the liberation, God, how her nursing body craved proteins and fats! Only the memory of her mother's clear, pretty voice advising her on manners prevented Gilberte from wolfing down everything. She left a wedge of omelette and most of her share of the baguette.

During the lunch, Ann initiated a conversation about the rue Daguerre and Madame Bernard's. Gilberte, awash in nostalgia, felt a modicum of her old trust seep back. Michel was contentedly gumming his second hunk of baguette when Nescafé was set before them.

"It seems so brutal," Ann said. "First to be punished by the Nazis, then by the French. Doesn't it make you bitter?"

Gilberte raised an eyebrow, then grimaced. "Yes. I'm bitter. But it's a gnat bite compared to how I feel about whatever pig denounced my father to the Gestapo."

"Any idea who it was?"

"No. But I'll find out. If it takes me the rest of my life, I'll find out."

"What about now?" Ann replaced the disintegrated crust in Michel's hand with a fresh piece of bread. "Any plans what you're going to do now?"

"When my hair grows out to a decent, patriotic length so that Frenchwomen will once again speak to me, I'll become a modiste."

"Make dresses and hats?"

"Dresses."

"You?"

"Sewing's not an arcane art." Gilberte looked away. "Oh, Ann, what else can I do? I can't leave Michel, but I must earn a living."

"It's a wonderful idea—Chanel had better watch her laurels," Ann said. "Won't you need a sewing machine?"

"That's the problem." Gilberte sighed.

"Look, we've known each other too long to horse around. I'd like to float a loan."

For a moment Gilberte couldn't speak, then she murmured, "It's very generous of you, Blakely."

"Stop being ridiculous." Ann touched her hand. "How much do you need?"

"Three hundred American dollars."

Ann's pay was seventy dollars a month, and she was improvident with it, splurging on movies, on gifts at the PX for her friends, her landlady, the cockney charlady. Her current net worth was three war bonds that would be worth seventy-five dollars at the date of maturation, and the five ones in her purse.

Yet without hesitation she said, "I'll have it at your place sometime tomorrow."

32

Having never borrowed money in her life, Ann had to prime herself to cadge loans from General Mannix and his staff, from other drivers—Larry, a consistent spendthrift, was broke. She accumulated three hundred dollars.

As Gilberte reached for the envelope stuffed with bills, her fingers stiffened. Charity is charity, no matter how warmly intended. "Isn't the next step to write what you Americans call an IOU?"

Ann, who had recently signed thirty-seven such markers, ached to slap the superior smirk from Gilberte's beautiful mouth. Then she glanced at Michel, who lay like a Buddha in the packing crate. "Only in movies," she said, smiling at the baby, who smiled back. "Pay me when it's convenient."

Two days later, Ann sat in one of the canvas seats that had been set up along the sides of a B-17, a Flying Fortress, shivering in a borrowed, too-large flight suit as she and her boss returned to England.

General Mannix's frown lines deepened and he spent hours at Fairfields, a highly guarded red-brick country house thirty miles north of London. There, other drivers let her know that her boss was strictly small potatoes. Indeed he was. Once she glimpsed

Churchill in his famous jumpsuit stumping across Fairfields' lawn and another day General Eisenhower strode by her car.

Returning to London one dismal November afternoon, they passed a freshly chalked newspaper placard announcing a British Canadian victory in Antwerp. The general told her to stop. Buying a paper, he scanned the front page, then took a pint of Southern Comfort from his topcoat pocket—to Ann's knowledge, he was a teetotaler. She watched in astonishment through the rearview mirror as he took a long, ritual gulp. Wiping the neck of the bottle, he passed it to her. "Drink to this Belgian shipping route, Ann. You've probably been wondering what we've been working on out there in the country. Well, we were planning convoys through to Antwerp."

German defeats were announced daily. Londoners greeted each other with fingers spread in the Churchillian V-for-victory sign. GIs made book on the date the war would end.

Then, on the icy, foggy night of December 15, panzer divisions penetrated the American lines in the Ardennes, spreading confusion and death. Heavily censored news bulletins concealed the interminable casualty lists from this German counteroffensive, but London had learned to read between the lines: carolers sang "Good King Wenceslas" and "O Come, All Ye Faithful" like dirges.

On December 22, Larry Porter phoned to say he was back in London, and there was a big splash at the Savoy.

"With the rotten news, Larry, I'm not in the mood for celebrating. Can't we just have dinner alone?"

Ann attributed the ensuing silence to disappointment. Larry sought out extravagant parties—he had a decided taste for the best hotels and restaurants.

Then he said, "At your service, shorty."

The blue, dimout lights of the motor pool jeep showed rain bouncing on the pavement of Weymouth Street as Ann stared toward the apartment building.

"Whose place is it?" she asked.

"An OWI buddy who's been shipped to Rome. And I'm getting soaked out here. Hey, you were the one to suggest we dine à deux."

"Larry," she sighed, "you know I meant a restaurant."

"I've laid in steaks the likes of which only generals get in restaurants. Ann, in view of my safe return from the combat zone"—he had been in Paris the entire time—"isn't it possible that you could relax that Wisconsin virginity fetish of yours?"

His use of the word *virginity* unleashed the routine guilts in her. "What makes you think I can cook?" she asked, and switched off the ignition.

The apartment, one room gerrymandered from a larger flat, was presided over by Betty Grable in a white bathing suit, while a spindly fir branch inadequately decked with paper chains paid tribute to the season. As Ann cooked at the high-legged, battered stove, Larry poured her two large bourbons-and-soda. As they ate the thick porterhouse steaks that would have been a month's meat ration for an English family of four, he uncorked two bottles of Bordeaux he'd brought back from France, filling her glass repeatedly. She willingly surrendered to his assaults on her sobriety. Wasn't it preferable to be blotto than to make the inevitable comparisons between this dinner and the meals shared in a book-filled cottage? She couldn't pinpoint when Larry started playing records, but "Green Eyes" was on the spindle when he held out his arms to her. Given the right dance floor, Larry was terrific, but there was no room here for his dips and swoops and twirls. Besides, she was far too unsteady on her feet for such fancy hoofing. Clinging to him for support as he shuffled her around in a tight embrace, she scarcely noticed the aggressive thrust of his pelvis against hers. When the record ended, he kept an arm around her as he slid on "Begin the Beguine," which had a clicking crack. His shaven, fragrant cheek glued to hers, he crooned the lyrics.

When this record ended, he turned off the gramophone. "Christ, am I ever nuts about you, shorty-baby. . . ."

"Like you too."

His kiss was deep, and his mouth remained glommed on hers as he switched off the lamp and eased her onto the bed. A faraway explosion set up a violent clatter of glass and crockery. Larry's caresses zoned in on her breasts and backside. She was so woozy that his erotic efforts translated into a game between affectionate children. She had never before permitted him to unsnap her rayon bra, but he was her friend and it seemed niggardly to refuse. Cupping her naked breasts, Larry made a peculiar whinnying noise, and his incursions grew rough. By a kind of alchemy she was naked under the eiderdown. When he started to rub her vulva, though, she was overtaken by an involuntary physical reaction. Nausea, sour and warm, traveled up her chest to her throat. She jerked backward, almost falling off the single bed.

"Toilet?" she mumbled.

"I'm so wild about you," he whispered. "Baby, I won't hurt you, I promise."

"Gonna upshuck." Holding a hand over her mouth, she gagged.

He rapidly crawled over her to switch on the lamp. Everything— his bare, lightly fuzzed legs, her strewn clothes, the uncleared table with its toppled tumblers and the mournful little Christmas tree— was shifting at weird askew angles. Wobbling to her feet, she gagged again. Larry whipped off his unbuttoned khaki shirt to cloak around her. Stepping into his shorts, he said, "This way."

She knelt on icy tiles, throwing up until only clear liquid came. She sank back on her haunches. Eyes watering, head throbbing, shivering uncontrollably, she was by no means sober, but far less drunk than she'd been a few minutes earlier. *What am I doing here, naked under a shirt that smells of Larry's Mum deodorant?* Kneeling, listening to the howl of sirens and the bells of fire engines, Ann berated herself with masochistic fervor for leading Larry on and at the same time absolved him of all guilt in his liquor-drenched seduction skirmish.

"Everything okay in there?" he asked, pushing open the door. Still clad only in his dog tags and khaki underwear, his face crimson-smeared with her lipstick, he peered sympathetically down at her. "Cookies all tossed?"

Nodding, she pushed to her feet. "Where can I rinse my mouth out?"

"Sink's right this way."

Fingering Colgate's on her teeth and sloshing water on her face, she accused herself of dwelling in concubinage with a memory.

Larry led her up the hall to the one-room flat. As she bent to retrieve her underwear, he curved himself around her back, cupping her breasts. "Straighten up the place later," he murmured in her ear. "First things first."

"It's all a mistake," she mumbled. "It's my fault, letting things get this far."

"Come back to bed." He kissed her neck.

She moved away. "I'm going home, Larry."

"You're leaving?"

"I must."

"There's a name for a female who does this kind of thing."

"I deserve it," she said, turning away to pull her panties on under his shirt.

Larry hunched on the bed watching her contortions as she dressed with her back to him. When she pulled on her raincoat, he said hoarsely, "If you walk out on me, we're finished."

"I'm sorry," she sighed.

"Cock tease!" he yelled.

She closed the door quietly behind her.

Larry buried his face in his hands, his body shuddering with sobs. He wept loudly and desolately for a long time.

By the middle of January, the counterattack had fizzled and the Germans were retreating across the ruined, snow-covered landscape of Belgium, leaving a trail of field gray and khaki corpses.

Arriving home at Polkingham Place after midnight on January 20, Ann found a letter from Larry. He was no longer in England: the censor had blanked out his boyish scrawl in several places, but there were enough humorous comments to tell her that he was chivvying a group of magazine writers through Paris. He did not even obliquely refer to the debacle at the Weymouth Street flat. Ann, weak with gratitude that she had recaptured his friendship, immediately scribbled an equally lighthearted reply.

On March 22 the Gestapo closed in on the remaining conspirators on Hitler's life. Field Marshal Count Bernd von Hocherer was strangled slowly in Berlin's Plötzensee prison. He could have vanished into the *Nacht und Nebel,* the night and mist of the Führer's enemies, however, because Allied planes had been bombing the hell out of Germany and morale was precarious. The Ministry of Propaganda gave out that the field marshal had died defending the

Rhine River just south of Mainz. The widow was permitted to pay her tribute to his swastika-draped coffin while Göring, wearing one of his gaudy Luftwaffe uniforms and heavy makeup, stood at her side inveighing all German *Volk* to follow the example of this gallant officer who had given his sons and own life for the *Vaterland.* The French press, short on paper and long on victories, devoted one paragraph to the death in combat of the archcriminal who had headed the Nazi Western Command in France. Gilberte stared a long time at the news report.

On April 25, Germany was cut in two. Patrols of the American 1st army met Soviet patrols at the Elbe River: GIs and Russians kissed, exchanged mementos, sang their respective anthems and toasted each other with vodka and bourbon. Field Marshal Montgomery's British forces were barreling across the German plains, the Canadians were sweeping the last Nazis from a starved Holland, and the French snapped the final Wehrmacht resistance in the Black Forest. On April 30, in the *Führerbunker* deep below the rubble that had been Berlin, Hitler shot himself in the mouth. (Eva Braun Hitler, the longtime mistress whom he had married the previous day, preferred the neater suicide of poison.) On May 7, Admiral Friedeburg and General Jodl signed an unconditional surrender on behalf of the ruined country that in twelve years had decimated Europe and ravaged much of the planet.

Ann's toes lifted from the floor as she leaned out the window to tear pages from the London phone book and scatter them confetti-like on the mass of humanity. Below her on Oxford Street, secretaries in drab Utility dresses were being hugged by staid old gentlemen wearing derbies, young enlisted men whirled housewives into the Lambeth Walk, horns of the stalled buses tooted, church bells chimed and a Scot in kilts stood atop one of the double-deckers adding the unearthly screech of his bagpipes to the cacophonous sounds of victory.

Larry pulled Ann from the window, and a tall infantry colonel grabbed her, bending her backward in a long, drunken kiss. "On behalf of the sovereign state of Virginia, I salute you, O embodiment of all that is fine and wholesome in our cherished womanhood."

A very young Canadian corporal slid another tumbler of champagne in her hand, "Come on, Yank baby, drink up!"

"Conga!" shouted a busty WAC. "Conga, conga! Everybody, make a conga line."

Larry planted both hands on Ann's waist, she held on to a Polish pilot who held on to a pretty English Wren and thirty or so people one-two-three-kicked around the flat, congaing down staircases, congaing across the foyer of the Mount Royal and out into the crush on Oxford Street, somehow managing to keep the line intact until Marble Arch, where it disintegrated against the solid mass of bodies.

"Boy am I dizzy!" Ann cried. "Too much champagne."

"On this day," Larry retorted, "it's not possible to have too much champagne."

"Let's go to the palace, I want to go to the palace."

"The palace it is," Larry said, taking her hand.

As they made their way through the crowds in Hyde Park and Green Park they were hugged by two tiny Chinese sailors, an Aussie private, a very inebriated French dowager, two gargantuan Slavs and a minimum of a hundred British, civilian and armed services. It was a long walk, and by the time they merged into the crush surrounding Buckingham Palace, the Mumm's had worn off and Ann was sober. A sticky web of thoughts had entrapped her.

The war in the Pacific still raged, but the European dance of death, the war that had started on a fine September morning in 1939, *her* war, was ended. Her life had been shattered into a hundred pieces, and now, finally, she would be able to trace down the kaleidoscoped shards. It flashed through her mind that she had never seen the same pattern repeated in a kaleidoscope, but then a group of nearby dockworkers began bestowing Guinness kisses on her, and her thoughts resumed their rubicund hue. She and her parents would return safe and happy to the rue Daguerre, and Quent would knock on the door.

A titanic crescendo of cheers deafened her. The royal family was emerging onto the balcony. Ann saw tiny pink ovals rather than faces, but she could make out King George's naval uniform, Queen

Elizabeth's and Princess Margaret Rose's pastel frocks, khaki-clad Princess Elizabeth, Queen Mary's large toque. The royal grouping typified to Ann all the English people who had treated her with such gracious generosity. The sweet-smiled landlady who used her own rations to bring up bowls of barley soup when Ann had bronchitis, the cockney charlady who insisted on ironing her clothes, the aged bus conductors who patiently gave her directions through bombed-out areas, the thin old woman in Shoreditch who had risked her own life to shove Ann out of the way of a toppling wall. As hundreds of thousands of voices raised in "God Save the King," Ann sang, too, tears runneling down her cheeks.

By now lights were blinking on.

After six years of darkness, lights!

Linking arms, she and Larry strolled the dusky, golden miles back to Weymouth Street—Larry had taken over his friend's flat and Ann had no reservations about going there. Nowadays Larry's kisses could pass the Hays Office censor. Ann was convinced that he, having gotten the sex business safely out of his system, perceived their relationship as she did, a solid amalgam of the old cliché "just friends."

In actuality, the failed seduction had convinced Larry that the object of his affections not only had the big eyes, retroussé nose and pert figure of the girl next door, but also possessed the moral virtue of that fictive creature. Though initially wounded to the core by Ann's rebuff, after a few weeks' absence he perceived that within the unassailable fortress of her chastity she wore the diadem of the highest level of womanhood.

Future wife.

33

On May 31, Ann drove General Mannix to the Southhampton dock where men were streaming aboard the *Queen Mary,* whose gray camouflage paint matched the lowering sky. Ann hugged the general good-bye emotionally and he planted a kiss on her forehead with equally fervent warmth. He was being redeployed to the Pacific, but had arranged a translator's job for her with SHAEF in Paris, where she would earn fifteen dollars a month more than her salary as a driver, a consideration since she was still paying off IOUs she'd incurred on Gilberte's behalf. After Mannix had disappeared into the vast belly of the ship, Ann didn't move. Oblivious to wolf whistles, she peered from gangplank to gangplank. It took her several minutes to realize that her eyes were peeled for a tall, black-haired captain.

Fool, fool, fool.

Her first morning in Paris, she rented a one-room flat. The toilet was down two flights, the furniture exuded musty odors, but the window overlooked the place Saint-Germain with its famous old church. Also she was near Montparnasse. Without unpacking the suitcase that held her earthly possessions, she set off for the American embassy. She was directed to a State Department official with a disconcerting tic, who took copious notes about her parents. His desk, however, was dishearteningly cluttered with other notes.

Forgoing lunch, she went to the rue Scribe offices of STEFMP. She found French workers packing the archives under the supervision of the only remaining American, a tall, horse-faced WAC officer whom Ann had not seen on her visits in 1944. After introducing herself, Ann explained her errand. Lieutenant Linda Dembock told her regretfully that STEFMP had been pronounced redundant now that the International Red Cross, Allied relief and various Jewish groups were tracing displaced persons. "But I can steer you to the right channels," she said. "Have you eaten yet?"

Across the street at the Hotel Scribe's restaurant, Ann told the little she knew about Horace and Dorothy's sojourn in enemy territory. As the story and the meal progressed, Lieutenant Dembock's long face became yet more equine with sympathy. "I'm on my way home next week," she said, finishing her coffee. "But an American couple shouldn't be difficult to track down. One thing I have to give the Jerries, they kept excellent records. Come by the office in three days." The restaurant had emptied out, and this remark put a *fin* to both the lunch and the interview.

"Lieutenant," Ann asked hastily, "have you any way to trace army personnel?"

"The army? You never mentioned your father was in the military."

"He wasn't. I . . . uhh. There was this captain in the OSS. He stopped writing, and I've been wondering what happened to him."

The lieutenant's mouth pursed knowingly. It was obvious what she was thinking: wartime shack-up gone sour. Raising a hand to the waiter, she called in near incomprehensible phonetics, *"L'addition, s'il vous plaît."* She turned back to Ann. "I'm only in Paris another week, so let's concentrate on your parents."

That same afternoon Ann climbed the stepped cobbles of the rue André-Antoine. She had no great hope of finding Gilberte and Michel—surely her loan had obviated their need to dwell in rat-infested basements—yet she anticipated that Gilberte would have left a new address for her. Again the door was answered by the frizzy-haired woman. "Since when," she snarled, "do *putains* leave forwarding addresses?"

"If she shows up, will you give her this?" Ann wrote her new address in Saint-German-des-Prés on a SHAEF card. The woman took the cardboard between her thumb and forefinger as though it were used toilet paper.

The following three days, when Ann wasn't translating documents at SHAEF she was tramping through Montparnasse inquiring about her parents. Dr. Descourset shook his head sadly. By now the only one of the neighbors and tradespeople to remember the Blakelys with any degree of accuracy was Monsieur Remigasse: the baker expressed disbelief that Madame and Monsieur had not returned to the fat, easy land of their birth. "They have never come here."

In a mood of stoic despair, Ann returned to STEFMP.

Lieutenant Dembock was beaming. "How's your *Deutsch?*" she asked, extending two slick photocopies.

The pair of facsimiles quivered in Ann's hands as she summoned up what little she'd absorbed at Madame Bernard's. In July of 1944, Horace Blakely, United States citizen of pure blood, had been employed as an accountant at Stroop Uniform Factory in Berlin. The second form, that of Frau Dorothy Blakely, held identical information.

She looked up with a puzzled frown. "Did internees get sent to Germany as forced labor?"

"I'm not sure they *were* forced labor. They had cushy desk jobs. And take a look at the stamp."

A swastika was surrounded by the words *preferential treatment.*

"It's so confusing," Ann sighed. "Why would they be given preferential treatment? They were enemy aliens."

"The Nazis held certain foreigners in high regard."

"Are you hinting my parents were collaborators?" Ann cried. "They were loyal Americans. Sure they obeyed the Occupation laws—our embassy in Berlin told them to! You don't know what it was like under the Nazis!"

"I'm as mystified as you," soothed Lieutenant Dembock. "The point is, last summer they were alive and well."

"But where are they now?"

"The most logical place is the Soviet zone. The Russkies are slow as molasses when it comes to processing people and papers. I've filed a request for information with them."

"That's wonderful of you," Ann mumbled apologetically. "I know how busy you are."

The lieutenant surveyed the normally ebullient Miss Blakely's slumped shoulders. More as an antidote to the young woman's distress than anything else, she said, "About that OSS captain you mentioned last week. He might have enough points to be discharged. Why not try his home address?"

Dear Quent,

I'm writing once again because maybe you didn't get my last million letters. The European fracas being history for nearly two months, I've been wondering. Are you redeployed to the Pacific? Do you have enough lucky points to go home? I don't mean to sound flip, but if I'm not flip, I'm in a mood indigo. My parents are still missing. And with the news from the camps, the Nazis turn out to have been far more monstrous than anybody imagined.

Anyway, I am vitally interested in knowing what has happened to you, hence this letter. Quent, you mean so much to me. In every possible way. Should this remark be out of date, ignore my little sentimental journey. On the less slushy side, I'm forever in debt to you for rescuing me. Without you, I might be one more grisly statistic.

As you can see from the Paris postmark, I'm back in my old stamping grounds. Don't be impressed by the SHAEF letterhead. I'm a humble translator of banally boring bureaucratic bunkum.

Hey, now for some good news. Last September I saw Gilberte, and she was terrific—if she hasn't told you her news, she will soon.

> *I am and will always be,*
> *your Ann.*

Without reading what she had written, Ann folded the sheets into an envelope, hurrying to the switchboard where telephone books from all over the United States were stacked. Looking up the main Manhattan branch of the Dejong Bank, she addressed her letter and dropped it in the slot.

The next few days her face remained permanently hot with embarrassment. Quent's vast inheritance, always a wall separating them, now was covered with mocking graffiti. *You dumb jerk! You idiot! How could you have written that slush? You're Miss Nobody and he's a multimillionaire.*

On Wednesday, the morning before Lieutenant Dembock was due to leave Paris, Ann arrived at work to find a message on her desk: *Be at the STEFMP office at three-thirty.* Ann rushed across the hall to her military supervisor, requesting the day off. She passed the morning dazedly wandering around the Opéra, then through Galeries Lafayette and Au Printemps, the large, meagerly stocked department stores nearby. At two she was already waiting in the courtyard of the building where STEFMP was housed.

Promptly at three-thirty, Lieutenant Dembock's footsteps echoed in the tunnel-like entry passage. After a muted greeting, she led Ann up the stairs to the empty office suite, unfolding two battered bridge chairs.

"It's bad news, isn't it?" Ann said.

The lieutenant's face grew yet longer and more horselike. "The papers came through from the Russian zone last night."

"Mother . . . ?"

Lieutenant Dembock rested a hand lightly on Ann's knee, then withdrew it, fiddling with the lock of her scuffed briefcase. "It's all in here." She drew out an envelope. "Ann, dear, last August your mother passed on."

"She's dead?"

"It says pneumonia. But the Jerries were big on euphemisms, especially when it came to death certificates."

"She'd been very sick twice." Ann's tongue was arid and shriveled. "And Daddy?"

"Late in 1944, he was transferred to Dachau."

"Dachau. God . . ."

Lieutenant Dembock sighed. "It happened March twenty-first, 1945." Extracting a typed sheet, she unfolded it. "Here's an interview with another prisoner. The original was in Russian, of course, so I had it translated." The lieutenant began to read aloud.

(The transcript did not include the information that Horace was one of the innumerable motes caught by random chance in the destructive rays of the Nazi bureaucracy. When Dorothy was near death, he had attempted to get medicine for her. The officer with whom he pleaded had not been issued regulations about those worthy of preferential treatment: rather than find out, he had dispatched Horace, as an enemy alien, to a slave-labor camp.)

The female voice, carefully emptied of emotion, droned through the paragraph in which the prisoner explained that he and Horace Blakely had been in the same barracks and shared the same backbreaking labor, loading barrels of strong acids.

"Daddy? But he had sacroiliac trouble."

"I still can't get it through my head how the Nazis treated fellow human beings." Lieutenant Dembock raised the paper again. " 'Horace Blakely was killed by overwork, starvation and lung-destroying fumes. I was with him at the end. He spoke about joining his wife. He was a man at peace with death.' "

Ann took the transcript. The rows of typed letters were as meaningless as the acrostics her mother (no, her late mother) had puzzled over.

How could I have left them?
They were so helpless—they couldn't even speak German. They needed me.
I'm alive because they're dead.
They're dead and I'm alive.

The guilt of the survivor, that irrational, ineradicable guilt, seared into her brain cells and the scars would never fade or diminish. Then something foul enfolded her, a dimensionless horror that clamped itself against the vulnerable new scars. She shivered violently, incapable of escaping what in earlier centuries would have been attributed to demonology, Satan risen to earth to invoke the landscape of hell. In this prosaic age, it was a gestalt of firsthand reports and newsclips of Auschwitz, Treblinka, Dachau . . .

The empty office and Lieutenant Dembock faded.

Ann was inside all that was malevolent, evil, cruel and vile, she breathed the indescribable stench of cadavers both living and dead, she tasted gray human ashes on her chapped lips, her stomach contracted with hunger that reached beyond hunger until each cell of her body shrieked for nourishment, she heard the shouts of black-uniformed SS guards, she cringed from their guns and whips, their Alsatians and Dobermans. She inhaled the acridity of chemicals until her nasal passages shrank and her burning lungs collapsed.

She didn't realize she was weeping until Lieutenant Dembock touched her shoulder. The sobs grew more convulsive. The lieutenant, who had job experience with grief and its attendant hysteria, slapped Ann's cheeks. When this measure failed, she drew the gasping, sobbing girl downstairs, hailing one of the taxis that were reappearing on Parisian streets and telling the driver to get them to the American Hospital in Neuilly.

Of those days in the hospital, only a few random sensory details would remain with Ann. The noisy sparrows chirping in the plane tree outside her window. The warm, breadlike smells of the nurse from Mississippi. The rough weave of the hospital sheets and pillowcases. Larry's forced, uneasy smile on that first visit when she'd asked him, *Am I round the bend?* She remained enmeshed in timeless heaviness, she couldn't swallow her food, words spoken to her made no impact on her brain, her own remarks trailed off in midsentence.

The heavyset major with the fleshy pouches under his eyes removed her untouched tray, pulling a chair next to her bed. "Ann," he said. "I'm a psychiatrist. Let's see if we can sort out your problems."

"Problems?"

"You do know why you're here?"

"I couldn't stop crying."

"Shall we talk about your parents?"

"They're dead."

"You've suffered a trauma."

"Are you measuring me for a straitjacket?"

"Of course not. Tell me about them."

For the next five and a half hours she told him. Obsessively. Repetitively. She told him over and over again of the sacrifices they had made on her behalf, scrimping for her tuition at Madame Bernard's, giving their meager rations to her. Her most repeated sentence: "How could I have left them?"

Seldom speaking, the major kept handing her Kleenex.

Beyond the windows, darkness had fallen. He switched on the light. "Ann, it's after eight. I have to go. But I want you to consider this. Your parents elected to stay in France. You had no part in their decision."

When he left, she collapsed back in the pillow, exhausted. His words in no way exonerated her. Her own outpouring brought no catharsis.

Yet from that afternoon on she became an actress. Miming enjoyment, she forced down whatever was on her tray. She "listened" to the bedside radio, she "read" whatever novels the Mississippi nurse lent her. She pulled her mouth into imitations of smiles, she put on lipstick for Larry's visits.

The role grew more familiar. The nurses began calling her "Sunshine." Dr. Gold, the harried internist with deep grooves in his forehead, said that she was the only patient who made him feel better.

After ten days she was released. Larry, his expression tenderly boyish, drove her home: the following Monday when she returned to SHAEF, the staff of her department welcomed her, the other two translators in her office treated her to lunch at Fouquet's. Nobody, including Larry, referred to either her parents' deaths or her haywire interlude.

In early August, she received a letter mailed that same morning from the working-class suburb of Saint-Ouen. The return address was that of a Fifo Jullien, but the writing on the envelope was Gilberte's.

Gilberte
Paris, 1945–1946

34

Fifo Jullien—Gilberte—lived in Saint-Ouen. Ann knew, of course, about Saint-Ouen's *marché aux puces*—the enormous flea market— but had never set foot in the suburb. Always impoverished, Saint-Ouen had not been treated kindly by the war. Ann passed rubble heaps that had been factories, craters where tenements had stood, destruction that paid impartial tribute to bombardiers on both sides.

Gilberte lived on the rue des Rosiers in one of the flats above a boarded-up metal shop. *Come immediately!* her note had said, and though she hadn't specified a reason for her summons, Ann, hav- ing recently translated a top secret documentation of France's towering infant-mortality rate, was positive the urgency was con- nected to Michel. She rapped loudly on the door with the hand- printed card:

MADAME FIFO JULLIEN
ALTERATIONS

So those hopes of becoming a modiste didn't pan out, Ann thought. Gilberte flung open the door. A piece of string tied back her jet hair, which had grown long enough to cover her ears. Splotches of moisture darkened her faded print housedress. Her long, slender feet were bare. As if sensing patronization in Ann's unwilled appraisal, she raised a thin black eyebrow, staring back. Immediately Ann perceived herself as a gaudy parrot in the straight skirt that she'd cut from a yard and a half of jonquil rayon and the white Swiss blouse whose fraying collar and sleeve-edges were bound with the same bright yellow fabric.

"Welcome to Saint-Ouen," Gilberte said. She gestured at an old woman asleep on the couch, her dentures on the rug beside her. "My esteemed landlady, Madame Pic. I rent the bedroom from her."

Then a child wailed tiredly. Gilberte's expression altered to naked worry and she darted away, Ann following her.

The small bedroom was jammed. Shabby, basted garments, predominantly black, hung on hooks behind the treadle sewing machine, a line of minuscule underwear and nightgowns sagged above a narrow bed while more small clothes, washed but unpressed, were heaped on the dresser.

Michel lay in his battered iron crib. "Hurts, Maman," he whimpered, rubbing the left side of his head against the sheet. His cheeks glowed like red coals. He had grown taller but was no plumper than when Ann had seen him nearly a year earlier.

"Hi, Michel," she said quietly, squatting beside the crib to smile through the bars at him. "I'm Ann. I knew you when you were a little baby."

Hiccuping, he looked at her with wary, tear-reddened eyes.

"A mastoid infection," Gilberte said, wringing out a rag in the washbowl. "Cold compresses seem to help."

"Shouldn't we get a doctor?"

"Only the tops of the medical profession practice here. The last doctor was drunk. The one before said he'd try leeches."

As Gilberte held the wet cloth against Michel's ear, his hiccups quieted into small whimpers. He dropped into a restless sleep.

She bent over the crib to touch his forehead with her lips. "Much cooler. I dragged you here on false pretenses."

"Why didn't you write sooner? Gilberte, I *want* to help."

"Staunch Ann, eternally true-blue."

Hearing her character traits dismissed with wry amusement once had brought Ann to a quick boil, but now she derived enormous comfort from the remark: of her life's fixed compass points, only

Gilberte remained. "Doglike devotion brought me here," she said, then sighed. "Gilberte, you're all I have left."

"Then you didn't find your parents?"

To avoid awakening Michel, they were whispering.

"Mother died someplace in Germany." Ann swallowed hard. "They said of influenza, but probably of starvation. Poor Mother . . . I always had to fight to keep her from giving me her rations. She got terribly run-down."

"Why was she in Germany?"

"I don't know."

"Where was your father?"

"There too . . . Oh, Gilberte, they sent him to Dachau. He was one of those slave laborers in striped pajamas. They had him lifting heavy barrels of acid. . . . But a man in his barracks said he died a good death. He was good, Daddy, law-abiding, so sweet and good. And Mother, she had this wonderful optimism, always putting the best light on everything. But you know how they were."

Gilberte, having considered Dorothy a dowdy, puritanical hypocrite and Horace an ineffectual little braggart, rested her sympathies solely with their grief-struck survivor. She touched Ann's hand. "It's rotten, losing one's parents, and especially both at once."

"It's my fault they died," Ann said, wiping her eyes. "I never should have left France."

At this, Gilberte spoke more loudly. "Spare me that nonsense. You're a rational being, Ann. No solipsism. Put blame where blame belongs. The Nazis killed your parents."

"Don't you feel guilty about what happened to—?"

"Papa and Maman? Yes, I feel guilty. But only because the person who turned my father in hasn't been punished."

"What good would that do?"

"Hocherer had a certain Gestapo captain and his orderly transferred. Also a pair of SS 'interrogators.' The quartet gave their lives for the Führer at the battle of Stalingrad."

"And did that make you feel better?"

"My, aren't you the good Christian? Yes, it made me feel a great deal better. Ann, my father's last words to me were to ask a promise I'd punish whoever informed on him. Nothing so pleasant as the Russian front for that creature."

"It seems so, well, after the fact. Futile."

"Believe me, this worm—and the entire worm family—won't feel the futility." Gilberte, who was smoothing and folding Michel's laundry, put a hand to the small of her back. "God I'm tired."

Ann attributed Gilberte's vengefulness to fatigue and worry about her child. "I brought along a few things from the PX," she said, opening her cloth shopping bag to extract a can of Chase and Sanborn coffee.

They were sipping from mismatched cups when Michel awoke with a sob.

"Michel, want to sit here?" Ann patted her lap.

He responded with an unhappy little nod, and she lifted him from the crib. Snuggling against her, he rubbed his ear against her shoulder. His stirrings and slight weight reached deep within her body until she could no longer separate herself from the child and his misery.

Ann's lively, outgoing nature decreed that she spend her affection not hoard it. She had already recognized a morbid, almost Egyptian quality to the excessive love she was lavishing on mental tombs for her parents. Cuddling Gilberte's feverish baby, she was experiencing something that, if it weren't for her clenched anxiety about his well-being, would have been release. Michel had unlocked the floodgates of her dammed-back emotions, and her love was pouring toward him.

Soon he dozed off: she replaced him gently in his cot.

"I know people at the American Hospital," she said. "I'll get a doctor."

"Your belief in your countrymen's ever-flowing bounty is touching. They won't treat the French."

"Where's the phone?"

Gilberte gave a muted, discordant laugh. "Let me look around. We have every luxury, so why not a telephone?"

"Where's the nearest?"

"Across from the flea market. In the crockery place."

The mustached secondhand dealer continued to glue together a faience bowl while commenting dourly on the degeneration of telephone service since the Germans left. As Ann waited long minutes for the operator, she silently concurred. When she did reach the American Hospital, the woman on the switchboard informed her in Parisian French that the doctors, they were all on their rounds, then cut Ann off the line.

She called Larry at OWI asking—no, begging—him to go to the hospital. "Find Dr. Gold, he'll remember me, tell him it's Sunshine. Larry, Gilberte's baby has this terrible ear infection. He's burning up."

"Kids get fevers. Take my word for it. I have three younger brothers." Though Larry spoke often of the eternal summer and easy living in Southern California, he seldom volunteered information about his family. "One or the other of us always had a temperature. Mom dunked whoever in a lukewarm tub. That snapped us out of it. Kids look way worse than—"

"Get Dr. Gold! Get any doctor!" Ann interrupted with such vehemence that tiny spots of saliva landed on the phone box.

When she returned, Gilberte had Michel in her lap. Suddenly his body stiffened and his spine arched outward. His lips turned blue. His eyes rolled back until only the whites were visible. Holding his breath while his face suffused with purple, he prepared for a shriek that when it finally emerged was as high-pitched as the cry of a jungle bird. His arms bent at the elbows, flailing like broken wings, his legs kicked with a total lack of coordination.

"He's dying . . ." Gilberte whispered.

Ann reached for the convulsing child, astonished at his slippery strength. *She's right, he is dying,* she thought, then her mind cleared and she heard Larry's good-humored soothing. "The bathroom?"

"This way."

In the bathroom, Madame Pic hunched over washing her face. Shoving the old woman aside, ignoring the whining complaints, Ann ordered, "Gilberte, fill the sink. Lukewarm water."

As the faucets oozed, Ann and Gilberte struggled to undress the terror-struck, contorting child. The chipped sink was full before they could get off his underpants. He was still wearing them as Ann submerged him.

After a couple of minutes the wild, uncoordinated motions eased. Ann murmured soft comfort, tugging off the sopping pants, holding the now flaccid baby in the water until the doorbell rang. Larry had arrived with Dr. Gold in tow.

Ann explained the convulsions.

"You did the right thing," Dr. Gold approved. In serviceable French, he said, "Michel, your mama's going to dry you and put you on the bed. Then I'll see if I can make you feel better."

During the examination, Michel lay inertly docile until the otoscope entered his left ear, then he struggled and shrieked. The doctor took a hypodermic from his bag, filling it.

"I'm going to stick a needle in your derriere, Michel. It'll hurt for a moment, but soon you'll feel better." Plunging the needle into Michel's thin buttock, he murmured to the adults, "Penicillin."

As Gilberte dressed the sobbing child, the doctor nudged Larry and Ann out to the gloomy, garbage-scented corridor.

"Now we'll have to wait and see," he said.

Ann, mildly elated at her successful treatment, took umbrage at the doctor's guarded prognosis. "What do you mean, wait? You gave him penicillin."

"It's not the miracle drug everyone likes to believe. Reactions vary. Michel's too thin—I'm no pediatrician, but I'd diagnose him as borderline starvation. If the penicillin doesn't work, he'll need to be operated on."

Ann's elation dropped from her. "An operation?"

"The bone's infected. And you can't neglect any infection that close to the brain."

35

That night Michel slept quietly under the vigilant gaze of Ann and Gilberte. He didn't stir until first light, then he lifted his head to give them a drowsily surprised look. He had stopped fretting at his ear. When Gilberte slid out the rectal thermometer that Gold had left for her, the temperature registered squarely on the red line. Normal.

Euphoric, Ann took the métro to SHAEF headquarters—she had rushed off to Saint-Ouen leaving a desk heaped with work.

The date was August 6.

She was typing the self-justifying deposition of a war criminal from Brittany when a masculine cheer went up in the corridor. She paid no attention. A minute later, a young adjutant stuck his head inside the door. "Hey, kid, there's big doings in Japan! Ming of the planet Mongo stuff! A B-29 dropped this futuristic bomb and it's totally pulverized some big city, Hirowhatsis or something. One bomb and nothing's left standing! It's not official, but everybody says the Nips'll have to surrender."

In the hall, people were embracing and bottles of champagne appeared, the corks popping joyous and loud. A deep, true baritone began singing "The Star-Spangled Banner."

"Oh, say, can you see by the dawn's early light . . ."

Other voices joined in. At this moment of impending victory, all the Americans were joined—those who had seen combat, those who had fought from desks, high ranks and noncoms, the civilian employees, and tears streamed down the cheeks of men and women alike. It was over, the war that had killed their brothers, their sons, their lovers, husbands, cousins, friends . . . the war that had embezzled four years of their lives. This bomb, God bless it, would surely put an end to the war that had devoured fifty million people and irrevocably altered the earth. Soon, soon, they would be going home.

The deep voice changed to "God Bless America," then swung into "America the Beautiful." Ann, who had never seen those alabaster cities gleam, found herself wondering whether New York, Chicago, Los Angeles could be evaporated by science fiction bombs.

Then the singing split into disorganized versions of "I'll Be Home for Christmas," "I'll Be Seeing You," "Sentimental Journey," "The Boogie Woogie Bugle Boy." Larry arrived, pulling her into his arms, kissing her.

"I'm taking you back home with me," he shouted over the bedlam. "A souvenir de Paree."

"Larry, you sentimental nut, you're blotto."

"Not entirely blotto. Listen, somebody's gotta make an honest woman of you, so why not join up with a charming, debonair, lighthearted guy?"

He bent her back in a vinous yet sweetly reverent kiss. Marry him? As the kiss lasted she closed her eyes. Behind the lids she saw Quent, a hallucination so vivid that she could make out the small chicken-pox scars near his eye and mouth. She drew away from Larry's embrace.

"What is it?" he asked. "Yes or no."

"Can that be Larry Porter? Or is my sight failing me?" boomed a red-faced captain, throwing his arms around them both, kissing Ann as he pounded on Larry's shoulders.

They were old buddies from OCS.

After five minutes of forcing laughter as Larry and the ruddy-faced captain chuckled about their snafus while learning to be officers and gentlemen, Ann slipped away. In her office, she buried her head in her hands and thought about her parents, about Quent. *Will there ever be a man who's not second choice?* She dashed away her tears as her direct line rang.

"I've been calling you and the other number there for hours," Gilberte said.

"We've dropped a new kind of bomb on Japan. They're about to surrender and—"

"The fever's up!" Gilberte interrupted. "I had to leave him! He's alone with that senile hag!"

"I'll be there with the doctor right away!" Ann said, addressing a prayer to Captain Arnold A. Gold, M.D. *Please be at the hospital.*

"I wonder how quickly," Gilberte said, "he would have rushed to Saint-Ouen if he knew who sired Michel."

"He's a good man."

"Undeniably. But how many good men who're Jews happen to love German field marshals or their offspring?"

It was three hours later. After shooting Michel with penicillin, the doctor had returned to his hospital celebrations.

"He said the infection had less pus," Ann said.

"Because of the penicillin. What Michel needs is an honorary United States citizenship."

"Maybe your family in America could invite you to visit."

Gilberte fixed her topaz eyes on Ann. "Quent's my American family."

Ann swallowed, asking what she had longed to ask earlier. "Have you heard from him?"

"Several times." Gilberte's unblinking stare did not waver. "His last letter was a couple of weeks ago."

"He's home, then?"

"Yes, in New York. Back in his old haunts, he tells me. Enjoying himself with *les femmes.*"

Ann's soft little laugh rang false. "Girls in the plural?"

"He's mentioned one particular debutante more often than the others."

"Serious?"

"It smells that way. Wife number one."

"Does he know how rotten things are for you and Michel?"

"He doesn't know there is a Michel," Gilberte said harshly.

"If you told him, wouldn't he help?"

"I despise beggars."

"But Michel—"

"Michel is a de Permont. He'd never beg either."

After Ann left, Gilberte stretched on her bed, her fists clenched.

She didn't know if Quent was alive or dead. No letters had come from him. She had lied. And was bitterly ashamed of herself.

With her emblematic self-honesty, she reasoned out her lie. She was indebted to Ann. She had been from the beginning of their friendship, when Ann had given up those girls at Madame Bernard's on her behalf—in Gilberte's mind no sacrifice, but then Ann, being Ann, could indubitably find something good in each of her jabbering, dreary classmates. Then there was the loan. Without that currency, she and Michel could not have survived. And now—Gilberte glanced over at her son, who was sleeping quietly— the lifesaving penicillin. God, how she despised being a supplicant! It was her pride, her stubborn if very human pride, that had pushed her into taking Ann down a few notches. She needed to have her benefactor a bit nearer to her own beggar's level. And she had indeed proved the full ridiculousness of Ann's adolescent infatuation for Quent—yea, verily, she had touched moisture on the large, luminous brown eyes. But knowing why she had lied to Ann did not mean absolution. Gilberte, filled with self-loathing, pounded a fist on her pillow.

Michel's ear infection responded surely if slowly to the course of penicillin: Gold gave him the last shot on August 9, when a second bomb destroyed the city of Nagasaki.

On August 15, V-J day, when the Japanese surrendered, Michel's temperature had been normal for four days.

"Shorty," Larry refuted, "there's not a chance of Gilberte and Michel getting across the Atlantic."

"The chargé d'affaires told me I could—"

"I was there, remember? Ann, you heard what you wanted to hear. He said, and I'm quoting, that though the war was over, shipping would remain tight for several years. Military personnel and certain United States civilians like yourself would have priority. Maybe in a few years, he said, when things loosened up, you could get them over for a holiday. And face it, if the chargé had known Michel's old man was a Nazi war hero"—the field marshal's part in three assassination attempts against Hitler would never become public knowledge. Gilberte had balked at telling Ann: it would have sounded like an apology for Hocherer and therefore a plea for exoneration for having lived with him—"he wouldn't have said that."

Ann sighed dejectedly. "It's all so unfair."

"I agree. He's a terrific little kid." Larry had formed a bond with Michel. On the previous day, the child, who had consistently turned his head away after a few desultory mouthfuls, had perched in Larry's lap finishing an entire can of PX Nestlé's condensed milk. "But given the circumstances, the two of them will get into the States shortly after a skating rink opens in hell."

They were walking near Ann's apartment. A fine August afternoon, students and writers crowded the exterior tables of the Deux Magots, and the warm, wine-scented air rang with passionate argument.

"Want a drink?" Larry asked.

Ann shook her head.

Larry halted, resting an arm around her shoulders. "There is one way we could get him over. Remember the little suggestion I put to you right after we dumped the mushroom over Hiroshima?"

He had not repeated his proposal: Ann had come to hope it was a gesture brought about by champagne and the day's historic excitement. "You mean about . . . ?"

"The holy estate of matrimony, yes."

Ann moved away from his arm.

"We could adopt him," Larry said.

"Adopt? Larry, you've seen Gilberte with him. She'll never give him up."

"She would if she knew it was strictly temporary. We wouldn't complete the formalities. When things improve here, we'd bring him back to her."

Ann touched his cheek. "Larry, it's very dear of you."

"Bull. I'm suggesting matrimony for the traditional reasons. When you're around, shorty, the birds sing, the bells ring."

Ann turned away, and they began to walk.

"You might as well know the worst." He spoke nearly inaudibly. "Dad doesn't have an Onyx distributorship, he sells the trade-ins, and before hostilities, not many of them. Who could afford college? I fudged about UCLA. I worked in a Standard station and took journalism courses at night at City College. And Mom dunked the fevers away in the bathtub because medical care was beyond our budget. So if you do take me up on my suggestion, all you'll have is a fun-loving liar with separation pay."

"It's not that, Larry."

"I know you don't love me," he said in a strange, humble tone she'd never heard him use. "But what's that old saying about wives falling in love with their husbands?"

She thought of a tall, handsome black-haired man in impeccable dinner clothes telling a debutante in a white custom-designed strapless about an asinine letter he'd gotten from this impossible girl in France whom he'd been trying to dump for two years. *I'll learn how to forget,* Ann thought. Marriage meant Michel would survive. Besides, Larry was a darling guy, and fun.

"Give me a little time, okay, Larry?"

He took her hand. "Take all the time you want. Take five minutes, ten, even."

"Larry and I are getting married."

"You didn't convince me to leave Michel with that toothless sow to drag me out here and tell me the obvious, did you?"

"Next Thursday."

"Congratulations. Now let's go back."

"Gilberte, I told you I'd try to figure out a way to get you and Michel to the States." A drop of summer rain splattered on the pavement. "He could go with us."

"Oh?"

"Uh, we'd, well, need to say we're adopting him."

Gilberte's hands clenched, and she asked harshly, "Three on a honeymoon?"

"Larry has a friend in the State Department who could cut through the red tape."

More drops were falling.

"And where do I fit in your little equation?"

"We'll be his foster parents. As soon as things are normal we'll bring him back to you. Gilberte, he was sick, so sick. And after we leave, you won't be able to get PX food or American doctors."

"That sounds suspiciously like blackmail."

"It's the truth, that's all."

Gilberte's face contorted, and she turned away, pretending to look at the shop they were passing, Gaston's Crémerie. There was no merchandise in Gaston's window, only a faded poster showing faded cows grazing in some pallid, prewar pasture.

"Go away," she said in a grating tone. "Go away!"

Gilberte sat watching Michel sleep flanked by his old teddy bear and the new Mickey Mouse that Larry and Ann had given him. When he was awake, his seriousness made him seem older and larger than he was. But now, with his butt pulled up, he looked small, extremely friable. She turned away. Misshapen black clothes hung around the room like omens of future mourning. The past two weeks she had missed all of her fitting appointments, and this morning a shouting vegetable woman had repossessed (without payment) the threadbare winter coat that Gilberte had relined. Ann brought nourishing food, Ann supplied medicine and if Ann hadn't paid Madame Pic the rent, she and Michel would be out in the summer rain.

Her life had no margins. Unless all the elements—her work, her health, Michel's health, the patriotic whims of her fellow Parisians —were tightly in place, disaster would overtake her. And Michel.

Dry-eyed she stared at her sleeping son. *I'll have to let you go with them, there's no choice,* she thought. A frisson of physical pain shifted through her chest. What she felt for Michel went beyond love and maternal sentiment, reaching directly to the blood that ran in both their veins. How could she survive the years without him?

* * *

Two mornings later it was sunny. Gilberte took Michel on his first outing. They walked slowly to the secondhand crockery shop. The smell of animal glue in her lungs, she called SHAEF.

"On that topic we were discussing," she started without preamble, "you'll be three on your honeymoon."

"We can take Michel?" Ann asked in that eager way of hers.

"Until things are better here," Gilberte said, and jammed the telephone mouthpiece into its holder.

Michel was staring up at her. Lifting him, she ran from the shop, carrying him all the way back to the apartment. In her room, she clutched him so tightly that he pushed at her face. "No want Maman. Down."

She held the small, wriggling body yet closer, pressing her lips to his healthily cool forehead. Struggling, he protested vociferously. Yet she could not put him down. She needed to hold him close for all the hours and days they would be apart. When he began to sob, she did too. Madame Pic, deaf as she was, opened the door. Was the baby ill again? Why all the weeping?

36

"Mademoiselle de Permont, there will be no repeats of the incident with Madame Dalmont." It was two months later and the speaker was the hard-eyed woman who called herself Mirielle Montargis. "You will not tell this client that my designs make her look like an overstuffed sofa. You will model and sell, sell and model. You will point out that the detail and beading are the *dernier cri*. Do you hear me, pretty girl?" Mirielle Montargis thrust a stubby finger at Gilberte. "Are you listening?"

She's a cheap, fifth-rate couturier who uses her models as vendeuses, Gilberte told herself. *I've lost two jobs already, I can't afford to lose this one. I've borne far, far worse.* "Yes, Madame," she said, allowing herself a faint mimicry of her employer's cadence. "I'm listening, Madame."

"That little lift of chin is perfect. A soupçon of disdain is good for business, just enough to intimidate the clientele, but not enough to chase them away." Madame Montargis gave a flip to the train.

Only someone as tall and slender as herself, Gilberte knew, could carry off this evening dress: the pointed train and the encrustation of silver bugle beads would make most women resemble an upright armadillo—but then again, it was unimportant to the tightly corseted bourgeoisie who patronized the House of

Montargis whether or not they looked like glittering reptiles: they selected their wardrobes for one purpose alone, to advertise their husbands' wealth.

"Glide," commanded Madame Montargis, leading the way to the luxurious fitting room where the alarmingly wrinkled customer sat waiting.

"Madame Treboul, allow me to present Mademoiselle de Permont," said Madame Montargis. "Possibly you were acquainted with her late mother? Baronne de Permont."

Mirielle Montargis never missed an opportunity to serve up her employee's illustrious name. None of the clients had ever met ViVi, none were privy to the *haut monde* scandal that had surrounded Gilberte's birth, but all had learned enough history in the schoolroom to be familiar with the patronym. From this day on Madame Treboul, like the others, would slip into every conversation the remark "My *vendeuse* at Montargis, Mademoiselle de Permont . . ."

Gilberte exhaled, undulating around the fitting room, with exactly the right amount of hauteur, and neither of the others had the least inkling that she was on the verge of tears. *I am not prostituting myself,* Gilberte thought. *Ann Blakely—no, Ann Porter—would consider this befriending a lonely old woman.*

The wrinkled, titillated client ordered far more extensively for the spring season than usual.

Gilberte hurried home along the rue Saint-Honoré paying no attention to the November chill or to the shops, closed for the night, dark as sepulchers behind their bars. She was immersed in thoughts of Michel. In the two months since Ann and Larry had taken him she had been like an amputee painfully learning to function again. She had made some small advances. Yesterday, though, the mail had brought a snapshot of him clinging to Ann's leg, his round, solemn eyes gazing with trust up at his foster mother. This three-by-five photograph manifested all that Michel had gained—he no longer looked frail or ill—and all that she, Gilberte, had lost. She was appalled at the force of her maternal jealousy of Ann.

With a bleak expression, Gilberte looked up at the classically pillared church of Saint-Roch then turned the corner. Her building was the grimiest on the rue Saint-Roch.

As she unlocked the front door, the whiny-voiced concierge called out that she had a visitor, a man. Gilberte began the long climb to her attic room expecting to find the big-bellied husband of a client. Three of these buffoons had discovered her address and presented themselves: each responded affirmatively to her indelicate hints that in exchange for a cash gift she would not be averse to an evening out and a "nightcap" in her room. On the pittance Mirielle Montargis paid her, she could not afford clothes, and after the Santé, what was the difference if a little more semen spurted into her?

The light went off on the flight behind her and she pressed the switch that lit the final unfinished staircase to her garret.

On the step in front of her door sat a tall, exceptionally thin American officer with his left arm in a sling. Too shocked to speak, she stared until the frugally timed light went out.

"Quent," she whispered.

She had not seen him since that rainy afternoon on the rue Daguerre. November 1941 and this was November 1945. Four years almost to the day. How many irretrievable losses had she suffered while traversing those four years?

She flicked on the light again. She had never seen him in uniform, and she wondered briefly if this was why he looked so different. Then she realized that he had lost a tremendous amount of weight—he was thin, so thin.

"I didn't mean to terrify you," he said. "But Gilberte, after the time I had finding you I didn't want to wait."

In this moment, hearing Quent's voice—that firm, low baritone, that Parisian French!—Gilberte accepted that she was still in love with him. She had loved him always. After those endless rapes in the Santé, it seemed a miracle that she could still love him like this, but she did.

She rushed up the high steps and just as the light went out again, embraced him. Under the uniform, he was emaciated, all bones. Yet for the first time since the SS had come to the rue Daguerre, she felt safe, utterly secure.

The injured arm formed a barrier between them, and from his

flinch, she realized her tight embrace must be hurting him. She pulled away.

"My God, Quent! I don't believe it!"

"Didn't the concierge tell you I was here?"

"She makes it a point of honor never to remember a name. Wait. Let me unlock the door."

In her slant-roofed attic, the light bulb was stronger. She could see that his high coloring was gone, and in the sallow, gaunt face his eyes were the enormous, sunken caves of a concentration camp survivor.

"You're all grown up. You look marvelous," he said.

"Merci beaucoup," she said with a mock curtsy, grateful for the maroon gabardine ensemble, purchased secondhand with the "gift" of the fattest husband.

"I was worried they might have hurt you in the Santé."

"That they did," she said, kicking off her wet shoes. "But what about you? That arm?"

"Gilberte, it's a long story. . . ." He turned away. "Let's have dinner."

At the Grand Vefour Quent requested that they be seated in the small, quiet room to the left of the large *salon.* He said very little, and Gilberte relaxed in her chair: she had always viewed the fact that he wasn't impelled to make conversation as yet another sign of his strength.

The waiter poured the Pouilly-Fuissé.

She held up her glass. "Your health," she said. "Quent, tell me about your arm."

"It happened at Mauthausen—"

"The concentration camp?"

"There were a lot of POWs there, but very few of our guys."

"The Germans didn't mistreat American prisoners, did they?"

"In some cases the Geneva Convention was ignored," he said offhandedly. Her father had once remarked that Quent's courage was as quiet and unyielding as the mountains on which he tested it.

"Bad?" she asked.

"It's over." He paused. "Gilberte, I heard about your parents before I was captured. It was the worst kind of blow. You know how

I admired André. And ViVi—you're the only woman I've ever seen who can hold a candle to her style and looks."

"You knew they were in the Résistance."

Closing his eyes as if a subterranean misery were rising too close to the surface and might be revealed, he said, "I knew."

"I expected it of Papa," she said. "But my mother came as a shock."

"That was why ViVi was perfect."

"I, well, I underestimated her."

Quent played with his trout. "Gilberte, there hasn't been an hour when I haven't worried that something I inadvertently said or did put the Gestapo on their trail."

Quent's motivations had always been mysterious to her. She had accepted that the code of noblesse oblige governed him, yet this knowledge had given her no insight into what made him tick. Now guilt and translucent pleading marked his face. *Forgiveness, he wants me to forgive him.*

She opened her mouth to relay the information that the family arrest had not resulted from any trail of bread crumbs unwittingly dropped by him but from a bona fide witness. An instinct froze her absolution.

"You see, I smuggled in the explosives for them. They used my last batch at the Gare de l'Est."

Gilberte was thrust back into the Santé beneath her parents' dangling corpses and Knecht was telling her of their culpability. She clasped a hand over her eyes.

"Gilberte," Quent said softly. "Gilberte, don't."

Swallowing, she composed her face. "When we've finished, take me someplace where it won't matter if I make a spectacle of myself."

After dinner, they walked on the gravel paths of the Palais-Royal gardens, empty on this chill, fog-patched night. Moving rapidly beneath dark, pollarded trees, Gilberte told of the arrest during the air raid, her voice remaining unemotional until she reached the events in the Gestapo interrogation rooms, then descriptions of torture and rape flooded out, her breath steaming in the darkness.

Yet even now, reliving the worst, she maintained enough control not to mention either the witness or her promise of vengeance.

Moving a little apart, she blew her nose, struggling to regain her composure. When she spoke again, her voice was normal. "They gave me six months for consorting with saboteurs. A profitable sentence for Wissman, the dwarf orderly. Every day he rented me out to his SS chums."

"Christ, how I'd enjoy killing him!"

"Hocherer arranged for that," she said.

"I asked him to help you."

"That he did. He got me released early, and after a year made me his mistress. Quent, I was neither willing nor unwilling. Now do you hate me?"

"God, no." He put his good arm around her, holding her loosely. When she looked up, she saw the glitter of tears on his hollow cheeks.

She felt a sudden hunger to tell him about Michel.

Later she would see this moment, this lost temporal chip, as her final opportunity to make her life whole again. But the snapshot had arrived the previous day and her pain was too fresh. Resting her forehead against his uniform overcoat, she said nothing.

As they started to walk again, she asked, "When were you captured?"

"Christmas Day, 1943. What with typhoid and complications from the arm, I was out of it when Mauthausen was liberated. Being OSS, I had no dog tags. I came to in the hospital facility at Château-Thierry and found the medics were about to cut off my arm. I cabled home. Appropriate strings were pulled, and I was transferred to a clinic in Stockholm where they do miracles with orthopedic disaster cases. So as you see, I'm intact."

"Neither of us is intact," she said.

"No, we aren't, are we?" He halted to light a cigarette. "Gilberte, I don't understand why your finances are so rotten. What happened about André's property?"

"I'm not the legitimate heir. His cousin Jean-Jacques inherited all."

"Once when I was a little kid, Jean-Jacques visited Grand-mère. I remember thinking he looked like Toad of Toad Hall."

"Exactly!"

"Hasn't he offered to help you?"

She stooped to pick up a pebble, holding it in her hand. "Jean-Jacques is a considerable patriot—now that the war's over. And I just told you I was a collaborator."

They were silent until they reached the rue Saint-Roch.

"At least," Quent said, "you didn't have a child."

There was only the echo of their footsteps.

"One of the nurses at the Frankfurt hospital was Belgian," Quent went on ruminatively. "She'd had a child by a German. She gave it to a foundling home. When anyone asked how she could give up her own baby, she would answer, 'Who needs a little *boche* around?' As far as I'm concerned, she has the same brand of patriotism as Cousin Jean-Jacques."

Gilberte gripped the pebble tightly. Because of some fault line in the geography of her soul, she felt obligated to pay Quent back for inflicting this unintentional wound. "Papa told me," she said slowly, "about the explosives."

Quent stopped walking. "He did?"

"It was the last time I saw him alive."

"Go on." He gripped her arm.

"Please, Quent . . . I don't want to make it worse for you."

The streetlight cast eerie shadows on the oval of his gaunt white face. "What did he say?" The question rang in the damp air.

"After the rape, they left us alone. Papa was in terrible shape. . . ." Releasing the pebble, she listened to it rattle in the gutter. She was crying. "Knecht . . . the Gestapo captain, he told Papa that . . . the Gestapo'd had spies on you."

"So they knew I was bringing explosives into the country for André?"

Gilberte wiped her eyes. "You're shivering," she said, taking out her key. "Come inside."

"Did the Gestapo trace the explosives through me to André?" Quent's voice rang with command and desperation.

Incapable of verbally affirming her falsehood, Gilberte nodded.

37

She sat in her room sipping the glass of her own cheap red wine that Quent had just poured for her, listening to him pace around the room—the leaks in the roof had warped the floorboards, so the footsteps creaked.

He halted. "What's this?" he asked in an odd, strangled voice.

She had thrust the snapshot of Ann with Michel into the frame of her mirror and he had taken it out. *At least you didn't have a child.* She could see his reflection. His face was bloodless and the parchment of his skin stretched over the bones of his jaw. Had he already deciphered in Michel a genetic resemblance invisible to her?

"My old school friend." Gilberte gave a false little laugh. "Remember Ann Blakely—no, Ann Porter?"

"She's married?"

"To Larry Porter. As a matter of fact, you're the matchmaker, you brought them together at our flat."

"The baby, is he theirs?"

"Not exactly. Generous souls that they are, they've adopted a war orphan." Summoning her every resource to form a slight smile, she reached for the snapshot.

He held on to it. "How long have they been married?"

Normally Gilberte would have put two and two together and connected Quent's peculiar insistence to Ann. Now, though, her skin prickling with anxiety, she thought only of protecting the secret she'd made of Michel's birth. Quent leaned backward and the bureau shifted.

"Quent, are you all right?"

"How long?" he repeated in a strained voice.

"Since September. But they were, as you Americans put it so coyly, dating. All the time they were in England. Ann somehow escaped through the unoccupied zone. Lucky for her. Her parents died in internment camp." *Am I babbling*, Gilberte wondered. *What does it matter? Say anything to keep his attention away from Michel.* "She and Larry are perfect together. Always smiling. Take my word, they'll be voted the good-natured, swing-loving, jitterbugging all-American couple."

"Are they here?"

"No. In sunny California."

"Larry's from there," Quent said. "California."

He was resting his full weight against the bureau as if he couldn't remain upright without support. *He's in terrible shape*, Gilberte thought. *I'll bet he can't see Michel's face properly.*

Firmly taking the snapshot from him, she shoved it in a drawer. "You need your beauty sleep, Quent," she said. "I never should have let you tramp around tonight. Go on back to your hotel."

After he left, she glanced at her cheap alarm clock. Nearly midnight. She should be undressing, creaming her face, her hands, her elbows and heels, readying her other outfit to wear for work. Instead, she sat on the edge of the bed, staring into the distance.

In the past hour she had lied about her son and lied about her father. Yet what importance did truth have when honesty would lose her Quent, her love, the one sanctuary remaining to her?

She dropped her head into her hands, plunging her fingers into her mass of thick, smooth hair, pressing against her skull to expel the image of his shadowed face as she'd told him that the Gestapo had followed his trail to her father.

The following evening, over dinner at the Ritz Grill, he told her he had an extended leave and planned to spend it in Paris. She cut his *gigot d'agneau* for him as he questioned her with solicitous tact about her job and how she managed. Once or twice his attention wandered but this she attributed to malaise and fatigue. His eyes were shadowed, as if he hadn't slept.

He suggested a nightcap in the hotel bar. Before the Nazis had commandeered the Ritz, this tiny bar had been one of the most elegant meeting places in the city, but now a group of half-drunk American officers were booming out the "Wiffenpoof Song" while a table of correspondents argued vociferously about the rights and wrongs of the Nuremberg trials.

"We can't talk here," he said. "Let's walk back to your place."

"Take a taxi, you mean. Quent, you look exhausted."

"I got in my two requisite naps," he said. Taking her arm, he guided her through the hotel foyer and into the harmonious square that is the place Vendôme. Circling the column, he said, "The problem is I can't find a way to put this so you won't take offense."

"Then why say it?"

"Let me finish," he said. "I'd like you to have money of your own. A million dollars."

She controlled her gasp. *A million dollars?* A fortune anywhere, but in postwar Paris, where dollars were the one hard currency, a rajah's ransom. With a million she could buy an estate in Saint-Cloud, she could establish her own fashion house, she could track down her enemy. But even with a million American dollars, she would be naked and vulnerable. Quent was her love, her refuge.

"You're right," she said. "You are being offensive." Her mind ranged over methods of utilizing the offer to bind him to her as they walked in silence to the rue Saint-Roch. She had splurged her savings on a bottle of Hennessy.

"Here," she said, giving Quent his glass. Her hand brushed his.

A faint color showed in his cheeks. Warming the glass in his hand, he said, "You always were a funny, proud little kid."

"Proud? Don't you see? It's blood money."

"Come on, Gilberte, that's crazy."

"Are you or are you not giving the money because of my parents?"

"I'm arranging what André would have arranged for you."

"Because you feel responsible for his death and Maman's."

He sighed. "Sure I feel guilty. But also I can't bear seeing you in this dump. Gilberte, you'll have enough to live quite comfortably in the United States."

Quite comfortably! How innocent the inheritors of great fortunes were about money. She went to the dormered window.

"In October," she said, "I took a jaunt to your embassy with the idea of getting on the waiting list for a visa. This mincing little official interviewed me. It wasn't easy answering his questions, especially the ones about my parents. I was idiot enough to tell him the truth about Hocherer. He smashed his hand on his desk and told me to stop right there. 'No Nazi bitch,' he shouted, 'has a hoot-in-hell chance of setting foot in God's country.' "

"What a nasty little jerk!"

"It's the truth, though." She rapped on the glass. She had glued *Paris-Soir* over the panes for privacy and the paper muffled the sound of her knuckles. "I don't have any chance of going to the States." As she rapped again, her sleeve fell back.

"Gilberte, what happened to your wrist?"

She glanced down at the thin scar, which had faded to the palest pink. "Nothing."

"I noticed it at dinner. Were you trying . . . ?"

She shrugged. "Let's just say the meeting with that nasty little man gave me black thoughts."

She had indeed attempted suicide, but earlier. It was three days after entrusting Michel to Ann and Larry that she had made a pass at her wrist with a razor blade.

"You've had a terrible time." Quent drew her gently from the low dormer to hold her.

She rested her cheek on his shoulder, feeling the chill metal of his captain's bars. *This is where I belong,* she thought. *Nothing else matters.* Arching her back to avoid hurting his wounded arm as she pressed her thighs against his, she kissed his throat lightly, then lifted her mouth to his. His breath tasted of brandy and cigarettes, his recently shaved skin smelled of aftershave. She could feel his erection. Her pulses raced, not with sexual passion but with a gambler's reckless hopes. She was risking everything in this single toss of hormonal dice. She touched the soft, slick flesh inside his mouth with her tongue.

He pulled away. "Gilberte—"

"I've loved you since I can remember."

"You're a beautiful woman, but—"

"Another rejection'll destroy me, darling."

"I care for you, Gilberte, but not this way."

"That's a lie, I can feel it's a lie." She was unknotting his tie. "Ah, Quent, if only you know how alone I've been, how terribly alone."

Stepping away, she unzipped the placket of her dress, slipping it over her head. Her brassiere fastened in front. Staring at him, she undid the snap. Clad only in her stockings, her black garter belt and black lace panties—all that remained of the magnificent wardrobe Hocherer had lavished on her—she touched her full, high breasts. The skin was velvet white, the flesh, thank God, gave no clue she had nourished a child. No stretch marks striated the flat, firm stomach below the delicately indented navel. Her long, shapely thighs lacked the sponginess that she'd witnessed in even the youngest of Madame Montargis's married clients. It was an astounding body, and she knew its aphrodisiac pull.

As she moved to Quent she saw lust and an expression rather like grief. Then, with a groan, he clutched her. She stepped backward to the bed, pulling him down with her.

"Ah, darling, darling." Straddling him, she undid his fly and lowered herself onto him.

She was at last with the man she adored, his hips rising to meet her spread thighs. For one moment the shadowed blue eyes peered into hers. Fearing that her face might reveal her complete and absolute lack of desire, she flung her head back, giving a cry of simulated ecstasy.

It was over quickly.

Sinking gracefully into his arms, she understood that although she had suffered many irretrievable losses in the Santé, she had emerged with one dubious asset. Frigidity. Never would she be the poor fly entrapped by illogical passions of the flesh, she would forever possess the immeasurable advantages of the spider who spins the sticky web.

38

He was sleeping when she awoke. She dressed, tiptoeing around, then, holding her shoes, returned to the bed. The universal blankness of sleep disguised him and whatever lay in his mind. Had she lost or won? She reached out a hand to wake him, then reminded herself that male-female strategy demanded he come to her. Leaving the saucepan of coffee on the hot plate, she tiptoed out.

Midmorning found her shivering in the *cabine,* the model's changing room, a curtained corner of the unheated atelier where the cutter, presser, trimmer and three seamstresses drudged away their lives.

"An American soldier to see you!" Her employer tore aside the dusty curtains. "A *blessé.*"

Excitement surged through Gilberte. "If his arm's in a sling he's my cousin."

"Cousin, hah! I informed him you were busy with a client. He persisted. In fact, he ordered me to get you."

"Madame Montargis, if you desire a better clientele than fat slugs who armor themselves with tinsel, you must accommodate yourself to our type of people."

Madame Montargis longed to tell Gilberte to get off her premises, but the snotty bitch was a gold mine. "I want him out!" she hissed. "I want you back with Madame Foucray."

Gilberte took her time fastening the sable-trimmed, beaded cocktail suit, then went into the warm, sleek anteroom. Quent stubbed out his cigarette, rising, cocking a black eyebrow at her outfit.

"The House of Montargis goes in for overgilding the lily," Gilberte said dryly. "In case you haven't heard, there's such a thing as work hours."

"When do you get off for lunch?"

"Today," she improvised, "I have a client booked at lunchtime. But I'll be home by seven."

"I'll pick you up."

"Do you want Madame Montargis to have a case of apoplexy? Quent, the truth is I've had three jobs since September, and I can't afford to lose this one."

"See you at the flat."

The small, tinny radio was playing and he did not hear her unlock the door. He had found the snapshot and was peering at it with painful intensity. Why hadn't she torn the damn thing up? She thought of putting him off Michel's track with a whimsical aside about Ann's crush on him, but decided to change the subject totally.

Closing the door, she asked, "Heifetz, isn't it?"

He jumped, whirling around, his fist clenching on the slick paper. Seeing her, he relaxed. "Never surprise an OSS man. It's likely to get you into trouble."

"I'll remember that little detail. Is that the Heifetz recording of Mendelssohn?"

"Good guess."

"Not a guess. Hocherer had a great fondness for decadent music."

A muscle moved by Quent's mouth. By now she had caught on that any mention of her war years whipped him. Yet her constant referral to the past was not entirely to establish her beachheads. There was enormous release in at long last giving vent to her grief and loss.

Sitting on the bed, she kicked off her pumps. "Been waiting long?"

"I came right back here."

She glanced at the few secondhand classics she'd picked up at *rive gauche* bookstalls. "Reading?"

"No, thinking." He paused. "Gilberte, has it ever occurred to you that if we were married, you would get into the United States?"

Somehow she prevented her visceral triumph from showing on her face. "Am I hearing," she asked with amusement, "a bit of polite regret?"

"I don't regret last night, Gilberte."

"Why else would you suggest matrimony like that, then?"

"I could have led up to the subject better," he admitted. "I've got a bad case of postwar syndrome."

"You're forgiven. But you must stop making these offers."

He came to stand in front of her. "Gilberte, look, I know how unique you are. With all of ViVi's élan and beauty, André's wit and intelligence. And as for me, I'm a lousy risk. Shot to hell physically —there's months of therapy ahead of me. And mentally—Jesus! Sometimes I'm a zombie, other times I'm so jazzed up I feel ready to burst out of my skin."

"Is this what is called the soft sell?"

He pulled her to her feet, resting his chin on her hair. "You're all I have left," he said, his voice muffled.

"And you're all I have left," she whispered. "I say yes, yes, yes."

The following day, Gilberte arrived at work after eleven-thirty.

"You're deducted two full days!" snapped Mirielle Montargis. "And this is your final warning!"

"I dropped by to give my notice. Wish me well, Madame. I'm getting married."

"That American 'cousin' waiting out there, is it? And here I thought you had more brains than the other girls! Don't you know these Yanks have nothing more than their easy smiles, their cigarettes, their uniforms? See how happy you'll be in a log cabin, wearing rags!"

"How kind of you to take an interest in my welfare, Madame Montargis, but I doubt it'll come to huts and rags." Gilberte extended her long, slender left hand, displaying an eleven-carat, flawless blue-white marquise diamond.

"Paste!"

"You've had more experience in beads than either of us. Still, it's hard to imagine that Cartier would pass off a fake to somebody whose family has patronized the shop for decades."

Madame Montargis's complexion attained a truly alarming shade of maroon under its coat of powder. She lifted Gilberte's hand to examine the engagement ring. "I see you have chosen your American wisely," she said. "I wish you both happiness. And when you select your trousseau, I will be delighted to take care of you personally."

Outside on the rue du Cirque, Quent said, "You look like the cat who swallowed the canary."

"Showing that old harridan my ring was so delicious. Darling, can you believe this? She actually thinks I'd buy my trousseau there!"

They had reached the rue Saint-Honoré and Quent was gazing at an exquisitely dressed young matron as she led a tiny boy into a shop called Pour les Bébés. The plump yellow-haired toddler looked nothing like Michel, yet Gilberte saw a resemblance.

"I want children," Quent said.

"How many?"

"A lot."

"Very patriarchal. Will they all be from one wife?"

He had been smiling, but now his expression changed. "Gilberte, first of all, I'm nothing like Dad."

"No multiple marriages?"

"I'm far too stodgy."

"Some might say stronger, more reliable."

"As far as I'm concerned marriage is a permanent state. And even if that weren't my philosophy, Grandfather Templar wanted eternal life for his money, if not for himself. The Trust is very inflexible, not designed in any way for the eventuality of divorce."

"Quent, what do you say to six?"

"Six what?"

"Children," she said, turning away quickly. No matter how many children she bore him, she knew she would always feel that one was missing.

Quent hailed a taxi, and they drove to the George V, where he was staying. After arranging rooms for her, he took her to lunch in the hotel restaurant overlooking the tree-lined courtyard. He had been released from the Stockholm hospital with the proviso that he take a lengthy postprandial nap. While he rested, she went out, stopping at a stationer's before taking a taxi to her garret.

Heaping her clothes on the bed, she shuddered. Every garment roused an unpleasant memory. When all her possessions were on the bed, she sat at the uneven-legged table with the snapshot and stationery in front of her.

Dear Ann,
What a wonderful photograph. Michel—or Michael as he's called in America—looks marvelous. He must have gained two kilos. The truth is, his life belongs to you two.

Her pen faltered. She peered at the photograph, shivering. It was almost a minute before she could force herself to dip her nib into the ink bottle.

I am willing to relinquish all claims on him. Forever. But I have conditions.
You must never tell him or anyone else the identity of his natural parents. You must never think of me as his mother. From now on, he will be one of the million nameless orphans of Europe.
Please write as soon as possible to tell me whether you agree to this.

Once more she picked up the black-and-white photograph, ripping it in half with a violent movement, then quarters, dropping the fragments in the wastebasket. Immediately she was on her knees, fumbling through the rubbish. Retrieving the four pieces, she put them together with shaking fingers, then bent over the picture as if her life depended on total recollection of Michel's body and features.

Downstairs, she told the whiny-voiced concierge that she could have the clothes in the attic. "I'll drop by from time to time for my mail," she said, pulling a ten-dollar bill from her purse—the American money would buy the concierge more than she earned in a month. "There's an important paper I'm expecting from California. When it comes, you'll get another ten dollars."

Near the mailbox, a barrel organ played stridently. Gilberte's hand clenched with an arthritic grip on the letter. Not until the tune changed to the "Habanera," and the organ-grinder's pathetic little monkey tugged on her skirt, did she drop the envelope into the slot.

From then on it was Cinderella time.

Quent opened an account in her name at the bank, transferring a hundred thousand dollars. "I want you to feel independent," he said.

He took her to Cartier again, this time to buy her a wedding gift. Their salesman brought out bracelets, brooches, necklaces, earrings. Emeralds with diamonds, sapphires with diamonds, rubies with diamonds, enormous pearls with diamonds. Gilberte rejected them all. The salesman picked up a large, flat leather case. "A client of ours has asked us to sell this for her. The stones were in her family but the design is ours. I believe it will suit you, Mademoiselle de Permont."

On the black velvet lay a glitter of yellow diamonds, some large, some small, connected by a web of platinum chains so fine that the lovely rose-cut gems would appear to have been dropped at random over her shoulders and bosom.

She turned to Quent. "What do you think?"

"The color's perfect with your eyes," he said.

Sometimes she shopped with him, sometimes she shopped alone. She bought three gold-and-ivory-handled umbrellas at LaFarge just off the rue Tronchet, she bought the softest leather gloves by the dozen pairs, scarves and purses at Hermès, perfumes at Guerlain, she ordered hats and shoes, she was fitted for dresses, suits, lingerie. It never ceased to astonish her that so many exquisitely made things could be obtained in a city where to her certain knowledge people starved to death, a city where shabby women and children queued shivering outside food distribution centers, and sad-eyed clerks unable to afford shoes clattered to work in wooden clogs. The drab misery from which she had just escaped forced her to accept that her love held an element of meretriciousness. Quent protected her not only from her personal demons but also from penury.

With each day she grew more accustomed to her cosseted life and, the other side of the coin, grew more fearful of losing her luxuries. When she had written the letter, she had been positive that the Porters would agree to her terms. Now she brooded. After all, they were newlyweds. Larry, with his hedonistic streak, would surely have second thoughts about being tied down by adoptive paternity, while Ann, though warmhearted and single-mindedly loyal, must nurse philoprogenitive dreams of her own brood.

Nightmares stalked Gilberte. Fearful of incriminatory mutterings in her sleep, after making love she would pull on one of her new satin negligees and hurry along the fifth-floor corridors to her own rooms.

The day after Christmas they took the sleeper southward. They were married by special license and the mayor of Antibes, who wore his sash over a tailcoat shiny with age, presented them with a string of garlic.

The first day after returning from her honeymoon, Mrs. Quentin Dejong took a taxi to the rue Saint-Roch. The concierge for once was smiling. Asking for her ten dollars, she held out a letter postmarked California. Gilberte's mouth was dry, her armpits wet, yet she restrained herself until she was back in the waiting taxi. Fumbling with the envelope, she tore the tissue-thin blue airmail paper inside.

Dear Gilberte,

Thank you, thank you.

You have given us the greatest gift, Christmas or otherwise. We adore Michael. Neither Larry nor I will tell anyone the identity of his parents. This is a solemn promise. As for keeping the truth from Michael, there will be no problem. In this country, adopted children have no access to information about their biological parents. . . .

This was the response for which Gilberte had been grinding her teeth every sleepless night of her engagement and honeymoon, so why was she reading it through a haze of tears?

"Oh God, God," she whispered. "What have I done?"

39

On April 30, the four-month anniversary of her wedding, Gilberte parked her stylish Jaguar on the boulevard Suchet, then sat staring at the borealis of colors cast by the morning sun on the shell-shaped copper canopy above the front door. Squeezing her eyes shut, she heard echoes of righteous speeches, angry shouts, snickering, heard the metallic click of scissors. Since that anguished humiliation she had avoided the home of her girlhood—had believed it unimaginable that she could ever again force herself over the threshold. But Jean-Jacques de Permont, toad-heir to her father's estate, had sent a brief letter informing her that two crates with her name on them had been discovered in his basement. The letter had crisscrossed the Atlantic, following her as she and Quent traveled to the United States for the formalities of his army discharge, then returned to Europe. Quent's elbow had not knit properly and he entered the Stockholm orthopedic hospital for further surgery, another pain-drenched convalescence. They had planned to return to New York on April 5. But on the third, President Truman had telephoned Stockholm, asking Quent to represent him at the Paris Monetary Conference, whose purpose, to work out means of stabilizing the yo-yo currencies of Europe, was top priority.

Jean-Jacques's letter had caught up with her at the George V this morning.

Over the breakfast brioches, Quent had said he would accompany her. "A lot of bad memories there, Gil. I'm not letting you go alone."

Temptation had gnawed her. With him at her side, she was instantly transformed into a shining multimillionairess impervious to doubt, fear or insecurity. Yet how could she risk having Quent with her? She might be opening a pair of Pandora's boxes crammed with Michel's things—who knew whether she could invent an excuse while holding back involuntary sobs? She was not a hysterical type, but her yearnings for her son were raw and beyond conscious control. Besides, it was possible that Jean-Jacques had retained the original staff, her ancient enemies, who would form a Greek chorus muttering of the bastard's bastard.

So she had said, "That's sweet of you, darling. But you have a meeting in a half hour at the Palais de Chaillot. And I need to practice driving." She had taken lessons on the snow-cleared streets of Stockholm. When he had persisted, she had said, "Do you want to give President Truman a black eye by playing hookey?" The president had already taken quite a bit of flack by appointing the commission's youngest member.

The sun disappeared behind a cloud, and in the sudden gloom she clutched the steering wheel, ordering herself to get it over with.

Anyone watching Gilberte Dejong emerge from the Jaguar would see an elegantly chic Parisienne—an uncommon sight in this first postwar year—casually adjusting her stone martens around the shoulders of her cream-white spring suit as she strolled to the entry. Her ring was answered by a bland-faced young manservant whom, thank God, she'd never set eyes on before.

"Monsieur le Baron asked me to convey his regrets but business has taken him away this morning."

"I imagine it was urgent," she said dryly. She had not expected Jean-Jacques to face her in the house rightfully hers!

The butler led her down to the basement and through crowded, dust-thick storage areas to a pair of small packing crates. With a start, Gilberte recognized Hocherer's calligraphic hand: *Gilberte de Permont.*

The servant picked up a crowbar. "Madame?"

"I prefer to be alone."

She waited until he'd been gone several minutes to use the crowbar. Prying up the slats of the larger crate, she found a dozen or so neatly stacked marbleized notebooks. She opened one. On the first page was hand-printed:

CHAPTER FIVE

I SURVIVE YPRES

When the light around Hocherer's door had shone until all hours she had assumed he was working on reports. *So he was writing his memoirs.* Dropping the notebook, she turned to the smaller crate without interest, fairly certain it contained more chapters. "Damn!" she muttered as she broke one of her long, crimson nails. She was still silently cursing her elderly lover and his memento mori as she peeled away the protective layer of brown paper.

Her pupils shrank as she stared. Two large manila envelopes. Each secured with unbroken red wax imprinted with the death's-head and swastika seal of the Gestapo.

One envelope was labeled:

Section IV, Geheimdienst
Terrorist acts at Gare de l'Est, October 6, 1941
André de Permont, closed case

The other envelope was labeled identically except that the typed name was Vivienne Cagny.

The basement storage room had been invaded by a hoarse, rhythmic sound. In her benumbed shock, Gilberte did not identify the sound as her own gasps. She picked up her father's envelope with violently shaking hands. It took her several minutes to break the seal and draw out the four pages of single-spaced typing. Her quivering muscles had lost every semblance of strength and she leaned her spine against a dust-covered, domed traveling trunk.

She ignored the headings, translating the first page slowly.

Having learned that Horace Blakely, United States citizen, greatly admired the suspect and possibly made a habit of following him, we deemed

*it necessary to interrogate Blakely in favorable surroundings. Accordingly
we requested the French police to pick up the wife, Frau Dorothy Blakely,
also a United States citizen. On the pretext of having her passport verified,
she was taken into custody on October 10, 1941, at 8:17 A.M. At 10:38
A.M., Horace Blakely arrived at the police station to make inquiry about
her. The police, again at our request, gave him no information, detaining
him on the same pretext. The two witnesses were then transported in
separate vehicles to headquarters at 82, avenue Foch. At 9 P.M. that same
night, Frau Blakely was brought to an interrogation room. After forty-two
minutes of questioning, it was determined that she knew nothing of the
terrorism, and she was returned to her quarters. At 11:10 P.M., Horace
Blakely was interrogated. First we informed him that Frau Blakely was
also being detained at headquarters. Agitated, he immediately admitted to
following de Permont in the hope of social contact.*

*Blakely proved a witness of the highest cooperation. He consistently
maintained he had seen de Permont enter the station just prior to the
terrorism, but then lost sight of him. He kept to the same story for the three
hours and forty-three minutes of questioning.*

*At 8:00 A.M. we returned Herr and Frau Blakely to the police station,
assuring them that if the information proved correct we would need them no
further. We guaranteed secrecy. We also offered preferential treatment
should it ever become necessary.*

Gilberte's lips formed an agonized smile at the irony of the
situation. Ah, the bitterest of jokes. While her father had risked
putting his head in the noose to get Horace Blakely out of the
hands of the police, Blakely, a neutral and therefore immune from
the Gestapo's torments, was denouncing him.

Horace Blakely?

That timid, boastful little nonenity? The betrayer?

He admitted to following de Permont in the hope of social contact. It
flashed into Gilberte's mind how often Horace Blakely had been
on the second-floor landing when her father was coming or going.
That dreadful little creature was like an idiotic teenager who
hounds a favorite film star. It was funny, yes, funny.

. . . a witness of the highest cooperation.

She whimpered as a sudden headache clamped above her eyes.
Through the staggering pain filtered inconsequential questions.

When, where and how had Hocherer obtained these secret Gestapo reports? Why hadn't he given them to her? Had he been trying to protect her from the facts? But if that were so, why store away the dossiers in her name? She shoved the rest of the pages back into the envelope, unable to read any further. Clasping both the opened and unopened envelopes against her jacket, she rushed past shadowy basement alcoves. On the stairs her ankle turned. She fell forward. The instinctive action would be to throw out her hands to protect herself, but she clasped her burden closer. A sharpness like ice touched her knee.

She limped into her mother's drawing room with its beaten bronze walls. Dropping the envelopes on the grate, she reached for a lighter. As she struck a flame she heard a discreet cough behind her. She wheeled around to see the young butler's bland face sag into premature jowls. "Madame is hurt. Might I be of assistance?"

She realized that blood was trickling down her torn nylon stocking.

"See to it that the crates in the basement are destroyed," she commanded.

When he'd left, she stared at the yellow flame with its tiny wisp of black smoke.

She had inherited neither her father's name nor his property, but Hocherer had reached out a ghostly hand. These Gestapo reports and the promise her father had extracted from her in the basement of the Santé were her sole legacy. She shut the lighter on the flame. Retrieving the envelopes, holding them tightly, she barged from the house she had not inherited.

On the avenue Foch, without realizing where she was going, she turned into the *contre-allée,* the inner road, scraping the side of the Jaguar against a parked delivery wagon. As she circled the Arc de Triomphe, a baker's boy had to swerve his bicycle out of her way, his long loaves scattering. She almost hit the liveried doorman at the George V.

In the bedroom, she slid the Gestapo envelopes into a drawer of the *garde-robe,* locking it. Still wearing her torn stockings and bloody, begrimed cream Patou suit, she flung herself on the bed gasping loudly.

She jerked up as Quent opened the door.

"Christ," he whispered.

Collecting her wits, she asked, "Why aren't you at the Palais de Chaillot?"

"It's our anniversary, I came back to take you to lunch. Jesus, Gil, what happened at that damn house?"

"Nothing. I found Hocherer's memoirs, dreadful stuff, suitable for burning."

"But you're hurt." Sitting on the bed, he pushed back her tangled hair. "Gil, you're hurt."

"Put it down to an inexperienced driver. On the way home, I braked too quickly."

"I'll get a doctor." He was reaching for the telephone.

The gray-haired hotel physician questioned her, shone his light in her eyes and cupped her skull with his hands before gravely pronouncing that there was no evidence of head injury. Dosing her with morphine, he cleansed and sutured her knee. While maids were changing the linen, Quent helped her into a nightgown.

"Thank you," she said, blinking drowsily up at him. The Mauthausen gauntness was gone, his color had returned. A tall, commanding man with hair the same true black as her own, a man whose concern showed clearly.

"You rest. I'll be in the next room."

"What about . . . afternoon session?"

"Gil, let the medication work."

She closed her eyes, listening to his firm footsteps retreat to the living room: he left the connecting double doors open.

Drugged, her thoughts came without protective irony.

Oh, God, my parents' only grandchild given over to Horace Blakely's daughter.

Ann . . .

Do I have to punish Ann, the only friend I've ever had?

The answer was unequivocal.

Yes.

Her father's final words had asked her to swear an oath of vengeance. That oath bound her—would bind her forever.

A peculiar idea came to Gilberte. The headache that had overcome her in the basement of the boulevard Suchet house was the symptom of a cancer as it began to metastasize through her brain. *The cancer's my promise to Papa,* she thought just before she fell into a dreamless sleep.

Ann and Gilberte
Los Angeles, 1949

40

The acreage had been owned by a truck farmer who raised a succulent variety of sweet corn, but the returning veterans' urgency for housing plus the generous financing the federal government offered to builders proved a far more profitable fertilizer, and the farmer sold. Instead of corn, a pastel tract sprouted. The Porters bought 109 Montecito Lane because there was no down payment, because of the superabundance of children for Michael and little Janey to play with and because the well-heeled suburb of Westwood was a couple of miles to the north so Larry could fudge geographically to say he lived there. His studied emulation of the rich Ann perceived as a sad yet endearing trait rather like a small boy's ache to play ball with the big kids.

On this particular summer evening, in her shorts and halter top, her auburn hair tumbling over her tanned, lightly freckled shoulders, she could have been an idealized amalgam of the women in the tract.

But appearances are well famed for being deceptive. None of the other wives had been born in France, none possessed vivid memories of fleeing an SS border patrol, none had an adopted child sired by a German field marshal on a French aristocrat. Not one had been inside the gates of a stately home like Greatleigh and though many had Cinderella dreams, certainly none had participated in a

love affair with a social register multimillionaire. But the neighborhood was confronted by a very obvious difference: unlike the other
women, Ann Porter was gainfully employed.

She sat with a twenty-two-by-thirty-inch sheet of sketching paper
tacked to the drafting table in the middle of the small dining room
that she had taken over for her work. Both children were asleep,
and silence ballooned the house, but beyond the open windows the
warm night was filled with sound, melancholy crickets in the new
shrubs, muted shouts from a detective show on the Fannings' new
television set next door, the distant, murmurous traffic. Though it
was almost nine Larry was not yet home. He worked for Purvis and
Associates, a small Hollywood public relations firm, and it was a
part of his job—the icing on the cake as far as Larry was concerned
—to sling the bull with members of the fourth estate while standing them to drinks at the bars of Don the Beachcomber's or the
House of Murphy or Mike Lyman's, and in the process to convince
them to mention Purvis clients in print.

At the sound of a motor coming up Montecito Lane, Ann tilted
her head, listening. The car went by the house. Stretching, she got
up to put two more pins in the rayon draped over the secondhand
dressmaker's dummy. The blouse ought to have considerably
more fullness and be made of silk, but Mr. Sever had given her a
wholesale price of $1.39 each. With a defiant glare, she pulled
more fabric over the bust. Her dream—her *fata morgana*—was
someday to design purely, by which she meant without considering
how much every inch of cloth, every seam, every fastening added
to the price. Then, reminding herself of her luck at finding any job
at all in fashion, she skimped the fabric again. When she and Larry
had first come to Los Angeles, she had taken a night class in
costume design at the Otis Art Institute. Her teacher had submitted several of her best designs to Mr. Sever, a sportswear manufacturer (what there was of a clothing industry in California centered
around sportswear) and he had offered her a job. *Part time,* he said.
By then she was pregnant with Janey and God knows Larry didn't
make enough to cover obstetrical bills, Michael's pediatrician, a
mortgage, payments on the appliances and a new Buick, the first
postwar model for which Larry had shelled out a large bonus from

his severance pay. When Mr. Sever reluctantly agreed that she could work at home, she had actually kissed his bald head.

Another car was coming up the street. This time headlights blossomed in the driveway.

While Larry washed up, she heated the spaghetti. Since the dining room was reserved for her work, they ate in the breakfast nook, which was jam-packed with Janey's Babee-Tenda, a feeding chair bulky and expensive but low to the floor and therefore safe.

Larry poured them red wine, telling her about a mishap between a client, a heavy-drinking character actress, and a columnist for the *Hollywood Reporter*, a story that made Ann laugh so hard, she nearly choked. He twirled spaghetti, holding up his fork. "Fabulous," he said. "How went your day?"

"Far more glamorously than yours. Michael refused to go to the play group and Janey threw up her liver."

"Is she all right?" he asked anxiously. Though he left the child-rearing chores to Ann, he was a worrywart about Michael and Janey's well-being—the untippable Babee-Tenda was his purchase.

"Afterward she ate her peaches and drank her juice, no barfing problem whatsoever."

He did not inquire about her work. Though he calculated on—and savored—a standard of living based on their joint incomes, her job was his albatross. Each monthly check signed by Mr. Sever transported him back to 1937, the year his father, a dourly unlikable boozer, had sold so few used Onyxes that his mother had been forced to find a job as a live-in maid: her wages had put food on the oilcloth-covered Porter table and, in Larry's eyes, also ratified his father's failure as a provider and therefore as a man.

After Ann finished the dishes, they went arm in arm to check on the children.

Janey sprawled on her back, angelically blond, with a dimple in her chin like Larry's. *Her father's daughter,* Ann thought, pulling the small, wet thumb from the cherubic mouth. Larry pressed an undone snap on her sleepers.

Michael curled in his youth bed, his light brown eyebrows drawn together, embattled and wary even in sleep. At five years old, he was an extravagantly intelligent loner. Ann loved him fiercely. And

Larry, who viewed life as an unceasing popularity contest, loved his son enough to forget his beleaguered, solitary ways.

In their maple double bed, Larry's fingertips traced Ann's shoulder, his signal. She went to the bathroom for her diaphragm.

He caressed her breasts before allowing his hands to move over her body. She had learned early in their marriage that if she caressed him in return he would brush her hand away. He sought her passivity, not her passion. She had decided that he believed her above that kind of thing. *It's my fault,* she thought. *I should have told him I wasn't a virgin.* But that confession would have involved her partner, and Mrs. Lawrence J. Porter had attempted to expunge all traces of Quentin Dejong from her memory.

Larry pressed his mouth over hers, a kiss that tasted of wine and spaghetti sauce, rubbing his finger on her clitoris. She was aroused when he moved on top—he never deviated from the missionary position. Once she had suggested entering from the rear, and for nearly two months he had not tapped her shoulder to initiate sex. She joined in his rhythm—sometimes she sneaked in an orgasm. This was not one of the nights.

He rolled over and instantly fell asleep. Staring into the darkness, she thought of his basic sweetness and how he loved Michael with the same concerned intensity as he loved his own Janey, of how amusing he could be. Rolling toward him, she curled around his back, kissing his pajama top between his shoulder blades.

Later, she would look back on this as the last uncomplicated night of her marriage.

41

When the telephone rang after lunch, Janey was napping. Michael, having established that such infantile routines were behind him, would only rest under the guise of listening to a story. Those ear infections of his babyhood, which had never recurred, lived on in Ann's consciousness. Besides, this was summer, polio season, and there had been terrifying stories in the *Herald.* To keep him stretched quietly on his youthbed she played the part of Scheherazade. Sometimes, like today, he rewarded her by dozing off. At the first ring, she hastily tiptoed out, darting across the small, sunny living room, reaching the kitchen just as the second ring began.

"Hello," she whispered breathlessly.

"Ann? Is that you?"

Silken French accent, dry amusement. The voice was unmistakable. Gilberte. They hadn't heard from her since that strange, quasi-legal letter. At first Ann had lived on the threshold of fear—what if Gilberte appeared to reclaim Michael? But the adoption papers were finalized, the years passed. Now, the fear returned so powerfully that Ann felt as if her carotid artery were being stretched taut.

Coughing to relax her throat, she said, "Gilberte. Where are you?"

"Sunny California. I'm in Los Angeles."

"Visiting?"

"You might put it that way. There's too much to catch up with on the phone like this. Can we meet tomorrow?"

"I have children."

"Children?"

"Janey, she's one. And Michael." Ann's soft voice rose defiantly. "My son! Michael!"

"Ann, you aren't thinking I'd interfere with *that*?"

"We've adopted him!"

"I can't believe that you're saying this." Gilberte edged each word with ice.

"It's not about Michael?"

"You put it in writing, if you recall, that there would never be this type of conversation."

Ann leaned against the counter, weak with the relief. "I'm pretty sure I can manage lunch," she said penitently. Jerking open the catchall drawer, she scrabbled among appliance guarantees for a pencil. "Where are you staying?"

"We've rented a house."

"We?"

"I'm married, Ann."

"Married! Tell me all!"

"Tomorrow. One o'clock. Six-ninety North Bedford, that's in Beverly Hills."

"I know right where it is," Ann said. On their arrival in California, Larry had driven her around the large homes north of Santa Monica Boulevard—north of the streetcar tracks—in Beverly Hills. *This is where we're going to live when I have my own PR shop,* he'd told her in a tone that mingled awe and hope. Had Gilberte come into her inheritance? Had she married rich?

"Mom?" Michael, sleepy-eyed, arms folded judgmentally, stood in the kitchen doorway. "You left in the middle of the story."

"The telephone rang."

"What dummy calls at nap time? It could've woken Janey." He and Ann both respected the convention that he never drowsed during story time.

Ann knelt, hugging him. "It was an old friend."

The small, sleep-warm body struggled to escape. "I'll bet she doesn't have kids."

Gilberte's hand trembled as she hung up. A long extension cord enabled the telephone to be brought onto the terrace—or, as it was called in Southern California, the patio—and she stared across the improbably green lawn to sunlight fracturing against the wavelets on the tiled swimming pool. She had waited so long, planned so meticulously, that it seemed impossible when she finally made contact she would feel anything beyond the mild boredom that a stage actress experiences at the end of a long run. So why these flutterings, this ridiculously misplaced hope for the revival of an old friendship, this anxiety about secrets leaking out?

Ann's just as eager as I am to forget Michel's antecedents, Gilberte thought. But she gave the name the softer, French pronunciation, and in bleakest honesty admitted that she would never forget he was her son, never.

A fly landed above her knee. She picked up her copy of the French *Vogue* to crush it.

"I'm back," Quent called.

Gilberte froze. Quent had said he'd be tied up all afternoon at the building site of what eventually would be the West Coast headquarters for Jason Templar Enterprises and the Templar Foundation.

His inheritance, always capitalized as the Trust, would pass on to the legal heirs of his body: it was administered by three lean and elderly investment bankers whom he and Gilberte privately called "the gray men," plus an army of accountants, real estate agents, stockbrokers and lawyers. Since the end of the war, Quent had joined the troika of the gray men on the Trust's board: he was not actively involved with Jason Templar Enterprises, which used the alchemy of wealth to produce yet more golden eggs, but spent his time administering the Templar Foundation, its philanthropic arm. At Gilberte's suggestion, they had flown out here so Quent could be *in situ* for the planning stage of the joint headquarters. This was the perfect opportunity for her to come in a natural way to Los Angeles, where Ann and Larry Porter lived. *He could have barged in when I was talking to her.*

"You're back early," Gilberte said. "The pool's winking at me. How about a dip?"

"You're on," he said. "I'll go up and change."

He fell in with almost all of her suggestions, and when he showed reluctance on issues of importance to her, she would obliquely refer to her parents or her time in the Santé to reactivate his guilts. Her circle had commented on his uxoriousness. (Bitsy Dejong Havemeier, her cousin-by-marriage, had put it succinctly. "What a love of a husband Quent turned out to be. When those standoffish types tumble, they tumble hard.")

What difference would it have made if he'd heard me talking to Ann? Gilberte asked herself. It was phase one of her plan that the Porters move onto the horizon. She wouldn't have waited this long, but she needed to insure that Ann had recovered from any lingering traces of that schoolgirl infatuation, and to be positive that she could control her own maternal yearnings, which, alas, time refused to obliterate or diminish.

"Ready?" Quent asked, extending a hand to help her up.

She averted her gaze. She seldom looked at him when he wasn't fully clothed. He was a well-built, muscular man, but his left arm from the shoulder to just above the wrist was roped with hard, red flesh. He'd volunteered only that the injury had occurred at Mauthausen, and because the scars repelled her, she had never delved further.

He climbed to the higher diving board, twisting down in a perfect half-gainer. She lowered herself from the edge. As his head came up, she said, "I spoke to Ann."

He tilted his head, pushing his palm against his ear to get out the water. "How is my cousin?" he asked.

He'd assumed she meant Anne Dejong Mayhew. Gilberte's extensive tribe of in-laws had introduced her to their circle, and even an occasional whisper of the old scandal of her birth did nothing to push her from this, the epicenter of American society. Her blue silk date book was filled. The women admired her clothes, and the men admired her breasts, both sexes admired her accent, her jewelry, her florist, her decor, her dinner party menus and—first, last and always—they admired her marriage. *They'd have admired a baboon if Jason Templar's heir had married one,* Gilberte would think, but then it was a characteristic of hers to inwardly denigrate any goal that she had achieved.

"As far as I know she and Fitzy are still on their boat in the Caribbean. No, I meant Ann Blakely—Ann Porter. My old friend from school. She lives out here."

Quent had been ready to climb out and repeat his dive: his hands tensed on the tubular rail of the steps. "Oh, Ann Porter. That's right, she lives in Los Angeles."

"She and Larry, yes. She's coming to lunch tomorrow."

"Sorry not to join you, but I'll be tied up."

He never intruded on her daytime activities. Gilberte didn't pursue the oddness of the remark: although she knew the keys to turn with Quent, she had never really understood him. She began swimming laps.

Before eleven, Ann took the children across the new black asphalt driveway to Mitzi Fanning's. Janey settled into Bobby Fanning's playpen without a whimper. Michael glared at Debbie Fanning, who was also five, scowled at Ann as if she were a criminal, and refused the carrot stick with peanut butter that Mitzi offered him.

"You're saving my life, Mitzi," Ann said as Mitzi handed her the keys to her old blue DeSoto.

"Gawd, think how many times you've taken *my* demons. I can't wait for a blow-by-blow of the reunion."

Returning to the empty house, Ann took off her white shorts and the sleeveless blouse with a rickrack yoke—Mr. Sever had turned thumbs down on the blouse because of the expense of this trim—and stood staring into her half of the closet. She had designed and made every garment hanging here, and now everything seemed loving-hands-at-home to her. It was important how she looked. After all, clothes were the armor she was donning to defend Michael—though often far too trusting, Ann did not fully believe Gilberte's avowed disinterest. She took out the black silk she wore when called upon to impress Larry's clients at expense account dinners, immediately rejecting it as too dressy. Her celadon green piqué, which turned her auburn hair a true red, had been let down to conform with the New Look: the line of the old hem scarcely

showed, but she was conscious of it. That left what Mr. Sever
referred to as *shlep* clothes, and her new pale blue linen. Ann had
bought the linen remnant for almost nothing, otherwise she never
would have chosen such a washy shade of blue. But there was no
other choice. After showering and dressing, she examined herself
critically in the bathroom mirror. Then, catching sight of her worried frown, she pulled both earlobes, crossed her eyes and stuck
out her tongue, laughing at herself.

In the Porters' tract, summer had browned the grass, but in this
part of Beverly Hills, heartland of Larry's aspirations, gardeners
turned on the elaborate sprinkler systems often and long, keeping
lawns a vivid green. Because this real estate was so overpriced,
each lot was jammed. Pillared, antebellum mansions like Tara
crouched between copies of the Alhambra and turreted châteaux.
Gilberte's half-timbered Tudor manor was the largest house on
Bedford. Ann pumped the brake vigorously, the only way to halt
Mitzi's DeSoto. She rotated her shoulders, drew a deep breath and
gripped the zinnias she'd plundered from her backyard.

Gilberte answered the door in an outfit similar to the one Ann
had been wearing earlier—but Ann was knowledgable enough to
realize that the simple blouse and pinch-pleated linen shorts came
from a top designer and cost maybe a hundred times what her own
would have retailed for. Gilberte thanked her for the flowers, setting them on the hall credenza, which was graced by sprays of
cymbidium—Ann had previously seen orchids only in corsages.

As she glanced around her expression was wary. "What a lovely
house," she said. In the two-story hall, the words sounded hollow
and inadequate.

"Ann, stop behaving as if frogs and toads are going to rain
down. I'm in California, I missed you, and that's all there is to the
invitation." Gilberte raised a hand. "I swear on Rabelais's grave."

One of the oaths they had invented on the rue Daguerre.

Ann burst into laughter.

"Did I forget to warn you to wear shorts?" Gilberte asked.
"We're eating by the pool."

42

Inside, each piece of dark, Italianate furniture massively conveyed its cost, but the garden was another story. On the patio, cheerful red and white Martha Washington geraniums, the most ordinary of Southern California flowers, exuberantly overflowed big terra-cotta pots while the chaises and chairs were padded with a naive Klee-like fabric. Three primary-colored beach balls bobbed in the pool.

"It's so pretty and fun out here," Ann said.

Gilberte went to the little wrought-iron rolling bar. "The place came furnished so we have to put up with those god-awful reproductions." She handed Ann a vodka and tonic. "But flesh and blood can bear only so much. We bought a few garden things."

"We, again the mysterious we—tell me about your husband."

"First, where did you get that dress? It's the most smashing thing I've seen this season, and I was at the Dior showing." Gilberte's head tilted appraisingly. "It's those big white buttons down the front."

"Oh, this? Just a little something I whipped up."

"You *made* it? A *Vogue* pattern?"

"Actually it's my own design. I'm a professional—that is, I pick up some extra cash at it."

"You can't kid me."

"No, really."

"Impossible! You couldn't manage without me to point out the error of your ways."

Ann laughed. "For that I have my boss. But Mr. Sever never makes remarks like 'That's hardly the thing for a regatta.' He says, 'What're you trying to do, ruin me with those fancy buttons?' "

"But doesn't he want style?" asked Gilberte, creasing her brow with befuddlement to show the delightful pecuniary ignorance of the ultrarich. A feigned expression. She had a four-and-a-half-page report from a local private investigator detailing Ann and Larry Porter's financial lives. She knew what Isadore Sever paid Ann and what Neil Purvis paid Larry, knew that Larry regularly exceeded his expense account, knew that the monthly mortgage check for the Montecito Lane house was $81.75, that Ann was improvident about collecting the loans she made to neighborhood wives while Larry was magnetized by every type of pleasurable extravagance.

"Sure Mr. Sever wants style," Ann said. "But at a price. His big sales are to Lerner Shops, that's a low-end chain."

"You work *and* manage your children. Ann, tell me about them."

"Michael?" Ann faltered.

"Of course."

"Gilberte, I would have written about him, but—"

"Why would you have written?"

"Because . . ."

As Gilberte leaned forward to grip Ann's wrist, the sunlight caught blindingly on her sole jewelry, a wedding band of diamond baguettes that covered her ring finger to the first knuckle. "Is this your idea of keeping a promise?" she hissed. "There is no reason you would have written to me about *your* son. I have no connection to *your* son. None. Do you understand?"

Ann could not look away from the cold topaz eyes. "You haven't told your husband about him," she whispered. "Have you?"

"No. And I'll kill anybody who does." The harshly muttered threat did not sound like hyperbole. Then Gilberte's grip loosened and she sat back.

A blue jay landed on the lawn, chirping its pugnacious call.

After a few seconds, Ann said, "Both Janey and Michael are monsters."

"Ann, this is me, Gilberte. I can see those darling buttons of yours bursting."

"No, they really are," Ann said, launching into innocently proud maternal stories that proved Janey's charm by her willful baby ways, and Michael's cleverness by his childish crimes.

They had finished their drinks when a Filipino manservant wearing a white jacket came to stand respectfully at Gilberte's side.

"Lunch is ready, Mrs. Dejong."

Ann's large blue tumbler slipped, fortunately not to shatter on the flagstones but into her lap. Bending her head as she dabbed her cocktail napkin at the stains, she said a bit too brightly, "How could you let me blabber on while you sit on this juicy news? You and Quent, married?"

"But I assumed you knew and were playing coy, asking about my mystery husband. It was in all the papers." One announcement only. The Dejongs belonged to a class that believed one's name should appear in the paper only at birth, at marriage and at death. "There'll be no shortage of lunch-table conversation, will there? First, though, would you like to freshen up?"

In the powder room, Ann's carefully composed smile melted and her face grew white and rigid as a Noh mask. *Why this feeling that Quent's betrayed you? What a dog-in-the-manger attitude. After all, you're married too.* Yet, and this was an undeniable if shameful fact, she never would have married Larry had Gilberte not told her about Quent, discharged from the army, giving a serious whirl to that New York debutante. Sooner or later, though, Quent Dejong would have been serious about somebody, and it sure wasn't going to be a SHAEF translator. And why not Gilberte, an aristocrat like himself? Only a visionary daydreamer of Ann Blakely's caliber could have romanticized a brave generosity performed because of her resemblance to his dead mother plus a few hot wartime couplings—most of them initiated by her—into the love affair of the millennium.

She carefully tissued the smudgy mascara from under her eyes.

Gilberte was waiting in the hall. Leading the way back to the patio, she said, "We're having a very simple meal, a little shrimp salad. I hope you don't mind."

"You're talking to a woman who lunches like royalty. Peanut

butter and jelly sandwiches five days a week," Ann said. "When did you get married? Engaged?"

"A true-life fairy tale."

Beneath a brightly colored umbrella, eating huge, marinated prawns on ivory endive, Gilberte wryly described how Quent had rescued her from the clutches of Madame Montargis. Ann maintained a brightly vapid yet convincing smile. The houseboy brought sherbets shaped like their flavor, a lemon for Gilberte, a peach for Ann.

"So you remembered how I used to hunger for peaches. Is Quent still a banker?"

"He's on the Dejong board, and also on the board of Templar Enterprises, but he's most active in the Foundation, which gives away a good portion of the money earned by Templar Enterprises. We're out here because he's planning the West Coast headquarters —the land's on Wilshire Boulevard in Beverly Hills, the building'll be the largest in the city. He's forever traveling in search of worthy recipients of funds. I'm not complaining. Actually, Ann, I'm proud of my husband. Imagine *me* confessing to a feminine idiocy like that! And without even a trace of irony! I'm honestly proud of him, he does an enormous amount of good. Sometimes I wish *I* had a more engrossing occupation than selecting patio furniture."

"It's called being a wife."

"I envy you your designing."

"And what a glamorous life it is. A ten-by-ten studio—it's really the dining room—and night hours, after the children are in bed."

"We both want a family. But so far, nothing. Oh, well, the trying's not *too* onerous."

Ann had visions of Quent entangled with Gilberte's slim body, his hands on those voluptuous breasts whose cleavage was visible in the unbuttoned top of the white blouse, of his caresses trailing up and down those long, slim, tanned thighs. Glancing at her goldwashed Bulova, she said, "Three already? Gilberte, I have to go."

"So soon? We haven't had coffee."

"In my neighborhood, parking children too long is a criminal offense."

At the front door, Gilberte said, "We must do this again. I'll be in touch."

Ann, positive that the final remark was strictly social, responded, "Marvelous!"

She turned right on Carmelita, driving the few blocks to El Rodeo Grammar School, which was closed for the summer. Parking next to the schoolyard's chain link fencing, she covered her face with her hands. The positive side of the lunch, that Gilberte had no designs on Michael, should have far outweighed the news of the marriage, so why this deluge of ragged tears?

Gilberte remained in the doorway long after the greasy exhaust from the jalopy had faded. She had primed herself to hearing about Michel—Michael—in his new life as an American boy, Ann and Larry's son, but she had been completely unready for the warmth and simplicity of the old affection between Ann and her. Until now, she hadn't comprehended the striving implicit in all her new friendships—or her power struggle with Quent. Being with Ann was like drifting on an air mattress across the swimming pool. Easy, relaxed, free.

She's Horace Blakely's daughter, Gilberte told herself, and slammed the front door closed. In the dim hall, she caught sight of the brilliant splash of zinnias.

"Joaquin!" she called. "Get rid of those weeds!"

"No," Quent repeated.

"But what's wrong with seeing the Porters? It's not as if we're booked up in California."

"I prefer not being booked up."

"Don't I know it!" Gilberte said dryly. Quent's desire for quiet evenings at home provoked most of their battles.

He lit a cigarette. "Did I tell you? I've cut down to a pack a day."

Nodding, she sipped her coffee, and let the Porter matter rest for the time being.

"I do feel rather bad . . ." Her voice trailed away.

"About tonight?" Quent asked. "I thought I was the antisocial one." They were dressing to go to dinner with some people from the Magnum studio, whose films the Dejong Bank financed.

"No, I was thinking of Ann. She was wonderful in my bad time—

both of them were. Will they think I'm snubbing them because they live in some dreary little tract house?"

He pulled on a black-ribbed silk sock, and said nothing.

Quent lit his postcoital cigarette. The curtains were open and the full moon glazed their naked bodies.

"This'll be the most difficult smoke to give up," he said.

"Quent, it was wonderful for me, and I vote you a little reward." Gilberte kissed his shoulder, then sighed. "Ann lent me money."

Her neck was on his arm. She felt his bicep muscles tense. "When?" he asked.

"Right after liberation."

"You never mentioned it."

"I didn't, no." *Because it involved Michel.* "When my head was shaved and I was living in a Montmartre cellar—actually a cave with one wall cut from the rock—God, it was cold down there. Her three hundred dollars rescued me. It must've been a lot for her."

"Did you pay her back?"

"I'm ashamed to say no. We were out of touch for years, and now it'd be an insult."

"Maybe we ought to see them," he said in a neutral tone.

"It'll only be once or twice, then the whole thing will die a natural death."

43

The following week, Gilberte phoned to invite the Porters to "a casual Saturday night supper."

Ann pressed the black telephone tighter between her ear and her shoulder. Seeing Quent again would be punishment enough, but spending an evening, now or in the future, with that indisputably married couple, Mr. and Mrs. Quentin Dejong, would constitute the most grotesque form of torture. She stumbled in with the one excuse able to bear the weight of permanency, the truth. "We can only do the big splurge for a baby-sitter when something comes up with Larry's work."

"What about the good neighbor who took over last week?"

"If we take Michael anywhere to sleep, he gets difficult." About as accurate as calling a ten-Richter-scale earthquake a tremor. "I'm sorry, Gilberte. But right now social evenings are just plain impossible for us."

"If anything happens so you can change your mind . . ."

"Yes, of course I'll call," Ann mumbled.

"What a day." Larry poured himself a Pabst. "My ass is dragging." He detailed his shepherding of Rosia Highwood, the Broadway actress, through a maze of morning, afternoon and cocktail interviews. Not until Ann flipped the burgers onto the buns did he ask, "How went it on the home front?"

Mr. Sever had okayed the blouse without modifications, but she did not relay *that*. Instead she informed him of Janey's new tooth, Michael's fisticuffs with Debbie Fanning, ending up, "Oh, and Gilberte called."

Larry's beer splashed. "About Michael?"

"I told you, Larry. Her main fear is that *we'll* talk." Ann set the coleslaw on the table. "She just wanted us to come to dinner Saturday night. I told her no, of course."

"By that 'of course' I suppose you mean you went into your soft-shoe routine about me not being able to afford a sitter?" Larry dashed beer from his chin.

Ann tried not to look at him. She understood that in his mind any suggestion they ought to put the brakes on monetarily proved his inadequacies—he longed for her to pretend both in private and in public that they could afford any luxury they desired. *Larry's changed,* she thought. But she knew that he hadn't: during the war he'd always behaved as if the best restaurants and the splashiest parties were his birthright. After visiting the crude, box-shaped, termite-ridden little bungalow in Van Nuys and meeting her bird-nervous, wrinkled mother-in-law who talked of nothing but what was on special at the supermarket and her alcoholic father-in-law who held his knife in his fist, she understood Larry's problem. But she still couldn't bring herself to invent excuses (as many of the neighborhood wives did) for skimping.

"Larry, dinner's on the table."

"What's with you? I've told you often enough that Templar's going to use a local PR shop to spread the word about their new complex."

"They will?"

" 'They will?' " he mimicked. "You're too damn occupied with your own hotshot sewing to listen to one word I say!"

He hadn't, of course, said anything. Nobody knew whether or not Jason Templar Enterprises, all of whose divisions kept a notoriously low profile, or the almost as reticent Foundation, would publicize the new West Coast headquarters, but every flack in

California agreed that if the press were so favored, Templar's own department rather than an outsider would do the job.

"I'm sorry," she said repentantly. "Please, Larry. The food's getting cold."

Larry took his time opening another bottle of Pabst, bringing it to the table. "I'm sick of eating in the kitchen like some kind of servant."

Putting down her fork, she looked across the table at his boyishly desolate expression. "Larry, I left it loose with Gilberte. I'll call her back."

"Why bother? You already told her I'm a big fat zero, haven't you? Or do you have in mind to make her stew over the incompetent she dumped her kid with?"

Ann jumped to her feet. "*Shut up!*" she whispered harshly.

Before this neither of them had ever mentioned Michael's parentage above a whisper, and these infrequent murmured conversations invariably occurred in bed. A restless sleeper, Michael could pop in at any minute.

With a stricken expression, Larry rose, stalking from the kitchen. A few seconds later, the front door shut noisily.

"Gilberte, I know I'm calling late. But is that invitation still good? If you still want us, we can come."

"Want you? You've just saved my marriage. If you could hear Quent on the dullness of California!"

The luminous green hands of their alarm clock showed two thirty-five when Larry's new Buick returned.

She switched on the bedside lamp. "Hi."

He grinned sheepishly. "Sometimes I'm a dumb shit, aren't I?"

"Let me give that question a moment's thought," she said, getting up to kiss his nose. He smelled of bourbon as well as beer. "I called Gilberte. It's on for Saturday night."

"Shouldn't we have brought candies or something?" Larry worried as they turned north on Bedford Drive.

"No. We should not," she said, clasping her gloved hands yet more tightly on her black silk lap. She was nursing her own anxieties. What if she fainted like some tightly laced Victorian maiden when she saw Quent, or burst into tears?

"Look at all these cars, will you," Larry said, whistling. "Somebody's having a big blowout."

The lights blazing at the Dejongs' windows told them who.

The Filipino houseboy opened the door. Gilberte, seeing them, excused herself from a group—could that mustached man on whose arm she was resting her hand be Clark Gable?

"Larry," she murmured, kissing his cheek. "A long time, a very long time. It's marvelous to see you. And Ann, that dress is gorgeous! Another Porter original?" She gestured at the crowd. "You inspired me to have a few other people."

Taking each of the Porters by an elbow, she guided them down two steps into the brightly lit living room, introducing them to casually dressed people whose names if not their faces were known. It *was* Clark Gable. In dizzying succession they met the film actresses Rain Fairburn and Ingrid Bergman, then the director William Wyler. The guests, famous or otherwise, greeted them cordially before returning to their own bantering conversations. Ann couldn't help glancing around—where was Quent? She decided he must be outside. But when Gilberte led them onto the patio, where the dinner buffet was being set up and waitresses offered trays of steaming, fragrant hors d'oeuvres to the noisy mob, he was still nowhere in sight.

After presenting the Porters to the novelist John O'Hara, who sounded drunk, an Oscar-winning screenwriter and a lanky young British earl, Gilberte left them. The guest list took Larry's breath away—none of Purvis and Associates' clients were instantly recognizable. And Ann, also bowled over, was further burdened by an acute case of nerves about seeing Quent—where was he? A less sociable couple would have clung together, floundering, but within a few minutes the Porters were part of two separate conversational groupings.

"No, we don't have one yet," Ann said, referring to a television set.

"Ah-hah, my kind of gal," boomed Joshua Fernauld, the Oscar-winning screenwriter, raising his thick gray eyebrows. "A purist."

"An impurist," Ann laughed. "The minute we have some spare cash, we intend to buy . . ."

The soft, moistly warm air had been sucked from the garden.

A tall man was emerging from the shadows at the far end of the patio. At first her mind refused to admit this was Quent. Not because he had changed so much but because these past six years she had imagined him in each tall man she'd glimpsed. What a blind idiot she'd been. Who else had this very black hair, the ever so slightly arched nose, the ruddiness of tanned cheeks? But he *had* changed. During the war he had been a boy, she realized, and this was a man, a man whose bearing proclaimed him accustomed to power as well as privilege. She was positive he saw her in that first raking glance. Yet he moved in the opposite direction, greeting a cluster of guests.

She forced herself to look away, pretending attentiveness to the talk of television programming, which, since there were so few sets, remained sparse and crude.

Then there was his voice. "Hello, Ann."

Emotions raced through her body so powerfully that she wondered if she glowed with their electric force.

"Gilberte mentioned she'd invited you and Larry. It's been a long, long time." He spoke rapidly, glancing over her shoulder.

The excitement flickered. She made a glottal sound that could be construed as agreement. Yes, it had been a long time.

"I just talked to Larry," he said. "You have children."

"Two. . . ."

"The baby boom," he said.

"A boy and a girl."

He wasn't listening. He was smiling broadly at the screenwriter. "And Joshua, I've been looking for you."

"Quent, mine host," Joshua Fernauld boomed.

"I'll have to drag you away. There's somebody I want you to meet." To Ann, he said, "We must catch up later."

And the two tall men, one gray-headed and corpulent, the other black-haired and well built, moved into another, larger grouping.

The voices and laughter in the garden had taken on a malevolent intensity. Ann couldn't bear another minute of the assault on her eardrums. She needed solitude. The pool deck was circled by tables, each with its luxuriant display of floral exotica. A loudly raucous line edged along the buffet, where caterers presided over vast roasts and chafing dishes a yard in diameter. No privacy out here.

She went inside. A half-dozen or so men were earnestly talking movie business in the living room.

The library was empty. Closing the door, she slumped in a chair, inhaling deeply to ward off tears.

The knob turned, and even before the door opened, she knew it was Quent.

"So here you are," he said with a cold smile.

She improvised, reaching for a heavy art book. "I wanted to see this, it's Van Gogh."

He was fishing in the pocket of his navy blazer. "This is yours," he said, extending a narrow slip of serrated pale green paper.

"A check? I . . . I don't understand."

"Gilberte said that after the war you floated her a loan. Three hundred, wasn't it?"

Ann blinked, wondering whether this subnormal emotional temperature and commercial tone were how he dealt with those applying for Foundation funds.

Forcing brightness, she said quite honestly, "I've forgotten."

"Was it more?" he asked.

"Who can remember? I'm rotten at numbers."

"No problem to tear this up and write you another."

Once he had held her naked in his arms and said he loved her. Well, wasn't that the correct phrase for an impeccably mannered man to use in that particular circumstance?

"How much was it?"

"There's no need to pay me."

"I dislike debts."

"Three hundred."

"Amen, then," he said, and with an aloof little smile dropped the check on a lamp table.

Alone, she tore the pale green paper violently, dropping the confetti-sized pieces in the caviar-bead evening purse that she had bought from a manufacturer in the same building as Mr. Sever. After that, she sat shivering, the book unopened on her lap. When she heard the guests begin to trickle back inside, she went to find her husband.

"Larry, I've got this headache."

"Ask Gilberte for an aspirin," he said.

"A real killer."

"That's what you get for drinking so many martoonies," he chuckled. "Drink some coffee, shorty, you'll feel better." He hurried after a squat, powerfully built man called Art Garrison who owned Magnum pictures. Larry was accumulating a dizzying number of names to drop.

The following morning, Sunday, Ann woke with a fever, aches, shivers. Her physical symptoms were firmly tethered to the emotional thrashing she'd suffered the previous night. Larry, however, diagnosed her illness as a case of summer flu. "And I made you stick it out until the end," he said repentantly. The next few days he came home early to help her put the children to bed. She had no appetite, so he bought her handpacked, ultrarich Wil Wright's ice cream, her favorite—one pint cost more than a fluffily stabilized half-gallon square Value Pak from a Van Vliet's supermarket.

By Thursday night, after her temperature had remained normal all day and evening, she had reached the conclusion that this illness marked a watershed in her life.

The Dejongs' Saturday night dinner had been the long overdue boundary between adolescence and adulthood. Resting in her bed whenever the children gave her a chance, she cringed from the image of Quent's smile. He was undeniably brave, but also a coldly unpleasant man who, for reasons embedded in his own subconscious, possibly her resemblance to his mother, had ferried her out of wartime France. Beglamored by his wealth, looks and a few incidents of wartime lust, she had clothed him in shining armor, then become infatuated with the glitter.

By Friday, her fever was gone and she felt strong, healthy, cleansed and mature.

In light of this new maturity, when Gilberte called to suggest lunch, she no longer waffled. What did it matter if she bumped into Gilberte's snob of a husband? She called Mitzi about baby-sitting dates, then dialed Gilberte back to accept the invitation.

44

Gilberte led Ann to a small, darkly paneled den whose somberness was increased by the tall cypresses that blocked sunlight from the narrow Tudor windows—a room more appropriate to men smoking cigars over business deals than to ladies' summertime luncheons. But Gilberte had no intention that this be a social afternoon. The time had come to instigate her plan. *It's going to be tricky,* she thought. And the trickiest part would be to zealously discipline her reactions to Ann, and to Michel. Opposite the desk, a gilt-framed mirror reflected the disparity between her inner turbulence and her casual smile.

"Before I start," Gilberte said, "give me your promise not to immediately turn me down."

"It's something sordid, isn't it?" Ann did her Groucho imitation, rolling her eyes.

Gilberte laughed. "No. An honest venture. I have in mind we should go into the rag trade."

"The what?"

"If you could see your face!" Gilberte laughed. "I intend to go into women's wear."

"Women's wear?"

"High-fashion *prêt-à-porter* for the American woman who can't afford Mainbocher or going to Paris—there's a lot in my circle, even, who want style and good fabric, but can't afford haute couture."

"You've knocked the breath out of me. But why? I mean, Gilberte, women's fashion is a rough, tough free-for-all. Ulcer country."

"I'm at loose ends. The other night you saw the full extent of my life—"

"This may come as a shock," Ann interrupted, "but there are some misguided souls who do not consider it the depth of adversity to lavishly entertain movie stars."

"Hollywood people! And New York's equally delicious. Oh, for God's sake, Ann! Charity board meetings interspersed with lunches at '21' and appointments at Elizabeth Arden aren't exactly my idea of fulfillment. And thus far nothing's come from the baby-making endeavors."

"What do the doctors say?"

"Next week I'm seeing a learned specialist. No more digressions, *s'il vous plaît.* It's beyond me why you're in a state of shock. Wasn't I always fascinated by fashion? And there's room for an American-French look—or should I say a French-American look. Witty, not too serious, yet *très elegante.*"

"But where do I fit in?"

"Isn't it obvious? I need a designer."

"Gilberte, you've forgotten more about style than I'll learn in two lifetimes."

"Knowledge and execution are different entirely." As Ann began a disavowal, Gilberte held up a long, slim, silencing hand. "In Paris before I enslaved myself to Madame Montargis, I was briefly an *arpète* at LeVos—yes, *c'est vrai,* for a few days I picked up the pins, the lowliest of the low. Then, heart pounding, I showed my sketches to the great designer himself. He thumbed through them, pulling a face as if I'd dropped a heap of *merde* in his office. No flair, he said. No freshness. No individuality. Oh, I was devastated. As you well know, one of my less attractive traits is a need to avenge a slight. Preliminary sketches for his spring showing were tacked to the walls, and I went around pointing out overdone details and unflattering lines. '*D'accord,*' he agreed. 'And there, Mademoiselle, is where your gifts lie. You are a born critic. Like the rest of that breed, you lack creativity—you lack every trace of creativity.' I can still hear the mincing dismissal in his voice. It hurt, I can tell you it hurt. Although I needed the job to eat, it didn't faze me at all when LeVos added that I was fired." The story was true and Gilberte winced in retroactive pain.

"LeVos is human," Ann said softly. "Even he can make mistakes."

"Ann, he was absolutely on target. I can't create something where nothing existed before. Remember? You always sketched. And I corrected the sketches."

"We were girls."

"Will you stop quibbling? Believe me, this isn't an exercise in self-denigration. My eye is excellent, and that's rare, exceedingly rare."

"Why me? You need somebody with high-fashion experience."

"Your clothes have a flair. They're fun, they're different. Of course they're a trifle obvious. Those buttons, for example, should be smaller, and real mother-of-pearl. The scarf as a belt is an innovation, and lively. But Ann, not in rayon, *jamais de rayonne.*" She tapped her nail on the desk. "That wild-and-woolly creativity needs shearing, Ann, and I'm the one who can do it."

"One thing. If you go ahead, you don't have to worry about backing, not with Quent." Ann prided herself on the ease with which she said his name.

"Quent hasn't a clue in the world what I'm up to. The capital is my own." The hundred thousand dollars he had given her before their wedding had been accumulating interest.

"You mean you haven't even discussed having a career with him?"

"This isn't the fifteenth century."

"That's where most men live," Ann said, on the brink of divulging her own spouse's shame of her job, then decided that the admission would smack of disloyalty.

"Is Larry like that?"

"He's very protective."

"I was counting on you both."

"Larry?"

"For the public relations aspect." Gilberte leaned across the desk. "If he wouldn't want to work for a woman or—" She broke off at a discreet knock. "Yes?" she called.

The Filipino's voice announced that lunch was served on the patio.

A warm Santa Ana wind rustled through the trees, carrying the fragrance of citrus blossom to the wrought-iron table as Gilberte outlined her plan. Haute couture was a dying beast, even in Paris the labor costs had soared until there were few who could afford an entire, individually designed wardrobe, yet nobody had stepped into the breach with the comparable mass-produced collections.

Though born of an ulterior motive, her filial obligation, Gilberte's venture had roused a passionate dedication. She had spent hours in the so-called couturier sections of department stores, she had carefully unstitched garments made by Mollie Parnis, Anne Fogarty, Claire McCardell and their ilk to examine the workmanship. She had studied financial reports. She had prowled the blocks bounded by 42nd Street, 34th Street, Ninth Avenue and Sixth Avenue—the area commonly referred to as Seventh Avenue. She had studied the pages of *Women's Wear Daily*. As she leaned over her neglected chicken salad, talking, her perfect features glowed. The house would be named Gilberte de Permont, and it would be her own signature on the label, a label that would become known by giving free wardrobes to glamorous young women whose doings the press followed avidly.

Ann caught fire. A separate line of finely crafted sportswear that featured the easy clothes that American women preferred. Maybe even slacks. Coordinated accessories.

"We always did cross-fertilize," Gilberte said.

"God, it's so exciting!"

"Before you make any decision, you have to know the worst." Gilberte jingled the cubes in her glass of iced coffee. "If you and Larry *do* decide to make the plunge, I won't be able to pay either of you what you're worth—at least not at the beginning. Say twelve thousand for Larry, nine for you." Because designers earn more than publicity hacks, she had originally planned the reverse sums— nine for Larry, twelve for Ann—but had switched after Ann's red face had told her that Larry, for all his boyish smiles, cherished archaic ideas about feminine inferiority.

Though twenty-one thousand dollars was slightly more than double the gross income on the Porters' 1948 joint tax return, Ann hesitated. "Larry makes way more than I do."

"That's my limit, but I'll divide it the way you tell me," Gilberte said.

As Ann drove Mitzi Fanning's old car home, she was glossed with a light sweat of excitement. Not to be forced to reduce her clothes to the cheapest common denominator. To see her designs executed by fine craftsmen. To use subtle colors and good silk or linen, not synthetics. Dresses and suits thronged in her mind. What luck that Gilberte hadn't suggested the idea before the party, when she, Ann, assuredly would have rejected the idea. That adolescent romance decently laid to rest, she could go ahead with Gilberte. Now her problem, a large problem, was how to convince Larry.

She yearned for skill in the fine art of working a husband. Bed, whispered the other wives in the tract, was the correct venue. Ann, however, knew she could never carry it off—and anyway, Larry, for a man who prided himself on knowing his way around, was remarkably conventional.

Luck was with her.

Neil Purvis had chosen this particular afternoon to inform Larry that he was good and sick of this blabbing about his new pals Clark Gable, Willie Wyler, Ingrid Bergman, Quent Dejong: "I'm in good with a few celebs myself" was the way he put it. "In case you've forgotten, buster, it's how you earn your daily booze."

Purvis had no intentions of giving the ax to the kid, who, with his cute little redhead wife, was a prime asset, he simply wanted to let the hot air out of his employee. But Larry, whose worst fear was being dropped back into the penury of his boyhood, arrived home badly shaken.

Naturally he didn't tell Ann about the reaming out, so she saw only that he was in one of his infrequent bitching, drinking moods. A wiser wife—like Gilberte Dejong, say—would have put off the discussion. But when had Ann been ruled by prudence? The dishes washed, she went into the living room, scenting the air with her Jergens hand lotion. "Larry?"

Larry remained stretched on the couch staring broodingly at the Scotch in his hands.

She perched on the easy chair by the small brick fireplace. "Gilberte has an idea about going into designer clothes. As a business."

"What's the matter?" Larry's laugh was humorless. "Dejong short on cash?"

"It's strictly her own sideline." Ann clasped her small hands. "She'd like us with her."

"Us?" Larry said. "What's that mean, us?"

"Me as a designer, you as a publicist to put her over," Ann said, launching into Gilberte's game plan.

By the time she finished, Larry was pacing around the living room. "I don't mind telling you that working with Purvis has gotten too damn predictable. I'm ready for a challenge," he said. "Besides, I'd be pulling down sixteen thousand. So as soon as you do your little number on the first show, you could drop out and rest on your cute little duff."

Ann nudged this remark from her mind. "What if you quit Purvis, and this doesn't work out?"

"Where's your faith, woman?" Larry went into the kitchen, humming. Returning with a fresh drink, he asked, "What did she say about shares? Will I have any?"

"We never got that far. I couldn't make any kind of commitment until we talked it over."

"It appeals to the gambler in me," said Larry, who had never even shot craps. "Now Mrs. Porter, see what I've got for you." He shot a meaningful glance at his slacks. The bulge proved the sexual quality of his relief.

When Ann called to tell Gilberte that Larry wanted to get together to discuss details, Gilberte did not seem particularly interested. "What he expects to learn is beyond me—at this point you know as much as I do. But if he wants, have him come over to the house next Wednesday."

Her father had taken her sport fishing in the Mediterranean and demonstrated how to tease the fish along. *Never be too firm with the line at the beginning, Gilberte. First let your hook be swallowed.*

* * *

Larry, himself aware of a thing or two, refused to meet on her
territory. He invited her to lunch at the Beverly Hills Brown Derby.

The Brown Derby's walls were lined with caricatures of the stars.
Larry, seated below the bug-eyed sketch of Eddie Cantor, had a
view of the entry. His planned speech demanding shares grew
shorter and weaker each time the revolving door circled to admit
somebody not Gilberte. At ten past one she swung inside. In a
large-brimmed white hat and the white plissé sundress that bared
the sumptuous upper curves of her tanned breasts, she magnetized
the gaze of every man in the crowded booths, no mean tribute in a
town where beauty is a commonplace.

Without apology for her tardiness, she slid into the booth, glancing at her gold watch. "At two, I have a doctor's appointment."

"We better order, then," he said with a nervous smile.

He remarked about the clothes of surrounding women, but she
refused to take the hint and bring up the business at hand.

Gulping his drink, he said, "Ann wasn't too specific about what
you have in mind. Shall I waltz you around a bit first, or ask my
questions?"

"Fire away."

"Where'll you be located?"

"New York, naturally."

Larry had always considered Manhattan the Isle of the Blest, but
he trusted his chary expression didn't show it. "Why naturally?
Adrian and Don Loper and some of the other studio boys have
more influence on what women wear than all your Adele Simpsons
and Ceil Chapmans put together."

"I can see you've been doing your homework," Gilberte said
with that wry little smile of hers. "You're right, of course. But
Seventh Avenue is the hub of the industry."

"It means uprooting my family," he said.

"Larry, I think you're perfect for the job, but Quent tells me
there's a lot of good publicists in New York."

"The kids are young," he said hastily. "At their ages, moving
won't be too rough on them."

The captain had rolled up the cart and they watched skilled

hands blend chopped avocado, chopped lettuce, crumbled bacon, chopped turkey, Roquefort cheese.

When her Cobb salad and his steak sandwich were on the table and they were alone, Larry asked, "Are you incorporating?"

She took a bite of her salad. "Delicious. Sorry. What did you say?"

"Are you incorporating?"

"I already have."

"Will it be a publicly held company?"

"Larry, you must taste this Cobb salad. They make it only at the Brown Derby."

"I know," he said. "Will you sell shares?"

"It's simpler to keep everything in my own name."

"What about . . . uh, employees?"

Head tilted questioningly, she put down her fork. "Larry, are you asking if you would be a shareholder?"

He forced a chuckle. "It's a logical question, if I'm going to give up a partnership."

"I haven't thought it through. I imagine, though, I'll have a profit-sharing program."

"What kind of percentage are we talking about?"

She shrugged her glowing, perfect shoulders. "Have your lawyers draw up what you have in mind."

Larry couldn't afford legal fees. "We're friends, Gilberte. Go ahead and have your people do it."

She glanced at her watch. "Two already?" she exclaimed. "You'll have to forgive me." Leaning over, she touched her lips to his cheeks.

Watching her move gracefully toward the revolving door, seemingly unaware of the gauntlet of masculine stares, Larry held two fingers to the place her lips had touched. The skin tingled oddly.

45

She had never visited Dr. Lassitter, whose office was a few short blocks from the Brown Derby. Not bothering to move the convertible, she strolled along Wilshire Boulevard humming. The meeting had proceeded triumphantly from its late start to rushed finish. Ah, how the sidewalks of Beverly Hills shone with specks of gold! Then her smile faded. She was recalling that as she'd kissed Larry's cheek the thought of seduction had occurred to her. Now she purged her mind of any such ploy. Not only was sex crudely obvious and distasteful, but it was also a perilous mistake. No matter how discreet she was, Quent might find out. He wouldn't divorce her—his guilts and the knots of his grandfather's estate were fiery swords guarding their marriage—but his perception of her would be irrevocably altered. She needed him, she loved him, she didn't want to hurt him. And besides, steamy panting was redundant. Larry, with his entwined yearnings for popularity and luxury, was the quintessential punitive instrument for a vendetta. Gilberte turned right on Roxbury Drive, her index finger drumming an unhappy, involuntary rhythm on her patent leather purse. That old, ruthless friendship with Ann gnawed at her even as the Gestapo reports whipped her onward.

Squaring her shoulders, she pushed open the door to the medical building.

* * *

In 1931, when James Lassitter had traveled to Stockholm to pick up a Nobel prize for work on hormonal changes in female primates during estrus, he was already acknowledged as tops in the field of human infertility. Now in his sixties, he had been canonized as the patron saint of child-deprived womanhood. With his ponderous cheeks and wide-nostriled nose, he was a remarkably unprepossessing man, yet the gleam of his small, hooded eyes ameliorated this ugliness, at least for Gilberte. Like her father, also neither tall nor handsome, Dr. Lassitter moved briskly with an aura of keen, virile intelligence.

He did not interrupt as she explained her plight.

"We've been married well over three years," she concluded. "My husband's getting edgy."

"What about you, Mrs. Dejong? How important is having a child to you?"

Michel, she thought, and felt a coldness in the back of her neck. "I'm even more disappointed than he."

"Have you had any miscarriages, spontaneous or induced?"

"Neither."

"Stillbirths?"

"None."

He pushed away the chart on which he had been writing. "I'll have a better idea how to proceed after the internal examination."

The chill at the base of her skull intensified. "Internal examination?"

"A pelvic. Surely you've had a pelvic before . . . ?"

"I'm a Frenchwoman, Dr. Lassitter."

"Mmm, yes. Well, there's nothing to be nervous about."

Gilberte submitted to the marauding fingers and speculum: eyes squeezed shut and heels braced in the stirrups, she unsuccessfully battled memories of the sweaty, ramming bodies in the basement of the Santé. When the gently persistent rummaging finally ended, she tissued away K-Y jelly, dressed, and returned to the doctor's thickly carpeted office.

"You've had a child," he said in a neutral tone.

"A living child, not a stillbirth. That's a question to add to your list."

"A difficult labor."

"I was alone. It was the last months of the war, and the doctor was caught in an SS roundup. He arrived after the baby was born."

"Did you hemorrhage?"

"Yes."

"I thought as much. Mrs. Dejong, this isn't pejorative, and I'm sure your doctor had no choice. But in saving you, he did a great deal of damage."

"Does that mean I need corrective surgery?"

"I doubt if surgery would accomplish anything."

"That sounds ominous," she said.

"The reproductive organs, though amazingly strong, are also very delicate."

"Are you saying I can't conceive?" Her color had drained until her tan appeared a cosmetic covering an exquisitely embalmed corpse. She had never anticipated this diagnosis. Never. Just as she'd believed herself barren before Hocherer had told her she was pregnant, so now, having borne a healthy son, she had not considered permanent childlessness. "Is that what you're telling me?"

"My receptionist will set up an appointment for a uterosalpingography."

Her hands gripped the strap of her white patent leather purse in an odd, relentless grip. "Answer my question. Can I conceive?"

"In my opinion, it's unlikely. Of course there are advances all the time."

"Ah, yes, those hoped-for miracles of science."

"Mrs. Dejong, make an appointment with my nurse."

Gilberte did not pause to speak to the heavy-faced nurse at the reception desk. She knew a placebo when she heard one.

"How did it go?" Quent asked.

"Larry's full of ideas."

He nodded absently: in the beginning he had been enthusiastic, offering astutely helpful advice, but his interest had waned the past few days, since Gilberte had put teeth into her serious intentions by offering both Porters a job—maybe Ann was right about men disliking career wives. "No," he said. "I meant at the doctor's."

"A lot of unmentionable poking and prodding by the Nobel laureate."

"And then?"

"He said to keep trying."

"Does he want to see me?"

"Lord, no. He told me three years isn't an unusual length of time. Oh, and I'm to take my temperature to discover when I ovulate." She had picked up this tidbit of advice from a well-thumbed pamphlet in the waiting room.

"That's all?" Quent's blue eyes showed relief.

"Afraid so." She took his hand, rubbing her thumb in a circular movement in his palm, adding huskily, "Darling, let's go upstairs and make a baby."

Two Sundays later when the Porter family set out, Montecito Lane was swathed in fog, but as they neared Beverly Hills the weather improved and, as if subservient to high property values, the sun beamed warmly down on Bedford Drive.

Michael leaned over from the backseat, breathing on Ann's neck. "Why do we have to go see these dumb poop guys anyway?"

"Daddy and I have to sign some papers, it won't take long." Ann's voice wavered.

Larry took his hand from the gear to touch her knee. The children, or rather Michael, were no adjunct to the trip, but its purpose. If they worked with Gilberte, it was inescapable that from time to time their son would be with his natural mother: better to discover her responses now, while they could still bow out.

As Larry parked, Michael announced, "I'm staying in the car."

"Oh no you're not!" snapped Larry. Michael blinked. Usually his dad left disciplinary action to his mom. "Now get out!"

At Larry's loud command, Janey awoke. Her face creased as if for tears, then she gave an uncertain smile that showed her four teeth, new and serrated.

Gilberte answered the door wearing a white nylon swimsuit that clung to her sumptuous curves and accentuated her tan, which gleamed with Coppertone. "The all-American family," she said.

"Backbone of the nation," Larry retorted, tousling Michael's brown hair. "This is Mrs. Dejong. This is Michael."

"Hello, Michael."

The child grunted something that sounded like "How'd'youdo," and moved behind Ann's leg, reaching up for her hand.

When she'd opened the door, Gilberte experienced a tearing sensation through her chest as if her rib cage were being pried apart. It hurt, oh, how it hurt, to see her son in the guise of Michael Porter, a lanky, scowling five-year-old American boy. As he sought protection from her with her oldest friend, her inherited enemy, the pain overwhelmed her. Summoning a mask of amusement, a skill acquired in earliest childhood and perfected through the years, she arched an eyebrow. "Your mother's told me a lot about you, Michael," she said. Turning her attention to the baby, she said, "Hello, Janey. Larry! She has your very chin, with the dimple. So sweet. Come on through to the patio. We're outside."

Quent rose from a gaily padded chair. He wore a tennis sweater over his swimsuit.

"What a dumb pool," Michael said. "Bixie's is better."

While Ann flushed and Larry remonstrated, Gilberte glanced over the child's head at her husband.

Obligingly, Quent asked, "Want to see if the water's as warm as Bixie's?"

"Nah."

"Let's try the dressing room and see if there's a suit to fit you."

The child looked at the bright, floating beach balls, then nodded.

"A first," Larry said, watching the duo disappear into the trellised pool house. "He never goes off with strangers."

"Quent has a way with *les enfants*," Gilberte said, moving to the wrought-iron table. "Here's the contract. Two copies."

Larry and Ann took turns holding Janey while they read the clauses. Ann's eyes kept straying to the shallow end of the pool, where Michael and Quent laughed and churned the chlorinated water. Every glimpse of Quent's left arm sent a chill through her. The OSS had not reported wounds to General Mannix. How and when had Quent earned his Purple Heart? Even though his movements were unimpaired, the arm was so . . . she could only think the word *vulnerable*.

"Shorty, quit worrying. Quent's not going to let your boy

drown." Larry chuckled, then whispered, "What about clause fourteen? The one that gives Gilberte de Permont exclusive rights to your designs in perpetuity?"

"Mr. Sever keeps the rights, too, he told me it's standard," she murmured.

They didn't need to lower their voices. Gilberte had moved to a chaise across the pool.

Eyelids almost closed, she studied Michel— No. This was Michael Porter. She found nothing of herself or Hocherer in the boy, nor any resemblance in feature or mannerism to either of her parents, no likeness to any of the de Permont ancestors who had gazed down on her blighted childhood from murky paintings in the Ile de France country place. Michel vigorously pushed a red beach ball through the water, splashing the deck around her. She didn't move. This was her unacknowledged, unacknowledgeable son, the only child she would ever bear, her wan, grave baby. Her arms again quivered with the emptiness of four years earlier, when she had relinquished him into Ann's waiting embrace.

"Gilberte?"

Startled, she jumped.

Ann stood over her, sunlight burnishing her breeze-blown curls a vivid red. "We're finished. At least I think we are." She made a face. "All that legalese."

Pushing to her feet, Gilberte could still feel tension shaking her arm muscles. "Quent darling," she called. "We're ready for the ceremonials."

Quent bent his head to one side, hitting his hand against his ear to get out the water. "Now? Today?"

"The champagne's cooling," Gilberte replied.

He lifted Michael from the pool, then hauled himself out, printing large, high-arched footprints across the flagstone. Picking up a patterned towel, he asked, "Larry, what about taking the papers to your lawyer?"

Reminded of professional services he could not afford, Larry glanced from the contracts to Gilberte. "Hey, lady, have you buried some nefariously underhanded technicality?"

She laughed. "*Mon dieu,* discovered in the act!"

"It just seems a good idea," Quent said, looking at Larry: he had scarcely glanced in Ann's direction since her arrival. "There might be a clause you'll regret later."

"Ole buddy, aren't we all friends here?" Larry asked.

"Right, right." Quent pulled on his tennis sweater and went to the kitchen door. After a few minutes he emerged, followed by the houseboy, who carried a large tray of drinks, and the cook with a platter of canapés.

Gilberte, Ann and Larry made a little ceremony of signing the copies, which the servants witnessed before returning to the house.

Quent poured Coca-Cola for the children, Moët & Chandon for the adults. His left arm around Gilberte's naked shoulders, he toasted, "To Gilberte de Permont. Incorporated and otherwise."

"To Gilberte de Permont," Ann and Larry echoed.

"We don't have a worry in the world," Larry said that night. They were whispering in bed with the lights out even though the children had been asleep for two hours. "She didn't even notice him."

"Yes, she did. She couldn't stand the noise he made playing in the swimming pool."

"Quent was terrific with him," Larry said. "But your old girl chum, she's one cold potato."

The following morning, Larry informed Neil Purvis that he was quitting, and then proceeded to clean out his desk, taking inordinate pleasure in the increasingly stupefied expression on his erstwhile boss's face as he turned down first a raise, then a ten percent partnership.

Ann continued to work on Mr. Sever's spring line for two more weeks, until he connected with a thin young man willing to work for peanuts. After that, in a ferment of creativity, she sketched hundreds of designs, mailing them in outsize envelopes to Gilberte in New York.

Gilberte had no problem locating her atelier. Jason Templar Enterprises owned a granite-surfaced building on 35th Street just off Seventh Avenue. She went around Quent, flattering and cajoling the nervous-eyed young agent into ousting the three leaseless manufacturers who occupied the third floor. She negotiated a highly favorable lease. (She took pride that she had accomplished all of this without her husband's help.) She conferred with architects and suppliers. She scoured the garment district, hiring in any way she could four top salesmen, Philip Mangone's best cutter, a half-dozen experienced sewing machine operators, pressers, finishers, packers, stock boys, clerical workers. She sneaked in a flight to Paris to spy out the collections.

There was never enough time. In January, when digging started on the foundations for the Jason Templar West Coast headquarters, she was immersed in selecting fabrics: it was out of the question that she accompany Quent to Los Angeles for the groundbreaking ceremony.

Ann and Quent
California, 1950

46

The family's impending shift to New York changed Michael from a pugnacious independent to a clinger. One afternoon during story time, he interrupted Ann.

"Mom," he asked, gripping her hand. "Is Dad buying my ticket for sure?"

"Of course he is. Remember we drove down to Union Station and looked at all the trains? The one we're taking is called The Challenger. You and Janey are sharing a compartment, and Dad's and mine is right next to yours, with a door between." Her voice singsonged as she soothed him with her well-worn verbal Baedeker. "At night a porter will come in and fix the seats into bunks—"

"How do I know you guys won't leave me behind?"

"Leave you behind? Aren't we going to the big zoo in Central Park?" Ann pulled the child onto her lap, cuddling him. "And what about building a snowman together? We'll explore together. Anyway, who else do I have to go with to the top of the Empire State Building?"

Tears welled in the clear gray eyes. "My real mom left me."

"Oh, Michael, baby, your real mom died in the war." This lie persistently refused to come out on a note of conviction and Michael, with his restlessly keen intelligence, had picked up on the waver. But Ann's next words were nakedly honest. "You're our son, we adopted you because we loved you very, very much. We'll love you forever and ever."

After this conversation she was Michael's patsy.

"Mom," he whispered, crawling into bed next to her, waking her. "I have this idea."

Larry snorted in his sleep, rolling over to the edge of the mattress.

"Go back to bed, Michael," she whispered with a hug. "It's the middle of the night."

"Ten past six," he said. He could tell the time, even on clocks with Roman numerals, the only five-year-old on Montecito Lane with this arcane skill. "Let's go to the beach."

Why not? She shared Michael's delight in an empty beach. And this was not only predawn, it was also January, a month when Los Angeles avoided stepping on its broad hem of yellow sand. Larry, a sackhound, never came along, and neither did Janey, an exemplarily late sleeper for a one-year-old.

Ann pulled on jeans and a faded army sweatshirt of Larry's, scribbling a note about her destination, taking the telephone off the hook to insure uninterrupted snoozing for father and daughter.

Sea fog held the early morning in thrall. Ann and Michael left their shoes in the Buick, running down the icy sand. There had been a storm far out in the Pacific. Breakers rose up, an endless invasion of giant waves whose translucent bowels entrapped logs of driftwood and mighty swirls of seaweed. Crashing thunderously, the furious water spumed and swept to the beach, retreating in a white foam that appeared innocent but in reality was vicious undertow. Larry fretted about the children every time they waded. As an adolescent he'd witnessed a little kid get swept away and dragged out of sight: the lifeguards never had found him. Ann positioned herself between Michael and the treacherous sea. Beyond the next lifeguard station—the stations would remain shuttered and unmanned for months—stood a solitary fog-smudged figure. Otherwise the beach with its wet, salty iodine odors was their private domain.

They ran hand in hand, scattering gulls and sandpipers.

"Michael . . ." Ann shouted. "Michael . . ."

"Mom . . ." Michael shrilled. "Mo-o-om . . ."

The furious surf swallowed their cries.

Jogging at the child's pace, Ann peered toward the horizon. At first she saw no demarcation between the gray-brown sea and the gray-brown fog, but then she perceived a hazy lavender line—no, more a luminous purple. . . . She visualized a tulle evening gown in this shade. Wrinkling her forehead, she fixed the subtle coloration in her mind.

"Mom!" Michael tugged at her. "Look, there's Mr. Dejong."

She stubbed her toe on a skeletally bleached hunk of driftwood. Quent was in New York, with Gilberte. Yet undeniably, the tall man was Quent. Gilberte once had mentioned he enjoyed early morning walks at the beach.

Ann's initial impulse was to drag Michael up to the distant boardwalk, an escape made impossible when Quent turned in their direction. Dreading the immeasurable courtesy that was worse than open contempt, she finger-combed her irrepressible curls and walked on cold, blue-orange feet up the sea-eroded embankment of sand toward him.

Michael ran ahead, throwing a punch of greeting that Quent deflected.

Grinning, he said, "No swimming this time, Michael, not in this sea." He turned to Ann with a rapid shift to a mouth-smile. "Hello, Ann. So you're an early bird too?"

Oh, screw you! she thought. Michael was sliding down the escarpment of dry sand. From this distance he couldn't hear them. "My sleep patterns can't come as any great shock," she said.

"I suppose not."

"We'll have to see each other from time to time, you and I. No big deal. Or do you honestly believe seeing me will ruin you with whatever gods may be, or damage your imperishable soul."

His face seemed more angular against the gauzy outlines of the domes and minarets of Santa Monica pier. " 'Invictus,' " he said.

"I know what poetry I'm misquoting! So for God's sake quit behaving like I'm on some other planet. Make the best of a lousy bargain."

"Ann, I've lost the drift of this conversation."

There was a pressure against her windpipe, she was trembling, yet at the same time shouting at him gave her immeasurable relief. "The goddamn drift is that something happened between us!"

"A long time ago."

"Who's denying that? But all the high-class gentility in the world won't cancel out a word—and don't tell me that's Omar Khayyám!"

"What's your point?"

"If we air the past, then you can behave normally when we're together."

He had been looking away from her. Suddenly his eyes widened and he whispered, "Oh Jesus!"

She wheeled around.

A wave larger than its fellows had traveled far up the beach. The foam whipped around Michael's legs. The child circled his arms, attempting to keep his balance. Still flailing, he fell.

Quent was already lunging across the wet sand, shucking his sweater and kicking off his sneakers as he sprinted. Energy rushed through Ann. Gasping, she pounded after him. The sand scattered by her feet half blinding her, she saw Michael inexorably sucked toward a moving, rising wall of water. His thin arms waved, his head bobbed. She imagined she could hear his terrified shrieks.

The soft, dry sand trapped her feet, slowing her. Quent was already in the surf. His body swiveled with the effort of battling his way forward. When rushing water reached his knees, he arced in, joining the now receding wave with powerful strokes. A mighty wall of water was gathering. This must be the chimerical seventh wave, the largest. It rose higher, higher, a towering mass that leaned forward like the flying buttress of a devil's cathedral, cracking with white far above Michael's head. Ann had reached the water. A tame-looking curve of retreating foam eroded the sand beneath her feet, forcing her into a struggle to maintain her balance. Impotently, she watched. The giant lashed down on Michael and at the same instant, Quent dived under raging spume.

They had both disappeared. Never, never had she felt such elemental panic. Not when German bullets whined by her head, not when she clung to the sheer rock face of the Salève mountain.

A sea gull wheeled above her, plunging into the baleful surf. To her drowning sanity, the bird was the angel of death.

Then, a surprising distance to the south of her, Quent pushed up, water streaming from him. He had Michael under his arm, a small, limp toy.

Ann struggled through the raging salt water in their direction. Quent shouted to her, she couldn't hear his words, but she understood his gestures toward land.

She returned to the beach, rushing along the sand. Quent had laid Michael facedown on his sweater, and was feeling the small spine. A streak of blood mingled with the water running down Michael's pallid face.

Dazedly blinking up at her, he whispered, "Mommy, it wasn't my fault."

"No, darling, of course not."

He vomited seawater.

"Michael," Quent said with reassuring calm. "Ever been in a convertible? Mine's right here. You, me and your mom are going to see a doctor to make sure you're okay."

47

In the hospital phone booth, her Levi's heavy with sand and seawater, her hands discolored with cold, she shivered so vehemently that she had difficulty dropping the nickel in the slot and dialing. This was the sixth time she had tried her own number. She was furious at herself for the compulsiveness, aggravated at Larry for yakking on and tying up the line.

At the busy signal this time, though, it suddenly hit her that she'd wanted him and Janey to sleep.

"I left the phone off the hook," she said in a defeated tone.

"Don't worry about it," Quent replied. His black hair was tousled with sand, his drenched twill pants clung to his long legs and he was barefoot, having forgotten his tennis shoes on the beach. "There's nothing he can do anyway."

"What if they need two parental signatures for emergency surgery?" Why was she exposing her demons? It gave her no relief and must be bitterly embarrassing for him. Squinting down the corridor in the direction that Michael, minuscule on the gantry, had been rushed a few minutes earlier, she said in the calmest tone she could muster, "He looked pretty awful, didn't he?"

"The bleeding had stopped."

Her attempt at control failed. "I should've insisted on going along. He's not well adjusted when it comes to strangers. He's only five and a half. I should've yelled, made a scene—"

"He's a tough little kid," Quent interrupted firmly. "I saw a percolator in an office. We could both use something hot. Be right back." He padded away.

Coffee was the last thing she wanted. She needed to pee, badly, but she was trapped in the waiting room area by a superstitious certainty that deserting her post would endanger Michael. Going into the sparsely furnished waiting room, she rested her forehead against the drab, greenish-gold paint. *It must have taken an effort to come up with such a hateful mustard,* she thought, and was incapable of bottling up her tears any longer.

"Ann." Quent had returned with the coffee. "What's happened?"

"Nothing, nothing." She took the paper towel he extended, blowing her nose in the rough brown paper. "But this whole mess is my fault."

Lines of sympathy showed between his eyes. "You didn't invite a twenty-foot wave to come up the beach."

"I let him wander off, I should've been watching him." Her voice was high and clogged. "Not trying to impress you. Correction. Trying to force you to admit that something had happened for you, when I knew it hadn't. . . ."

"Here," Quent said, handing her another paper towel.

Blowing her nose again, she took the coffee and sat with both hands curved around the warm mug.

"Is it wrong? Don't you still use a lot of milk?"

A tacit admission of their shared past that rolled over her unnoticed.

"It's fine." She sipped. "I haven't said thank you for saving his life."

"Hey, should I have just stood by watching?"

"That undertow was brutal—you could have drowned."

"I'm a pretty fair swimmer," he said.

"It was brave, you're always brave. Oh, God, what's taking so long? They must have found something awful. A concussion. A broken neck or—"

"Ann, stop it!"

"Sorry. You see before you a prime specimen of Worrying Mother North Americanus." Her attempt at levity rang with intimations of hysteria, and she forced herself to take a sip of coffee. "So tell me, what is the correct remark to make to somebody who saved your son's life?"

"The best way is not to keep mentioning it." His tone was kind. "Gilberte told me Michael's a war orphan."

How had Gilberte summoned up a normal tone to relay this information? *She had to, you idiot. Look at what a swell liar you turned out to be.* "We've adopted him. He's ours. He's just as much ours as Janey." The coffee had increased the ruthless pressure on her bladder and she set down the pottery mug. "Quent, I'm going to the john—will you yell outside the door if the doctor comes?"

"Sure, but it'll be a while yet."

As she washed her hands in the rest room, she glimpsed herself in the steel mirror. Her color resided solely in her rat's nest of hair. *I look like death,* she thought, making no attempt to restore life to her appearance.

Back in the waiting room, Quent was rubbing at his bad arm.

"Quent, what happened?" Without such a severe case of emotional diarrhea, she never would have asked. "I mean, I couldn't help noticing your arm."

"Nothing very pleasant."

"The war?"

His eyes were a darker blue as he studied her. "Yes, the war," he said, and went to the window to stare out. The mist had lifted, leaving the quiet street softly hazed. "Stop me if I'm wrong, but you seem to feel I walked out on you?"

Surprised—no, stunned—she took several shallow breaths before replying. "No letters."

"Yes, I stopped writing," he agreed.

Between them lay miles of frozen tundra: he had always possessed the power to conjure up this barren ice to separate himself from her.

"You'd been behind enemy lines before, and I always heard from you eventually. After a few months I was bonkers. Not being family or anything, I had no way to find out what had happened. It got so bad that General Mannix helped. He had this friend, a colonel, in

Grosvenor Square." The OSS was centered in this area, close to the United States embassy. "He pulled rank to find out if you were missing, captured or . . . well, dead. They were ultradiscreet at OSS, of course, but they let him know that you were broadcasting messages on schedule."

"It wasn't me."

"It wasn't you?"

"Trust me," he said. "It wasn't."

"Quent, I'm not doubting you. But that's what they told General Mannix."

"Our cryptographers never believed that their opposite German numbers might be as bright as they were. It didn't occur to them that messages might be phony."

"Where were you?"

He turned, his face as uncommunicative as his back had been. "Mauthausen."

"You were a prisoner?" she whispered.

"For nearly two years."

Gilberte had never mentioned his being captured, although she had reported concisely about that debutante he had whirled and waltzed at Manhattan coming-out balls. *Mauthausen?* Though the Germans had treated most of the American prisoners of war with reasonable decency, at the Nuremberg trials terrible stories had surfaced about the few unfortunate enough to land in Mauthausen concentration camp.

"Two years . . . That means right after—"

"More like a year and a half. Right after I took you down to Greatleigh. In December I was dropped back into the *zone interdite* near Dieppe. The Nazis had a welcoming committee on hand."

"Quent, I wrote a million embarrassing letters."

"Prisoners at Mauthausen rarely got their Red Cross packages, or their mail."

"I sent one to the bank right after V-E day."

He shrugged. "Maybe they forwarded it, maybe they didn't. Several months aren't very clear. As a matter of fact, I was completely out of it."

"Oh, Quent . . . I . . . I'm so sorry." What a woefully inade-

quate cliché to cover her empathy, her sympathy, the yearning
regret flooding through her.

A nurse bustled by. They were silent until the squashy sound of
her white rubber-soled shoes had faded.

"You never cashed the check," he said.

"Check?"

"The three hundred I bestowed on you at the party."

She winced at the memory. "Oh, that."

"I was a sweetheart, wasn't I? That's me, no grace under pressure."

"Pressure? You've lost me."

"It's quite simple. In the camp, I'd built you up, you were all that
kept me going, and when I got out I heard that this wondrous
heroine had jilted me—"

"I didn't."

"Anyway, my mood was bitter, and that's putting it mildly. I'd
made up my mind never to see you again. And then Gilberte came
up with her Hollywood party."

"I turned her down, but Larry . . ." Ann paused. "When did
you get back to the States?"

"In January of forty-six."

"But Gilberte had told me . . ." Again her voice trailed away.
Gilberte had lied. Standing in that shabby, overcrowded bedroom,
in the presence of Michael sweating with fever in his iron crib, she
had lied.

Quent was watching her with narrowed eyes. "What was it
Gilberte said?"

Gilberte was her friend, Gilberte was the sole survivor of her
girlhood. Gilberte was Michael's mother. Gilberte was her employer—and Larry's. *Isn't there a statute of limitations on the ways one
can be joined to another person's life?*

"Mrs. Porter?" A young, soft-looking doctor with a blue smear
of stubble across his face stood outside the waiting room.

Trembling, she rose to her feet. "I'm Mrs. Porter."

The doctor turned to Quent. "Mr. Porter?"

"Dejong," Quent corrected. "A friend. How's Michael doing?"

"The patient suffered contusions and a flesh wound that needed
suturing."

"Stitches?" Ann whispered. "What did you say about a concussion?"

"I said contusions. Con-tu-sions. In layman's language, that means bruises. The X rays show no cranial or spinal damage."

"None? You're positive?"

"I can read an X ray," the doctor said testily.

"Mrs. Porter is concerned," Quent said.

He had neither raised his voice nor altered his expression, yet the resident grimaced apologetically.

"In point of fact," he said, thrusting both hands in his white coat, "the chief of pediatrics happens to be in the hospital. He also did an examination and read the X rays. He concurs with me."

"What's his name?" Quent asked.

"Dr. Gerardson."

"Will you please tell Dr. Gerardson that Mrs. Porter would like to speak to him."

The fleshy blue jowls quivered. "I assure you that he'll repeat what I've told you."

"Tell Dr. Gerardson that we're waiting."

The two men stared at each other for a second or two.

"I'll ask him," said the resident in a subdued tone. Starched coat flapping, he hurried away.

Ann's legs shook and she sank into a chair. "Why did you insist on seeing the doctor?"

"Because in a minute or so you'll be doubting that pompous little creep."

"You're worried about Michael! You brought him to the hospital because you were afraid he'd—"

"Ann, I want you to stop this." Quent squatted in front of her, taking her icy hands in his warm grip.

At his touch, her fears faded, or at least became manageable. He was staring into her eyes. Her lips parted in a shaky little sigh.

A stretcher was being rushed down the corridor, and there were rapid, excited commands, but they didn't look away from each other.

"I meant it when I said you saved my life." He spoke with quiet intensity. "In Mauthausen dying often seemed a fine idea. Thinking of you kept me going."

"I feel so rotten about . . . Quent, I'm sorry."

"So am I," he said. "Ann, I'm going back to New York on Thursday. Could you get away for a couple of hours?"

She knew precisely what they would do in those hours, yet a breathy voice beyond her volition whispered, "Yes."

A siren was howling into the Emergency entrance and neither of them heard the footsteps.

At a cough, Quent released her hands. They both reddened. The chief of pediatrics repeated in plain English what the Emergency Room resident had told them. Other than needing three stitches in his forehead, Michael appeared fine. As a precautionary measure, however, he should be watched and kept quiet for a couple of days. He would be out in a few minutes.

48

Angry bruises bulged from Michael's right cheek and gauze bandaging invaded his hairline, but otherwise his brush with the Pacific apparently had left him undamaged. Ordering that the top of Quent's Cadillac be lowered, he squirmed around, alternately raising both arms into the wind then leaning his head back to peer up at the sky. When Larry opened the door, he flung himself at him. "Daddy! Guess what? I was in a real hospital!"

He frisked about like a bear cub after a winter's hibernation until Ann picked him up and deposited him in bed. Only the combined efforts of both parents kept him there. That afternoon, when Quent returned the Buick, Joaquin trailing him in the Cadillac convertible, Michael rushed into the living room demanding another ride with the top down.

Panicked screams awoke Ann and Larry.

Together they darted to the back bedroom.

In the dusky shadows that the night-light slanted across the linoleum, they saw Michael crouched on all fours. His yellow sleepers with the left toe sticking out in no way matched his horror-contorted, unchildlike features.

"Oh, my God," Larry whispered.

Neither he nor Ann could know it, but in this position Michael

bore a marked resemblance to Bernd von Hocherer as a relay team
of SS beat him to death under the impersonal eye of a movie
camera—the film was later flown to Berchtesgaden where the Führer viewed it with highest satisfaction.

"Michael, darling." Ann squatted by the child. "It's all right,
Mommy and Daddy are here. Come on back to bed." She bent to
pick him up.

Michael cringed away, shaking his head, gasping out his screams
with rhythmic hoarseness.

Larry sat on the floor, stroking the small, heaving shoulders and
back as one would gentle a colt, continuing to caress and murmur
as Ann brought a coverlet that he wrapped around the hysterical
child. By now Janey had awoken and was crying too. Taking her
from her crib, Ann called their pediatrician. By the time the balding doctor arrived, pajama top showing under his sport jacket,
Larry had Michael, sobbing quietly now, in his arms.

Watching them, Ann had difficulty catching her breath: it was as
though she were on a high mountain peak where the air was too
thin.

The following morning, Larry took Michael to the radiology lab.
Soon after Ann put Janey down for her morning nap, the doorbell
rang. Quent stood on the steps with three large boxes in the
lollypop-and-ribbon wrap of Uncle Bernie's Toy Menagerie.

Taking the packages, she said a subdued "Thank you," and did
not invite him inside.

"One's for the baby."

"That's really nice of you."

"How's Michael?"

"He woke up screaming last night. The doctor came and said it
was a nightmare, there were no concussion symptoms. But to be on
the safe side, Larry's taken him in for more X rays."

Quent took a step toward her. "Ann, what is it? What's wrong?"

"I just told you."

"No, I mean, yesterday you were terrified, but you were *there*.
With me, I mean."

The Good Humor man was tinkling around the corner.

"Last night, Michael was a total mess. And Larry was fabulous. They're very close. He wouldn't let me do anything, only Larry."

"He's a great little kid."

She clutched the large boxes closer. "Quent, I don't know how big a deal our date is for you. But, well, you know me. A dyed-in-the-wool romantic. I've never quite gotten over the way we were." How odd, to be making this flat-toned averment of imperishable love in broad daylight while the ice-cream truck proceeded slowly up Montecito Lane.

"The wound's always there, isn't it?" he said.

"I wouldn't tell Larry. Would you tell Gilberte?"

His mouth tensed, and after a moment he shook his head. "Only about fishing out Michael from the surf."

"So."

"Yes, so."

"So because I want to keep our date too much I'm begging off."

"Do you want me to argue you out of the decision?"

"No."

"Okay," he said, his expression unreadable. "Tell Michael he rode on record-size waves."

She clutched the brightly wrapped gifts, closing the door. Through the glass panel she watched him walk to his convertible without the least sign of dejection. When he got in, though, he sat rubbing both eyebrows for several minutes before starting the engine.

Gilberte
New York, 1950

49

The unfinished showroom smelled of sawdust. The carpenters had gone to lunch, leaving their tools near the shells of four plywood office booths. The big sheets of plate glass that would give the booths windows into the showroom were to be installed this afternoon.

Gilberte and Quent stood peering at the half-dozen slashes of gray paint above a sample of gray carpet. She and Ann had talked on erratically buzzing long-distance lines about the decor. Gilberte had been set on a showroom that oozed elegance, but Ann had argued, *Do you want the buyers to see chandeliers and boiserie or Gilberte de Permont clothes?* So there would be simplicity and a monochromatic color scheme. Arriving in Manhattan yesterday, Ann had taxied directly from Grand Central Station to blend these samples.

"The painters're starting tomorrow." Gilberte moved the sample square with her toe. "What do you think? Is the carpet better with this shade?"

"Aren't they all the same?"

"Darling, I'm aware you're smiling indulgently at my career," she said. "There's no need to press the point."

"Come on, Gilberte, I'm your biggest fan. But you know me. The nearest thing to color-blind there is."

Undeniably Quent lacked an eye for color. And equally undeniably, once she had convinced him that Gilberte de Permont, Incorporated, was no whim, he had given staunch moral support—he was better than her lawyer at explaining the ramifications of the agreements she signed. (Refusing his offers of financing, a point of pride with her, she doled out funds with the tight fists of a Breton peasant.) Yet there was something wrong between them.

She couldn't put a finger on what this unsettling something was. She couldn't even recall when she had first become aware of the subtle undercurrents. Though he remained what her so-called friends called "an absolutely most divine husband," by which they meant exceedingly rich, well-mannered, nonabusive either physically or verbally, and also willing to go along with her outrageous new interest, he had become . . . well, absent. The innermost workings of his mind had always remained a mystery to her, so the best description she could come up with was this nebulous word *absent.* At this minute, while he talked to her, his spirit had taken off to parts unknown.

The sawdust made her cough. "This one," she said, greasepenciling a large *X.*

"It looks the pinkest."

"And you say you have no eye for color! It *is* the pinkest," she said, going to the folding chair to retrieve her golden sable coat. "Darling, let's get out here."

As they lunched side by side on the blue and white zebra-striped banquette at the front of Le Soleil, the new restaurant on 53rd, they were greeted by a flow of people being escorted to the lesser tables. Gilberte began noticing how many of the women gave off signals to Quent. Betsy Mappen darted eager glances at him. Lynn Hutchinson, in from Grosse Pointe, smiled mistily as she thrust out her breasts, Eleanora Risconti held her glasses to her mouth, playing her tongue at the frames. Then, during the entrée, a thought exploded inside her brain. *He's having an affair.* A sudden trembling afflicted her.

Without him, I'll be back in the Santé.

Though she loved him, though she was hotly, territorially jealous of this real or imagined woman, though being Mrs. Quentin Dejong gave her the backbone to face the world, this irrational fear shrilled above the other emotions. *Without him, I'll be back in the Santé.*

Quent interrupted her mental maunderings. "Isn't your veal good?" he asked solicitously.

She realized that she had set down her knife and fork. "It's delicious."

Taking a bite, she tried to think rationally. Even if Quent were indulging in a little fancy footwork—and she had no proof of this whatsoever—it would in no way signal the end of their marriage. Glancing at Quent's strong profile, she once more listed the reasons why he would never divorce her. First and foremost, he was locked into guilt about her parents. Then there was his own rectitude, plus his distaste for the paternal pattern. (Her bloated, handsome old father-in-law had recently left his fourth wife for a twenty-year-old manicurist.) A tie more mundane but equally serviceable was the Trust. Jason Templar's legacy made it virtually impossible for any heirs of his body to divorce outside the borders of New York State, where for all intents and purposes adultery was the sole grounds. Quent had no way out unless she complied.

But what was the voice of pure reason against the shrilling of fear? *He'll leave me and I'll be back in cell 8. I must keep him. But how?*

He wants a family.

A child was impossible.

He doesn't know it.

That evening Quent ate dinner at the Metropolitan Club.

As usual when alone, Gilberte had a light supper in the sitting area off the master bedroom. Apple logs crackled in the black marble fireplace. A small Renoir nude hid the safe with her jewels and the Gestapo dossiers. She nibbled a bit of sole, then could eat no more. Until now their bedroom suite had delighted her. But . . . Mightn't the black lacquer chairs and tables she had selected with such care seem fussy and uncomfortable to a large man? And wasn't the antique fabric her decorator had found for the curtains, iridescent green silk woven with gold bees, the Napoleonic emblem, a reminder that Empress Josephine had been divorced in favor of a younger, fertile woman?

A juggernaut of fear was flattening Gilberte's conscience.

She bathed until the scented water cooled. Using her nail scissors, she trimmed her explicit black pubic triangle. She fingered a lubricant into her vagina. After slathering Chanel perfume on her breasts and thighs, she went to her dressing room, where one section of the forty-foot length was given over to nightwear. The fragile drifts of lingerie were made for her at Odile, just off the place de la Madeleine, the same house that her mother had patronized, and, like the baronne, she had three fittings for each negligee and gown, an attention to detail that nowadays was unobtainable even elsewhere in Paris. Gilberte finally selected a beige silk mousseline that veiled yet did not hide her large-nippled breasts.

It was just after midnight when the car stopped on the Fifth Avenue side of the house.

Dabbling more Chanel on her rushing pulses, she turned out the lamp. The glow of the fire danced around her as Quent came in. She kissed his cheek, which was cool with the night air, inhaling the scent of his clothes. Havana cigars. *He hasn't been with a woman.*

"A good dinner?" she asked, nuzzling against him.

Though he put his arms around her, she sensed a reticence. "Fine. How went your evening?"

"Slowly. . . . Without you, time passes slowly."

"I meant to be home a couple of hours ago, but Chester and I started hashing over the Nagasaki hospital, and time sort of ran away. Looks like I might have to go there."

She sighed. "You will? To Japan? When?"

"Maybe sometime in March."

She'd unbuttoned his suit jacket. She started to unknot his tie.

He pulled away. "Gilberte, it's late."

"It's been weeks, darling."

He stood unmoving as she undid his shirt, but when she licked down the line of dark hairs that bisected his chest, she could feel the beating of his heart. Kneeling to work his belt, she pressed her cheek against his erection. "What's this talk of being tired? Ah, darling, how I've missed you. . . ."

He sat on a chair and, her long, slender legs straddling his, she sank slowly onto the hard core of him. As he thrust up toward her, she rotated and shifted. It was the same as always. No matter how needy her love, no matter how yearningly she tried to respond, she felt nothing. The fire washed them with living red shadows, she simulated passion, the antique black lacquer chair creaked fiercely, and Quent gave a cry.

They moved to the bed. As his lighter flared for his cigarette—these postcoital puffs remained his sole indulgence with tobacco—she saw the bleak hollows below his cheeks.

On March 25, she saw him off at La Guardia. His flight to San Francisco, the first leg of his three-day journey to Japan, had been called, but they had not moved.

". . . Quent, I shouldn't bother you with this, not now."

"You're twitchy, Gil, and that's understandable. But there's no reason. Larry tells me you're a shoo-in." Quent's solicitous tone was devoid of the impatience he must feel.

She had sublimated her anxiety about her marriage by vocalizing her catalogue of misgivings about Gilberte de Permont, Incorporated. Would the showroom and the collection be ready by market week? Would the salesmen write a single order? Would the press ignore her even though she had salted her showing with names like Mary Martin, Babe Paley, Ethel Merman? Would she be a world-wide laughingstock?

"Larry's been here a few weeks, his finger's not exactly on New York's pulse."

"Gilberte, if you're worried about dropping money the first few seasons—"

"I know a banker."

The metallic voice was announcing the flight again. Taking her arm, he guided her toward the gate where Chester Houston, who integrated the Foundation's philanthropies, waited with his own new gold-cornered briefcase and Quent's battered old one.

"I went to my gynecologist." Gilberte's throat tightened. "Yesterday."

Quent halted. "Yes?"

"At this moment," she murmured, "a rabbit is dying."

His eyes sparkled, his skin glowed, his expression took on vitality. She hadn't realized how anesthetized he had appeared, and her mind's eye saw an idiotic vision lifted from the *Frankenstein* film: the sky had opened, loosing bolts of lightning that imbued her husband with life.

"Hey," he said. "Gil, why didn't you tell me?"

"What? That I have *quelques jours de retard*?" As she said that she was late, she felt overgirdled, breathless.

"I would have canceled, Chester could have gone alone."

"Didn't you get a letter from General MacArthur, the Great God of the Pacific himself?" she asked. "Didn't he say unto you that it's urgent you be in Nagasaki? The Japanese lose enough face as it is, accepting the hospital from the Templar Foundation, and if the top man isn't there for the discussions, the plans will be stymied."

"The hell with that noise."

"Quent, it's too soon to be positive. Besides, you'll be back in less than a month."

He put his arms around her. "When'll we know?"

"The day after tomorrow."

"Damn. My flight'll have taken off from San Francisco." He kissed her hair. "The minute you find out, Gilberte, call the office. I'll arrange for them to radio the clipper."

"Darling, stop being such a stereotype."

In response, he put two fingers in the corners of his mouth, giving a loud, boyishly exultant whistle. As the passengers turned toward them, he pulled a straight face that matched his pinstriped topcoat.

Two days later, she telephoned the headquarters of Jason Templar Enterprises. In a curiously high whisper, she gave Marian LaRosa, Quent's gray-haired, efficient executive secretary, a one-word message.

Yes.

50

"That apartment near Columbia University was twice as big," Ann said.

"Myself, I prefer this," Gilberte said.

"Who wouldn't?" Larry said.

The three of them were in the narrow, unfurnished living room of a tenth-floor apartment on East 67th Street, the most elegant residential area in Manhattan. Ann's footsteps echoed down the room's length and along a windowless, dogleg corridor. The others followed her into a small, dark bedroom.

"Michael and Janey'll have to share this," she said.

"Michael's of an age where he can survive the excitement of mixed sleeping arrangements," Gilberte said dryly. She often astonished herself with her ability to talk as if Michel were indeed the Porters' offspring. Her chest was taut.

"It's so small and gloomy."

"A coat of yellow paint'll fix that, shorty." Larry, having picked up Manhattan's geographic declensions, hadn't the least intention of living in Nowheresville, as he termed the West Side. "Next year we'll move to something bigger."

"The rent on the other place is way less."

"If it's money you're worried about, think of what it's costing us per diem at the Ranaleigh." They were temporarily esconced in the Ranaleigh Apartment Hotel, where the elderly residents complained about the children's noise and Michael chased fat dachshunds down the corridors. "Besides, a live-in'll be less than the sitters."

"I have friends nearby with children," Gilberte said. "I'll see what I can arrange to get the tykes together."

"We'll take you up on the offer," Larry said eagerly. With a long stride, he thrust his face toward Ann's. "I'm not about to sacrifice Michael and Janey so you can save a few bucks."

"That's not fair!" Ann cried.

"I leave you two lovebirds to argue it out," Gilberte said, buttoning her mink. "I have an appointment."

Her car was waiting, and she gave Jordan an address on 78th near Madison.

Quent had been in Japan for two weeks. Each day he had placed a phone call, a near impossibility. A pair of sapphire ear clips then a diamond bracelet had arrived from Cartier. The collection had been presented. In the frantic turmoil of the as yet unfinished *cabine*, Ann, wearing faded slacks, had pinned last-minute adjustments on her designs before the models paraded along the raised runway. Gilberte, clad in the crimson Velázquez suit—it turned out to be the collection's hot number—had stood in a corner of the gray showroom with her hands clenched to hide the quivering. Though she had incorporated with an ulterior motive, the business had grafted itself onto her ego, become part of her, and she panted after its success and recognition. None of her pessimistic fears had come to pass, but then again neither had Ann's optimistic dreams. No instant big time. Buyers from Saks and Bergdorf's had bought timidly, but they *had* bought, which, as Ann had pointed out, was a foot in the door. While there had been no orders from Bonwit's or Lord & Taylor, Neiman-Marcus in Texas had taken a flyer with several styles. The salesmen had worked long and persuasively in their four freshly painted, glass-fronted cubicles, between them hustling up a respectable number of orders from women's specialty shops. Larry had lured reporters to the showing with Gilberte's background, and though the inches of copy dedicated to her aristocratic forebears and her husband's wealth had been triple those detailing the clothes, still, five major newspapers had printed a photograph of her in the Velázquez suit.

The car pulled up outside a smart, black-painted door inset with a gilt plaque.

J STONEHAM KREIGER, MD
CLINIC SPECIALIZING IN OBSTETRICS AND GYNECOLOGY

Gilberte had checked out Dr. Kreiger with the same care that she had vetted Lassitter, the Nobel laureate in Los Angeles, but for opposing qualifications. Kreiger, tall, slender, with an imposing head of pewter-gray hair, had carved a fashionable practice out of his willingness to accommodate his patients. He was freehanded with prescriptions of every type, his facilities delivered infants with a maximum of anesthesia, and D&C's that never would have been permitted in larger, more carefully regulated hospitals were performed, thus keeping down the birthrate in various socially prominent families. Word was that Kreiger had affairs with his patients.

On her first visit, Gilberte had proved the veracity of this particular rumor. While her new physician made out her chart, she had engaged in meaningful eye contact: he had not requested his nurse to step into the examining room. Black alligator heels thrust into stirrups, Gilberte had taken part in intimacies definitely not part of the gynecological routine. Though all she had heard of J. Stoneham Kreiger assured her of his cooperation, her own life's experience had taught her that whenever possible one should avoid dealing from weakness.

Later, dressed with her ankles decorously crossed, she had inquired, "Am I correct? This is my second month."

"Mmm," he had responded noncommittally.

"My husband does so hope I'm pregnant."

"I see," Kreiger said, still uncommitted.

"He's quite set on it," Gilberte had said, and stared across the desk for a long moment, her clear, yellowish eyes narrowed like a tigress's.

Kreiger had shivered perceptibly. "Yes, you're correct," he'd said. "Definitely the second month."

Today, on her second "prenatal" examination, Dr. Kreiger palpated Gilberte's empty uterus while repeating to his nurse the responses normal for the first trimester of pregnancy.

"Well, Mrs. Dejong," he announced, "you're doing splendidly. I'm happy to report that you're almost past the danger period. Not quite, but almost. Soon there'll be only a minimal chance for a spontaneous abortion."

At a little past midnight, the red lights of an ambulance were flashing outside the Dejongs' house on Fifth Avenue. The five live-in servants, bathrobes over pajamas and nightgowns, watched as their groaning, weeping mistress was wheeled out on a stretcher.

The sirens howled along Fifth Avenue to 78th Street, then cut over to Madison Avenue and Dr. Kreiger's clinic.

The private nurse ushered Ann in with the warning that "our girl is still quite out of it." Impressive floral tributes already crowded the dresser and the nurse shoved Ann's roses in water, putting the vase in the hall, returning to goggle at a grainy wrestling match on the ten-inch screen. Dr. Kreiger's was the only health-care facility in Manhattan, possibly the world, with the amenity of television.

Ann sat by the bed. She had never seen Gilberte like this. Her expression was slack and only the faint line above the left side of her mouth showed the location of that armoring little smile of amusement. The whole situation had come as a shock to Ann. This morning, when she'd learned of the miscarriage, her stomach had plummeted and she had fallen into the deep cavern inhabited by the green-eyed monster. Now, though, watching her pale, conked-out friend, she berated herself for her jealousy. She had children, why shouldn't Quent? After a minute or so at the bedside, she felt only sadness for Quent, who'd had dreams of fatherhood since he was fifteen, and for Gilberte, who'd been forced to give up Michael and now had lost out a second time.

Gilberte's eyes flickered, then opened.

"Ann," she whispered without surprise, as if she'd expected to see her.

"I'm sorry, Gilberte, so sorry. If I'd known I wouldn't have let you lift a finger during market week."

The nurse bustled to the bed with a tumbler, raising the bent glass tube to Gilberte's lips. "Here, honey. Take a sip of water."

"Get out," Gilberte whispered.

"Honey, I'm Mrs. Braithwaite, your nurse—"

"Don't call me . . . honey." Gilberte's labored diction was low but autocractic. "Turn off . . . noise. Then . . . get out."

The woman retreated to switch off the television. Chin raised, she stage-whispered to Ann, "I'll be right here in case our girl needs me." The door swung shut behind her.

"When you didn't come in this morning," Ann said, "I called the house and the butler explained what had happened. Right away Larry put in a call to Quent's office, but they'd already heard about the miscarriage."

"Wasn't a miscarriage," Gilberte said drowsily.

"Gilberte, you lost the baby."

"No baby . . ."

"Shh."

"Never was one . . ."

"Don't try to talk. You're still doped up."

"No baby," Gilberte repeated.

"It's okay," Ann murmured.

"Not pregnant . . . never was pregnant," Gilberte said. Then her eyes closed. Her jaw tensed. Beads of sweat broke out on her forehead. "Yes, of course. Lost my baby."

"You'll have more."

"Quent was delirious. Whistled like a boy. . . . Not like himself . . . He wants five or six . . . he didn't want to leave me . . . so crazy about me . . . so excited I was having his baby . . ." The sweat was dripping down into her black hair.

"I better get the nurse," Ann said thickly.

"Fill in for me," Gilberte mumbled, and fell asleep again.

When Ann emerged, streaky clouds were hiding the sun and the temperature had plunged ten degrees. It was almost three miles to Seventh Avenue and 35th, but without thinking she started to walk. Unless stuck for time, she walked everywhere. The island of Manhattan fascinated her—the diverse population, the unceasing energy, the exotic foods, the smart, inexpensive merchandise in shop windows. Today, however, she plodded along, her eyes fixed on the pavement. She wasn't thinking of Gilberte's weird remarks, which she had immediately categorized as drug-induced babble: Dr. Kreiger had spoken with medical concision about the "aborted fetus." No. She was brooding about the fetus's father.

Since coming to New York, she'd seen Quent infrequently and briefly. His pleasant courtesy lacked the abrasive aloofness that had characterized his manner before Michael's rescue. Their episodes in wartime France and England, that dawn dive into the Pacific and their subsequent conversations might never have taken place. Well, this was not entirely accurate. He had struck up a friendship with Michael, requesting permission to take him to the Central Park Zoo, and to a revival of *Pinocchio*. Both times Michael, who since the move had alternated between truculence and rambunctiousness, had returned to the Ranaleigh with chocolate and pleasure staining his face. Ann had wasted a good deal of time musing that the pair were second cousins once removed, and did shared blood make for an affinity?

She was shivering hard and her feet were numb by the time she reached the garment district. Dodging around two boys who jauntily shoved racks of identical navy dresses, she was tempted to get a mug of coffee and a hot sweet roll at one of the long, narrow counters that exuded the spicy aromas of pickles and pastrami. But it was after ten, and she must take Gilberte's appointments.

Gilberte's office resembled a charming sitting room with English antiques, green-and-white upholstery, the bowls of fresh flowers that arrived daily. Color-coordinated samples of wool crepe were strewn across the love seat and Ann's first draft sketches (unsigned) were heaped on the lowest of the lacquerwork tables, an artful clutter that, like the flowers, was changed daily and all for show. One wall was decorated with framed sketches of the collection. Wincing at the large, imperious *Gilberte de Permont* slashed below her work, Ann took off her winter coat but kept on her pertly feathered hat—it was the custom of women in the industry to wear hats while they conducted business.

She met with a Mr. Sam, whose consonant-crowded Siamese patronym was impossible for Westerners to pronounce. Mr. Sam, a dapper and round-cheeked Thai, having survived the Japanese occupation, had reestablished his hand looms in Chiang Mai: his opulent silks cost about a fifth the price of less exciting goods in the United States. Holding a sample of astonishingly vivid azure, Ann envisioned models parading in a cruise collection. A cruise collection? She had never even thought of a midseason line, much less broached the idea to Gilberte. Yet the vision remained clear. On impulse, she decided to go ahead. Because of the manufacturing difficulties and the distance, Mr. Sam was explaining, there could be no reorders. Drawing a deep breath, she used the back of a sketch to jot down the yardage she would need in the emerald, the azure, the pink so bright that it looked hot.

She didn't have time for lunch, so she sent out for coffee with lox and bagel—a new delicacy for her.

At three-fifteen, the fashion editor from *Life* arrived with Larry, who had just lunched her magnificently at the Colony restaurant. Ann asked Gilberte's leggy young secretary to model the Velázquez suit and the editor admired the wide belt, the peplum, semiguaranteeing a page.

Ann settled an argument between the cutter and the patternmaker, she hired a new presser, she hurried a slow-delivering trimming supplier, she telephoned the Ranaleigh twice to make sure the children were okay, and the clinic once, finding out that Gilberte's progress was satisfactory.

By six, it was raining. Every cab was occupied. Ann, though, had acquired a native New Yorker's verve about leaping off the curb with an upraised arm. Within five minutes she was on her way to the apartment on 67th, where Larry was waiting. The two of them went over the rental agreement with the realtor.

"What's this about a three-year lease?" Larry asked.

"So you think it was easy getting the landlord down from a five-year lease?" countered the broker, a smartly minked widow. "Three years is his absolute minimum."

"And my absolute maximum," said Larry with his most boyish smile, "is one year."

"And then, hocus-pocus, you'll be commuting from a large colonial house in Darien?"

"Darien . . ." Larry lingered over each syllable as if the Connecticut suburb were a magic rune. "Yes, Darien."

His salary alone wasn't enough to assure the landlord of the one year's rent, so Ann signed her name beneath his.

51

As Gilberte and Larry emerged from the St. Regis (she had dropped by the hotel's King Cole Room, where he had been lunching with a fellow Californian, Cyril Magnin, head of snazzily chic Joseph Magnin's), she indicated a narrow store across the street. "That's Quent's man," she said.

It was two months after Larry had moved to New York, and he was still catching on to the city's fabled delights. He peered at the single bolt of white cloth in the window and the name MORTON'S in bronze lettering above the door. Neither offered a clue as to the merchandise purveyed. "Morton's?" he asked.

"Quent swears by Mr. Morton, says he's the only shirtmaker on this continent with the same quality as Turnbull and Asser in London. Come on across, I'll introduce you."

Morton, a tall, round-shouldered man with an Oxford accent, greeted Gilberte congenially.

"Mr. Porter would like to see a few fabrics," Gilberte said.

Mr. Morton's congeniality extended to Larry. Soon the counter was heaped with fabric. Egyptian cottons as fine as silk. Magnificent linens. Whites of every shade and variety. Striped blues, striped grays, a diminutive maroon check.

Gilberte held up a white-on-white cotton. "This would be perfect on you."

Larry already had his eye on a narrow blue stripe similar to one he'd seen on Quent.

There was no problem about choosing between them. Mr. Morton was explaining that the minimum order for a new client was one dozen shirts.

"The other day, Larry, weren't you mentioning you wanted to have shoes made?" Gilberte asked. He had never brought up the subject. "Have you heard that the Goforth man is in New York?"

"Goforth?"

"Quent's bootmakers, they're on Jermyn Street in London. This is the first time they've sent a representative over. He's here to make foot models for new clients."

"Mmm. Where can I contact him?"

"I'll have Quent recommend you."

"Larry, next time you send flowers to Diana Vreeland"— Gilberte pronounced the first name Dee-ah-na— "please call Constance Spry. I've learned the hard way that their arrangements are *never* boring."

"You don't have tickets for the opening of the new Rodgers and Hammerstein? Here, let me write down the number of our ticket broker."

"I heard of a marvelous new caterer."

". . . the most reliable limousine service in town . . ."

Although Gilberte had no compunctions about leading Larry on to greater and greater extravagances, guilt twisted through her every time she saw Ann. Ann's lively eagerness publicly appeared intact, but when she thought herself alone, she took on a beaten, frazzled look. Gilberte had to constrain herself from inquiring if there was anything she could do to help.

Approximately six months after Ann and Larry moved from California, Gilberte invited them to a dinner party.

* * *

If it were possible to set Jason Templar's block-long, 137-room mansion, which had been demolished in 1923, beside his grandson's red-brick Federal-style house, the latter would appear modest in the extreme: standards of grandeur, however, had been lowered in the intervening three decades and the Dejongs' place on Fifth Avenue facing Central Park was considered to be one of the city's finest private residences. Inside, lighthearted paintings by both known and unknown Impressionists mingled with the somber Gainsboroughs and Goyas that Quent had inherited, and a cigar-store Indian presided over the entry to the billiard room whence the guests spilled into a glassed-in terrace and then out to a charming little city garden. Unlike at the Beverly Hills party, there were no famous faces, and the women's dinner dresses were understated. The men wore custom shirts, hand-cobbled shoes, British tailoring, and none of these items appeared new. Gilberte had composed her guest list so that the Porters were the only couple not included in the New York Social Register or tethered by marriage, schools, clubs. At the Beverly Hills party, Larry had been awed yet also convinced that, given any kind of luck, he would join the pantheon of big shots. Here, after introductions to a Roosevelt, a Rockefeller and two Dejongs, he was cowed. The exalted names, which would be terrific to drop later, indicated an aristocracy whose sole entry was by birth. He stood on the fringe of a masculine conversation with a fixed little smile. Since in this crowd being with one's wife did not appear to be social suicide, after a few minutes he joined Ann. She seemed at her bubbly best in a group that included Quent and several illustrious patronyms. When Larry diffidently mentioned that Ann was an old friend of Gilberte's from Paris, questions flew at her: Had the hostess shown a precocious interest in fashion?

"Absolutely," Ann retorted with a laugh. "This was during the war and clothes were impossible to come by, so we invented a game called Design—we sketched ourselves wardrobes. I drove poor Gilberte round the bend. My ideas were cribbed from the movies. She, of course, knew everything there was to know about couture from her mother. *My* mother had one new dress every other year from the *modiste* around the corner—Madame was incredibly untalented and half blind, but very, very cheap."

Larry, reddening, joined his bray to the laughter.

As Gilberte and Quent were undressing, he asked, "Why didn't you invite the Porters with a more arty crowd?"

"You're right, they didn't fit in, did they? Well, I've done my duty. After this we'll let them seek their own level. At dinner, Larry never stopped asking Mittie and Charity the most ridiculous questions about schools in Darien. As if *they* were experts in Darien!"

Darien, Connecticut, was an hour or so commute on the New York, New Haven, and Hartford. As Gilberte had pointed out, none of her guests would dream of living there—but the executives who ran their corporate enterprises viewed the suburb as their Valhalla, their ultimate goal. At the turn of the century Darien had been a summer beach resort, and this image remained. Large houses, almost all of them built of white clapboard and pretending to be older than they were, nestled along the hushed, tree-shaded roads that wound toward Wee Burn Country Club.

Ann, having heard stories of the town's exclusivity and the so-called gentleman's agreement that barred selling to colored people, Jews and Catholics, would have turned thumbs down on the house on Hollow Tree Ridge Road even if it weren't far, far out of their price range. As they drove toward it, Larry stared hungrily at a stables, a big Cape Cod almost hidden by massive white firs, a quaint carriage lantern, the equally quaint street names. It never occurred to him that Gilberte, who was accompanying them on what the Darien realtor called "a second lookie look" at his dream house, might consider herself slumming. Certainly he would never have suspected from her manner. As Jordan smoothly chauffeured them in her car, she pointed out jungle gyms, tree houses, wood-paneled station wagons filled with children.

The house, with its overgrown acreage, weathered roof shingles and peeling paint, appeared venerable. In actuality, it had been built a scant thirty years earlier, but had stood empty for the past two.

As they toured the rooms, Gilberte admired the hand-hewn

beams and the fieldstone fireplaces. When they had finished the inspection, she asked, "What'll you do with those third-floor rooms?" There was a maid's room next to the kitchen, but two cubicles for additional servants were tucked beneath the curling shingles.

"My plan is to break down the partition to give Ann a room to play." Larry spoke too archly. It shamed and rankled him that they relied on his wife's income more rigorously than ever. "What think you, boss lady? Is this or is it not the value of the century?"

"A steal," Gilberte said.

"We don't have the down payment," Ann said.

"The realtor's positive the owner'll take a second."

"Larry, she wasn't at all sure," Ann said. "And anyway, even without a second, the monthly payments would be way beyond us."

"So we'll tighten our belts a bit."

Ann looked at the warping, hand-pegged floorboards, the large water stains that splotched two walls. "There's a monumental amount of work. The roof, the pipes—"

"Exactly why it's a bargain," he interrupted.

"The shingling alone'll be a fortune." Ann's voice shook. She was on the verge of tears.

How she loathed the role of miserly spoilsport! During the war she had seen Larry's lavish tips and the rapidity with which he reached for checks in the same way that she had viewed the dashing tilt of his lieutenant's cap: he was a happy-go-lucky guy. Now, though, forced into being the family Scrooge, she had learned to dread his improvidence. Their current expenses were astronomical enough, what with the steep rent and the maid's wages, but even so they could have cut it—if it weren't for his charge accounts. Gifts for her, gifts for the children, gifts for friends, gifts to his parents to impress them with his success. His personal bills, which included the time payments for the suits he'd bought at Chipp and also invoices from merchants so exclusive that she'd never heard of them—at a shop called Morton's he'd purchased twelve shirts, each one costing more than a dozen Arrows! He owned hand-cobbled shoes, a tailor-made hacking jacket. He wrote substantial checks to a ticket scalper, and to the limousine service who delivered them to the Broadway openings. He had hired a caterer for three "buffet suppers" that had cost a bloody fortune. (How he sniffed out these discreet provisioners to the upper crust was beyond Ann.) Their gross income was more than double what it had been in California, yet on Montecito Lane they had been reasonably solvent and on 67th Street they were sunk into a morass of unpaid bills. She was forever robbing Peter to pay Paul, one month putting off the landlord, the next ignoring the pediatrician. The subsequent dunning phone call or threatening letter brought on a painful tightness in her neck.

And now Larry had set his profligate heart on this house.

Her skin felt bruised by the weight of so many future bills.

Gilberte moved to the window, gazing out at the tall grasses, unpruned trees and bramble-choked shrubbery. "What a marvelous garden," she said.

"Isn't it, though?" Larry agreed with a triumphant glance at Ann.

"Look, far be it from me to interfere," Gilberte said. "But since I'm along for my opinion, I have to say Larry's right. This is but the perfect place for children. And if the down payment's a problem, I'd be willing to take on a second mortgage."

"We can't let you—" Ann started.

"Gilberte, you're an angel!" Larry broke in excitedly.

"No gratitude necessary. I wouldn't make the suggestion if my tax attorney hadn't told me that second mortgages are a sound investment." She paused. "Quent mentioned something new called a balloon payment."

"Balloon payment?" Larry pushed back his thinning blond hair. (Last month he had written a check to a salon on 49th that treated incipient baldness.)

"It's quite simple," Gilberte said, and extemporized on a new theory of financing that she had heard the president of the Dejong Bank explain to Quent. "You pay nothing for say, five years. At the end of that time I get my money back, plus interest, of course. Long before that Gilberte de Permont, Incorporated, will be solidly in the black and there'll be substantial bonuses."

"Gilberte—" Ann started.

But Gilberte cut her off. "Talk it over while I go explore that garden. It reminds me of our country place in Ile de France."

Larry struggled to open the warped side door for her.

Gilberte trod through the tall weeds, getting her pumps wet. Nothing here reminded her of the gemlike gray château in Ile de France. But this big, untended garden, surrounded as it was by a low stone wall, with its semi-impenetrable mesh of raspberry bushes and its large trees, many of which had branches sturdy enough to support a tree house, might easily be mythologized into an enchanted kingdom by a small, imaginative boy.

Gilberte could not escape her nemesis—that long-ago promise. Yet neither could she relinquish Michel. And there was the rub. Though tormented that her actions were inflicting harm on her son, she could not stop her scheme. *At least he'll have a place to be happy,* she thought. A squirrel, holding its tail aloft, darted away as she rounded an overgrown rhododendron bush.

Larry peered through the filthy window as his employer moved out of sight. "This balloon payment idea," he said, "it solves our problems."

"Sure!" Ann retorted. "All we'll be stuck with is the first mortgage, the taxes, a new roof and God knows what other repairs."

"You heard Gilberte!" His face was red and sullen. "The house is perfect for kids."

"Larry, as it is, we can scarcely keep afloat."

She expected a shouted reproach. Instead Larry slumped on the crazed paint of the windowseat. "Shorty, you don't understand what this place means to me. I had to turn over every cent of my paper route money, so I never had a dime for the movies. My buddies would open the emergency exit and I'd sneak in. On-screen there'd be houses like this. Big, full of prestige and furniture, yet comfortable. And the fathers—Jesus, those screen dads. Old Judge Hardy was my favorite. All that white hair and decency. He wanted the best of everything for his family. You know my old man. Whenever he scrounged up enough to get loaded, he'd take off his belt to Mom and us. Afterward I'd lie on my stomach with my ass bleeding and swear that my kids wouldn't grow up like me."

Ann sat next to him. "There's other nice suburbs," she said gently. "We could buy a smaller, newer house."

"Don't you understand? I want them to grow up in the right place, have all the right things. I don't want them to work their tails off getting people to like them."

"Larry, you're the most popular person I've ever known."

With an incoherent sound, Larry sank to his knees, his arms around her waist, his head pressed to her belly, a supplicant position.

Later, when Gilberte pushed open the difficult side door, Ann told her that they would be eternally grateful for her help.

Gilberte couldn't look into the huge, frightened brown eyes.

52

One morning in the winter of 1951, Ann sat in what the real estate broker had called the "keeping room," a tiny room off the front hall. It was furnished with a secretary's swivel chair and a battered gray metal desk that Ann had bought at Goodwill. (When guests were expected, Larry would lock the keeping room door.) She was playing an onerous form of solitaire with the bills stacked in front of her, placing the urgent ones to her right, shuffling the ones that could be put off to her left. She frowned for nearly a minute at the statement of Henry Bennet, DDS, of Darien. A handwritten addendum threatened a collection agency, so she placed it to her right. The payment on the new Lincoln also to her right. The quarterly dues at the club—Larry had joined Wee Burn, the most desirable club in town with the excuse that taking up golf would help him in his career—she set down on the left. He would be furious, but the utility bills, due the previous month, had to be paid. She waffled between Robinson's Antiques in Darien and the decorator, Willis Zode, whom Gilberte had insisted on bringing out to the house, in the end dropping them both on the left because the two mortgage payments were inescapable: already the bank had tacked on a ten percent late penalty for the previous month.

She would pay the neatly typed yellow statement from Galway's Darien Grocery. No matter how rigorously she determined to drive to the supermarket in Stamford, after the twentieth of the month she invariably ended up stony broke and thus was forced to patronize Galway's, which charged—and overcharged. On the back of an envelope she scribbled *Coriana, Mr. Popescu, commute tickets.* She was spartan about paying both Coriana, the beaming, ample-waisted Jamaican who cooked and tended the children (Sundays, Ann put on large blue latex gloves to tackle the cleaning) and Mr. Popescu, the bent, seventyish gardener. Sighing, she closed her eyes. Numbers preceded by dollar signs danced behind the lids.

She forced herself to count the ways in which the move to Darien had been beneficial. Janey no longer wet her bed, and Michael, that proud loner, actually had a friend, Timmy Popescu, the youngest son of the gardener by his third wife.

The numbers refused to go away. She could only truly expunge her sense of dread while she worked in the clammy chill or simmering heat of her never-finished attic studio. Up there, she also forgot her misery about Quent. She seldom saw him, she missed him constantly. Once a romantic, always a romantic.

Shoving the bills to her left into a drawer, aligning the ones to her right, she opened the large maroon checkbook. She ordered herself not to be so rough on Larry. He was a terrific father and, discounting his compulsive spending, a great husband—*he* wasn't mooning after somebody else.

A little over a year later, on a sunny afternoon in April of 1952, Gilberte called Larry into her office.

"I'd like you to meet Marjan," she said.

"The face is familiar." Larry grinned into the small, angularly distinctive features of the strawberry blonde model who had three times graced the cover of *Vogue.*

"And the body?" Marjan asked, striking a pose that thrust a hipbone toward him. Modeling, she showed the demureness that matched the current ultrafeminine fashions, but her smile to Larry invited carnal consideration.

"Marjan's going to do our ads," Gilberte said.

"All of them?" Larry asked.

"That depends on you," Gilberte said. "What sort of coverage could we get if Marjan were the Gilberte de Permont Girl?"

"A Gee de Pee Gal," Larry said, nodding.

"I'd be your symbol," Marjan said, fluttering mascaraed eyelashes at him.

"That'd mean we'd get a double whammy. Our name'd be mentioned whenever I get you into the columns. Hey, boss lady, a sensational idea. I mean it."

"Why don't you two go think up publicity angles," Gilberte said.

She sat gazing thoughtfully at the door long after they had left her office.

"Clever, using one name," Larry said, blinking as they emerged into the bright, invigorating afternoon.

Marjan smiled. "Our discussion, where d'you have in mind?"

"The Colony? '21'? Lindy's? I'm yours to command."

Marjan continued to smile.

Larry, who had never tumbled from the marriage bed, felt his ears burn.

"I know a place a few blocks away," she said. "Opposite Madison Square Garden."

That area was given over to seedy bars and hotels with day rates. "Oh?" Larry took an involuntary step backward.

Marjan's smile altered, becoming subtly derisive.

Horns were snapping viciously on Seventh Avenue. Larry felt as if his hands were double their normal size. Then he asked, "What's so special about this place, hmm?"

She gave a throaty laugh.

The Montague was precisely what he had anticipated: a fleabag. The immensely fat desk clerk, knowledgeable in the ways of garment district expense accounts, inquired whether Larry wished to charge the room.

"A lot of guys put it through." Marjan removed a fleck of tobacco from her lipstick. "It's up to you."

Again Larry imagined catcher's-mitt-sized hands dangling at his sides. After a brief hesitation, he started the formalities of opening an account for Gilberte de Permont, Incorporated. The Montague's linens weren't clean, room 405 smelled of dust and stale perspiration, and Larry, nervous enough anyway, had a problem

maintaining his erection. But Marjan was an endlessly innovative
nympho.

Late in the winter market week of 1953, Gilberte stood with one
hand on the microphone, watching the bouquet of models, headed
by Marjan, now officially the Gilberte de Permont Girl, pirouette
up the temporary runway to the strains of a Liszt Hungarian Rhap-
sody. The flowered cotton of the stylized peasant skirts belled out
to display flounced, beribboned petticoats. Light caught the gilt
embroidery thread of the trompe l'oeil necklaces on the fitted
bodices. The three hundred people squeezed together on rented
chairs burst into spontaneous applause, a rare accolade during this
hectic week.

Resentment percolated through Gilberte. She had battled
against these peasant dresses, reminding Ann that although this
might not be a *maison de couture,* neither did milkmaids and swine
girls buy Gilberte de Permont clothes. But Ann's pretty jaw had
clenched with tenacious doggedness in defense of her brainchildren. Staring down at the women's hats, the gleaming bald heads,
the applauding hands, Gilberte reflected that Ann did seem to
possess a kind of voodoo prescience about fashion. There had
been a serious article in the esteemed French periodical *Le Jardin
des Modes* about the Velázquez suit. That Thai silk cruise line had
hacked a path into the buyers' budgets, last year's summer knits
had flown out of the stores. All Gilberte's vaunted logic cried out
that only a moron would be reduced to ignominy by this sustained,
heartfelt ovation—but logic would not still the lost, resentful child
within her.

Raising a silencing hand, she said, "These delightful little cottons were designed when I had need to cheer myself." Sympathetic
whispers rippled through the audience. The cognoscenti knew
about her sojourn in Dr. Kreiger's a few months ago, when she had
suffered a second miscarriage. (*Poor Quent,* Gilberte thought, gripping the microphone with both hands. *He still hasn't forgiven himself
for being away on that climbing expedition in the Himalayas.*) "I saw
myself on a hot night dining on the terrace. But now it seems to me
that I could wear one on the boat, barefoot, for cocktails."

At this Marjan kicked off her sandals and, still dancing, pulled up one side of her skirt, tucking it into her sash, a seemingly impromptu act planned by Ann to show off the lavish petticoats. Now Gilberte's smile masked perverse fury. Although she had thrown Larry and Marjan together, she was experiencing the twisted ambivalence that colored her entire relationship with Ann. How dare this skinny blonde tramp sleep with Ann's husband!

The trio ran up the staircase, laughing like naughty schoolgirls at the renewed applause.

It's a smash collection, Gilberte told herself. *I'm a success, I'm a success.* But her cheeks drew in as if she were sucking a lemon.

That evening Gilberte went to bed early. The frantic work and doubts surrounding the collection, the strain of presenting the show herself (another of Ann's ideas, to break the tradition of an MC impersonally calling out numbers and present the line herself, with appropriate small talk) had exhausted her, yet she did not skip her nightly routine. She never neglected either her appearance or her work. She was jotting down the following day's *must do's* when Quent arrived home from a business dinner. He paused at the open doorway of her room.

When he had returned from his climbing expedition to find her recuperating from her "miscarriage," he had suggested he move to the large, paneled study. At the time it had appeared another example of his thoughtfulness. Now, though, it seemed to her that he had retreated yet further behind a moraine of husbandly consideration. She missed his large, warm body at her side, she missed their late night conversations. She brooded that he might have affairs—he was too much a gentleman to let word of his indiscretions get around, so her angst remained speculation.

"How did it go?" he inquired.

"Very well. Salesmen writing orders all over the place. And the gift, as usual, was smashing." At the beginning of each market week, he sent a piece of jewelry to her office, this time a ruby and diamond brooch in the shape of a rose. She patted the side of her bed to indicate he would be welcome.

"For some reason it seemed very you," he said, not moving.

His smile was fond, yet he remained at the threshold. The warmth of the cashmere blankets, her immense wealth, her much-envied marriage, her carefully arranged social life, her fame and business success, all these fell from her. She felt as stripped and shorn as she'd been under the shell-shaped copper canopy on the boulevard Suchet.

"Maybe because Papa had a rose pin designed for Maman," she said, sighing. "I wonder what Bonn *Hausfrau* treasures it now."

Quent came to sit on the bed.

"Darling," she murmured, running her fingers through his black hair, so like her own, twining her arms around him, pulling him onto the Porthault sheets that were changed daily. Her simulation of passion involved acrobatic slitherings that could have been reported in the *Kama Sutra.*

Afterward, while he smoked his postcoital cigarette, he asked, "Were the Porters at the showing?"

"They always are. Larry swarmed all over, spreading my name. And Ann was in the *cabine* checking on the models. Why?"

"Just wondered. At that party of theirs"—every few invitations, Gilberte and Quent made a token appearance in Darien—"they seemed a bit frayed around the edges."

"The results of being host and hostess. And poor Ann, she'd just love to hear your description."

"Does she do your designs?"

Another shiver passed through Gilberte. "Of course not. Whatever gave you that notion?"

He squinted through the smoke at her. "Didn't she use to?"

"Never. Probably you got the idea because sometimes when I'm tied up, she watercolors my sketches."

Quent blew out smoke, inhaling again. "Next week I have to go out to San Francisco."

"The bank?"

"Yes."

"How long this time?" she asked.

"No way to pin it down. And since I'll already be out on the West Coast, I might as well zip on down to Los Angeles to settle that grant to UCLA." The Templar Foundation munificently endowed universities across the country.

"I'll miss you."

In lieu of a response, he touched her cheek, and it occurred to her that this gesture was more intimate than anything that had passed between them this evening.

"I have to admit you were right and I was wrong about those damn peasant dresses," Gilberte said. "Too bad for you. Now you'll have to come up with something astonishingly like them but totally different for the next collection."

"I've been thinking . . ."

"There's a novelty." Gilberte often teased Ann about her inability to work out designs in her head—she needed to sketch or drape to discover her ideas. "Go on."

"Denim . . ."

"What?"

"Denim."

"Like workmen's trousers."

"Exactly. But washed until the fabric's as soft as Michael's pants."

"You're serious, aren't you?"

"The idea's all vague. I'll have to try it."

"Denim . . ." Gilberte raised a finger. "Wait. I do remember seeing something that looked like denim skirts in Santa Fe."

"New Mexico?" Ann asked, surprised. "You've been there?"

"When I first came over. Quent had always rhapsodized about the Southwest, so in my naïveté I let him drag me out there for a couple of days. Long enough to turn my skin to leather and to enjoy a highly romantic interlude."

"Hmm?" Ann leered suggestively across the desk.

Gilberte noticed that the responding smile was forced. As Quent had pointed out, Ann seemed doused. That sense of joy, that passionate commitment to all life's promises was gone. She looked sad, burdened, the freckles were more pronounced.

Gilberte then committed an inexplicable generosity. Why? What had happened to her vow? After the years of forcing herself to invent and secretly inflict methods of everyday torment on Ann, why would she long to return Ann's smile to its former gleaming happiness?

Yet she was saying, "We have a little place near Santa Fe. Why not confer with your muse there?"

"That's fantastic of you, Gilberte, but I can't leave Michael and Janey."

"Larry'll be here. Besides, that Jamaican of yours usually takes care of them."

The phone rang. "Boss's orders," Gilberte said over the jangle. Why was she pushing it? Later she could uncover no ulterior motive in her invitation beyond twisted and misplaced lines of compassion for the enemy who was her only friend. "Boss's orders, a week in Santa Fe for you." She picked up the receiver to forestall further argument.

Ann and Quent
Santa Fe, 1953

53

The house was a few isolated miles east of Sante Fe. Built in the pueblo style, its weathered beams projected out below the flat roof. The four-feet-thick adobe walls needed replastering annually, and this gave them a patina like much-worn gold. The five raffishly askew little windows that pierced the front of the house as well as the large territorial-style windows along the rear *portál* were painted a vivid blue known locally as Taos blue. Beyond the huge old cottonwoods that shaded the free-spirited rear garden, the stables and caretakers' quarters stood like sentinels against the harshly beautiful desert.

The house was small, but the interior appeared spacious because of its simplicity and because of the sculptural quality of the recesses and *bancos* that in many places assumed the function of furniture. Ponderosa pine *vigas,* massive ceiling beams, served as ornamentation, augmented in the living room by a curved-topped niche that displayed antique Hopi kachinas.

Ann emerged from the smaller of the two bedrooms, tightening her robe against the chill that was rapidly being dissipated by blazing mesquite logs in the corner fireplace. Worry no longer haunted her eyes, her nose and cheeks were tanned to a light apricot. Standing at a territorial window, she gazed out. In the three days since her arrival she had been unable to get enough of the landscape—the sawed-off flatness of the mesas that extended to the Rio Grande to her west, the continents of clouds that cast great, drifting purple shadows across vast stretches of high desert. The air here was so crystalline that she felt able to reach out and touch the Sangre de Cristo mountains, which now, in the early light, were bronze, but this evening, when the setting sun touched them, would blaze red as the holy blood for which they were named. After a few minutes she smelled coffee, and went into the kitchen where Rosie was fixing her breakfast. (Rosie and her husband, Juan, Indians from the Peñasco area, lived in the caretakers' weathered wood house.) Ann doctored the potent brew with Carnation evaporated milk. As Rosie brought plate after plate of steaming sopaipillas, golden-fried airy puffs of dough, Ann drenched them with sage honey, justifying her appetite with the thought *I won't need lunch.*

Juan had given her keys to the Ford pickup, and, wearing jeans and an old sweater set, she bounced along the unpaved ruts toward Canyon Road, where the artists lived, then wound into Santa Fe on the narrow corridors between one-story adobe buildings. Emerging at the Plaza, which she loved for its honest yellow grass and dusty old trees, she parked on its north side in front of the Palace of the Governors, a long straggle of unprepossessing adobe that dated back to 1610. In the chill, crepuscular shadows of the deep *portál* sat Indian women in bright velvet blouses. Ann knelt to examine their neatly arranged, handmade wares: pottery, leather and silver belts and *bolas,* turquoise bracelets and necklaces, geometrically patterned rugs, kachina dolls. The prices were painfully low, but she warned herself sternly that she couldn't afford anything. On the other hand, she couldn't go home without gifts, could she? She found a squash blossom necklace for Coriana: the silver wasn't heavy, but the turquoise was a perfectly matched greenish shade. She hesitated for a long time over a gleaming, onyx-black pottery bowl from the village of San Ildefonso, admiring the elegance of the stylized deer running around the rim: in the end she decided that the possible recipient, Gilberte or Larry, would consider it junk. For Janey, she chose two small animal-headed dolls that were descendants of the antique kachinas at the house. She bought an openmouthed pottery storytelling woman with children crawling all over her because it would tickle Michael. She paid a few pennies for a half-dozen necklaces made of brilliantly dyed corn.

By now it was nearly one, and, despite her resolutions to avoid lunch, she was ravenous.

Stowing her purchases—except for the corn necklaces, which she was wearing—in the pickup, she crossed the Plaza to a diner whose sign proclaimed CHILI AND EATS. Sitting at the counter, she fingered her corn necklaces. *Another morning shot to hell,* she thought unrepentantly. She was no closer to designing a collection than when she arrived.

"Yeah?" The countergirl stood with her pencil poised.

"Green chili and a tamale," Ann said.

"The chili's very hot here, you'll need a beer," put in a masculine voice.

She wheeled around.

Quent sat on the stool next to her. In his faded jeans and faded plaid flannel shirt worn with a *bola,* with that Indian-black hair, he could have been a local.

"What're you doing here?" Her voice squeaked.

"Having lunch," he said, and set down a small, newspaper-wrapped package. Lounging against the aluminum-tube back of his stool, he grinned at her.

"You knew what I meant," she retorted with belligerence worthy of Michael. "In Santa Fe."

"I happen to own a place near here."

"I know, I'm staying there—I'm meant to be designing a collection there."

"Like it?"

"It's marvelous. But now you're here, of course I'll move." She glanced primly across the Plaza in the direction of La Fonda, a Harvey hotel.

The waitress cracked her gum loudly.

"Give me the same as the lady," Quent said. *"Y dos cervezas, por favor."*

In the few seconds while he ordered, Ann understood what she would have known immediately—if she'd taken time to think before she spoke. He had followed her in here.

As the waitress bawled out the order, pinning it up, Ann asked, "How long have you been watching me?"

"About an hour. I'd never have thought you'd be such a careful shopper."

"You were spying on me!"

"Given my stint in the OSS, why the shock?"

"Will you stop grinning like a cat with a canary inside?"

"Aren't you carrying this redhead's temper act a bit far?"

She shifted to get coins from her pocket.

"What're you doing?"

"Paying. I'll go pack my things."

He straightened, his smile faded. By alchemy, he transformed himself into the uncommunicative aristocrat.

"How did you know I was in Santa Fe?" Ann asked quietly.

"Rosie. I was in Los Angeles, and phoned to say I'd be in for a night or so."

"I wish she'd told me. I could have brought my stuff into town with me."

He swiveled his stool to face her. While the voices around them bleated and the waitress bawled an order, she stared into the deep blue eyes.

"Do you want to leave?" he asked.

Her mind flooded with reasons to say *yes*—her marriage, her friendship with Gilberte, all the decently monogamous virtues that Dorothy had instilled in her. Looking down at the beer bottle, she fingered away the moisture and shook her head.

"You'll stay?" he asked.

Suddenly she smiled at him. Sucking in her cheeks, pushing her pretty white teeth forward to denote idiocy, she said, "I must have brain damage."

He laughed, then pushed the package toward her. "For you," he said.

It was the black pottery bowl.

"This was the end of the Old Santa Fe Trail which ran a thousand miles from Missouri," Quent said. They were crossing the dusty Plaza to the pickup.

"Know what? I imagined this would be a smaller Los Angeles, I guess because of the Spanish background. I still can't get over the difference."

"It's the Indian heritage," he said. "New Mexico's history is deeply rooted in the Indian culture. Ever hear of the Anasazi, the ancient ones?"

"Weren't they ancestors of the Pueblo tribes?"

"Right. There's ruins of their cliff dwellings not far from here."

Her eyes sparkled. "I'd love to explore some."

"No problem about that." A black feather lay on the dirt path and he bent to pick it up, smoothing it carefully. "So you do some of the designing?" he asked.

"All of it. Then Gilberte goes over whatever I come up with—she has a terrific eye, wonderful taste. Sometimes I agree with her suggestions, sometimes I give her a rough time, refusing to compromise." Ann laughed, exhilarated by this public announcement of her creations. Then she added, "It sounds rotten that way. But it's how we work."

They had reached the pickup. He opened the passenger side for her. "Keys?" he asked.

She reached in her jeans pocket. "How did you get into town?"

He raised a hand, jerking his thumb.

"Hitchhiking? You?"

"Let's have one ground rule," he said. "None of that, okay?"

She stared up into his eyes. And felt as she had this morning, that in this clear, crystalline air, all things were within her grasp. "Deal," she said, touching his cheek, smiling.

"Back in the diner, I was shaking," he said in a chesty rumble. "I thought it'd be the same as in Los Angeles, when you turned me down. God, Ann, you don't know how crazy I've been without you."

54

"You're another person," she murmured.

"From during the war, you mean?"

"No, New York."

"Him. He *is* another guy. He's all Jason Templar Enterprises, the Trust, the big philanthropist. A *Fortune* magazine type. Sometimes I leave him."

"What are you doing when that happens?"

"Thinking about you."

She smiled.

They were lying under the wedding ring–pattern quilt, arms around each other. Without discussion they had come in here, the larger of the two bedrooms with Quent's unopened suitcase on the painted Spanish bench, silently throwing clothes on the tiled floor, clasping each other on the bed with drowners' urgency. Afterward, they had slept, and now, three hours later, twilight shadows padded the corners.

Ann touched his left arm, a wandering caress that traced the levels of hard, slick flesh.

He moved the arm.

"Did I hurt you?" she asked.

"I can't feel anything. No nerves there. But if you get rough, the bones'll twinge."

"Darling, what happened?"

"A bald-headed Kraut at Mauthausen wanted to know a lot of things that I couldn't tell him. . . . You don't want to hear ancient history."

"Would you rather not talk about it?"

"I never have. . . ." he said.

"You don't need to."

Rolling onto his back, he clasped his hands under his neck. "I told you the Dieppe Gestapo was waiting for me when I parachuted back into France?" he asked in a flat, expressionless voice.

"Yes, the morning you rescued Michael."

"One of my contacts had been tortured, and spilled everything he knew. Which was more than I knew. But the Germans assumed that an American would have very hot information—I like to think I wouldn't have given it to them if I did." He rubbed his bad elbow.

"The radio code?"

"That they figured out for themselves. After the interrogations, they turned me over for 'special treatment.' "

"Special treatment?"

"It had a lot of meanings. I could have been shot as a spy. Instead, I was transferred to Mauthausen. Right after I arrived, the SS guards put me in with twenty-nine other Americans—most of them were downed pilots. They took away our shoes and marched us to the bottom of the quarry. They loaded seventy-or-so-pound slabs of granite onto our backs, and we carried them up a hundred and eighty-six steps. Then we carried them back down the hundred and eighty-six steps. They loaded more rocks on our hods. It began to rain. The steps were very steep, and now they were slick, too. If you fell or didn't climb fast enough for them, they kicked you and beat you with truncheons. They had two shifts, and they kept us carrying the stones all night. After two days and nights, when the rain stopped, there were three of us left."

"Left?"

"Alive. The others were dragged away in a handcart hauled by these skeletal Russian POWs and Polish Jews. I'm pretty sure by the next morning the other two were dead."

"Oh, God," she whispered.

"He wasn't much in evidence at Mauthausen. After that I was

shoved in a subcamp called Gusen with the French POWs. We were starved and worked twelve hours a day in the quarry." He was silent a long, brooding minute. "Then, toward the end of the war, I caught the attention of Rottenführer Ulrich Hoelzhoener. I doubt whether Hoelzhoener was a really sweet guy to begin with and, understandably, he'd become embittered—his wife and three small children were killed during the fire-bombing of Dresden. He ordered that I be kept in something called a kennel, a cement cell three feet high and five feet long. The only time I could stretch out was when they hosed me off for questioning. Hoelzhoener had acquired a medieval torture instrument, a real antique. An iron vise. He kept it locked on my elbow, turning the screws every day when he interrogated me."

Ann bit back a whimper. She longed to hold him, but understood from his rhythmic rubbing at the bad arm that touch would be unbearable for him. "Quent, you couldn't tell him anything useful. By then France had been liberated."

"The lieutentant was convinced that even though I'd been captured in France, I'd been working with the Dutch underground." Holland had remained part of the Third Reich that last winter of war. "He felt he was breaking new ground for the Fatherland. It wasn't humanity's finest hour, believe me."

"That sadistic bastard." Tears were oozing from the corners of Ann's eyes.

"The arm festered and I had spotted fever. I was delirious when the camp was liberated that May by Patton's Third Army. Being in the OSS, I had no dog tags, but I must have been babbling in American. I came to in the military hospital to hear I was about to part company with my arm. The family knew the right strings to pull, and I was off to Stockholm and Dr. Lindstrom's clinic, he's an orthopedic genius, but Jesus, the operations were painful. Sometimes I begged to have the damn arm amputated and get it over with."

"I'm sorry, darling, so sorry," Ann murmured.

"I like to think," he said musingly, "that your New York buddy would be different if none of this had happened, but probably I'm kidding myself."

"You've always been the bravest, the best person I've ever known."

"Did I say that thinking of you kept me going?" He reached for her hand, gripping it tightly.

The evening breeze rustled over the endless sea of sage, the peaceful, redemptive music of the high plains. She dried her eyes on the sheet and rolled toward him, massaging between his tensed shoulders. Consoling. Comforting. After a few minutes, they were pressed tight together, his leg over hers.

When they had made love earlier, it had taken him a long, tender while to coax her to climax—to cut through the barrier of her guilt. Now, though, as he entered her, she gave a high, astonished cry, then gasped out, "Quent, Quent . . . ah darling, Quent, Quent, Quent . . . I love you . . . always, always. . . ."

Later, when they put the lights on in the living room, Rosie carried over a tray of covered dishes. *Posole*, which looked like popcorn soup, *poblano* chicken, enchiladas. As they ate, Ann said, "Rosie seems to know what to do."

"Natural tact." He tore a blue-corn tortilla, buttering the smaller piece. "If you're asking if I've brought anyone up here, the answer's no. But if you're asking about women, the last two years I haven't been actively faithful."

"I have," she said. "Until now."

This oblique exchange was as close as they came to mentioning their spouses for the next several days.

Holding hands, they hiked in the desert, she lay in his lap in front of the raised fireplaces while they stared at the flames, they held hands watching the setting sun redden the Sangre de Cristos. It was as though the vestigial, animal gift of silent content had been restored to them. When they talked, it was about the concern of the moment—Rosie's tantalizingly spiced southwest cooking, the lazy flight of a fringe-winged hawk, the electric storm that ranged the night with the brilliance of Fourth of July fireworks.

They made love a lot. They made love with guileless swiftness and artful, prolonging skill. They made love with uninhibited wildness in the bathtub, they made love fully dressed in the chill night under the huge, glittering stars. Ann floated in time, seldom glanc-

ing at the painted Spanish colonial clock as it ticked away the
minutes until her Sunday morning flight.

When they awoke on Saturday, Quent said, "Today's your last
chance to visit the Puyé ruins."

"I'm ready!"

They wound through hills, passing long, shabby Indian villages
then emerged in a tremendous flat valley. At the junction of the
road, Quent pointed toward the Jemez mountains. "Los Alamos is
tucked away there."

Shivering at the intrusive name of the secret, closed city, birthplace of the atom bomb, she moved closer to him on the pickup's
seat, glad they were heading in the opposite direction. They turned
north into a desolate canyon. After a few miles, Quent pulled over,
parking on the shoulder.

"There," he said.

At first she didn't recognize anything that could be caves. Then,
following the line of his finger to a stratum of rock near the flattened top of the mesa, she saw a series of dark marks that might
have been a natural formation. "That's the cliff dwellings?" she
asked.

"Disappointed?"

"No, surprised. How do we get there?"

"Walk," he said, pulling out the picnic basket and a folded Navajo blanket.

As they left the truck, the sky was a dome of blue with a few
frayed white puffs, but as they trudged up the slope, darker clouds
swarmed over the Jemez mountains, covering the sun. The temperature dropped swiftly, but the exertion of hiking uphill around
tumbled rocks at an altitude of five thousand feet kept Ann warm.
Reaching the base of the brown cliff, she looked askance at the
rough-hewn log ladder. Several rungs were missing and it stopped
a good distance short of the ledge.

"No fair. I'm a city gal and you're a mountaineer."

"I've gotten you up and down a worse place than this, haven't
I?"

He climbed the ladder swiftly, depositing the Navajo blanket and
the basket, returning to boost her up until she sprawled on the
loamy brown soil that covered the rock of the ledge. This was the

first chance she'd had to look at the panorama. The pickup far below was a toy, trees and brownish greenery fringed toy villages. A beam of light protruding from a cloud showed the snow salting the creases of the Jemez mountains.

"Oh, Quent," she breathed, holding out her arms as if to embrace the vista.

The dwellings that ranged along the ledge had door holes and cutouts like windows. Peering inside the nearest, she laughed aloud. Some centuries-dead inhabitant had carved a *nicho* and a *banco* in the hollowed-out space. "All very familiar," she said, her eyes shining. "Your architect wasn't very innovative."

"Now you believe me when I tell you the Anasazi started it all." He raised a hand, peering at the sky. The towers of dark cumulus clouds were trailing a curtain of rain. "Ann, we better get inside."

"This one's too low for you," she said, moving to her right. "Let me find us a proper home."

The ledge had crumbled to a few inches, so she hugged against the palisade, then scrabbled over a protruding bone of the cliff, rejecting three caves as too small, another as too low and the next as lacking in charm. Quent laughed, joining in the game.

She peered through a semicircular hole. "This one. We'll buy this one—that is, if you can stand inside."

He had to stoop to get through the entry, but his head didn't quite reach the domelike center. "Sold," he said.

He spread the rug on the soft dust of the *banco,* and Ann covered one end with Rosie's Tupperware bowls of tortillas, salsa, cold roast beef and hard eggs. As they ate, wind rushed along the side of the mesa, then lightning flashed. They both counted aloud, and as they chorused "Ten," thunder boomed. Rain sluiced as if the sky had opened. The freshness of wet earth and the smell of electricity combined with the aroma of food.

Sharing the last of the coffee that remained in the thermos, she said, "Listen to that rain. Maybe we're trapped here forever. I won't have to think up an excuse for going home without a single sketch."

It was dark inside the cliff dwelling, but she saw the change in Quent's expression, as if his warm flesh had become as impervious as the rock that swallowed them.

"We still have hours and hours left," she said quietly. "I shouldn't have ruined it."

He wrapped his arms around his upraised knees. "We're going to have to discuss the future, so why not now?" His voice was low yet angry. "I don't think I could leave her."

"Quent, it's been heaven, but there are no obligations."

"Most of the time I hate her."

"Gilberte?" she asked bewildered. "I know you're not wildly in love, but you've always seemed perfect together. The same friends, you both like classical music. And Gilberte cares for you—she always has, Quent. Always."

"You sound like a marriage counselor."

"Or Pollyanna. But it's true."

"All week I've been thinking, 'My life could have been like this.' "

"Me, too. But what's the use?" Sighing, she pushed back her hair. "It's impossible. There's the children—Larry's crazy about them, and they adore him. And though I never loved him, I've always liked him. Everybody does. He's very sweet, very dear. . . ." Her voice trailed as a streak of lightning showed Quent's tightened lips. At this moment he had no wish to hear her softer emotions toward her husband. "I can't just walk out on them."

"I married her when I was still all nerves and in rotten shape physically. I'd just heard about you and Larry. But looking back, my guess is I'd have married her without any of those reasons. I'm so damn guilty about what had happened."

"Quent, you really still believe that you gave away the baron and baronne?"

"I've got proof."

"Who gave it to you? Gilberte?"

"She plays on my part in it, sure. But in Dieppe they knew I'd given explosives to the Résistance."

"My guess is that particular crime was on every OSS prisoner's record."

"André was my friend as well as my relation. Oh, hell, I idolized him. When I was a lonely, bewildered kid, he treated me like a friend, which Dad never did—was incapable of doing. He paid honest attention to my ideas. And I killed him and ViVi."

"Any number of people could have betrayed them."

"Ann, I'm not arguing, I'm trying to explain why I'm so damn confused about Gilberte—why in spite of everything, I stick around."

"She's always been complex, different."

"Don't tell me! And the hell she went through turned her into a very sick woman." Pushing to his feet, he flattened both hands on the brown rock at either side of the entry. "She wasn't pregnant."

Startled, Ann took a moment to realize what he meant. "She was," she denied.

In the sheepskin jacket, his back was strong and adamant. "No, she's a compulsive liar. She lies about everything. Her orgasms, her feelings, her designing." He thrust a hand into the rain. "Having a child would have made a rotten situation endurable. The first miscarriage shook me plenty. The second was worse. I blamed myself. The problem might lie in me. My less pleasant wartime experiences, I decided, might have done damage. I told you I was just in Los Angeles. I made an appointment with the doctor she used out there, his name's Lassitter, and he's an expert in fertility. He was astonished that Mrs. Dejong had been pregnant. As a matter of fact, he was incredulous. He said, given the state of her uterus, it was a miracle greater than the virgin birth."

A blast of wind drove rain into the cave. Quent shifted to avoid the rush of water. Ann remained immobile. She feared the least shift in her equilibrium. If she moved, maybe she would blurt out that Gilberte was not barren, that Michael was her child by Field Marshal von Hocherer. And if she said this, the unsayable, then Gilberte would take her son from her.

Quent came slowly back and sat facing her. "I didn't intend to spew this over you."

"Darling, you must know how crazy I am about you."

"Yes. And I love you. And you like Larry, and I'm probably tied to Gilberte for the rest of my natural life."

Ann sighed. Guilt, remorse, moral code, children, decency, idiocy, call the combination whatever, each of them was tied into a loveless, luckless marriage.

"The storm's passing," Quent said, and this marked an end to the conversation.

Ann, Larry and Gilberte
New York, 1953

55

There was no airport in Santa Fe. As Quent drove her the sixty miles to Albuquerque, she stared out at the wind-hewn formations and stumpy mesas. Their silence, unlike the serene quiet of the past few days, had a ponderous, waiting quality, like the thunderheads that cast black shadows across the tawny landscape. They both were thinking of what must be spoken. Finally, Quent said the words. "What about New York?"

"I want to see you."

"But?"

"Quent, I'd be sure to give myself away. And we agreed that our marriages both seem pretty irrevocable."

"Should I talk you out of that decision?"

She shook her head.

Gazing at the endless posts strung with barbed wire that were a ubiquitous part of the western landscape, she remembered him cutting the thickly strung wire at the Swiss border. Then they both had been so young and unencumbered. Without warning she began to cry. Quent pulled into the rutted shoulder, reaching over to hold her. The tears seemed inexhaustible, she could not halt them, and he stroked her hair, from time to time kissing her forehead.

"I wish . . . I wish we were a different kind of people," she wept.

He pressed his cheek against hers. The cheek was as hot and wet as her own.

This was their good-bye. They did not kiss at the airport. Reaching the top of the aluminum ladder, she turned, and saw him standing with his hands in the pockets of the disreputable sheepskin jacket. He did not raise his arm, and neither did she.

Her flight arrived at La Guardia more than forty minutes late, but Larry, who had promised to meet her, was not at the gate.

She had already retrieved her suitcase when he arrived, liquor and apologies on his breath.

As they walked toward the car he chattered about the children— Janey had cried for her, so he'd taken a day off and bought tickets for himself and both children to *The King and I*. Also he'd taken in a Dodger–Cards game with Michael at Ebbetts Field. (Michael considered baseball a moronic game, but since he adored his father, Larry did not know this.) He'd gone to a PTA meeting put on by the March of Dimes: three doctors had discussed ways to protect children in the upcoming polio season. Ann wasn't fooled. Larry was attempting to take her mind off his tardiness by waving his Daddyhood. But she also knew that while she had been in Santa Fe making love to another man, *he* had been dear and doting with their children.

Two days later, Gilberte was on time to meet Quent at the same gate. While Jordan went to retrieve the baggage, Gilberte said, "You look tired. Bad flight?"

"Rocky," he said.

In the car, he leaned back and closed his eyes.

As they were crossing the bridge into Manhattan, he said, "Ever think how much of the time we spend apart?"

Gilberte, who had assumed he was drowsing, felt a jolt of adrenaline tighten her muscles. Sitting erect, she said, "You were gone longer than you intended."

"That's not what I meant."

"Both of us travel a lot."

"Yes, but why?"

"If you're angry about my career, why not say so?"

"I'm not blaming you. It's my fault too. But it's gotten so that

we're only together if we need to put in an appearance someplace."

Sweat broke out, chilling her body, and she shivered under her
creamy lynx coat. Terror, terror out of all proportion to his few
quietly spoken words. Forming an acid little smile, she asked,
"Who is it this time?"

"Who is what?"

"That well-worn other woman, as in *cherchez la femme.* As in your
father's divorce suits."

"This is about us."

"I have it! You've committed the ultimate cliché. While you were
out there in Hollywood, you fell for some stupid little starlet."

Quent turned, giving her a long, level look. "Why did you lie
about the pregnancies," he asked.

He might as well have dropped her in the icy black water far
beneath them. The blood rushed to her heart while her body froze.
"I'm having difficulty following you. . . ." She was shivering so
her voice shook, as if with rage. "I must say this is a difficult
conversation to follow."

He drew a breath. "You can't have a child."

"That's an interesting theory, but methinks a mite dishonorable
for *you* to have invented. Did your new girlfriend, the dedicated
young thespian, dream it up? Tell her from me that's she's welcome to see my records at Dr. Kreiger's."

"Dr. Kreiger's a six-foot piece of shit!"

"An evocative metaphor," she said.

"He's an unethical quack." Quent's voice had returned to its
normal incisive calmness. "He's been slapped on the wrist by the
AMA for every sort of shady gynecological dealing."

"I was pregnant twice. And you can tell that to the lady in
question."

The windowless corridor stretched endlessly as she plodded
along. Her mother's disembodied voice, high, charmingly malicious, informed her it was a gaffe to continue, and from behind a
closed door screams rang out. She longed to run in the opposite
direction, to escape, yet she was powerless to prevent her feet from

trudging forward. The air in the corridor grew colder, and was filled with the flat, salty smell of raw game, of used menstrual pads.

One of the doors was ajar, and she knew that inside some unimaginable horror awaited her. Her heart crowded her chest so that she could scarcely breathe, and she stared back at the surreal perspective of the corridor. "De Permonts do not run away," her own voice informed her. She pushed the door open wider. Her father was sitting in a chair, his small, quick dark eyes sad.

"Gilberte, you shouldn't have come here," he said.

Then she saw his flesh was muddy, and there were little flecks of blood on his shirt. And he was tied to the chair.

A moment before he had been talking to her, but now a filthy cloth was stuffed into his mouth. She heard a distant thump-thump, as of hundreds of booted feet goose-stepping in unison. As the cadence grew louder, filling the cell, forcing it to expand, she saw the endless line of soldiers, faceless under their helmets, alike in their black uniforms as dragon's teeth. At a command, one stepped forward, taking from his bayonet a pair of long, glittering scissors. She heard the loud rip of cloth as he cut her blouse and skirt from her. Naked, shivering, she heard the men's laughter, pulsating and inhuman as their boots. Another command. Four soldiers stepped forward in formation, spread-eagling her on the icy stones. Another command, and a fifth soldier stepped forward, unbuttoning his trousers. To avoid looking at the phallus, pink as a dog's but enormously thick and ropy, she looked up at the wall. And saw her father's dangling, bloodied corpse. . . .

She screamed and screamed.

She awoke with a violent jerk.

"Gilberte." Quent prodded her shoulder. His hair was rumpled over his forehead, his pajama top undone. "Nightmare?" he asked sympathetically.

The terror receded.

"I was back there . . . they'd come to rape me. An army of them. And Papa was dead . . . dangling, all bloody and awful, his eyes bulging out."

"It's okay, you're safe," he said.

"I'll never be safe. Never, never, never," she said. "Quent, stay here a bit."

He sat on the bed stroking her hair. Her shudders lessened. Until now the terror had been unfeigned, but as she recognized his expression of culpability and grief, the calming beats of her terrified heart told her she mustn't lose her advantage. She continued to sob. He lay down next to her, and she pulled the blanket over him. Though she kissed his neck, his jaw, and pressed close to him, he did not react. Still, he slept all night in her bed.

In the morning when he got up, she locked her door and went to the Renoir nude. Swinging the painting open on its hinges, she worked the combination of the safe and pushed aside jewelry cases. She removed a large Florentine leather box. Inside lay the Gestapo envelopes.

The *cauchemar,* for all its distortion, had an element of warning. The shades of her parents were trapped in some ghastly, shadowy land, waiting to be properly avenged.

It wasn't yet seven, but she reached for her green faille telephone book, looking up her travel agent's home number. Staring at the sheets of yellowing paper, she ordered the arrangements she wanted him to make for her.

56

Ann, feeling a displaced person amid the society bustle of lunch hour at the Colony restaurant, fidgeted with her silverware and wished that she smoked. A cigarette would make a fine prop as she waited at the table always reserved for Gilberte. A threesome of overly thin women were following the captain, and as the trio glanced toward the table, she responded with a smile, having met them often at the various benefit fashion shows that Gilberte put on. All three women peered blankly, as if she were part of the table setting. Ann looked down, pretending to be occupied with her portfolio. The large flat case held her sketches for the Santa Fe collection. She had not yet discussed her designs with her boss.

That same night she had arrived home, she had started to work in her attic. The next few days ideas had streamed from her fingers, but she had been unable to report in. She knew she could not carry off a conversation with Gilberte. Her burst of high inspiration had never fully expunged her awareness of infinite loss. At the end of the week, when she had nerved herself up to call the office, the new secretary had told her that Madame was in Paris—yes, an unexpected trip. This morning the secretary had rung back to say that Madame had returned and would like to meet with her over lunch.

There was a little rustle at the nearby tables as several men got to their feet. Gilberte, smiling at them, glided after the captain. While most of the other women in the restaurant had cropped their hair into the new, short poodle cut, Gilberte's black mane was intact and drawn back into a chignon that emphasized her ivory skin and exotic topaz eyes. Her unadorned black *tailleur* (not designed by Ann, who knew it was a Balenciaga fresh from Paris) capitalized on her lushly sensual breasts and hips.

She was trailed by a youngish man. His barbering was longer than an American's, and his pin-striped suit cut tighter to his thin, short body. Ann knew he was French even before Gilberte introduced him.

His name was Yves Roland.

As they sipped aperitifs and ate, they chatted *en français* about the cold weather in New York, and about Paris, pre- and postwar. Yves Roland knew everybody who counted, from Piaf to De Gaulle, from Jean-Pierre Aumont to Jean-Paul Sartre, Cocteau to Coco, and he passed on amusing tidbits about them. He did not drop any hint for his presence in New York. His glasses magnified his owl-round eyes and he looked at Ann intently whenever she spoke, an appraisal neither condescending nor subservient yet sensitive as a sponge. He was soaking up her character, her personality.

This baffled her. She knew intuitively that women were not Yves Roland's preferred bedmates—and she also guessed that, unlike many homosexuals, he preferred his own sex as friends.

She wondered why Gilberte, who seldom did anything without a reason, had included him at this lunch.

Gilberte glanced at her watch. "It's two-thirty!" she exclaimed. "I must rush. An appointment. But you two stay, enjoy your coffee." And, as Yves rose to say good-bye, she added, "Ann, Yves worked with Cortini."

Cortini and Schiaparelli were spoken of in the same breath, two designers, both women, both Italian, who had put their mark on French fashion.

"Cortini!" Ann said as Gilberte hurried away. "How I envy you."

"Don't. She's cruel to all her protégés, and most cruel to those with a soupçon of talent." Leaning toward her, he said in a low voice, "Madame Dejong has told me in strictest confidence that you aid her in her work?"

"I do all the original designing," Ann said, her face reddening.

But why this sense of blowing her own horn? She was simply telling a colleague the truth. "Then she discards and alters. I go back to work again."

He nodded. "Cortini works the identical way. She can't sketch, can't drape. Seven years with her house taught me a lesson. Before I would sign a contract with Madame Dejong, I insisted she put in a clause that acknowledges me. All advertising, press releases and labels will say, 'By Yves Roland for Gilberte de Permont.' "

"You're here to work for Gilberte?" Ann whispered.

"But surely you knew that she came to Paris to interview?"

Ann shook her head. Her hands were clenching and un-clenching, and she did not realize that she had pushed the napkin from her lap until the waiter, with a small flourish, returned the starched damask to her.

"You've gone pale. I didn't mean to shock you." A moment earlier, Yves Roland's sympathy had been unctuous, phony, but now his concern rang true. "Some water perhaps?"

Ann took the glass he extended, setting it down. "Where do I fit in?"

"Of course you'll continue in your sphere."

"What's that?"

"She said she wanted to devote more time to something called 'the big picture.' "

"I've always worked with her."

"*Exactement.* And you'll work for me."

"My collections have always sold."

"I assure you mine will also." Yves Roland bristled. "Madame told me that she desired somebody who didn't smell of Spam and peanut butter."

Ann's outrage turned to misery. Why had Gilberte committed the gratuitous cruelty of having a stranger, a rival, spell out her new position? Through her mind flashed the thought that Gilberte knew about Quent's being in Santa Fe. But how would Gilberte have found out? The guilty flee when no man pursueth.

"I should not have repeated this," Yves Roland apologized.

"It's not your fault."

"She's a bastard, that one."

Ann assumed Yves Roland was using a figure of speech to make up for his outburst of spite. (Not for several days, during which the two of them hashed out the Santa Fe theme despite his vacuum of ignorance regarding New Mexico, did he exhume the bones of the long-dead scandal.)

They parted with a neutral handshake beneath the restaurant's canopy, he hailing a taxi, Ann on foot. She had intended returning to Darien immediately—she had promised the children they would go to the library and then have a treat at the coffee shop. But as she plodded through the chill afternoon toward Grand Central Station, hurt snapped at her like a mean little dog. All these years of silently going along with Gilberte's pretense that she was some kind of human mimeograph machine and here was Yves Roland with a contract that guaranteed him credit for his designs!

I can't go home before I have this out with her.

She used a pay phone to explain to Coriana that she'd be taking the 5:32, not the 4:32 as planned, then she trotted into a subway entrance.

When she emerged on Seventh Avenue, a cold drizzle was falling. Pulling up her coat collar, she walked more and more slowly along the sidewalk opposite the gray granite building, finally stopping in the entry of a wholesale trimmings supply shop to stare up at the light that flowed through pinch-pleated sheer curtains. Gilberte's office.

She had been drawn here by her need to get her accusations out in the open, but now she was asking herself, who was Ann Porter to accuse Gilberte Dejong of betrayal?

Ann shrank deeper into the shadows as Larry and Marjan emerged. His left arm was snaked around the twenty-and-a-half-inch waist. Ann knew the model's measurements. She had often knelt in the *cabine* pinning in seams at the leanly narrow waist now adorned by a tightened raincoat belt and Larry's caressing fingers. Marjan bent closer to Larry, whispering something in his ear. He smiled, his hand rising fractionally toward the flat bosom.

It didn't take an expert in the field of human relations to realize they were on their way to a bedroom, in either a hotel or a borrowed apartment. Marjan, for all her glamorous occupation and sexual foraging, lived with her father and mother in Queens.

After the couple disappeared around the corner of Seventh Avenue, Ann stood shivering until a stout, mustached man came out of the trimmings supply shop. He smiled at her. She barged into the drizzle, running back to the subway entrance.

57

Ann was silent as she drove Larry home from the Darien station, but he talked enough for both of them, resting his hand on her knee. His episodes with Marjan increased his affection for his family and therefore, or so he rationalized, improved his performance as husband and daddy. The children were in bed but still awake. He said lengthy good nights, stroking Michael's soft brown hair, kissing Janey's warm, Ivory-scented neck. Downstairs, he poured himself a large Scotch, then went to the kitchen. Despite his blandishments that Ann keep the maid up to serve them in the dining room, his wife stubbornly insisted on letting Coriana turn in while she herself reheated or fixed the meal. Tonight, though, there were no pots on the Roper range, and Ann was sitting at the breakfast table with her head bent. "If we're eating out, it's fine with me," he said irritably. "But let's get a move on."

She lifted her head, staring at him as if he were speaking Esperanto. When she had arrived home from New Mexico, she'd had a glowing tan, Larry recollected, but now she looked as if she'd powdered herself with whole wheat flour.

He stalked to the refrigerator, with elaborate gestures taking out a carrot, biting into it.

"I've been thinking about this a lot," she said, as if continuing a conversation. "Maybe we ought to get a divorce."

Divorce?

The carrot dropped from his hand. He felt the heat rising in his face, a guilt he told himself was irrational. He might have been screwing around a little, but in an uninvolved way that was therapeutic to their marriage.

"I'm not blaming you," she added.

The rhododendron bushes rattled outside the window, then he found his voice. "What sort of shit is this?" he yelled. "Divorce? Blame?"

She glanced up at the ceiling, toward the second floor where the children lay in their big, sparsely furnished rooms, then at the service porch, from beyond which came the sounds of Coriana's radio.

"I walk in after a hard day's work and get a soap opera riddle," he whispered roughly. "Will you kindly explain what in hell is going on?"

"Things haven't been the same since we left California."

"By that do you mean you miss our days of scrounging around in Levittown west?"

"Oh, Larry," she sighed.

She must have been dieting. She was thinner. She looked as fragile as she had in the hospital bed following Janey's birth. His wave of helpless pity for her made him bluster louder.

He shouted, "There's somebody else!" A statement that was patently ridiculous.

"There was," she said.

The sudden pain bursting through his head frightened him. Guys his age had strokes. He gaped at her. "There was?"

"It's over."

He gulped the remainder of his Scotch. "Are you sitting there calmly telling me you've been laying another guy?"

"It's over," she repeated.

"I don't believe this!" And he couldn't. His cute, wholesome little wife, his virgin bride, his open-book Ann, putting out for some other guy?

"I hate all the subterfuge."

"Right. Let's square it all up, my wife goddamn opening her legs for the populace!"

"It had nothing to do with us, Larry." She was weeping.

"Nothing to do with us? You bitch, miserable cunt."

Larry knew the requisite actions that inevitably followed these words, actions that had been burned into his brain from earliest childhood. He should yank her to her feet, slam either side of her face, then either pummel her with his fists or take off his belt to her. But Larry was not cut out to be a wife beater. Clutching his head, he rushed out to the garage, gunning the Lincoln down the gravel driveway.

The following evening, he drove home with a dozen long-stemmed red roses. Ann was in bed.

"Here," he said helplessly, and handed her the flowers.

"Thank you," she said, getting up to take the ginger jar from the bedroom fireplace.

He followed her into the bathroom, watching her fill it. He averted his gaze from the missing floor tiles. No matter how he nagged at her, she kept forgetting to call a tile contractor.

"Ann, this other guy, is it really finished?" He looked at her in the bathroom mirror.

She nodded. Busy moving the roses from their cardboard coffin to the blue-and-white ginger jar, she did not return his reflected gaze.

"Then why did you say that about"—his larynx tightened and he had difficulty speaking—"a divorce?"

"You have somebody too."

"The hell you say!"

"Larry, let's not put each other through this," she said. She had stuck her finger on a thorn, and she sucked at the drop of blood. "I know you have a girl."

"Your damn crystal ball is cloudy today, kid."

"I saw you. Two days ago."

"With Marjan?"

"Yes, Marjan."

"It so happens we were on our way to a shoot."

"I leveled with you."

After a beat or so, he muttered, "It means nothing."

"Larry, I'm not accusing you, I haven't got the right."

"You and the kids are all I've got." Sinking down on the edge of the tub, he buried his face in his hands.

After a minute, he heard her murmur, "Hush, hush." Her tone was husky, comforting.

As Ann stroked his hair she thought: *Poor Larry, poor, poor Larry.* Neither vicious nor cruel, he didn't burn for power, he didn't lust after wealth. His compulsive extravagance was not an attempt to impress the world, but a plea—approve of me, like me, see me as a great guy, love me. How hearing of her defection must have slashed his poor fragile ego. No wonder he'd run out of the house. Trapped in the web of her pity, Ann forgot the damage he did to her by acting the child. She kissed the thinning hair.

"Shorty, you and the kids are my life," he said brokenly.

Later that evening, as he ate the supper she'd fixed him, a cheese omelette doused in canned Hormel chili the way he liked it, she stood at the sink washing the pans telling him about yesterday's lunch with Gilberte and Yves Roland.

"She didn't explain it to me herself. That's what hurts. She left us there in the Colony and let him explain. A man I'd never seen before."

"Doubtless he's something new and unique in the history of fashion," Larry said sympathetically, "but I never heard of him."

"He must be good. He worked with Cortini."

The toaster popped up two pieces of rye toast, and Larry buttered one. "Schiaparelli, Cortini, who can keep them straight."

"Larry, her name's on all my sketches. But she's giving *him* credit. His clothes will say 'By Yves Roland for Gilberte de Permont.' "

"Big deal. Shorty, listen, you signed a contract that everything you had was hers."

"Coffee?" Ann asked in a thin voice.

"None for me, thanks." Larry watched her take his dishes to the sink, then said ruminatively, "I know this Paris designer guy has you shook, but have you considered that Gilberte's your friend and she's trying to deliver you a message?"

"Message?"

"Like you should stay home with the kids and take it easy."

Ann gripped the sink, staring at a pear-shaped hole in the plaster that they'd never had the money to fix. She was too distraught to speak. Larry's persistent refusal to admit that her work was anything more than a personal whim infuriated her, as it always did. But now for the first time she was considering that Gilberte might slash her salary.

58

For the next few days Ann couldn't force herself into the garment district. She had often worked at home, so there was no reason for concern, yet she received twenty-seven phone calls inquiring whether she felt okay. Everyone from Moe Sbicca, the head salesman, down to the new messenger boy, Maisl—his first name was unknown—called. Not one of them mentioned Yves Roland, yet she understood that each call expressed solidarity on the raw deal she was getting. During these conversations she experienced a visceral heave of humiliation, and quite a few times after hanging up, she rushed to the toilet to vomit.

Ideas of quitting swarmed chaotically through her mind. Quitting, alas, was impossible. Who would hire a nobody on her own say-so that she had done the designing for Gilberte de Permont when everyone knew from the extravagant advertising, the publicity campaigns as well as the horse's mouth that the proprietor was a fashion innovator? And if by some fluke she, Ann, could find a job, who in this cutthroat business would shell out the handsome salary that the Porters now required more desperately than ever?

Larry attempted to cheer her up with a crimson satin box of Godiva chocolates, a black alligator pocketbook with the expensive name of Henri Bendel stamped inside. (Ann returned the purse but the chocolates, alas, were non-negotiable.) He also raided

F.A.O. Schwarz on behalf of the children—she didn't have the heart to take away their gifts. With homicidal thoughts about her husband and a near hysterical laugh, she finally asked herself what difference a few more bills could make? There were already enough in her metal desk to prove indentured servitude for the rest of her natural life.

On the day she returned to work, she stopped feeling paranoid about her growing conviction that Gilberte knew about Santa Fe.

She found another name painted below hers on the door of her frosted glass office. CARTWRIGHT POLLITT.

A young man, handsome as a male model with overly blond hair, was kneeling to pin the skirt on a dress form. He introduced himself. "I'm Cartie Pollitt, Mr. Roland's assistant," he said. "And I'm trying to get a bead on this denim idea of his."

Ann wedged her portfolio and her purse next to her crowded drafting table. What difference did one more theft of her brainchildren make? Besides, who knew, maybe humiliation was good for the adulteress's soul. "Here," she said. "Let me show you."

One evening in the middle of April, Ann and Larry missed their train home: since there wouldn't be another for nearly an hour, they trotted downstairs to the Oyster Bar. The crowd had thinned out and they got a table.

Larry, who was being abnormally uncommunicative, stared into the Scotch he'd ordered. Ann took out her compact. Before March, she had seldom used more than lipstick, but now she had on Pan-Cake, mascara and eyeshadow. And even with this disguise when she glanced into the powdery mirror she imagined she could see the signs of both her pining for Quent and the incessant mortification at work.

By the time the waitress set down Ann's bluepoints and Larry's chowder the tables on either side were vacant.

Larry reached over and touched her hand. Since the debacle he had been affectionate but hadn't made love to her. "She's turning into a vampire," he said.

"Who?"

"Who else? Gilberte." He glanced around to make certain there were no eavesdroppers. "Word is she's been talking to Davis and

Benton." It was a point of pride with Larry that even during market weeks, Gilberte had never resorted to Davis and Benton, the highly influential publicists referred to as the mouth of the fashion industry. "They say she's going to call in outsiders."

"You know how everybody in the business loves to gossip," Ann said consolingly. "It can't be more than a rumor, Larry. You've done a fabulous job."

"You're right, why would she change?" But he continued to crack his knuckles and didn't pick up his spoon.

It was Gilberte's custom to start her workday at ten. On Monday, May 4, though, Jordan delivered her to the gray granite building at nine. When she had taken over the fourth and fifth floors, her office had been expanded to include a spacious antechamber. The flowers had already been delivered, and her secretary was clicking at the typewriter.

"Good morning, Madame, how nice to see you so bright and early." There was no surprise evident in the greeting. She was ugly and compulsively thin, but Gilberte had hired her because even under stress her voice remained as soothing as that of a radio announcer doing laxative commercials.

"The minute Larry Porter comes in, tell him I want to see him."

"He never gets to work at this hour, Madame."

"Never?" Gilberte asked coldly.

"So far as I know, but I've only been here a few months." The secretary's rouged cheeks drew taut against her jaw, giving her an expression of hostility. Gilberte had heard enough swiftly truncated conversations to understand the resentment she had aroused with Ann's de facto demotion. She shook with a sudden burst of rage against the world, her old enemy, as personified by the skull-faced secretary.

"Hold my calls," she said icily.

"When Mr. Porter comes, Madame, or starting now?"

"I've been told my English is excellent. *Now.*"

Closing the door firmly behind her, Gilberte stood immobile, her breath coming raggedly. She seethed with fear, desolation, panicky helplessness. *Oh, God, it's* la p'tite bâtarde *all over again.*
. . . She unlocked the desk drawer where she kept the Miltown.

When she stopped trembling, she told herself she had over-reacted ridiculously, and went to the small table with Yves's sketches. She pored over a design for a suit. Her critical function told her it would be handsome—and without the least spark of originality. She had long ago conceded inwardly that she lacked the intuitive jump. She could not tell Yves Roland how the jacket might be altered, the skirt cut differently to give the suit the pleasures of the unexpected that showed in Ann's designs. *Those denims will be the only interesting numbers in the collection.*

From her drug-shrouded calm came a grieving nostalgia. Oh, she would give her soul (if she still possessed that inutile item) to return to the guileless friendship of two adolescent girls playing Design—such a dear, silly game.

How lonely I am, Gilberte thought.

Since his trip out west, Quent, who was home less than ever, spoke to her with constrained politeness. On her part, the marriage had eroded to a raging need to keep it intact and jumpy watchfulness whenever he spoke to a woman. Her husband had become a stranger, her father was dead, her son belonged to Ann. Her employees scorned her. Forming a slight, involuntary rictus, Gilberte carried Yves's sketches to her desk and began making notes.

She had one remaining friend.

Gilberte de Permont, Incorporated.

The hands of her Fabergé clock, once the possession of a Romanov princess, pointed at five to twelve when the secretary buzzed her. For half an hour Gilberte let Larry cool his heels, then she told her secretary to send him in.

He pushed the door ajar, peering around it boyishly. "Hi, boss lady," he said. "Can we stall off our powwow till after lunch? I should be at Sardi's. Major groundwork for a fashion show on Ed Sullivan and—"

"This can't wait," she interrupted.

Turning, he asked the secretary to contact his party at Sardi's and explain that something major had come up and he was delayed. Then he started to talk ingratiatingly about the growing importance of television coverage.

Gilberte interrupted. "Larry, I have very little time."

"So let's start the music and dance."

"I've been going over your expense account," she said, opening a drawer to get a file heaped with white, pink and yellow receipts.

"There's the living proof that I've been hauling bananas for you," he said.

"What an unusual phrase. I assume it means attending to business?"

Forcing a smile, he clicked his tongue, aiming his index finger at her. "You got it, boss lady."

"Hardly company business. This one"—she slid a receipt across the desk—"is from the Hotel Montague."

His Adam's apple turned white. "Forgot what we did there. Must've been a bash for out-of-town buyers."

"I'm quite certain not," she said coldly. "I had Jordan drive me past on the way to work. The Montague's a flophouse for assignations."

"Places change, they get run-down—"

"The most recent bill is dated April 28, 1953. Places seldom run down in less than a week."

"You caught me with my hand in the cookie jar," he said with a pale little smile.

"The accounting department has verified paying bills for thirty-two visits to the Montague."

"I'll make it up to you."

"That goes without saying." She selected other bills. "Constance Spry. You seem to have sent an inordinate number of flowers in the course of the year."

"Jesus, Gilberte, you know the lady buyers, they expect wall-to-wall flower arrangements."

"And what about the models? I see these orchids went to Miss Mary Jane Petersen in Queens."

Marjan, who combined and truncated her names, took a prom queen's delight in having orchids delivered to her parents' apartment.

"I'll cover all of those. I'll cover everything not totally connected with my job." He gave a laugh. "Gilberte, you and I both know expense accounts are meant to be a bit elastic."

"Being a prudent Frenchwoman, I lack your financial resilience." She tapped the heaped invoices. "You've run up exorbitant bills at restaurants and bars all across Manhattan, but there's no way to verify who you were entertaining, so I ignored them. The expenses that have no connection whatsoever to Gilberte de Permont add up to twenty-four thousand three hundred and twenty-nine dollars."

Larry's face drained of color. The sum exceeded his annual income—in this mental equation he included Ann's checks. "I'll pay," he said loudly.

"Now there's a less costly but more serious problem. The last few months my stockroom's been consistently robbed."

"Jesus! You know me better than that."

"I noticed Marjan wearing a lot of our clothes. Yesterday I spoke to her. She said you gave her things."

"Isn't she the Gee de Pee Gal?" Larry's question ended with a muffled sound.

In this moment Gilberte remembered the young American lieutenant with his cap pushed jauntily back as he lugged cases of PX delicacies up to that awful flat in Saint-Ouen. She longed to ease up. Yet the compulsion was beyond her control.

"Larry, my merchandise is expensive. We're not discussing petty pilferage. This is a criminal offense."

"I'll pay for whatever she says I gave her."

"As far as I can tell from the items that Marjan mentioned, it's around fifteen hundred dollars' worth—of course that's with your employee's discount."

"She *should* be wearing our clothes," he mumbled with a trace of defiance.

"That is up to my discretion, don't you agree?" Gilberte closed the file. "Between stolen merchandise and your illegal charges, it rounds out to twenty-five eight."

"You don't have to worry."

"It goes without saying that I can't keep you on. Or Ann either." She paused. "So your loan is due."

He stared at her with blank, bewildered eyes. "What loan?"

"The second mortgage on your house."

"But the payment's not due until 1956!"

"You and Ann signed papers. Didn't you read them? Clause five, section B states that in the event that your employment with Gilberte de Permont, Incorporated, is terminated, the loan must be fully repaid."

"Have you thought about my family?" Larry's voice rose. "Have you thought about Ann? She's your friend."

"I'd say from your visits to the Montague and your gifts to Marjan, Ann hasn't been uppermost on *your* mind."

"I'm talking about Paris. I'm talking about going into hock to help you."

"You're only embarrassing yourself."

"I'm talking about Michael."

Michel. Under her antique desk, Gilberte's hands were clamped together. Her son. If Quent ever found out about Michel, he would leave her. She had always known that Michel would eventually be an innocent victim of that long-ago vow, and now she felt as if the sacrificial knife were piercing her own chest.

Not betraying her lacerating turmoil, she stared Larry down. "If you ever say what you just said again, I'll have the police on you."

"You bitch," he said, his voice choking and low. "You cold, bloodsucking bitch—" His voice broke and he rushed from the office.

As the door slammed, Gilberte shuddered. She sensed she had crossed over a hair-fine line to some other place, but where this place was, she didn't know.

59

That same afternoon Ann drove Janey through bucolic, spring-green Darien to visit a friend who lived on the Sound near Holly Pond. Michael, who at almost nine had determined to devote his life to the study of insects, was staying at school to complete a project on spiders—arachnids, he called them. It was Coriana's day off. As Ann unlocked the front door, a tranquillity came over her. For unto her was granted an empty house with several quiet hours to work: it didn't matter that she would be attempting to put a little zip into Yves Roland's ball gown, which at the moment was sedate enough for a dowager empress to wear in her coffin, all she cared about was the work that inevitably rescued her from her own thoughts.

Reaching the landing, she heard odd, snoring noises in the master bedroom. Pushing open the door, she saw Larry sprawled on the candlewick spread, a bottle on the upended orange crate that she had painted to serve as a bedside table. She shook his shoulder. His jaw remained lax. He was out cold. Larry, a highly socialized man, was no solitary tippler. Besides, he never came home in the middle of a weekday afternoon. With a baffled frown, she returned downstairs to perk coffee.

* * *

"And then the bitch fires me!" It was an hour and a half later. Larry, not fully sober, was talking with loud indignation. "She tells me I've spent too much for Gee de Pee and fires me. If she wanted a lid on my expense account, why didn't she damn well set a limit?"

"She actually said you're through, Larry? It wasn't a warning?"

"Shorty, we're canned."

"We? Me too?"

"Both of us, the damn refrigerator bitch."

"God . . ."

"I don't believe it myself. She gives me the boot even though I promise to pay for every damn tab she questions."

"But why should you do that? The money was spent doing your job."

"Just because she's a malicious bitch," Larry said in a righteous tone, "doesn't mean I can't be a gentleman."

"How much is it?"

"Around fifteen thousand."

"Fifteen thousand dollars!"

"Maybe a buck or two more."

"How much more?"

"Twenty . . . uh, more like twenty-five."

Ann stared at him with suddenly shadowed eyes. Thus far Larry had gone through life with the not uncommon belief that if he avoided his problems, why, then those problems did not exist. Even the most optimistic ostrich, however, could not keep his head in the sand when confronted by these huge, bruised eyes.

Unwillingly, he added, "And she's calling that balloon payment thing."

"You mean our second mortgage?"

"She put it in the fine print that if we no longer work for her, the loan's due."

Ann was on her feet, her expression yet more desperate. "I'm going in tomorrow morning," she said. "I'll talk to her and—"

"Won't do any good. She's got it in for me, don't ask why, but she does. Maybe it got back to her that you're bitter about this Yves Roland."

Ann clenched her back teeth. Larry's inability to accept the consequences of his own actions, to shift the blame, was his least attractive trait. But then again, maybe he *was* the whipping boy for her. "What'll we do?"

"Have a little faith." His smile had inebriate edges. "Shorty, anybody interested in making it needs their name plastered in front of the public. So she fired me, big deal. Probably the best thing that ever happened to me. Old Larry-boy's in the right time and right place and the right industry . . ."

His hopeful words faded as Ann left the sunlit bedroom.

Closing the door of the keeping room, she hunched at the Goodwill desk. If Larry had poked his head inside, she would have attacked him physically. For several minutes she slumped there, breathing unevenly, then she straightened, muttering one of Dorothy's favorite adages: "No use crying over spilled milk." She fumbled around for scratch paper, finding one of Yves Roland's blue memo slips. In his spiky French hand he reminded her that all designs for the next collection would be worked out on living models. *Maybe I ought to send this on to Cartie Pollitt,* she thought as she turned the small blue square.

She wrote:

$25,000.00

She stared at the zeros, blanching. Tightening her jaw, she opened the top left-hand drawer where she stored the jumble of unpaid bills. She had never been able to force herself to add them together. Now she copied the long rows of numbers. The grand total was $9,763.26. She added this to the money they owed Gilberte, staring at the sum.

$34,763.26.

She did not include the second mortgage with their obligations. She had already given up on the house. Property values in Darien had shot up, and with any luck they could clear nine or ten thousand dollars on the sale, money, God knew, they needed. On another bit of scratch paper, she figured their minimum living expenses. With nothing coming in, they could no longer pay Coriana to mind the children or Mr. Popescu to tend the garden—not that they had ever been able to afford either a gardener or a maid. They would need to live meagerly for the rest of their lives—and maybe when the grim reaper arrived, he'd need to haul along their remaining bills.

What about filing for bankruptcy? She immediately dismissed the question. What could be more morally reprehensible than shirking your debts to the people who had trusted you? Besides, there would be an indelible public stain on their reputations. (Throughout her Paris childhood, Horace and Dorothy had clucked and muttered over a long-dead Blakely who had gone under in Wichita in the recession of 1910.)

There was a loud, metallic clang outside her window. Michael, home from school, had let drop his Schwinn bicycle—one of the few items for which Larry had ever paid cash. Ann jumped up, tapping the glass, waving at her son. Michael lifted his right hand two inches and turned away. At this new masculine disdain for mothering, she chuckled. In her own way, Ann was as tattooed with optimism as Larry: she couldn't add up her debits without counting her assets, the greatest of which were two healthy, terrific kids.

"So we'll have to sell the house," Ann said later that night as she and Larry were getting ready for bed. "Right away."

"So you just said." Larry aligned his black wingtip shoes, made by Goforth, under his clothes valet. "You're getting boring with it, you know."

"What other choice do we have?"

"You've never believed I could cut it, have you?"

The next few days, Larry turned a stony cheek whenever Ann mentioned selling. Losing his job was ego-shattering enough without the symphony of psychological woes that boomed into his mind every time she brought up banishment from his dream home in Darien.

Before ten the following Monday morning, Ann drove to the Salt Box Realty Office in Darien. On Wednesday afternoon a platoon of corseted, middle-aged brokers trooped through the rooms, then sipped iced coffee and nibbled sweet rolls as they advised Ann to get this or that fixed.

Coriana wept when she heard she must leave the Porters, hugging her lamb, Janey, to her ample waist: within hours the Jamaican had lined up a job with the Newcombes, who lived on the Long Island Sound in Tokenoke, and when Mr. Newcombe came for her and her tin trunk, she, Ann and the children wept. (Larry, unable to face the dismantling of his life, was seldom around.) Mr. Popescu showed no emotion. However, Timmy Popescu, Michael's one friend, refused to speak to Michael in school except in taunts. Michael, naturally, didn't tell his parents. He became a behavior problem to his teacher and changed from a voraciously advanced reader to a surly television addict.

Quent was constantly in Ann's mind. Before this, his Trust had frightened and awed her. Now, for the first time, she envied it. What she wouldn't do with those mountains of cash! By night, she dreamed of the real Quent holding her in his arms.

Two weeks after the dismissal from Gilberte de Permont, Incorporated, a letter arrived from Kemp and Schuyler, attorneys-at-law, to inform the Porters that they represented Mrs. Quentin Dejong in the matter of recovery of legally incurred debts.

"Mrs. Porter? I know you've overlooked Dr. Skaggs's bills. . . ."

"Mrs. Porter? The payment on your roof repair was due the first of November, 1952."

"Mrs. Porter? This is our third warning. After this we have no recourse but to turn your bill over to a collection agency."

There had always been dunning phone calls, but now creditors seemed to have sniffed out the demise of Ann's and Larry's employment: she felt as if she were surrounded by the rustling cries of vultures. She loathed the phone and sometimes let it ring without answering. She also loathed the arched metal mailbox with its burden of windowed envelopes.

She sold the few antique pieces that she had lovingly refinished, for double what she had paid. She got twenty cents on the dollar for the gold-rimmed Lenox china dinner set on which Larry had splurged two Christmases ago. The desperately needed proceeds she kept in her desk top drawer, for food and a commuter ticket.

That unusually cold May, Larry went into town every weekday to spread the word that he was available. He arrived home buoyed by hope and liquor, telling Ann at length how everyone had stood him drinks and there were fantastic offers firming up. Two bills arrived simultaneously on the second of June. Gallagher's and Lindy's both requested payment for the substantial tabs scrawled with the signature of Lawrence J. Porter.

"How could you?" Ann asked heatedly.

"Just like you, taking it out on me because there's a goddamn recession!" he yelled. Immediately thereafter he kissed her repentantly and was sweet and helpful with the children.

Ann filed these new bills with the old.

The next day she asked Larry to hold down the fort while she tested the job market for ghost designers.

Milt Copeman rubbed his sizable schnozz as he thumbed through her sketches, nodding as he came to the easy-looking coats—he was a midprice ladies' coat manufacturer. For two weeks she had been showing her portfolio to everyone she knew on Seventh Avenue, and Milt was the first to express interest.

"These're tops, honey," Milt said finally. "The truth is, Dessie" —Dessie Copeman, his wife and chief designer—"has in mind to retire as soon as we come up with somebody to take her place."

"I'm willing to take very little if I can work mostly at home."

"This smells like a hot number." Milt Copeman peered regretfully at the three-quarter-length jacket with the push-up sleeves. "Ann, I don't need to tell you that everyone in the *schmatte* business depends on factoring. I bank at Dejong on the corner of Seventh and Thirty-third, I have good rapport with the manager. So you can see why I can't hire you?"

"Gilberte has nothing to do with the bank." Ann's mouth was dry.

"There's a whisper going around, and you know how it is, if something's whispered in people's ears, they tend to believe it. The whisper is that the manager at Dejong won't sign notes for anyone who hires either of you." Copeman raised his hands. "You kids ain't about to find work, not in this town."

On the commute home, Ann drafted a letter to her old boss in Los Angeles.

Mr. Sever's affirmative reply came rapidly, on June 24. On June 25, a chirpy realtor brought over an offer from a White Plains couple. It was considerably less than Ann had hoped for. They would clear just under five thousand eight after paying the bank, the balloon second and the commission. Still, as the chirpy realtor pointed out, there had only been this one nibble. Ann trotted upstairs to discuss the offer with Larry.

"What do you think?" she asked.

"You already know my opinion, so why ask?"

She went slowly down the stairs to inform the chirpy broker that they accepted.

The buyers requested a sixty-day escrow.

Ann and Michael
Summer, 1953

60

Ann, packing bric-a-brac in the den, wore cutoff jeans and a halter: on that night in early August no breeze came off the Sound to dispel the muggy heat. Staring appraisingly at the duck decoy in her newsprint-blackened hands, she thought, *It should be sold.* But she had an affection for the weathered wood, and besides, wouldn't taking the duck to California be her act of defiance for this entire lousy day? This morning a snaggletoothed man in a drip-dry suit had rung the front doorbell. Thrusting the pediatrician's bill at her, he had said, "I'm not your kindly Dr. Skaggs, Ann, my outfit don't play footsie. My advice is to pay what you owe, Ann. Otherwise you'll see legal action so fast it'll make your head spin. Ann, you won't like your neighbors reading about it in that paper of yours, what's it called, the *Darien Review.*"

Janey and her friend had gotten into her makeup: the pair of five-year-olds then the bathroom tiles and woodwork had to be scrubbed clean of kiss-proof lipstick. Michael, afflicted by a hoarse throat the past few days, had chosen this afternoon to forsake the television and race about the tall yellow grass with the hose. Overexertion mingled with icy water was a dire no-no during polio season, but he had been going through such a lonely, belligerently miserable phase that she lacked the heart to ruin his fun.

She wrapped the decoy in newspaper, packing it. Glancing at her gold-plated watch, she realized it was seven minutes to nine. She and Larry had an old rule that if he hadn't phoned that he'd be on an earlier train, she was to pick him up from the 8:03. The children were already in bed, and she would have to leave them alone in the house for twenty minutes or so. Filled with vague worry and active resentment, she went out to the car. The dealer had been about to repossess the Lincoln, so she had traded the big luxury car to the realtor, who was willing to make the payments and give her a hundred dollars—Ann used the check to buy this tremulous, pre-war Chevy sedan with torn upholstery. Larry loathed it.

As she turned the ignition, she saw that the gas gauge was almost on empty. She had no cash left to fill the tank. Pondering what to sell next, she felt her eyes fill. She despised her weakness, and reminded herself that this was a snap compared to when she'd had to beg neighbors on the rue Daguerre to buy her mother's wedding silver so there'd be money for scraps of food.

She pulled into the unpaved area that was down an embankment from the small station. The majority of corporate executives who were the heart blood that pumped through Darien rode the 5:32. When the brightly lit 8:03 pulled in only a few weary men with briefcases stepped off.

Larry wasn't in the contingent.

Driving home with her mouth set, she returned to her packing.

"Mommy?" Janey had come downstairs. In her white nightgown with her cloud of pale curls, she was a sleepy, Pre-Raphaelite angel.

"What are you doing up, baby? Bad dream?"

"Michael woke me. He'th making monthter noitheth." Upset, Janey reverted to her babyhood lisp, and when truly distraught, she spluttered with this adorable earnestness.

Ann knelt to embrace the small, warm body. "Baby, he can't turn himself into a monster." Michael's teasing sometimes took the form of pretending to be a werewolf.

"He'th really mean."

Ann carried her daughter up to bed, extemporizing on *Wind in the Willows*. Janey kept interrupting in a drowsier and drowsier voice until she fell asleep.

Before Ann went downstairs, she looked in on Michael.

"Mom?" he mumbled. "I feel crummy."

She went to his bed, touching his forehead. The skin burned wetly under her fingers. "You're hot, I think maybe you have a little fever. I'll get the thermometer."

She had reached the second bathroom when he cried out—was this the sound that had frightened Janey? The drawn-out groan terrified Ann.

Rushing back, she asked, "Michael, what happened?"

"I tried to get up," he whimpered. "It's my neck, Mom."

"What's wrong?"

"Every time I move, it hurts."

A stiff, aching neck was the symptom that terrified every mother in the United States: it portended the onset of poliomyelitis.

"I'll go call Dr. Skaggs," Ann said in as calm a tone as she could muster.

She dialed wrong twice before reaching the exchange. "If you'll give me your number," said an androgynous voice, "the doctor will get back to you."

"This is an emergency!"

"Please give me your number."

For a paranoid moment, Ann decided this was Dr. Skaggs's method of repaying her for her long-delinquent bill. She gave her message, shrilly repeating Michael's symptom of painful neck. Returning to his room, she smelled the sour odor of vomit.

"Tried to get to the bathroom," he mumbled, hoarsely apologetic. "S'polio, isn't it?"

"More likely stomach flu," she said lightly.

Her mind was jumping through blazing hoops. Of course it was polio—acute poliomyelitis, infantile paralysis, the scourge, the plague, the dread unthinkable. Every article stressed the vital importance of prompt medical attention. Last week, she had seen a report in *The New York Times* about Mount Sinai Hospital's well-equipped polio unit.

"Michael," she said, "we have to get you someplace where they can help you."

"No moving . . ." Michael began to cry. Proud loner, he never wept.

"It hurts, I know, but you'll be with the driver of mighty generals. Smoothly Blakely they used to call me." How could her voice sound so vivacious?

She couldn't leave Janey alone, but how could she take Janey in a car with Michael puking polio germs? Churning at Larry's absence, she was ready to weep at the impossible task of finding a sitter at this late hour. Then she thought of Coriana. Luckily, her new employers, the Newcombes, were an elderly, childless couple unlikely to cavil at their housekeeper baby-sitting at the home of a possible infantile paralysis victim.

Coriana succumbed to the terror in Ann's voice, and Mr. Newcombe sped her over.

By then Ann had changed Michael's pajamas. She carried the heavy child, groaning and sobbing, down to the old car—if only she could have the Lincoln for this one trip! There was no traffic this late, otherwise she would have had an accident as she broke speed limits along the finished sections of the thruway. In New Rochelle the car began to cough, and she realized she was out of gas. She oozed into a Paloverde Oil station. She had only a few pennies in her change purse, but the attendant, mercifully, cashed her check—she was beyond considering the morality of passing bum checks. While the tank filled, she stroked Michael's slippery, burning forehead.

"Mom . . ." he muttered hoarsely. "Polio's my own fault . . . playing with hose . . ."

"Hush, it's all right, darling."

His skin was yet hotter, and when he mumbled something about *Ivanhoe,* she knew that he had lapsed into delirium.

She went through every red light in Harlem and Manhattan.

Pulling into the Mount Sinai emergency entrance, she saw by the eerie brightness that Michael's thin neck was drawn rigidly downward, turtlelike, between his narrow shoulders, and his face was a strange, bluish magenta as he struggled for breath. Impossible to believe he had been his normal pugnacious self at dinner. As the white-uniformed orderlies lifted him from the car, he gave a high-pitched screech that sent her reeling back to Saint-Ouen and his early brush with death.

She registered him, saying silent prayers of gratitude for the March of Dimes, the organization that made polio care available to all who needed it. She was directed to a large waiting room. A stout couple murmured over their rosaries. Two elderly blondes talked with resolute cheer to a pale, hunched-over young man. When a weeping girl came in, the young man gripped her hand. The blondes—by their conversation, mothers to the young couple and grandmothers to the stricken baby—moved to sit near the pay phone. One or the other of them answered the constant ringing, speaking to whoever was on the other end in muffled whispers.

Ann called Darien. No, Mr. Porter, he had not come home or called, the little lamb was sleeping, and how was dear Michael? Hanging up, Ann sat with her icy hands clasped, her eyes closed. *How is dear Michael?*

"Mrs. Porter?"

"Yes?"

A white-coated man with a gray crew cut and a seamed yet somehow youthful face came to sit near her. "I'm Dr. Levinson," he said quietly. "Could you fill me in about Michael's activities and health the last few weeks?"

She told him about the hoarse throat, and this afternoon's game with the hose, ending in a shaken voice, "I knew about the polio outbreak. Why didn't I stop him?"

"Mrs. Porter, there's no point blaming yourself. None of us knows that much about polio."

"Then he does have . . . it?"

"The symptoms all point that way. We're running tests, of course, doing a spinal tap."

"What about Janey—my little girl, she's just five."

"Have whoever's baby-sitting take her temperature twice a day, watch her carefully, and make sure she washes her hands with soap and water very carefully after she uses the bathroom."

"Will she get it?"

"No need to borrow troubles, Mrs. Porter. We have our hands full with Michael."

61

When a subtle gray tinged the window glass, a rotund, cheerful volunteer in a blue-striped uniform wheeled in a cart with a coffee urn and a platter mounded with doughnuts. Breakfast revived the worry-crushed little group somewhat, and they exchanged information. The very young couple, Joy and Artie Liebman, had a two-year-old baby girl in an iron lung. Artie's mother lived on Riverside Drive while Joy's had driven up from Philly. The Catholic couple, Aurora and Joe D'Amato, were parents of six, and their youngest, Dommy, their only son, had crawled into their bedroom two nights ago, unable to use his legs: he was afflicted with spinal poliomyelitis, the commonest form of paralytic polio. The D'Amatos were praying that his case was the mild, transitory type of infection in which the paralysis passed. "Dommy's been first baseman on the Saint Ignatius baseball team for two years," Joe D'Amato kept repeating, as if this athleticism were an amulet to prevent atrophying of boyish muscles—in truth, many of those crippled by polio, like the late President Roosevelt, had been in superb physical shape before contracting the disease. Ann called the house again. Coriana reported that Janey she was still sleeping and Mr. Porter he had not called.

* * *

"Mrs. Porter?" Dr. Levinson beckoned her into the hall.

A stethoscope dangled from his neck and his lined face no longer appeared youthful as he sank into the one of the ladder-back oak chairs that lined this section of the corridor. Ann nervously took the chair next to his.

"Michael?" she prompted.

"I'm sorry it's not better news," he said. "We've verified that he has the spino-bulbar strain."

Ann felt her skin grow cold. Having pored over the National Foundation for Infantile Paralysis pamphlets in the waiting room, she knew that spino-bulbar was the most virulently dangerous type of poliomyelitis. It combined the paralyzing effect of spinal polio-myelitis with the bulbar type, which attacks the brain stem, thus impeding the muscular ability to swallow. *That's the reason he was hoarse,* she thought.

"Mrs. Porter, are you all right?"

"I'm not going to faint," she said. "If only I'd been more careful, gotten him here sooner—"

"Mrs. Porter," Levinson interrupted firmly, "putting yourself through the wringer won't help anything. Once the virus has invaded the body we have no drugs to stop it. All we can do is keep the patient breathing while his system battles the disease."

"Can I see him?"

"Yes. He's in a respirator. You can only stay a minute or so."

As he led her down the corridor he was telling her about a man he'd worked with, a Dr. Salk, who had developed an inactive virus vaccine that had been tested encouragingly this March, about a Dr. Sabin, who was doing research on a live virus vaccine. Ann paid no attention. In the supply room, an attendant handed her a green surgical gown that was far too big, green paper booties to cover her sandals, a shower-type cap with elastic for her hair. Ann refused the mask.

"I'll terrify my son," she explained.

The attendant shrugged her fleshy shoulders. "If you want to get inside the polio unit you'll wear it. We can't be spreading germs, can we?"

Tying the double straps so the fabric covered her mouth and

nostrils, Ann followed Dr. Levinson through a door painted in large black letters:

ISOLATION
POLIO UNIT

They were in a corridor similar to the one they'd left, but there were far more pieces of equipment and nurses. Glancing into a room, she saw a nurse removing a steaming cloth from a washing machine while two other nurses adjusted more steaming cloths on a small, wailing patient. "Kenny packs," Dr. Levinson explained. Ann tried to recall what she knew of the Sister Kenny method, which included wrapping hot packs on polio-tortured muscles.

The corridor ended in double swinging doors. Even before Dr. Levinson pushed them open, she could hear the rhythmic pulmonary droning. The sound of three rows of respirators.

Though Ann had seen numerous photographs of the iron lungs that mechanically inhaled and exhaled for paralyzed human lungs, she was momentarily disoriented, imagining she had strayed into some futuristic automobile dealers' lot. The streamlined two-tone green steel boxes with rounded lids and shiny chrome fixtures resembled cars, a lineup of weird cars. The patients' heads, which protruded beneath angled mirrors, were incongruously mortal.

Michael's face was small and frighteningly white.

She crinkled her eyes reassuringly. "Who is this masked rider?" she asked, paraphrasing the closing words of *The Lone Ranger.* "It's your mom."

He blinked, showing he'd heard.

"Michael, you're going to feel better soon."

An uncertain blink.

"You're one terrific guy, and I love you so very much," she said softly.

He mouthed, "Dad?"

"He'll be here practically any minute."

The doctor took her arm. Shrugging free, she touched her fingers to the cloth over her mouth, indicating a kiss. Michael blinked again.

Beyond the double doors, she leaned against the wall to support herself. It took several minutes before she was able to undo the straps of her sterile clothes.

The waiting room was crowded by now, and conversations about muscular damage, Warm Springs, braces, physiotherapy swirled around her. Once again she telephoned Darien. Janey, she was crayoning, and not a word, not one, had come from Mr. Porter, but Mrs. Newcombe had called to see how Michael was doing, and to tell her to stay as long as necessary. And did Mrs. Porter want her to clean up or do more packing? "You're wonderful, Coriana, but just be with Janey."

She was wild to see Michael, to hear a progress report from Levinson. She had always been impatient, and now impatience combined with her intolerable anxiety for Michael to give her an unscratchable itch that made her grind her teeth and fidget in her quiet corner. Suddenly she thought of Gilberte, normally immaculate Gilberte in a dirty print housedress, her black hair tied with a string, Gilberte keeping watch over the escalating fever of her year-old, feverish illegitimate son. *I ought to tell her about Michael,* Ann thought. She did not move.

In the weeks following their dismissal, she had phoned Gilberte a half-dozen times. The secretary had taken messages. The calls had not been returned. Ann then had drafted a three-page letter requesting that they be allowed to repay their debts in installments. Gilberte had not responded: instead, a missive had arrived from Kemp and Schuyler to inform the Porters that unless the entire sum owed their client, plus legal charges, was forthcoming within sixty days, action would be taken. The day the house sold, Ann had mailed a brief note to say that the check for the balloon payment would arrive when escrow closed on August 27. No answer had come to that, either.

A group of stout young women swarmed in, engulfing the mother of a patient: their Brooklynese and the smell of fresh cinnamon coffee cake filled the waiting room. One of the new arrivals used the phone. When at last she hung up, Ann got to her feet.

The mellifluous-voiced secretary informed her that Madame had just stepped out of the office on her way to a luncheon appointment. *Excuse number thirty-six,* Ann thought. "Please tell her I'm at

Mount Sinai Hospital. Michael's very ill—he has polio." She gave the number of the pay phone.

Gilberte didn't call, Larry didn't call. Where the hell was he? Dr. Levinson didn't come, and none of the nurses she spoke to had any information on the polio unit patients.

By four-thirty, the left side of her forehead ached as if the skull had cracked: she had reached the pitch of fear that banishes inhibitions. She looked up Jason Templar Enterprises in the Manhattan phone book dangling from the phone by its metal cord. She was passed along a chain of switchboard operators, who politely inquired her business with Mr. Dejong. Doggedly repeating that she was a friend, she finally reached a Miss LaRosa, Mr. Dejong's executive secretary: Mr. Dejong was out of town, but if Mrs. Porter left her number, he would be informed of her call.

Ann stumbled back to her chair.

That evening when she was allowed to see Michael, his face was taut and his eyes glazed. The fever was up.

"Mrs. Porter?" Aurora D'Amato extended the earpiece to her. It was after ten and the rush of evening visitors had departed: the blonde grandmothers had left with promises to return at dawn. The D'Amatos and the Liebmans and she were voyagers marooned in the latitude of fear.

Ann stared at the phone. Gilberte? Larry? Quent?

It was Larry. "How's Michael?" he asked anxiously.

"In an iron lung . . ."

"An iron lung? Jesus, I could kill myself."

"Where are you?"

"Home. I'd be there in a flash—but Coriana wants to get back to the Newcombes and—"

"She'll stay."

"Shorty, you've got the car."

"Call a taxi."

"I don't have any cash." Larry began to cry. "I don't have one thin dime. I had to walk all the way from the station."

"Write the cabbie a check," she snapped.

After that, she stood at the doorway, watching down the corridor. Polio units pay no homage to night, and nurses and orderlies swung briskly in and out of the door behind which Michael's immune system struggled against the polio virus.

62

Gilberte had risen about one to turn off the air conditioner—they had had units installed throughout the house two years earlier. At three-thirty, the temperature in her bedroom was well over eighty, yet she still felt the cold, clammy air. She sat holding the Florentine leather box. It now contained not only the Gestapo envelopes but also a heap of telephone messages from the Porters. She had felt compelled to save these desperate unanswered calls as an insane kind of proof of her good faith to her parents' reliquaries—she was fulfilling her obligations. The vast majority of the messages were from Larry. At first he had contacted the office four or five times a day, slacking off until last week when he had phoned only twice. She picked up the latest message. *Ann Porter called at 1:15: Michael is in Mt. Sinai with infantile paralysis.* In the space MAY BE REACHED AT was a neatly printed telephone number.

Gilberte peered at the pale ivory memorandum. Years ago, on a dingy street in Saint-Ouen near the *marché aux puces,* hadn't she made her decision about Michel? Hadn't that decision been sealed permanently by Quent's remarks? She had no son. This ailing child was Horace Blakely's grandson. And someday he, Michael Porter, would inherit her revenge. Her eyes squeezed shut, her lips pulled taut over her teeth, and the tendons in her neck showed. It didn't matter what she was telling herself. The discordant interior music of her biology refused to be silenced. She jammed the messages away, hastily locking the box in the safe. Rushing to her immense, meticulously organized dressing room, she yanked out a navy linen chemise.

Gilberte halted at the entry of the falsely cheerful yellow waiting room. Five people slept in the utilitarian aluminum and Nauga-hyde chairs. A fat, shabby couple from whose hands drooped ro-sary beads, a girl in a white cotton piqué (crumpled though it was, Gilberte recognized the dress as part of her rival, Jo Copeland's, summer collection) slumped with her head on the shoulder of an equally young boy.

And Ann.

Ann wore faded Levi pants, chopped off at midthigh, with a faded blue halter top that might have been cut from the denim of the successful Santa Fe outfits. The auburn hair was longer than Gilberte remembered, spilling in curls to her freckled shoulders. Asleep, she looked as naively defenseless as she had on the rue Daguerre.

Then her eyes opened. Either she had not been asleep or she had come instantly awake. Seeing Gilberte, she raised a finger to her lips, signifying silence, and tiptoed to the hall, leading Gilberte a few yards. Two interns glanced at them before returning to a conference over a chart.

"Thank God you're here," Ann said with quiet intensity. The shadows under her brown eyes made them appear yet larger and more luminous. "It's the spino-bulbar virus."

"Spino-bulbar? Whatever are you talking about?"

"Didn't you get my message?"

"It's a habit of mine to do the rounds of hospitals in the wee hours of the morning." *My God, what am I saying? How can I be making wisecracks?*

"The spino-bulbar's the most deadly type of polio virus there is."

Gilberte's chill was reactivated and goose bumps broke out on her sleeveless arms. "You're quite the medical expert."

"His lungs are paralyzed, so he's in an iron lung. He can't swallow and they couldn't pump out his throat properly, so he's had a tracheotomy."

"Next you'll be giving lectures for the March of Dimes."

Ann's face contorted. "If you don't give a damn how Michael is, why come here?"

"That's my role in life. Giving aid and comfort."

"Yes, I know," Ann said, her eyes suddenly glinting. "You've made Larry and me off-limits to Seventh Avenue."

"Where *is* Larry?"

"On his way."

"There, you see? The father's not concerned enough to rush. Ann, you've always been overemotional."

Ann ached to slap Gilberte's smile, then recalled that she had always hidden her deepest misery behind this acid little smirk of amusement.

She sank into a chair. "The fever's up, and the second time they let me in, I'm pretty sure he didn't know me." She bent her head into her hands.

Gilberte took the next chair, touching Ann's wrist. She wanted to hack off her consoling fingers, she chastised herself for breaking her promise to her father, yet her compassionate touch remained on Ann's trembling wristbone.

"Children get deathly ill and pull through," she said.

"Gilberte, he's only nine. Maybe he'll be in an iron lung the rest of his life."

"He'd be better off dead."

"No—" At a man's hurried footsteps, Ann broke off and Gilberte turned.

Larry Porter was jogging toward them. Ann jumped to her feet, but instead of running to him, remained where she was, hands tensed to her bare, lightly freckled thighs. Larry's pace slowed, and he smiled tentatively. His face was bloated and red as if he had been drinking, yet he was freshly shaven and wore a clean shirt with a carefully knotted tie.

"Greetings and salutations to you, Gilberte," he said brightly. Then he leaned toward Ann to kiss her. She moved so his lips did not brush her cheek. Blinking as if with hurt, he said, "Shorty, I'm sorry it took me so damn long, but the cab took hours getting to the place. Well, how's our boy doing?"

"I haven't heard anything since I talked to you."

"Like they say, no news is good news," he said. "Come on, gals. Let's see if the coffee shop's open. I'll treat you to a cup."

"Why not champagne?" Ann asked with a bitchiness that startled Gilberte.

Larry's dissolute boy's face crumpled, and for a moment it appeared as though his bloodshot eyes might ooze tears, then he formed a smile. "Bubbly's in order, isn't it, now the three of us are pals again?"

"Oh God!" Ann cried, running back into the waiting room.

Larry made a whimper deep in his throat. "As you can see, we're pretty upset about this," he mumbled, following his wife.

Gilberte poised in the corridor. One hand at her pulsing throat, she watched the unhappy couple hurry away, continuing to stare at the empty corridor after they had disappeared. Her vision was hazed by tears. She became aware that the interns were watching her. Raising her chin, she wound through corridors to the exit where Jordan waited. As he sped down night-empty Fifth Avenue, she shivered in a corner of the backseat.

"Shorty, I would give my right arm to have been with you," Larry was saying. "But yesterday afternoon I dropped by Gallagher's and who should be raising a drink but Wolf Englemark, *the* Englemark of Englemark and Bowes. How could I rush away? He set up an interview for me this afternoon. By the time we finished yakking, the trains had stopped, so I sacked down with Bill Johansen. I spent all morning prepping for the interview. It went fabulously well. You mark old Larry's words, they'll make a top-notch offer." He spoke too smoothly.

Had he been with Marjan? Had he been running up another unconscionable bar tab? She found herself hoping it was Marjan. Better in the night and two days that he'd been incommunicado for him to have been with another woman than standing greater Manhattan to drinks.

He was looking at her as if expecting a response. Unable to think of anything to say that would not start an argument or strip him naked, she nodded and closed her eyes. As usual, falling in with his subterfuges made her feel as awkward as if she'd been the liar.

He slept soundly until the rotund, cheerful volunteer wheeled in her cart. Taking a crumb and a sugar doughnut, he explained to the D'Amatos and the Liebmans that he'd been on a business trip and out of touch. Around ten o'clock that morning, Dr. Levinson arrived to tell Ann she could visit the respirator ward.

Larry asked, "When can *I* see my boy?"

"I'm sorry, but only one parent at a time."

Ann, half insane with the need to touch base in the polio unit, said, "Larry, you go. He asked for you."

A minute or so after Larry and the doctor left, the telephone rang for Ann. She heard the droning, undersea rumble of long distance.

"I just got your message," Quent said. "Ann, what's wrong? Who answered the phone? Where are you?"

"I'm so frightened," she whispered.

"You'll have to talk louder."

"I'm at Mount Sinai Hospital."

"Did you have an accident? Are you ill?"

"Michael's got polio."

"God . . ."

"The spino-bulbar kind."

For a long moment there was silence. Then he said, "I'm in Boston. I'll be there as soon as I can."

"Thank you."

"Ann, every single day I've wanted to call you—every hour."

"I know, I know."

"I kept hoping you'd get in touch with me, but not this way, never this way."

63

Larry came back a few minutes later with his shoulders bowed. Gripping Ann's hand, he said with desperate cheer, "Shorty, we pulled him out of worse than this back in Paris."

"How does he look?"

Shuddering, Larry took out his handkerchief, blowing his nose and wiping his eyes. "What sort of medication have they given him?"

"A serum made out of blood plasma from recovered patients," Ann said. "It's a one-time thing."

"Nothing else?"

"That's all there is. And they aren't sure if *it* works."

"Hey, none of that defeatist talk. Attitude's important," he said. "What I don't understand is how he got sick so quickly."

"His voice has been hoarse for a few days."

"Why didn't you take him in to Skaggs?"

Because he's turned our bills over to a collection agency and now his nurse asks me for cash. Her sudden irritation was so acute that she felt as though another entity had hunkered down between them. Not trusting herself to speak, she returned to her brooding fears.

Three hours later, when the waiting room had emptied out for lunch, Quent arrived.

Larry jumped to his feet to shake his hand. "Quent, this is terrific of you, you're a real buddy."

Quent put his arms around Ann. For a moment she stiffened, then, realizing this was a normal gesture for an old friend to make, reached her arms around him and briefly permitted herself to relax against his muscular warmth. When she pulled away, Quent stared at her an instant too long. She stifled an impulse to put a hand to her hair. What must she look like in her rag-bag clothes after two sleepless nights?

"How can I help?" he asked.

"There's nothing anybody can do," she said.

Quent turned to Larry. "It's a long drive to and from Darien. We're so near—it'd be no problem at all if you stayed with us."

"We might just take you up on that offer," Larry said.

"Janey—" Ann started.

"Of course she'll come too," Quent said. "Tell you what, I'll run out to Darien and bring her and your maid back."

"That's just it," Ann said. "Coriana's been baby-sitting with Janey for nearly two days. She and the Newcombes—she works for them now—have been fabulous, but she can't stay indefinitely."

Larry peered down at the shiny, narrow toes of his custom-made shoes. "Ann decided a maid just cluttered up her life," he mumbled.

"Mrs. Kalinska, she's the cook, has seven grandchildren. I'm positive she and Janey'll hit it off. Give your sitter a buzz that I'm on my way."

"No!" Larry said vehemently. "I mean, thanks all the same, but this has been plenty tough on Janey and she doesn't know you all that well. Besides, we'll have to throw some things in a suitcase. And Ann needs to change."

"I can't leave the hospital." Ann's voice rose anxiously.

"Janey really is a mess, poor baby," Larry said. Though Quent had moved up the hall to give them privacy, he lowered his voice. "Don't mention anything about putting the house on the market."

"Oh, for God's sake, Larry."

"It's important, shorty. I realize Quent's doing this for Michael, they've been buddies since the big rescue. But let's not push things. He might take any mention of selling the house as criticism of Gilberte. And the last thing we want to do is queer my chances for getting back into Gee de Pee."

She wanted to scream at him that he was a perfect phony with his talk of terrific interviews and out-of-town business trips, his clean shirt, his smell of aftershave, but he was staring at her with abject pleading. She fished out her fountain pen and began listing what she wanted him to bring for her and Janey. She handed him the car keys and a five-dollar bill, the folding money from the check she'd cashed at the Paloverde Oil station. "This is for Coriana," she said.

He hurried away. Alone, she tried not to stare at Quent, who was engrossed in a conversation with one of the polio unit nurses.

After a minute, he walked over to Ann. "Come on, let's have some lunch."

"You go, Quent. I'm not hungry."

"That nurse promised to watch out for Michael. If there're any changes, she'll send a volunteer to the cafeteria." His cheeks were ruddy, his eyes clear. He spoke authoritatively.

She was too drained to resist.

The cafeteria was crowded with nurses and doctors in starched white coats. Spotting an empty table in the far corner, he said, "This way." He draped his jacket over the back of a chair, going down the line, returning with a tray jammed with club sandwiches, coleslaw, milk cartons, melting scoops of chocolate and vanilla ice cream. Her anxiety about deserting her post made her flesh feel raw, as if the skin had been removed by a third-degree burn, and it was all she could do to swallow a few dutiful bites.

"Why didn't Larry want me to go out to Darien?" he asked.

"The house is full of cartons."

"Cartons?"

"Boxes. We're moving on the twenty-fourth."

"To another house?"

"No." She clipped off the word.

"Ann, I'm only asking."

"We're moving because we can't afford the first mortgage much less the second, which Gilberte holds and is calling. This can't be news to you."

"It is. Ann, we don't talk much."

"She fired us. Larry's been a nut case. He's positive he's turned into a pariah, so he spends his time proving he's not."

"Why did she fire you?"

"The excuse was that Larry overspent on his expense account, and took some stuff."

"Excuse? Ann, I don't understand any of this."

She pushed away her plate with a jerky motion. "Isn't it obvious? Gilberte's punishing me for being with you. Larry's just the fall guy."

"She has no idea I was in Santa Fe."

"Oh, no, not a clue. That's why she's been so adorable to us the last few months."

"The night I got back she pulled one of her episodes. She accused me of having a girl in Hollywood. Since then she's made snide little comments about my starlet."

"Come on, Quent. She hires a new designer without telling me, she gives *him* credit for helping with the collection. She fires us. Then sets out to queer our chances with everyone else, not too difficult when she reminds the garment industry at large that her married name is the same as the bank that holds Seventh Avenue's purse strings. I mean, what friend wouldn't do that to a friend, with no reason?"

"Take it at face value. She's furious at Larry," he said. "It has nothing to do with us."

"Have it your way."

"Ann, believe me, if she thought it was you, she'd wouldn't have kept it a secret from me." The skin under Quent's eyes looked stretched.

Unable to stand another moment under his intent, caring eyes, she jumped to her feet. "Thanks for the lunch," she said, and bolted around tables where Mount Sinai personnel lingered over coffee.

"Ann—" he called after her.

She ran up the steps, and had reached the landing when he caught up to her. Ignoring the afternoon visitors flooding by them, she put her arms around him.

"Oh, God, Quent, I'm so frightened."

He stroked her hair. "The Foundation's been pretty generous to different polio groups. I'll call in a specialist."

"Would you?"

"I wish I could do more." He touched his lips to her forehead. "One thing you have to promise me, sweet. You won't camp here tonight."

"I can't leave—"

"Let Larry take the watch for a few hours. We're only minutes away. Let *him* put in some time."

Gilberte had never been at ease with people, and since her visit to the hospital she had felt as if she were performing in a play with a cast who knew their stage business and had learned their lines while she was forced to improvise as she went along. Positive everyone was snickering at her, she fretted endlessly about the correct moves, the right words.

She cued herself at each sentence as she praised the detailing on a peau de soie blouse to the young woman who bought for Patricia's, the top women's specialty shop in Southern California. (Since Yves Roland had taken over, every major account had needed Gilberte's personal coercion before placing an order: his clothes lacked the liveliness of Ann's designs.)

The phone rang, and Gilberte snapped into the mouthpiece, "No calls."

"I'm sorry, Madame, but it's Mr. Dejong."

The winter's over, Gilberte thought. Relief brought spontaneity. "Put him on," she said.

"He's here, Madame."

"Here?"

"In the outer office, Madame."

Smiling warmly at the California buyer, Gilberte said, "If you'll excuse me just a moment, Miss Wace. My husband's back from a business trip."

Quent was standing. He did not respond to her smile.

Gilberte's pleasure faded. "Darling, you've taken me by surprise. When did you get in?"

"This afternoon. Michael Porter's in Mount Sinai."

"Yes, polio. I dropped by. So you visited too." *Before you saw me.*

"The Porters're staying with us."

"What?" Gilberte couldn't control her surprise. Although Quent sometimes took Michel out, she could tell that he looked down on both parents—a condescension that was atypical for him. He showed a definite reluctance to be with them.

"Mrs. Kalinska is taking care of their little girl."

Aware that the secretary, arranging two carbons under a sheet of stationery, was listening, Gilberte murmured. "Thanks for consulting me."

"Darien's too far for them to shuttle back and forth."

"I don't remember if I mentioned this or not," Gilberte said, "but they don't work here anymore."

"No, you didn't mention it." He was regarding her through narrowed eyes. "Michael's critically ill."

Michel, not Michael. My closest living kin. My baby. Gilberte formed what she hoped was a smile. "It's very kind of you, darling." She kissed his cheek. The flesh felt warm but ungiving. "Ann's my oldest friend."

64

Quent returned around four with Dr. Cashagian. Cashagian, a specialist from the March of Dimes, concurring with Michael's treatment, was guardedly optimistic, but Ann worried that his hopeful prognosis was to prove the advances in polio treatment to the Jason Templar Foundation.

Expecting Larry back, she insisted Quent leave before six.

Larry didn't walk in until after eight. "Janey needed a lot of reassurance, she's one confused little girl. She kept asking whether you were sick, like Michael. Shorty, you better get on over to the Dejongs'."

For the first time in almost two days, Ann left the hospital. Cars moved along Fifth Avenue with radio music blasting from their open windows, men in shirt sleeves and women in cotton dresses strolled, children crowded around an ice-cream truck. The placid, normal summer night seemed wrenchingly surreal to Ann as she hurried around the block searching for the dented Chevy: it was nowhere. Frustrated to the point of tears, she recalled Larry's telling her that the Dejongs' car was waiting for her. Sure enough, she had passed the chauffeur on her way out.

At the house, the front hall with its pedimented statuary and paintings made her feel yet more displaced. What was she, un-bathed, uncombed and wearing makeshift shorts—a total slob—

doing amid this perfection? Why wasn't she at Mount Sinai where she belonged? Then Janey, in her pink flowered nightgown, burst through the shadows of the landing, holding on to the curving banister as she raced down the staircase. "Mommy, you're here! I missed you, I really missed you."

"I missed you worse, Janey-Janey." Ann held up her palms to warn off the child. "We'll hug and kiss after I've had my bath."

A thick-legged older woman with a kind smile had followed Janey. Introducing herself as Mrs. Kalinska, she said, "Mrs. Dejong asked me to tell you she's in her room."

"Mommy," Janey interrupted, "just wait until you see the bathroom. It's huger than my whole bedroom."

The enormous bathroom was carpeted in white, the faucets were stamped *sterling silver,* a tray held a variety of perfumes and shampoos. While Ann washed her hair, Janey sat in the wicker love seat chattering. "This house is so big and scary. It's got infantile bugs."

"Janey, you're not going to get polio." Ann splashed from the tub, pulling the thick white terry-cloth robe from its hook, kneeling to hug the child fiercely. "I won't let you."

"Anyway, I'm sleeping in your room." Janey ran to the bedroom, plopping onto the nearest bed.

Ann stretched out on the other, positive she could not fall asleep. But the warm bath had unknotted her muscles and after two wakeful nights, she dropped into an exhausted slumber.

"Ann?"

At her first glimpse of Gilberte standing over her in her loose white peignoir, Ann decided she was enmeshed in one of those recent nightmares in which Gilberte screamed accusations of adultery. Then she saw Janey peacefully slumbering with her thumb near her mouth and remembered the polio unit. For the extremities of fear and wretchedness, reality could outclass nightmares.

"What time is it?"

"Eleven-thirty."

"I must get back."

"How is he?"

Ann was fishing underwear from the suitcase Larry had packed. She and Gilberte had always been physically modest with each other, and Ann expected Gilberte would go away. Instead, she sat in the flowered slipper chair. "Well?"

"The same. Breathing oxygen through a tube in his throat."

"Ah, yes, the tracheotomy you mentioned."

Ann was turned away, so she did not see Gilberte's tensed fingers yank a pearl button from her neckline.

They had been whispering, but Ann's response came clear and tight. "I'd like to get dressed."

"By all means. I'll get Jordan to bring the car."

Gilberte listened to the car ease away. Vengeance through the generations, her father had asked. And here it was in spades. Ann's talent lay in useless shambles, her marriage to that sad, vain weakling had sentenced her to a lifetime of penury and debt. Her child was sorely stricken. She looked like absolute hell. Could any woman on this earth be more destroyed?

Yes, Gilberte thought.

Me.

The D'Amatos' son was off the critical list, the Liebman baby's fever had dropped: both families had left for the night. Larry, alone, stretched out sleeping. Waking him, she asked for news— there was none—then told him the chauffeur was waiting at the Fifth Avenue entrance. She had settled down and was thumbing through a pamphlet on the Sister Kenny treatment when Quent arrived.

"Larry's at your place," she said.

"I left when I saw him come home." Quent sat next to her, putting a consoling arm around her shoulders.

After that the August days blurred together. Michael's fever would drop slightly, then rise higher. Always higher. Sometimes Larry was in the waiting room, sometimes Quent. Gilberte came too: whenever Ann returned to the house for a brief nap and to reassure Janey, Gilberte always managed to be around, inquiring in brittle tones about Michael's condition.

* * *

The Benefactors traditionally gave their charity ball in mid-August, a month when members and those select friends to whom they sold tickets were out of town. Since the ball was one of the major social events of the year and attendance proved one to be top drawer, there was a mass return that particular weekend. Gilberte ached to stay home. She needed to check in with Ann and to be available if any change occurred. External signs of her terror, however, were a luxury she could not afford. Edouard arrived with the tools of his trade. As he coiffed her hair and applied cosmetics, she listened tensely for Ann's arrival. At eight, she could no longer stall her departure. Yellow diamonds glittering at her ears, wrist and throat, the full skirt of jonquil satin ball gown rustling around her, she crossed the hall. She could hear the elegaic chords of the second movement of Beethoven's Seventh Symphony coming from Quent's room. He answered her tap wearing the trousers of a gray business suit and a shirt with rolled-up sleeves.

"You were meant to be ready a quarter of an hour ago," she said. "Remember, darling? I told you that we're going to Cary and Deepie's for cocktails."

"I'm staying home."

Unaware of the night hours he put in at the hospital, Gilberte said, "You're on the board."

"What if I were still in Boston?" A steady, nonbaiting tone, accompanied by a steely glint in his blue eyes.

"You aren't in Boston, and your family knows it." Three Dejong cousins and an uncle sat with Quent on the board of the Benefactors.

"Tell them the truth. I'm not in the mood for celebrating."

As if *she* were in the mood! "What a tiresome hermit you've become," she said, and clicked rapidly down the stairs.

Where was Ann?

Ann was at the hospital alone.

Usually Larry ate with Janey, but tonight his daughter was at a rerun of *Snow White*—Mrs. Kalinska, the cook, a generous-hearted woman, conjured up ways to distract the bewildered little girl. Solitude was not Larry's metier, and his anxieties spilled over.

Having cashed a check with Quent, he went to Gallagher's where, as he'd hoped, he ran into a couple of acquaintances. He ordered a porterhouse but barely nibbled at it. He sought forgetfulness in round after round of drinks.

65

As Gilberte unlocked her front door, she exhaled, and her shoulders slumped. Her jonquil satin gown was uncreased, her hair as sleek as when Edouard had pinned the French knot, her makeup and diamonds in place, yet the released tension gave her a disheveled look. She had reached the staircase when Quent emerged from the library.

Forcing herself erect, she said, "You were sorely missed."

"I was on the way to get coffee. Do me a favor, will you, and make some? Larry's plastered. Ann and I are trying to sober him up."

"Has Mrs. Kalinska suffered a coronary?" Gilberte asked.

"She took Janey to the movies, and then let her sleep in her room. No need to wake them up."

"I'm exhausted," Gilberte said. "And though there's not much use in trying to discourage the original good Samaritan, my advice to you is to back off. Larry prefers life with a buzz on—possibly that's what launched him into such a hollow career."

He continued staring at her impassively.

"D'accord, d'accord," she said, starting for the kitchen.

Waiting for the coffee to brew, she sat with her elbows propped on the marble pastry table. Concern for Michel hovered as always in the wings of her mind, but she was brooding about her husband's behavior. She couldn't remember his ever asking her to perform a household task. And for Larry Porter, of all people! She smelled the aroma and realized that the coffee was percolating dark as her thoughts.

Outside the library, she called, "The waitress."

Ann came to the door, taking the tray with a wan smile. "Thanks, Gilberte. Sorry your houseguests are such a pain."

The library was lined with massive Duncan Phyfe bookcases from Greatleigh. Behind the glass doors stood old tooled-leather sets, first editions and brightly jacketed new books—mostly nonfiction, Quent's preference. It was he who used the room, he who had insisted on the old pieces and heavy, comfortable upholstery.

Larry, in the deep embrace of a leather club chair, attempted to push to his feet then sank back. "My once and future bosh . . . sorry, boss lady," he said.

"Come on, Larry," Quent said, pouring the coffee. "Get some of this inside you."

"Both of you real folks," Larry said. "Good old Quent, trucking in the learned medicos by the carload, spelling me in a few of the wee hours with shorty . . ."

Gilberte, who had been poised to escape upstairs, let her hand drop from the doorknob. "You've been at the hospital?" she asked Quent.

"Yes," he retorted tersely.

Holding his cup and saucer at an angle, Larry elaborated, "There lo's of times. Gilberte, you're good people too. Inviting us t'stay here, having cook take over Janey . . . Maybe should s'pect this kind of treatment from you. After all you're Michael's—"

"Larry!" Ann cried sharply.

Gilberte's heart was beating as if she had just lifted a hundred-pound sack above her head. "We go back a long time, Larry, a long time, so gratitude's not in order." She crossed the red-and-blue patterns of the seventeenth-century Oushak rug to stand over Larry. "But I did fix that coffee," she said. "The least you can do is drink it."

Larry gulped noisily at the steaming black liquid, then set his cup precariously on the arm of his red leather chair. "Sorry 'bout you slaving in the kitchen. Not queering it about taking me back . . . ?"

"Now you're being silly," she said.

" 'Member that four-page spread I got Marjan in the March *Harper's*? Four goddamn pages of Gee de Pee clothes. Isn't easy to get, everybody knows that, four pages. But I dood it, I dood it, four big, slick pages of your suits and gowns. Oh, I was riding high. And how about that *Vogue* cover in December? That's me, th' wheeler-dealer who put Gee de Pee on the map. Can't buy my kind of publicity. Takes long, hard work. And the big layouts in all the papers—L.A., New York, Chicago—for those peasant outfits of yours, 'member? And all the television news shows with those hot-damn Santa Fe things. And what about . . . ?"

As he rambled, Gilberte nodded, fear racing through her as if she faced a dangerous animal. What should she say? What response was least likely to jolt him into blabbing out the unsayable?

"Larry." Ann picked up the coffeepot, taking the cup from him. "Come on upstairs."

"I'm talking to Gilberte 'bout something important," he snapped.

"I need a catnap so I can get back to the hospital."

"Tha's my loyal helpmate. Never thinking about anything but herself. Goddamn career woman. If you'd only thought of your family for once, Michael wouldn't be in this trouble. If you'd only gotten him to hospital sooner."

"I told you what Dr. Levinson said," Ann whispered. "It wouldn't have made any difference."

"Or, if you'd called old Skaggs to th' house, not been such a skinflint—"

"Cut it out, Larry," Quent said in a low, quaking tone.

"You don't know her, you don't know my wife, Quent ole buddy. Didn't get the doctor. In polio season, for Chrissakes, in the goddamn polio season doesn't have th' doctor. And why? I'll tell you why. Money, money, money."

"If you don't shut your drunken, fucking mouth, I'll kick your shitty ass out of my house!"

Gilberte swiveled around to make certain this growl of obscenities came from Quent. Hands clenched, muscles tensed, he stood glaring at Larry.

For as long as she could remember, Gilberte had admired

Quent's calm, potent control. He didn't bounce like a Ping-Pong ball in the bubbling geyser of his emotions the way she did. He never permitted the biting concerns of the moment to affect his decisions, he never let any kind of baiting get to him. How often had she envied him his mastery over himself? How often had she taken the gods to task for not bestowing this gift of measured logic on her? How often had she wondered what it would be like to possess her husband's aloof, aristocratic control? Wondered how it would be to live without resentments, without striving ambition, without inferiorities, without her maddening, needful love of him, without gnawing vengeful urges—and yes, without agonizingly unbreakable maternal ties. How often had she longed for Quent's well-ordered interior landscape? For the first time she understood that her husband was not carved from wondrously smooth marble. *He's as frayed and torn as I am, maybe more so. He just hides it better,* she thought. *I don't know him at all. We're the same blood, we've been married for years, and I don't know him at all.*

Larry shrank backward, as if to obliterate himself in the deep chair. "Don't mind me, Quent ole buddy. This polio thing's got me nuts." His voice was placating and far less slurred.

"Why weren't you around to call the doctor?" Quent demanded. "Where were you?"

"Lining up work."

"For two days and nights? And how was Ann meant to pay the doctor? The check you gave me bounced."

"Damn bank's always goofing up my 'count," Larry blustered. "I'll make it good."

"Save the bullshit."

"Quent, what's the point?" Ann said. She wore no lipstick, and her mouth was white.

"He wasn't there when you and Michael needed him," Quent said in a low voice. "Now he's turned it inside out, blaming you."

Ann stared down at her hands. "A couple too many drinks, that's all."

"Ann—" Quent started.

"He's right. We've all been under a huge strain."

Gilberte was looking from Quent to Ann and back to Quent as they spoke.

And all at once, in a far more subtle way than the revelation of her husband's tumultuous inner life had come to her, she accepted a truth more vital to her existence.

He's having an affair with Ann.

Her dignified husband, the closest thing to American royalty there was, and lively, bubbly, fatally bourgeois Ann?

Yet even as her mind denied the affair, memories were short-circuiting its improbability. Incidents that, since they had occurred at widely separated intervals, had roused none of her suspicions. Quent's mysterious wartime assistance to Ann. Quent, pale and cadaverous from Mauthausen, holding a photograph of Ann and Michel, and she too intent on hiding Michel's identity to question his interest in Ann. His original desire to avoid the Porters, his later too-pointed indifference to Ann. When he'd rescued Michel from the Pacific surf, Ann had been there. His return from "out west" with talk of a separation had neatly dovetailed with Ann's trip to Santa Fe, a vacation that *she* had lifted the embargo on deathbed vows to bestow! This invitation to the Porters. And now his out-of-character, obscenely worded blowup at Larry.

It's not an affair. He's in love with her.

Smoothing the rich satin skirt of her ball gown, she sank gracefully into a wing chair. She felt as if she were carved from ice.

"Larry, how blotto are you?" she asked brightly.

"Not t'all."

"Good. Now *we'll* have a private little chat, the two of us. You and I. Like Ann and Quent just had." She drew out the single syllable of both names.

The long windows were open on the city garden, and into the suddenly quiet library came the distant howl of a police siren.

Quent broke the silence. "What was that remark supposed to mean?"

"Darling, lighten up a bit. As they say, the truth will out." Gilberte glanced at Ann, who swallowed sharply. "I was wrong about your little starlet."

A muscle jumped at his eye, but he spoke decisively. "We'll go into it later. Michael's fever's up. This isn't the time."

"Sir Galahad Dejong," she retorted.

Larry guffawed as if this were a scintillating witticism. "Anytime,

Gilberte, talk to me anytime you want. Ready to talk terms of returning to Gee de Pee right now, right this very moment I'm ready."

"Larry, dear friend, our conversation isn't going to be about business."

"Huh?"

"It's more personal. We need to discuss your wife." Gilberte winked thick lashes coated with Edouard's mascara. "And my husband."

"Ann and Quent?" Larry frowned.

"Exactly," Gilberte said. "Ann and Quent."

Larry's shifting emotions showed clearly on his drunken, boyish face. Bafflement, comprehension, then disbelief. "Ann and Quent?" he muttered. "You're talking crazy."

"The deceived spouses are invariably the last to know, dear heart."

"The hell you say!" Larry gripped both arms of the chair, struggling to his feet. "What in rat's hell's going on here?"

Ann, who had turned yet whiter, reached for his arm. "Come on upstairs."

"So *he's* the guy you've been putting out for."

"Larry—"

"Been doing it with old moneybags Dejong, have you?" His face red and swollen, he appeared on the brink of bursting into angry tears as he shook his fist at her. *"Cheating bitch!"*

The intensity of his rage and misery forced Ann backward a step. One of her ankles twisted outward. Gripping a library table, she kept herself from falling. She looked as dazed as if she had fallen. Quent took her arm, guiding her through the French doors into the garden.

66

As Gilberte watched the shadows merge and disappear into the blackness, she felt an odd click behind her forehead, almost as if she were undergoing some painless yet totally traumatizing surgery. She couldn't gauge what damage was being done to her central nervous system, yet her mental processes remained active.

He's married to me, she thought. *He's out there with her, but he's staying married to me.*

Back in March, when Quent had talked about divorce, Gilberte had unconsciously followed her old, unhappy method of working him with his own guilts by having that nightmare. Afterward, trapped in the fear that the old constraints might soon no longer keep him, she had readied herself for the eventuality in a manner that filled her with self-hatred. Secretly obtaining copies of Jason Templar's two-hundred-page will and the small library that set up the dynastic Trust, she had handed the documents over to Patrick Kemp and his partner, Otis Schuyler: after a cursory study, they ordered the thorny labyrinth of legalities trundled over to a Wall Street firm that specialized in major estates. The experts corroborated what Quent had told her when he had proposed. Working out a property settlement for a divorce would be a seriously complicated enterprise. Her lawyers added that should she choose to put obstacles in her husband's way, the litigation could be dragged through the courts for decades.

While Gilberte considered these unsavory methods to maintain her marriage, she was peering through the open French windows at the impenetrably shadowed garden.

Larry also was staring at the darkness. There was no hint of his easy charm in the embittered, bloodshot eyes and the mouth stretched with pain. Ann could not have chosen a partner more ruinous to his ego than Quent Dejong. From the first time they had been introduced at the Hotel Pyramide, Larry had paid Quent the compliment of unbridled envy. He envied Quent's ancestors, his English-tailored clothes, his manners, the accent that reeked of class, his innate and quiet courage, the casual way he sometimes left the top button of his shirt undone. Most of all he envied Quent's fortune. Though Ann was the least meretricious woman he'd ever known, he now placed the full burden of her defection on the money. With a whimpering sound, he moved unsteadily to the tantalus, pouring what remained in the crystal bottle with the dangling silver label etched *Scotch.* For some freak metabolic reason the drink had a sobering effect.

He jerked his head toward the garden. "How long has *that* been going on?"

"Who knows? It's not recent. Maybe since the war."

"She was a virgin when I married her, a virgin, I tell you!"

The diamonds at Gilberte's throat winked as she shrugged. "You asked a question and I gave my opinion. In any case, it's obviously hot and heavy now. So he's been at the hospital with her?"

"To spell me, he said, the bastard." Larry took another gulp. "What a time to get in her pants!"

"A rendezvous in a doorless waiting room? Larry, you're not *that* drunk." Gilberte paused, adding harshly, "He cares about her."

"That cold fish?"

Gilberte, ready to cut Larry down again, recalled her own similar assessment of her husband's emotional temperature, and said nothing. The curtains belled inward. They both stared expectantly. It was only a sudden gust of the hot night breeze.

Larry sighed. "Crazy about that girl, did my damnedest to make a good life for her and the kids. But how could I compete with Mr. Bigbucks? Even if I'd known I was competing, how could I have?"

"Larry, listen to me. I. Am. Staying. Married."

"What about—?" He gestured at the garden, asking in an aggrieved tone, "Or didn't you just see what I saw?"

"How about you? Do you want to keep your marriage intact?"

"Jesus, how could she hit me with this now? When my boy's so sick."

"Is the fever up?"

Larry's brow furrowed. "Ann said something, but I can't remember if it was up or down."

Gilberte closed her eyes. After a couple of moments, she said, "I'll never give Quent a divorce."

"Give? Man like him buys everything he wants."

"Except a divorce," she said. "Besides, he'd never walk out on me. He's the world's last moral man."

"D'pends on your d'finition of moral. Screwing other people's wives." He shook his head. "You know Ann. She's not going to stick with me if she's involved with him."

"He's too much the gentleman to keep her as a mistress." *Is that true? I don't care, I can't afford to care. Let him sleep with her, let him do whatever he wants with her. Without our marriage, I'm nothing. . . .* "You said you're mad for her. Well, fight for her."

Larry gave a shuddering sigh followed by a yawn. "Too beat to think," he said.

Watching him weave across the library, Gilberte was appalled at herself for joining forces with this pathetic, self-deluding drunken jellyfish. Briefly she recalled the bright, winning young officer he had been, and her scalpel-sharp self-honesty told her she was responsible at least in part for his depressing transformation. His uncertain footsteps faded up the staircase and there was only the rustle of leaves, the lullaby of late night traffic. The dark garden remained inscrutably still. After a minute she followed Larry up.

Shedding her gown, she creamed away her burden of cosmetics and pulled a silky wisp of nightgown over her head. Her terror for Michel was thicker and more anguished because she'd been compressing it into a tighter corner of her consciousness. As she got into bed she felt the thickness invade her chest. She couldn't get her breath. Gasping, her chest heaving, she was once again trapped in the agony of the *baignoire* treatment. *Help me! Won't somebody please help me!*

Ann and Quent didn't speak. The tall old copper beech soughed overhead and he held her. Too weary and worried to consider the implications of what had just been said, she pressed her face against his shirt, smelling the starch and perspiration, feeling the strong, solacing beat of his heart. When she finally pulled away, she could see that Larry and Gilberte were no longer in the library. Reluctantly she said, "I better go up to the room."

As she came in, Larry was bent over the dressing table, peering at his reflection as if searching for signs of a melanoma.

"Larry, I'm sorry," she said.

"Shove it!" His breath clouded the mirror. "So that's what you've been doing there all night—how many times've you two been flitting off to some fancy hotel?"

Ann thought of those interminable dark hours at Mount Sinai when only Quent's presence had kept her sane. "He sits with me, that's all."

"Yeah, sure. Gilberte's curious about us. Is the redheaded adulteress staying with her hubby?"

"What about you and Marjan?" she asked.

"Wondered when you'd bring that up." He sighed deeply. "Makes me feel stinking. He was getting sick and I . . . I was with her. Couldn't stand what you were doing to my house." He began to sob. "I'd've been home where I belonged if you'd just left me my house. Why did you have to sell my house?" He staggered to the bathroom.

Ann lay down. After a couple of minutes her entire body itched with desperation to be near Michael. She was smoothing the bedspread when Larry returned.

A few strands of water-dark hair hung over his blotched forehead—he'd obviously sloshed water on his face. Yet he appeared far more drunk. "Where d'you think you're going?" he demanded.

"Back to the hospital."

"With your sugar daddy, yeah." His voice was hectoring, loud.

"First getting to the bottom of this! Find out what gives with you and that rich bastard."

"Shh."

"How long has he been humping you?"

"It's never been just that."

"Since when?"

"France."

"France? Jesus. A school kid?"

"There was a border patrol, we were in a lot of danger—"

"I's in the war, too, 'member? Told me you were cherry."

"I never said that, Larry."

"Yes you did." He gripped her shoulders.

"Stop that! You're hurting me."

"Prick-tease with me, not with *him*!"

She twisted but couldn't escape his digging fingers. "Larry, I cared for you, but it was different—"

"Yeah, Mr. Billiondollars didn't marry you, so next time, with me, no ring, no nookie." He released her suddenly.

Falling backward, she hit the wall with a cry. A moment later Quent flung open the door. His eyes narrowed as he stared at them. Taking three swift strides, he engulfed Larry in his shadow. Larry backed away, breathing stertorously. Quent's back was to Ann. She saw his shoulder muscles bunch, straining his shirt. He raised his hand, holding it flat and level a few inches from the side of Larry's neck. OSS personnel dropped into occupied territories had been taught that vulnerable spot in the neck where a silent blow can kill.

"Quent!" she screamed, "Quent, stop it!"

The levelly measuring hand did not move. Ann charged at him. Clutching his arm, she felt the implacable muscular strength.

Then he turned, blinking at her as if he hadn't realized his own murderous intent.

Larry collapsed slowly against the wall, his back propped, his legs sliding forward on the white carpet.

67

"So here we all are." Gilberte stood in the open doorway, her long black hair, untethered from its elaborate twist, streaming around a face as pale and oval as an egg. "Watching Larry take a rest."

Larry attempted to rise, then sank back on the thick beige carpet. "Need a hair of the dog," he muttered.

"You've had enough," Quent said.

At the same moment Gilberte was responding, "Drink coming up."

Later, Ann would wonder why Gilberte, whose character was a mosaic of deviousness and biting honesty, had increased Larry's alcoholic haze—did she at some subliminal level want the truth to out? At the time, though, consumed with the need to return to the hospital, Ann didn't give consideration either to her husband's blotto state or to Gilberte's motivation. When Gilberte returned, Larry had maneuvered himself into the slipper chair. She handed him the highball, then closed the door. "No need for the servants to hear what I have to say."

"Gilberte, whatever it is, I don't have time." Ann took out a striped top. "I've been away from the hospital for ages."

"This will only take a minute, then you and my husband can dash off to spend the wee hours together. It's something you both need to know." Gilberte drew a breath. "I'm not getting a divorce. There'll never be a divorce."

Larry drained the glass. "Wassat 'bout divorce?" he asked plaintively.

"Other states," Quent said, "have different divorce codes."

"Agreed. But with the Trust, you'll be tied up in court for the next thirty or forty years. So what will you do? Set up Little Orphan Annie here in an apartment with jewelry and poodles, or whatever men give their doxies? Go ahead. The legal profession will get rich."

"Doesn't it matter that I'll end up hating you?" Quent asked.

"Hatred's a common response when people feel guilty, or so Papa often told me."

"Michael's fever might be up again," said Ann, whose anxiety had peaked above the press of other emotions loose in the guest room.

"Is my point clear?" Gilberte asked her.

"Yes, yes," Ann said, going to the closet. "Now let me change."

"I imagine both gentlemen have seen you *en déshabillé*." Gilberte's negligee floated behind her as she left the room.

Quent stood over Larry's low chair. "I'm not leaving you alone with her," he said, grasping Larry's free hand, hauling him to his feet. Larry squinted contritely at Ann as if he were about to speak, but Quent shoved him from the guest room.

Released, Larry stumbled along the broad hall with its dark seventeenth-century Dutch landscapes. With a phlegmy cough, he sank onto the top step of the handsomely curved staircase. Quent and Gilberte remained on opposite sides of the hall: Gilberte visualized them as scouts from opposing armies peering through spyglasses at the other's encampments.

Larry broke the silence. "Out to ruin our lives," he muttered as if continuing a conversation. "Has been for months. Probably years. Yes, since California. Always putting temptation in our way. Like Faust . . . was it Mephistopheles? Always showing us how life should be, right clothes, restaurants, limos, 'spensive furniture—"

"Larry," Gilberte interrupted, "am I cast in the starring role of Lucifer?"

He turned to squint up at her. For a moment he attempted his ingratiating smile, then thrust out his lip petulantly. "Why'd you build us up then lower the boom?"

"What a truly amazing gift of self-justification you have," she said, her heart beating faster. This was no conversation to continue under Quent's cold gaze.

"Why'd you fire me?"

"You need a memory course. What about your bloated expense accounts and merchandise pilfered for your lady friend?" She paused. "This isn't quite the intelligent approach, Larry. That is, if you're coming back to your old job."

Larry's face struggled visibly between hopes of reinstatement and the certainty that she'd wronged him. "You've led me on, then dumped me. Set your legal hounds on us."

Quent, who had been watching intently, asked, "What's that? Lawyers?"

"Darling, don't encourage him. The next step is the obligatory crying jag."

"Plenty to cry about. Being sued for big bucks." Larry was too far gone to dissimulate for pride's sake. "And what about my house? Man's house meant to be his castle. 'Tween you and my wife, I'm shoved outta my house."

"A brief, fond moment for self-pity," Gilberte said. "Now come on downstairs. You need more coffee."

"Thing I can't figure out is why? Always been decent to you. Didn't we help you 'nough in Paris? Didn't shorty go into hock deep 'nough for you? And, remember? I dragged over doctor from American Hospital with penicillin for your kid."

"Kid?" Quent was no longer lounging against the inlaid wood panel. "What kid, Larry?"

"The offspring of his pink elephants," Gilberte said with a dissonant laugh.

Ann, wearing a fresh blouse, opened the guest room door.

"Enter the other woman," Gilberte said.

"What child?" Quent persisted. His narrowed gaze moved from Gilberte to Larry to Ann.

The three remained absolutely still, as if electrical currents had passed through the warm, wax-scented air, connecting each with the others.

A quavering note whistled from Gilberte's throat but she did not hear it.

Ann gripped the brass door handle. Eerie backlighting from the guest room showed the freckles standing out in her pallor.

Larry, once he'd mentioned Michael, had covered his mouth as if to force back the revelation. Now the hand dropped. "Wha's the hell's the difference? Can't yank him out of the iron lung, can she?"

Quent stared at his wife. "Michael's yours?"

Gilberte gazed back at him, her chin lifting fractionally, the old defiant stare even though fear was being pumped into every cell of her body, fear so intense that it was depleting her of the ability to stand erect. Leaning against her door, she looked away.

"So he is." Quent turned to Ann. "You lied to me."

His expression was so naked with hurt that Ann almost cried out. She understood then what she should have considered from the first. That he inevitably would view her keeping the secret of Michael's birth as an act of betrayal. He wasn't naive, as she was, about easy consignment of trust, yet he had given her his trust wholeheartedly. In this single minute the universe they had forged together had been laid waste. Yet what else could she have done? Lost her son?

Then his mouth hardened and his expression became formidable. He turned back to Gilberte. "Aren't I entitled to an explanation?"

"What's the question?"

"First, who's Michael's father? Or do you know? Did it happen in the Santé?"

"Darling, count on your fingers and get the answer. He's Hocherer's." Gilberte's arrogant drawl was hoarse, as if she'd been shouting for years. "He's the son of the archfiend war criminal, Field Marshal Count Bernd von Hocherer."

"Is that why you gave him up?"

"No," Ann said. "She couldn't help it. Michael, he—"

"I prefer talking to my husband without *your* advocacy."

"Go on," Quent said.

"With all the work you've done with UNRRA and the Marshall Plan and the other relief organizations, I'm surprised you've forgotten the veritable glut of food and medication in Europe immediately after the war. You surely recall those rosy-cheeked, plump, well-dressed children playing amid the rubble. Michel—that was his name then—was malnourished. Easy prey for every type of infection. There was no medicine available to anyone but Americans. Michel had a worse mastoid attack than usual. Ann called Larry, and as he blabbered, he brought an American doctor she knew. But obviously that wasn't going to be the last time Michel needed miracle drugs. So my greathearted friends here offered to take him back with them to the land of the free and the home of penicillin manufacturers." As the misplaced archness spilled out, Gilberte felt as if a massive blister growing within her for years had burst—the consequences might be unspeakable, but, ah, the relief of finally speaking the truth.

Quent looked at Ann with eyes as expressionless as flat blue stones. "All these years you've kept up the pretense that he was a war orphan."

"He's our son."

"I never thought *you'd* resort to sophistry. All right, you adopted him to save him."

"No," Ann whispered. Her saliva tasted bitter. "Because we loved him—we love him."

"And it never once occurred to you that I should have been told? He's André's grandson. My cousin."

"Quent, I should've told you, but I couldn't. We'd given our promise to Gilberte."

" 'N she'd take him away if we let the cat out th' bag," Larry added.

"Do stop glowering," Gilberte said. "What else could I have done? It was you, my love, or him."

"You've told me everything else about your time during the Occupation. Repeatedly. Endlessly. Why not this?"

"Cast your mind back." Gilberte was shivering. "Can you recall your quaint morality regarding women who gave up their children?"

Larry burped and suddenly his head drooped onto his chest. He began to snore gustily. Ann ran to the staircase as if he had been shot.

"Larry, please get up! Come on!" Her voice shook. She was on the verge of hysteria. "You should be in bed."

When he didn't move, she descended a few steps to pull at his hands in an attempt to drag him to standing position. He slumped to one side, flaccid. If she did yank him to his feet, he might well fall down the stairs.

She looked around. "Quent?" she asked. "Can you help?"

Quent's expression was impassive: Ann and Larry might have been two out-of-place pieces of furniture. "I'm sure you know how to handle him better than I do," he said. His firm steps sounded along the hall to his room.

Ann made a whimpering sound, like a small, voiceless animal as it dies, then returned to jockeying her snoring husband.

Gilberte watched, wondering why she should continue to feel drained and depleted. She should be kicking her legs and waving her arms in a primitive victory dance. Quent might be furious at her—but what was one more step in his alienation? Hadn't it just been made abundantly clear that his heart had become disentangled? Ann remained her secret enemy, but Ann was no longer her rival.

Larry's arm flopped as Ann attempted to drape it around her shoulder.

After a minute Gilberte, too, returned to her room.

Tears flowed down Ann's cheeks as, alone amid priceless Rembrandts, she panted and struggled with the inert weight of her husband.

68

Ann halted outside the empty waiting room. The cold glare of the eggshell lighting, the ugly tubular furniture, the tattered polio pamphlets and the harsh aroma of Lysol made the place so inhospitable that without somebody to share her burden of dread and worry she was unable to force herself across the threshold. A student nurse and an interne were sauntering up the hall. He said something about borrowing a car to drive out to the country on Sunday, and the girl replied, "Fabuloso," with a happy laugh. It was difficult to remember that couples spent carefree days picnicking and stealing kisses under shady trees. As the two disappeared in the direction of the nurses' station, Ann went inside. Her head was bowed and her spine curved as if she were suffering from osteoporosis.

How could I not have told him? she thought, and automatically took her usual seat on the corner couch. Bleary-eyed and frantic with worry for Michael, her stomach quivery because she'd lost Quent forever, she ignored the letter that had arrived from Paris nearly eight years earlier, forgot Gilberte's threat. It now seemed a crushing indictment of her love for Quent that she had kept the truth from him. She closed her eyes, seeing that cold, superior expression as he'd ignored her plea. When had her *chevalier sans peur et sans reproche* refused to extend a helping hand?

She had been drenched with perspiration by the time she finally hauled Larry onto his bed. Then, galloping downstairs, she had realized she didn't have any money, not so much as a nickel for a phone call. She had run back to the guest room, shifting Larry around to rifle his pockets, appropriating the two crumpled ones from his wallet, leaving him a quarter and three greenish wartime pennies. Two dollars and twenty-eight cents—all that remained of the rubber check Larry had given Quent. The grand total of the monetary resources of the Porter family.

In the well-mannered calm of the Dejong ménage, she had been permitted the luxury of worrying solely about Michael, but now the real world intruded with its petty but overriding concerns.

They couldn't stay on at the Fifth Avenue house.

Tomorrow they must return to Darien. But there was no money to put gas in the Chevy, currently parked at some astronomical cost a block from the house, where the Dejong cars were garaged. There was no money for food, no money to pay a baby-sitter. (Ann raced by their indebtedness to Gilberte and others, incapable of struggling with the abstract future and large sums.) In three weeks —no, it was now two—the escrow would close. They would have to move. But where? What landlord would take them with no money for the first month's rent, much less a deposit. She couldn't take her job with Mr. Sever. Los Angeles was out of the question. Michael would be in Mount Sinai for months. His stratospheric hospital bills here were covered. *Thank God for the March of Dimes,* she thought for maybe the hundredth time.

She shifted in the chair. What about Larry? Would she stay with him? Would he stay with her?

I can't think about that now.

Another problem was whether Gilberte would carry out her threat. Probably. Gilberte had been an intransigent girl, and she had grown into an intransigent woman. She never forgot a slight, she never forgave a wrong—or what she might consider a wrong. True, Michael was legally adopted, but justice, blindfolded, permits her scales to dip heavily under the weight of cold cash.

"Oh, what does any of this matter?" she whispered aloud, then prayed silently: *God, please, just let him live. Let him live.*

Having forgotten to wind her watch, she had no idea how long she had been sitting there when high heels clicked down the hall.

It was Gilberte.

Her beige linen dress was set off by a coral choker and coral earrings, her hair had been swept up in a gleaming mass, she wore short beige kidskin gloves. Yet to Ann there was something poignant about her compulsively flawless attire for a middle-of-the-night hospital visit.

"I'm sorry," Ann murmured in French.

The topaz eyes flicked over her. "I imagine you are," Gilberte finally retorted in English. "You've just given up my son. And my husband's disenchanted."

"I feel so rotten about lying to him."

"Anyone bred to a fortune like Quent has become accustomed to a few lies. And to having his own way."

"He's never had what he really wanted."

"And that, I suppose, is lo-o-ove. Darling, you don't understand him at all."

"You're the one I don't understand."

"Is that," Gilberte asked, tugging off her gloves finger by finger, "the onset of a critique of my character?"

Ann shook her head wearily. "No. I honestly don't understand you. Once I thought I did. Back on the rue Daguerre, when I took something to heart, you'd say that life is a comedy to those who think, a tragedy to those who feel, and that you belonged in the former group."

"An inexact quote, but let it pass."

"Privately I decided that you were the exact reverse of what you said. You weren't amused by life at all. You felt everything far too much. In some way I never could figure out, you'd been hurt very deeply when you were little. And you shot out hedgehog prickles of sarcasm to protect yourself from more hurt."

At this accurate summation, Gilberte shivered. "What a youthful psychologist you were," she said. "Did you dream of training with Freud?"

"I was dead wrong, wasn't I? You have no emotions at all. If you did, you couldn't be blitzing away at me now, when Michael's so ill."

"Isn't laying the blame elsewhere Larry's forte?"

Ann went to the window. Shifting a slat of the venetian blind, she peered out. Random yellow oblongs shone in the darkness of the opposite wing.

"What've you heard?" Gilberte asked quietly.

"Nothing since I got back."

"How was he when you left?"

"The fever was down a bit, but he looked terrible."

It was a few minutes before three, the hour when biological clocks slow, when the circadian rhythm is at its lowest ebb, the hour when death is most common. Dr. Levinson came to the waiting room. Ann rose stiffly to her feet.

He glanced at her with professional impersonality. "You really need to rest," he said. "I'll have a nurse bring you a pillow."

"Michael?"

"The fever's up again."

"How high . . . ?" Ann whispered.

"Just under a hundred and five."

A groan came from Ann's throat.

Gilberte watched from her chair, hands clasped composedly on her slim Hermès purse. After a lifetime of schooling herself, she betrayed none of the sick horror erupting through her.

"We're trying a new serum," Levinson was saying. "Dr. Stratton brought it with him." Stratton, one of the specialists Quent had summoned, worked at the polio research center at Johns Hopkins. "It's still in the experimental stage, but . . ." The unspoken words *there's nothing to lose* hung in the disinfected air.

"Can I see him?" Ann asked.

"Dr. Stratton?"

"No, Michael."

"That's why I came. We're hoping it might help."

Gilberte had stood.

"Gilberte, this is Dr. Levinson," Ann murmured. "Doctor, Mrs. Dejong."

"Mrs. Dejong," he said, pausing. "Your husband's been a tower of strength. Now, if you'll excuse us—"

"I'm coming too," Gilberte interrupted peremptorily.

"We have a rule," Levinson said. "One visitor at a time. And only the immediate family."

"Then that includes me," Gilberte said.

The doctor glanced from Ann to the elegant woman with the French accent. Gilberte lifted her chin, staring back.

"I suppose it can't hurt," he said.

Ann's hands were shaking so badly that Gilberte had to tie the straps of both sets of sterile garments.

Inside the respirator ward, Gilberte halted to stare at the mechanisms, tubes, dangling bottles, mirrors angled above patients, the automatic pens zigging across oxymeter charts. Ann, aware she had only a brief time, hurried to Michael. The head protruding from the chrome neck of his mechanical monster was subtracted of flesh, a small white skull from whose caverns gray eyes looked beseechingly up at her.

"Hello, Michael. I brought a visitor, Mrs. Dejong. She's sorry you're sick too." Ann spoke in a normal conversational tone. "Dad sends his love, and he'll be here next time."

Michael nodded.

"We both love you very much."

The sunken eyes closed.

"Remember when you were little and sometimes you liked me to sing you to sleep?" Ann asked, softly singing, " '*Frère Jacques, Frère Jacques. Dormez-vous, dormez-vous?*' "

Gilberte's higher, less true soprano joined in, "*Sonnez les matines . . .*"

Levinson motioned to them, and still singing softly, they backed away between the streamlined respirators.

69

Quent was in the garishly bright waiting room. As they came in, he rose to his feet. Tall, broad-shouldered in his shirt sleeves, he had a look of athletic vitality. His greeting to Ann, spoken with the same courtesy he would give an inconsequential stranger, could not dispel the comfort she derived from his presence.

"You *do* enjoy the ambience here, darling," Gilberte said. Her pupils were enlarged and glittery, as if she'd used belladonna drops.

"Were you just with Michael?" he asked.

"It was on our agenda, yes," Gilberte retorted.

"How's he doing?"

"I lack a base of comparison. Ann?"

"The fever . . ." Ann coughed rustily to clear her throat. "The fever's nearly a hundred and five."

"A hundred and five? Good God!"

A broad-hipped nurse waddled in with a pillow. Peering at the two women, she moved toward Ann. "You must be Miz Porter. Dr. Levinson asked me to give you this."

Thanking the nurse, Ann set the pillow on the scarred little table next to her. Quent and Gilberte took seats at a distance from each other and Ann, ruling out conversation. Whenever Ann glanced at Quent, he was staring at a remote point in the hallway. Gilberte's thin, perfectly shaped and painted lips remained set in a slight knowing smile.

The nurses changed shifts at six. The corridors were abustle with uniforms when Levinson returned to the waiting room.

His mask was pushed down around his neck like a detached green clerical collar.

Shakily, Ann pressed her hands against the pillow on the table, pushing to her feet.

"Mrs. Porter," the doctor said. "Ann, perhaps you'd better sit back down."

"I'm okay."

His steps lagged as he came toward her. "Right after you left," he said quietly, "Michael went into a coma."

Still staring at him, she wet her lips. Those damn, mercilessly cheerful nurses. "From the serum?" she whispered.

"It doesn't seem likely, but we can't be positive. Mrs. Porter, we tried everything we know, everything. But he slipped away from us. . . . Your little boy is gone."

Ann saw a kaleidoscope of images. A grave-eyed baby staring at her across a rat-infested Montmartre basement. A toddler pawing at his ear. A tiny boy, his feet straddled far apart with belligerent courage. A three-year-old stumbling over words as he read a Little Golden Book to her. A child breaking into unwilling sobs as he asked if she'd leave him the way his real mom had. A skinny, wet-haired boy racing across a stretch of unmowed grass as he formed shifting rainbows with a hose.

These images circled and the feminine voices seemed to be singing, *Dormez-vous, dormez-vous* . . .

Quent caught her as she fell.

Gilberte, slender ankles crossed and spine erect, sat in the manner her mother and governesses had trained her to sit. She dealt with grief in the way she always had, by bottling it up. But this, the second time that she lost Michel, her agony was too unendurable to be bottled up without something giving way. She understood exactly what was happening to her. Her mind was being divided in the same way that the Nazis had partitioned France. On one side of the boundary, beyond the *zone interdite,* lay the dark, loamy agriculture of her spirit—her *ka,* her *anima divina.* On the other side, the heavy industry of her intellect that was now commenting on the scene before her: the doctor holding an ammonia phial to Ann's nose, Quent squatting next to the couch, chafing a small, limp hand. Worry transformed his face, tears runneled down his cheeks.

In all the years she had known Quent, had she ever seen him break down like this? How odd that this restrained man would show his emotions to the doctor and passing nurses.

The tears are for Michel, Gilberte decided. *The concern is for Ann.*

His attachment had in no way lessened. But this loaded information did not ignite Gilberte with flames of jealousy, fear of desertion, anger. *He loves her.* The thought was a calm statement of fact. *Dead. My son is dead.*

She recalled the blazing, angry blue eyes of a Jewish doctor reduced by the Nazis to performing abortions. *If I had gone through with it, Michel never would have existed.* The thought was unencumbered by grief, bitterness, regret. How she had yearned for this mathematical precision of thought! And now her son's death had cut her loose from the tyranny of her emotions.

There was no need for her to stay in this ugly waiting room and watch Quent and the doctor attempt to revive Ann.

"I'm redundant," she said, rising. "See you at home, Quent."

"There's so much to do," Ann said as Quent drove along Fifth Avenue to his house. Since she'd come to, she had been oscillating erratically between sonorous biblical phrases like *my son, my son, would that I had died for thee* and mundane practicalities.

"Take it easy today."

"We have to go home. To Darien."

His hands tightened on the steering wheel. "Today?"

"Yes."

"It's not necessary."

"We can't stay at your place. Under the circumstances."

The morning rush hour had begun and the convertible oozed, then stopped, trapped in the traffic that waited for signal changes ahead. They passed pedestrians hurrying to work on the sidewalk beside the iron fencing of Central Park, and then the same pedestrians passed them.

"I'll make arrangements for the funeral," Quent said.

"Would you? I'll pay you back—we will."

"No, Michael's my relative, so let me do it," he said, adding expressionlessly, "Under the circumstances."

Turned away, eyes wet, she couldn't see his expression of remorse. Fumbling through her purse, she came up with a tattered bit of Kleenex.

He shifted in the leather seat to get out his rumpled handkerchief.

"Thank you," she said, her voice muffled by the fine linen. "We don't have the money."

Larry was still sprawled on the bed in the same position she'd left him. Pulling the cord of the inner-lined curtains, she let sun flood into the room. With a complaining snort, he awoke, resting his forearm over his eyes.

"Sleeping," he muttered.

"I have to talk to you."

"Later."

"It's Michael."

"Michael?" He lifted his head a few inches, then fell back groaning. "Jesus, I really tied one on last night."

"Can you remember?"

He pressed his fingers to his forehead. His face shone with sweat. "The little revelation about you and mine host? Thanks for reminding me. Now let me sleep it off some more."

"Michael . . ." The tears were oozing down her cheeks and she went blindly to the bed, sitting next to him. "Michael's . . ."

"What about Michael?"

"He died. . . . Oh, Larry . . . he's dead."

Larry's eyes squeezed shut and he started to cry in loud, gasping sobs that involved his entire body. She pushed the thinning damp hair from his forehead. He clutched her waist, and she lay down next to him. Arms around each other, they mingled their tears for their son.

As Larry clutched his wife in their mutual grief, he wasn't fully sober, and he knew it. Even so, his actions took him by surprise, as did his sudden arousal.

Shoving her onto her back, he shifted on top of her, jamming his open mouth, which smelled of liquor-soaked sleep, on hers.

He hadn't approached her sexually for months. He'd always had a tame technique. For a moment Ann assumed him to be in the throes of a yet more intolerable surge of grief, but his pelvis began crushing and grinding on hers in an unmistakable rhythm. His teeth cut into her lips as his tongue crammed and rotated. She tried to pull away, her body instinctively battling. She was a small woman, weakened by lack of sleep and losing so much weight. Her struggles were ludicrously inadequate.

He shoved up her skirt. Clogged by tears, gasping under his mouth, she pushed at his hand. With a violent effort, she turned from his mouth and tongue. "Please, please," she whispered. "The door's unlocked. The others—Janey might—" Her words rose in a gasp.

He had jammed a knee upward. The pain between her thighs momentarily stunned her and she ceased struggling. He fumbled with his fly. The agony as he thrust into her made her scream. The scream went into his foul-smelling mouth. His furious pounding forced air into her lungs. This must be how Michael had felt, terrified, something else breathing for him, she thought. Larry collapsed on top of her, drenching her with his tears and sweat.

Edging from underneath him, she waddled to the door, pressing the lock catch, then went into the bathroom, locking that door also. Sunlight came through the dormer windows to glint on the sterling silver fixtures. Ann pressed her forehead against a thick, monogrammed towel.

"My baby. . . . Mi-ichael . . ." came her cry of irrevocable loss.

70

When the physical upheaval lessened, she scrubbed up the drops of blood that had trickled onto the thick white carpet with water and a bar of Roger & Gallet soap. Then, turning on the shower full force, she let the scalding water beat against her. She was combing her dripping, tangled hair in the steamy mirror when Larry tapped.

"Ann?" he called softly, then tapped again. "You okay?"

"Be right out."

With a huge effort, she pulled on the terry robe. Not glancing at Larry, she stumbled across the guest room, collapsing on her bed, neatly turned down the previous night.

"You look zonked," Larry said in a sympathetic tone.

"Take the covers from your bed if they're bloodstained and put them in the hamper," she said. "And shove the clothes I left on the bathroom floor in the suitcase."

She closed her eyes and listened to Larry moving around. When he came to sit on the edge of her bed, the mattress springs shifted beneath her and her near catatonia lifted.

"Get away from me!" she said thickly.

He jumped up. "What's wrong?"

"You *raped* me!"

"It wasn't anything like that," he said. "Shorty, you're all crazy about Michael."

"That's right, blame him. You always blame somebody else."

"It's a rotten time for both of us."

As he sat on her bed again, she aimed a punch at his side. The force of her outrage hummed behind her blow. He grunted. Holding a hand to his kidneys, he moved to the stripped bed and sat with both hands dangling between his knees, head bent.

"Shorty, look, I honestly don't know what happened before. Maybe I did jump on you. But you're right about me, I always do blame somebody else." Larry balled his hands into fists. "Dad took his belt off to us if we broke any of his fucking rules. Or if he got drunk. Or if the boss ate him out. In our happy, loving home, the first rule you learned was keep your nose clean if you don't want to be beaten bloody." Larry stopped, shaking his head. "Is that blaming somebody else?"

"I don't know," she sighed.

"Look, I know how lucky I am having you. You're such a giving person, you make people feel happy with themselves. I never want to hurt you. I know I sometimes overspend, but that's because . . . well. It's as if somebody inside me takes over and says to me, 'This is how to be a truly good guy.'"

"It's okay, Larry," she said in a flat, thin voice.

After a full minute, Larry said, "This isn't to excuse myself. But this thing with you and Quent, it's more than I can handle."

"I told him we'd go back to Darien today." She shuffled awkwardly to the closet, taking out a clean cotton dress that smelled of a starched ironing by the Dejongs' laundress.

Larry asked, "How about the funeral?"

"Quent's taking care of that."

Larry gave a bitter little snort. "Tell him that the tombstone should read: *My Dad the loser couldn't afford to bury me.*"

"Oh, Larry."

Larry's shoulders slumped, then he said, "That's through, isn't it? You and him?"

"For him it is." Because Larry had just attempted complete honesty with her, she added, "Not for me. I'll always care about him."

Larry peered at her with an expression that mingled pleading, jealousy and active resentment.

* * *

Gilberte, hatted and gloved, came down the stairs. As she crossed the hall she glanced into the dining room and saw Quent. She always had a breakfast tray but he, a substantial breakfaster, ate down here. Today only a coffee cup was in front of him.

Looking her over, he asked, "You're going to work?"

"Naturally. I gather you're taking the day off."

"I would've anyway. And there's the funeral to arrange."

Aware that the servants might be listening, she came to sit at the table. "Isn't that up to the Porters?"

"You're pretty unnerving," he said.

"Why? Because I mention that the family normally makes burial plans?"

"You know they can't afford to. That's what gets me. To drive into bankruptcy the people who were raising your—who were raising Michael."

"Something happened when I was very young. A child came of it. That was years ago." Astonishing how simple marital differences became when one's mind was cleared of the sentimental, cleared of past defeats, of cluttering emotions. Equally astonishing, how in her new state she could relegate Michel to history. "Why should it affect me now?"

He peered at her, then leaned back in the Hepplewhite chair. "I've been wanting to talk to you," he said.

"So long as it's not about divorce."

"There's an issue on which you've made your position abundantly clear," he said. "I was wondering how much Larry owes you."

"There's no need to be so judgmental about my collecting it. He embezzled from me. I could've gone to the police."

"Tell me how much."

She smiled faintly, and a redness showed on his throat.

"I'll have the accountant look it up," she said. "Offhand, around twenty-five thousand. Though why you want to know is beyond me. I'd never accept a check made out by you."

"I know that," he said.

* * *

Late that afternoon, the Porter family returned to Darien.

The house might have been deserted for years. August showers had come through open windows to dapple the dusty floorboards of the near empty rooms. A spider had spun webs between two packed cartons. The smell of rotten oranges came from the lidded garbage pail under the sink.

Janey was being religiously monitored for signs of polio: after a barely touched supper of scrambled eggs, Ann took her little girl upstairs to put a thermometer under one plump arm. The front doorbell rang, and Larry got it. After Janey fell asleep, Ann returned downstairs. Larry was watching an old Jean Harlow movie.

"Who was at the door?" she asked.

"Messenger service."

"From whom?"

"Guess. Who do we know who's above using the U.S. Mail?"

He pointed to a folded paper on piled-up books.

She opened the heavy linen business stationery. Underneath the letterhead *Quentin Dejong, One Templar Plaza* were two paragraphs outlining funeral arrangements. *Mr. Dejong asked me to assure you that anything can be altered.* It was signed by Marian LaRosa, executive secretary to Mr. Dejong.

"This was all?" she asked.

Larry gazed intently at Harlow's peroxide hair. "No billet-doux," he said. "If that's what you're asking."

"Janey wants me to sleep with her."

"No problem about that, is there?"

71

The afternoon of Michael Porter's funeral it rained. The warm downpour didn't discourage a surprising assortment of mourners from crowding the air-conditioned chapel at Frank E. Campbell's undertaking establishment on Madison Avenue. Many Gilberte de Permont employees took off the afternoon. Ann and Larry were well liked, and this showing was intended not only to express sympathy but also to prove alliance. It was generally conceded that Madame had done Ann the dirty. Opinions on Larry were sharply divided: those with expense accounts edgily said that giving him the ax was punitive and a slap on the wrist would have been adequate, but those without such fringe benefits spoke militantly about playing the big shot on company money. The chic, angular Better Womenswear buyers came in their black linen chemises with good brooches affixed to the right shoulders. The D'Amatos shared a cab from Mount Sinai with the Liebmans, each couple offering up grateful prayers to the God of their denomination that theirs wasn't the child in the white coffin. The Newcombes drove the wet roads and highways from Darien with Coriana, and Michael's teacher took the train. A contingent of Larry's fourth estate buddies arrived amid the aromas of lunchtime steaks and martinis. Milt Copeman, the coat manufacturer, showed up with his wife: that cute, nice, bouncy little redhead had been dealt enough rotten breaks, and to hell with the Dejong Bank, he whispered as Quent and Gilberte slipped into the rear pew.

Gilberte had fully intended to be a no-show.

Her newfound ability for pure reason informed her that she had given up Michel years ago and the Porters were ex-employees so therefore this funeral bore no connection to her.

She had been at her desk picking at the cold poached salmon that the Colony delivered to her office if she had no luncheon engagements, when Quent had opened the door without the routine secretarial buzz. The shoulders of his dark suit had glinted with drops of the tropical rain.

"You're wearing that?" he had asked, surveying her short-sleeved white piqué. "To a funeral?"

"It's impossible for me this afternoon. I'm tied up with a silk manufacturer from Lyon."

"The car's double-parked."

"Mainbocher's the only American house Monsieur Wolfe supplies and he wouldn't be talking to me if he weren't a friend of Yves Roland," she had explained calmly.

"I'm not here to argue," he had retorted with yet more deadly calm. "We're going to the funeral."

She had insisted on stopping at the house to change to black.

Since they were seated in the back, many of the somber-faced latecomers—employees, business connections—stopped to say a few words. Gilberte heard none of the muted conversations. Her newfound faculty for logic had abruptly deserted her. Overwhelmed by incalculable grief, she could concentrate on nothing but the small white coffin blanketed with white roses and delicate white orchids. This was the first time Gilberte had been at a close relative's funeral. *La p'tite batârde,* had been persona non grata at the last rites of her own grandmother and aunt, she had been serving her term for "consorting with terrorists" when her parents' Gestapo-sealed coffins were wheeled through the Santé gates to waiting family members: by the time Hocherer had obtained her early release, her father lay beneath an elegaic stone angel in the de Permont enclosure of the rustic Ile de France graveyard, and her mother had been reinstated among the Cagnys in a marble recess of their mausolem in Père-Lachaise Cemetery.

The pastor of St. Bartholomew's Episcopal Church, where the Dejong and Templar families had worshiped for more than half a century, appeared wearing clerical vestments. He addressed a few words of comfort to Ann and Larry, he quoted "To An Athlete Dying Young" from *A Shropshire Lad,* he said very little about the deceased, whom he had not known. Gilberte battled her desire to stand and tell the assemblage about her Michel, to inform them in detail of his career with boxes, how gravely quiet he had been when she'd placed him in his first, a suitcase into which she'd punctured airholes, how nicely he had played in his U.S. Army crate, how she had sung *Frère Jacques* to him as he lay in his streamlined breathing box, she wanted to tell everyone how intensely she loathed this final box, which looked like a petit four frosted with rosettes.

Then the tears that she had not shed in the hospital erupted in unstoppable waves. As she gasped and shuddered, Quent put his arm around her: he was not the husband who longed to be rid of her, but her consoling cousin, kin to Michel.

The organ swelled, pulsating, and ushers tapped the rows of mourners to rise and file past the casket.

Quent and Gilberte were among the last. By the time it was their turn, her weeping had quieted somewhat. Stepping between the massive floral arrangements on easels, she halted. The upper half of the coffin was open. She saw a small boy in the jacket of a new dark suit—Quent must have bought it. Under bright embalming makeup, he showed no sign of the torments of his last days. Neither did he look at peace. As she looked down on the vacant, painted little mannequin she felt a sharp physical pain, as if one of her organs—possibly her heart—were being ripped roughly from her. Visible tremors ran through her body, and the wrenching sobs started again. Quent's arm guided her away from the small casket.

At their approach, the group surrounding Ann and Larry melted. Tears were streaming down Larry's cheeks. Quent grasped his rival's hand. He kissed Ann's cheek, and there was no sign, none, of any emotions other than sadness and sympathy.

Gilberte murmured, "Larry, I don't know what to say." Her tear-clogged voice was devoid of sarcasm, chokingly sincere. "There's no consolation in words. . . ."

Then Michael's two mothers stared at each other. Gilberte, wiping her eyes, could not connect this small woman whose black silk dress hung on her, this pale mourner, with the excitable, freckled Ann who sometimes slammed down a hand to emphasize her point that by God she intended to keep her design exactly as it was, the Ann who could mark an end to the bitterest argument by making a face. This was a wraith whose vibrant, uncontrolled auburn curls struck a jarring note.

Gilberte spoke first. "I'm sorry, Ann," she murmured.

"He was such a terrific little boy . . . I loved him so."

"I always did. The love refused to go away. . . ." Gilberte was crying again.

Ann held out her arms. They hugged each other.

In this moment of shared maternal grief, pressed against Ann's fragile, quaking body, Gilberte perceived that their relationship was shaped like an hourglass. The top half was the lost innocence of girlhood shared in the worst bloodbath ever taken by the human race, yet nonetheless those years had nurtured a joyous friendship. The glass narrowed on the day that Ann had carried Michel down the apartment steps. The tiny point through which the sands of their joined lives trickled was those minutes in the basement storage room on the boulevard Suchet when she'd translated a Gestapo report. After that the shape swelled with that malign imperative, the obligation placed upon her by her father.

Releasing Ann, she moved with Quent to their waiting car, where they joined the funeral cortege.

The Porters sat far apart in the long black limousine that glided through the rain-drenched streets, the first in the line of cars following the hearse.

Larry wiped his eyes. "That Gilberte is one peculiar dame."

"The funeral must've been torment for her," Ann said. "She hates showing her feelings."

"Amen to that. Jesus, who would have ever expected the snow queen to melt?"

Thinking of Quent's arm around Gilberte, Ann stared out the dripping window. "I hope it stops."

"What?"

"The rain."

"Oh," Larry said, and blew his nose again. "The sixty-four-dollar question is, will she call her dogs off of us?"

"We owe so much to everybody." The conversation was taking place apart from Ann.

"One thing I can promise you. In a few months we'll have no financial problems whatsoever. Ann, you can forget that Los Angeles idea of yours. There's a terrific new star on my horizon, and right here in Manhattan."

Ann let his words slide from her in the same way that the drops were sliding down the windows.

By the time the cortege reached the cemetery, the summer storm had ended. The sun was showing in a patch of blue as Michel, illegitimate son of a Prussian aristocrat who had received his field marshal's baton from the Führer's own hand, grandson of an equally high-born French Résistance fighter, beloved adopted son of a middle-class, dead-broke American family, was laid to rest in the soaked brown earth near the three white Italian marble obelisks that soared above the white bones of Jessamyn Templar Dejong, Mathilde de Permont Templar and Jason Templar.

When Gilberte arrived home, she was once more engulfed by a tidal wave of grief. She lay on her chaise sobbing. With all her heart, she wished for the empathy of that moment when she had embraced Ann, when Ann had embraced her, that cojoining of maternal grief. *Ann, Ann, only you can understand what this is like, you're the only one on this earth who knows what I'm going through. . . .*

As Gilberte's uncontrollable tears seeped through her fingers, it came to her that her long apprenticeship in the poisonous art of revenge was inane if not insane. Ann was the only friend she'd ever had, and despite all that had come between them the affection abided, irrevocable and honest.

Now that Quent no longer loves her, what's the point of all this enmity? Let the dead bury the dead.

Gilberte's sobs quieted and she dried her eyes. Locking the door to her room, she moved the ornamental screen that stood in front of her fireplace in summer. She opened her safe and took out the Florentine box. Carefully she removed its contents—the telephone memorandums, the envelopes with the Gestapo seals, the musty, tattered sheets with their single-spaced German typing—arranging everything on the antique brass grate. She got the silver lighter that Quent had used for his postcoital cigarettes. It had been nearly a year since they'd had sex, but one of the servants must have refilled the fluid. The lighter flicked on immediately. Kneeling, she held the flame close to the papers. Her hand began to shake.

I can't.

Why couldn't she? Today, the day of Michel's burial, was surely the day of absolution, the day when the tyranny of grudges and hatreds could be cast off. Yet her hand now shook so convulsively that the flame almost went out. Kneeling back on her heels like a nun, she stared at the shifting, smoke-tipped light. She could hear her father's hoarse, drained voice telling her that whoever had betrayed him was his true enemy, hear him extract her promise to carry out the vengeance through the generations. With a click, she closed the lighter.

The old memos that charted the Porters' desperation she crumpled into her wastebasket. Her lovely, tear-wet face coldly assured, she replaced the dossiers, relocking the Florentine box in her safe.

Logic had returned. How could she have even considered violating the oath that her dying father had elicited from her?

Early the following morning she phoned the office of Kemp and Schuyler.

Three days later, on Sunday, a gum-chewing young process server knocked on the Porters' front door with a document that informed them that Gilberte de Permont, Incorporated, was instituting legal action for nonpayment of debt.

72

"I saw this two-bedroom today," Larry said. "Has a pantry that could be fixed up into a bedroom for a live-in maid. Good-sized rooms, a uniformed doorman. Prime location on East Seventy-fifth between Madison and Park." He broke the seal on the fifth of Black & White that he'd carried home in his briefcase. "Join me, shorty?"

"No thanks."

"Just a little nightcap," Larry coaxed with his winsome smile. "I'll drown it in soda, the way you like." He was already at the near empty refrigerator.

It was quarter to nine: he had roasted Oscar Mayer wieners on the battered portable barbecue then blackened marshmallows with Janey to make s'mores. In the week since the funeral, he had been considerate and tender with his best girls, as he called Janey and Ann. Each morning he commuted into Manhattan, returning without fail on the 5:32. Ann never inquired how he spent his time in the city. The day following their departure from the Dejong house, he'd handed her five crisp new twenties. "For food and gas, and whatever," he had said. She had never asked which of his friends was sport enough to "lend" him a hundred dollars. She didn't question the muffled telephone calls he made behind the closed bedroom door in the evening. Anesthetized by grief, trying to hide her leaky tears from Janey—the poor baby was wetting the bed and waking up with nightmares—Ann had no emotional capital left to invest in curiosity about Larry's doings.

Had she defined her feelings for her husband, she would have discovered a radical change since her race with Michael to the polio unit. Her affection remained—albeit a bit tarnished—as did her pitying exasperation. Yet a vital glue had melted. Her sense of obligation was gone. She no longer felt duty-bound to recompense Larry for his deprived boyhood. She was not responsible for any psychological debts but her own.

"Here," he said, handing her the watery Scotch. "The three of us'll take an early train in to see the place."

"Why waste the broker's time?" she asked. "We're leaving for Los Angeles the day after tomorrow."

"Shorty, I've told you over and over we'll only go back there for vacations." He raised his glass. "You're looking at the president and CEO of Porter Public Relations."

She gripped her glass. How could he cling so doggedly to self-delusion?

"This afternoon," he said, "I signed the lease on three hundred and eighty-five feet of office space in Rockefeller Center."

She could feel her jaw sag. Larry's flights of fancy were invariably pie-in-the-sky stuff. Never specific.

He chuckled. "I wish I had me a camera to catch that expression. Yes, Rockefeller Center, the big time. On the thirty-third floor with a view of Central Park."

"Didn't they ask for a deposit?"

"The first and last months' rent." His eyes slid away. "I've got backing."

"Larry, anything that comes in now is legally tied up. Those lawyers—"

"The bitch'll be paid back a hundred cents on the dollar. And so will the other bloodsuckers." His frown was brief. Taking another sip, he said, "Shorty, this is the jackpot. You're going to be draped in sable and loaded down with diamonds. For the first time in my life, I've got all the right ingredients at the right time. With this Korean thing behind us, the country's about to explode. And who's sitting in the catbird seat high atop Rockefeller Center?"

Hearing this old, old refrain roused Ann from her oppressive inertia. "Lawrence J. Porter," she said. "The celebrated dead-beat."

"It's no secret you've never believed in me," he snapped back.

"That was below the belt," she agreed.

"You'll love the apartment, Ann."

"Janey and I," she said slowly, "are leaving for Los Angeles the day after tomorrow."

In the kitchen, her words seemed hollowed out, like the biblical quotations uttered by the voice of God in wide-screen religious epics. The faraway train whistle sounded faintly, then stillness prevailed in the warm night. Ann felt a sense of calm, as if her words indeed had been sacrosanct.

"I'm signing the lease," Larry said irritably. "You've got to snap out of it, Ann. You'll have only yourself to blame if the place doesn't suit you."

"Where are you getting all this money?"

"I told you. Backing. A silent partner."

"Who?"

"Why so picky? What matters is I have the moolah." He gulped at his drink. "Look, I know that this is a rough time for you. But we're a family. You don't just break up a family because you've got a sudden yen to see palm trees and the Pacific."

"I'll be able to make a living in Los Angeles."

"And I'll be making a damn sight more in Manhattan." His voice rose. "There's no way I'll let you pick yourself up and cut me off from my kids—" At the plural, he halted abruptly.

Ann's tears oozed. Setting down her untouched glass, she picked up a sponge, urgently scrubbing Ajax on the stained porcelain of the sink although she knew that the buyers planned a total remodeling job on the kitchen.

Larry poured himself a fresh drink, downing it. "You were happy with me," he said. "I know you were happy before that fucking rich bastard showed up."

There was a hard core of truth in what he said. If she hadn't been exactly happy on Montecito Lane, she had been content.

Larry, who had been watching her face, snorted angrily and wrenched open the difficult back door. A minute later, the noisy Chevrolet vroomed, digging down the driveway.

* * *

He returned the following afternoon. He gave Janey a good-bye present, a lavishly dressed Madame Alexander doll—Meg, from the *Little Women* collection. He again pressed five twenty-dollar bills into Ann's hand. "This should get you there," he said. "I'll send you a lot more."

He didn't stay for supper. Ann and Janey drove him to the station. All three of them were weeping as the train pulled out. "I'll come see my best girls soon," he called from the window. "Bye, Janey. . . . Bye, shorty. . . . Byeee. . . ."

Earlier in the day the Bekins truck had picked up their things—Ann had sold her pink-gold bracelet watch to pay the freight—so she made a game of camping out in sleeping bags.

Before six the next morning, she was closing Janey into the jammed Chevrolet. As she walked around to her own car door, she gave a farewell look at the white clapboard house. The sparrows that nested in the rhododendron were chirping, dew glinted on the long, yellow grass, the unwashed windows of her "studio" reflected back the pink rising sun. The Schwinn that she had not had the heart to sell was propped against the garage where Michael had left it. Ann's eyes misted. She had never wanted this pretentious replica of colonial gentility, yet now she accepted that there had been moments of incredible sweetness here.

Swiping her knuckles across her eyes, she got into the car.

As they joined the traffic that already was streaming into the city, Ann had a vexing sense that she had overlooked something important. But what? In Stamford she pulled over, checking her purse. Driver's license, marriage certificate, Janey's birth certificate, the money Larry had given her. Everything in place. They had crossed Manhattan, burrowed through the Holland Tunnel and reached Newark before she realized what she had neglected. Pulling into a Shell Oil station, she bought a Bireley's Orange from the machine, giving it to Janey while she went to the telephone booth.

"Quent," she said when she finally reached him. "I've never thanked you for all you did."

"That's not necessary." A car honking loudly for service drowned out his politeness, and the next thing she heard from him was a more relaxed, "Hey, what's going on there?"

"I'm in Newark."

"Newark? At a jalopy derby?"

"Janey and I are on our way to California."

"By car?"

"Yes, driving."

"Just the two of you?"

"Larry's staying. He's got his own PR firm."

"That's new."

"Yes, he's very excited about it." Glancing at Janey, who sat on the running board playing with her straw while bright orange liquid dripped onto the beautifully made silk crinoline of her new doll, Ann added in a low voice, "Quent, I never meant to keep secrets from you, but, uh, well. . . . I'm not trying to be oblique, but Janey's right here."

"You don't have to tell me this."

"I should have trusted you."

"Ann—"

"You're far more reticent than I am, and I expected you to be open with me. Quent, I'm trying to say I'm sorry."

"Hey, come on," he said, and his voice sounded close, the timbre low and deep.

"And grateful for all the arrangements and the support."

"You're embarrassing me," he said. "Listen, I'm the one who should be apologizing. I was pretty damn vicious to you. Sometimes I don't understand myself. I knew how loyal and honorable you are. How could I have been angry at you for keeping your promise?"

"It was an awful time."

"Are things getting better for you?"

"No," she said simply. "But life goes on, and there's Janey."

After a pause, he said, "Do you have an address for when you get there?"

"Only at my boss's plant."

"As soon as you have a place, will you let me know?"

"Yes," she said. "But I need time to sort things out."

"Who doesn't. Ann?"

"Yes?"

"Drive carefully," he said.

"I made my living driving big brass, and don't you forget it, buster," she said.

He laughed.

She hung up, allowing the simple force of relief to pulse through her for a few seconds before she touched Janey's cloud of near white curls. As the hot, crowded car edged into the stream of traffic going westward, the two of them were singing "Ca-al-iforn-ia, he-ere I come . . ."

Ann, Gilberte and Quent
Los Angeles, New York, Paris
1953-1954

73

Because Gilberte had made a career of disguising her emotions, nobody would have suspected that for over three weeks now, since Michel's death, she had alternated between that eerie state of magisterial clarity and a tornado of emotions that made her light-headed, as if she might topple. It was in the second, overwrought state of mind that she went into the music room where Quent was listening to the Emperor Concerto. They were having guests this evening and his black tie hung around his collar.

"Let me do that," she said, bow-tying it for him.

"Thank you," he said, lowering the volume on the Beethoven. "Gilberte, sit down a minute. We haven't talked in a long time."

"Does that remark have an ominous ring to it?" she asked, hoping her voice reflected amused superiority rather than the skipped beat of her heart.

"It's just that I—" He stopped at the front door chimes. "We'll go into it later."

She greeted her guests, she accepted compliments on her appearance, her home, her party, she deftly edged congenial groups together, she made dry jokes, sipped dry Chablis, nibbled lobster salad, beef Wellington and cherries jubilee, but all the time fears howled within her.

Because it was a Thursday evening and the guests were all departing early the following morning for country places or sprawling beach "cottages," everyone left in a cluster before the hall clock chimed eleven.

When they were alone, Quent said, "Let's have a nightcap."

"Ah, yes, our tête-à-tête. I'd forgotten," lied Gilberte, going to pour the brandy. Sweat broke out under her arms, and she was grateful to Yves Roland for insisting on dress shields. "It went well, don't you think?"

"Your dinners always do." Sitting, he swirled the brandy between his palms. "Gilberte, we can't keep on like this."

"Are we still talking about the party? Or have we changed the subject?"

"I'm moving out tomorrow."

Her hand jerked, and as Courvoisier sloshed on her long beige dinner skirt she blurted out the words that had been in her head all evening: "You're going to her." A thin, unwanted accusation, followed by, "It's beyond me what you see in that little nobody!"

"I'll be at the Pierre," he said, getting to his feet.

"My apologies for the cliché responses, but darling, you honorable types just don't say abracadabra to a wife and then vanish."

"This isn't sudden, I haven't been inscrutable. You must've guessed I've only stayed around until you got on your feet after Michael."

"Ever generous."

"I can see that you're in fine fettle again!" He drew a breath before saying in a tight voice, "You'll have the house, the use of any of the other places you want. I still care for you, you're my cousin—"

"*I am your wife!*"

"It's not much of a marriage for either of us."

"Why not admit what's really behind this? You've always resented my miscarriages." The wrong words kept leaping from her mouth, like ferocious gray rats.

"You never used to lie to yourself," he said coldly.

"Whatever *you've* decided, I did miscarry. I've become pregnant more times than your dear little redheaded sweetie pie."

"Ann has no part in this conv—"

"Are you going to deny you're sleeping with her again?"

"I haven't seen her since the funeral."

"Michel was *mine!*" Sweat was running down Gilberte's face and she was panting.

"If you need me," he said, rising to his feet, "you can reach me at the Pierre."

"All right, go! But remember, there'll be no divorce, at least not until you're too old to get it up."

"You've never been crude."

"Yes, do let's be civilized. We won't mention your little dumpling, the one woman alive who happens to have the key to your valiant youth, when you went in for rescuing damsels from the cruel Nazis."

"Michael's death hit you harder than I realized," he said.

"Should I call Ann at the Pierre too? Or don't you have the guts to live openly with her?"

"She happens to have a husband and a child, and for us dull, gutless types that presents a problem."

"Not to worry, darling. You can hold her hand while her husband's in jail for embezzlement. Or maybe she'll hold something of yours. As I recall from our more active days, it always did respond to fondling."

"You're a real bitch."

"I wasn't when my parents were alive!"

He winced, hesitated briefly, then strode from the library. She wiped the back of a hand across her forehead, and drops flew. A minute or so later, he came down the stairs carrying a suitcase. He kept clothes at their houses as well as the Templar Enterprises hotel suites, so she had seldom seen him with travel gear. The largeish pigskin suitcase brought home the reality that he was moving out.

"You're all I have left, Quent," she said in a thin, childlike voice. "Don't leave me."

His face was very white, but he said quietly, "You know where I'll be."

"Oh, get out!" she screamed, for once not caring whether the servants heard her. "Get the hell out!"

The front door closed softly. At the metallic clink of the iron-work doors of the vestibule, she drew a long breath. Her panic suddenly left her, as if a subterranean part of her had ratified his departure. As she climbed the staircase, her mind cleared. All right, Quent was gone. She must plan how to proceed. In her room, she dismissed Yvonne—who must have overheard at least the finale if not all of the argument—then opened her moire-covered telephone book to the letter *B*. Bernard, the name of that frumpy Montparnasse headmistress, was her private code for Jack Convy, the bald ex-paratrooper who ran the detective agency that she had originally used to map Ann and Larry's financial status. She had retained Convy in her business from time to time, and he had entrusted her with his home telephone. Dialing, she arranged with him to have her husband followed.

The next evening, when she arrived home from Seventh Avenue, she found a handwritten note on the salver with the other mail. *I meant it, Gil. If you need anything, call me at the hotel or my office.*

The first inkling Gilberte had of Ann and Larry's split came one blazing Indian summer afternoon in October. Her lawyer Patrick Kemp phoned to inform her that since neither the Porters nor their counsel had contacted them, they had checked to make sure that the couple hadn't skipped. He was still in Manhattan. He had somehow managed to come up with the funds to lease space in Rockefeller Center, where he had set himself up as a specialist in public relations. He was also in the chips enough to be living at the St. Moritz. Did she wish them to get a court order with an estoppel? "That would mean any payments he receives would be turned over to you."

"They're staying at the St. Moritz?"

"Porter is. He's evaded our phone calls. But a new wrinkle's come up. This morning we received a letter from Mrs. Porter to inform us of her new address in Santa Monica, California."

"California!"

"She and the little girl are living out there," the lawyer said.

Was Quent's shift to the Pierre linked to this? Jack Convy's weekly reports mentioned no women, and the only time Quent had left the city, he'd told her about it. He'd spent ten days climbing near Grenoble. Yet she was positive that the two were connected.

"Has she filed for divorce?"

"I didn't look into that."

"Why not?" Gilberte barked.

"Mrs. Dejong, I understand your reservations, but there's no reason to be concerned. Mrs. Porter sent you a cashier's check for the house loan. She's quite willing to assume liability for the entire remaining twenty-five thousand. That's covered in her letter. She asks to be permitted to return it in monthly increments. Small ones at first, increasing with her ability to pay. She didn't mention any exact sum. Frankly, I suggest you consider her offer. It'll take years getting your money back, but Porter's a slippery customer and you'll have difficulty ever collecting from him."

"I don't have time to discuss this now," Gilberte said breathily, and hung up. The air had been punched from her. She had just realized that after all these years of aiming her heavy artillery at Larry to score direct hits on Ann, she would have to find an alternate method of warfare. It had been a gross tactical error to push Ann so far that she left him.

Hurrying into the outer office, Gilberte brusquely told the skull-faced secretary to cancel the afternoon's appointments. As Gilberte trotted across the thick gray carpet of the empty show-room, another thought occurred to her. Gilberte de Permont, Incorporated, constructed as a punitive instrument, no longer served this purpose.

Normally her chauffeur, Jordan, took her everywhere: she was unused to hailing taxis. Darting onto Seventh Avenue to wave one down, she was almost hit by a slow-moving delivery truck. By the time she reached the house, she was so distraught that it crossed her mind to call Quent at his office. In the weeks since he'd moved out, he had behaved with what she could only term *gentillesse.* He had showed up with her at a party for the dowager Duchess of Kent. He had driven with her to Newport for Jacqueline Bouvier's wedding to that handsome Irish senator. He had stilled the worst of the gossip about the breakup of that admirably suited couple, the Quentin Dejongs. But of course she couldn't call him. How could she, when her panic symptoms were caused by her sudden loss of weapons against Ann?

She took a sleeping pill—one would not put her to sleep but would act as a tranquilizer.

After a few minutes, a dark, soothing calm passed like a curtain across her agitation. She was no longer shaking and gasping. Her mind had returned to logic. She recognized that a jury of her American peers would assuredly sentence her to the loony bin for her obstinate, impractical pursuit of a second-generation vendetta. But what did her American peers know of the naked heart, of families with centuries-old traditions of honor, of *la p'tite bâtarde*— what could they know of vows extracted in the basement of the Santé?

She paced slowly up and down her sitting room considering methods of harming Horace Blakely's daughter. With Larry out of the picture, it wouldn't be as easy as before, she told herself, but there was no rush. They were both young women.

74

It was raining, the torrential California rain that gouges canyons into hillsides and plunges mud slides into swimming pools. Ann peered along the yellow brightness cast by the Chevy's headlights at the huge drops ricocheting between her and her old-fashioned arched front door. Larry wouldn't approve of either the declassé apartment or this palm-lined, shabby street in Santa Monica, but the semifurnished one-bedroom was cheap and the architectural excesses of an earlier decade tickled Ann. The elderly landlady, Mrs. Podell, had fallen for Janey's smile and (another bonus for the apartment) baby-sat gratis every Friday evening while Ann taught Costume Design Workshop 106, a UCLA extension class.

Ann mailed her UCLA salary directly to Gilberte de Permont, Incorporated. She and Janey eked by on Mr. Sever's biweekly checks. The second hundred that Larry had pressed into her hand in Darien was the last money she had received from him. Through September and October, his long-distance calls had been larded with mention of sums he was about to put in the mail: he had employed the same richly expansive tonalities when talking of his plans to fly out and scoop "his girls" off to Palm Springs for Christmas, an unkept promise that had infuriated Ann because it involved Janey. He swore to be out for Janey's birthday, but wasn't.

She no longer felt rotten about putting a continent between father and daughter.

As she darted through the driving rain, she half expected Michael to open the front door—her mind refused to accommodate his death, and no matter how she dazed herself with work she dreamed every night of him, waking in tears. Stamping her wet shoes on the cracked red tiles of the patio, she called, "It's me, Mrs. Podell."

Quent opened the door. "I told her I'd take over."

Stepping over the threshold, Ann let her dripping carryall fall to the thin brown carpet, and he wrapped his arms around her.

"You'll get all wet," she whispered huskily.

In reply, he kicked the door shut behind her and held her tighter as they kissed.

Quent had visited Santa Monica twice before, shaving a few days off business trips. They were of necessity circumspect. There were laws against unmarried couples cohabiting, and Mrs. Podell, though friendly, didn't want to get in bad with the police. Besides, Ann would be tagged an unfit mother—if Larry found out, he could take Janey away from her, as could the local authorities.

Quent ran his hand over her drenched curls. "I missed you."

"Me, you."

They kissed again lingeringly, then he pulled away. "You're drenched," he said. "After you've changed, there's some chili in the kitchen."

In her quilted robe and matted-down blue fleece slippers, she reheated the Chasen's chili. This type of snack or a couple of pints of buttery rich Wil Wright's ice cream were the extent of his presents to her, and Janey's gifts were a book or a small toy. Gilberte's prediction that he would make Ann his mistress had poisoned his generosity.

Ann left the dishes on the kitchenette table and they moved to the couch. Lightning flashed, thunder grumbled and the downpour drummed fiercely as they kissed more and more passionately.

Because of Janey, they had never made love here. But tonight, the rain a noisy curtain insulating them in this snug, shabbily furnished apartment, though they whispered hoarse, useless warnings to each other, it happened. A hasty, madly exciting coupling.

* * *

The rain had stopped by midnight when Quent left.

When he arrived a few minutes before eight the following morning to take her and Janey to breakfast, the sky was a brilliant, clean-washed blue with a grave indigo curve marking the horizon. The Pacific, striated with gaudy aquamarine and purple, reflected the sun in thousands of bronzed platelets. They walked the few blocks to Wilshire Boulevard, Ann clasping Janey's hand, not touching Quent yet feeling the warmth of his body near hers.

At Biff's, Janey ordered little thin hotcakes and sausages, then, irritated by hunger, kicked her once-white sneakers at the central stand of the Formica table. "How come you don't live in California?" she demanded of Quent.

"Because I live in New York."

"You said you lived on your airplane." Her accusatory *s* sound sputtered.

"I sleep on it sometimes, and that's fun," he said. "But it's not truly mine. It belongs to the business."

"Janey, drink your orange juice," Ann said.

"All those seeds, yech!" Janey said. "Mrs. Podell thinks you're Mom's boyfriend."

"I'm her friend," Quent said carefully. "And yours, too."

"Grown-ups aren't friends with kids," Janey said flatly. "Anyway, if you're my friend, why do you take Mom out without me?"

"Sometimes we need to talk about grown-up things that'd bore you."

"Mrs. Podell's an old dummy."

"I thought you liked her," Ann said.

"Oh, who cares," Janey said, not turning from Quent. "She wanted to know if you're going to be my dad. I told her I have my own dad."

"You sure do," Quent said. "And he'll always be your dad."

"There's a girl in my class, Kathy." Janey's worried lisp intensified. "She and her mom are divorcing her dad."

The waitress set down their orders.

"Does Janey talk much about divorce?" Quent asked.

"That was the first time."

"What about you?" he asked.

"I've never brought it up."

"What I meant is, you must have thought about what you're going to do."

Ann had been dreamily pulling on her stockings. Now she turned to look at the bed where he lay with the sheet tangling around his chest. They were in his bungalow at the Miramar Hotel. Templar Enterprises maintained a suite on the top floor of the Beverly Wilshire Hotel convenient to the West Coast headquarters, but Quent stayed here because Ann lived three blocks away— and because the bungalows could be reached from the street without going through the lobby.

"Nothing specific," she said. She never considered going back to Larry, yet her thoughts of a final break were nebulous. She was not recovered enough from Michael's death to be decisive. Besides, she was too strapped to consider hiring a lawyer.

As if guessing her thoughts, Quent said, "I'd find you somebody good."

All at once her seminudity disturbed her and she pulled her slip over her head. "The way we are is fine with me."

"Not with me." He paused. "Ann, you might as well know this. Right after Michael died, I gave Larry a cashier's check."

She turned to him. "You gave him money? Why?"

"To pay what he owed Gilberte."

"That much? Quent, did he understand what it was for?"

"I sent an explanation with the check. It was in the envelope with the funeral plans."

Ann picked up her blouse. "So you're his backer?"

"Unintentionally."

She reddened, unreasonably humiliated by Larry's actions. "Why're you telling me now?" she asked.

"I'd give him more if it'd free you," he said in a cool, dispassionate tone.

"And what about *your* freedom?"

Quent's momentary remoteness faded and he rubbed his scarred elbow. "Ann, don't get angry. It would just be easier, that's all."

"For who?"

"Both of us."

"Have *you* talked to a lawyer?" Her eyes challenged him.

He looked away. "Before Thanksgiving I made an appointment. After that I couldn't stop thinking about André. How good he'd always been to me, how much I admired him, what a terrific person he was—how terrific he'd been to me. When I was a kid I used to wish he was my father. I couldn't get him out of my mind. You know how he doted on Gilberte." Quent paused. "Ann, this thing with Michael's been terrible for you, but in a way it's worse for her. She can't show her grief, it's all bottled up inside her, fermenting."

"You know she's always played on your guilt."

"Try to understand how you'd feel if you had inadvertently dropped part of your own family into the Gestapo's hands. In the Santé, one of the Germans used to sell her. Day after day she'd be gang-raped. It wasn't enough that André and ViVi were murdered, they had to brutalize her. And that's on my conscience."

"So you didn't keep your appointment with the lawyer?"

"My not getting a divorce means so damn much to her."

"But you're separated, you don't live in the same house."

"God knows I can't pretend to tell you what goes on in her mind, but I think it has to do with her sense of security. As long as I'm her husband, she feels she's safe. Maybe you're right, maybe I do play into her hands. But I just couldn't do it to her." His voice had dropped as if he were exhausted. "Sweet, I'm so damn confused."

Ann sat on the bed next to him, stroking his shoulder. "You don't have to feel guilty about *me*. I owe you. You saved *my* life."

The rest of his long weekend in California neither one of them brought up the subject of divorce.

One of the architectural flourishes of her apartment was a walled patio too narrow for outdoor furniture. In fine weather, Ann would work out there. On a warm afternoon about five weeks later, in early March, while Janey was making chocolate chip cookies at Mrs. Podell's, Ann knelt at the dress form, staring morosely at the stiff white nylon piqué. After years of selecting from the most opulent fabrics, she felt a physical revulsion for the yardage that Mr. Sever had provided with instructions to design a matching skirt and blouse. An actual nausea. *Whatever I do with this junk it'll look like a uniform. I'll call and tell him exactly that,* she thought. She pushed rapidly to her feet. The sunlight danced and her head felt disconnected. Fearing she might pass out, she sat cross-legged on the warm red tiles, breathing deeply.

And she connected the nausea, the sleepiness of the last days, her period being late.

She was pregnant.

That sweet, romantic quickie, of course. She snapped her fingers like castanets and laughed. Then decided she must share the good tidings with the other partner. Long-distance calls were not in her budget, but anyway she called Quent's private number at the Pierre—it was three hours later in New York, and he would have left the office. Hearing the first static-laden ring she was catapulted back to his initial visit: he had asked in an awkward tone whether she would do honors with the "precautions." She had promised to use her diaphragm. He was stuck in his marriage and didn't want accidents. Unlike her, he had a hard-edged sense of morality. Oh, he would acknowledge the baby, but did that mean he would share her excitement in having a bastard? Her heart was beating fast as he picked up the phone.

After the greetings, he asked, "Ann, what's wrong?"

"Not a thing."

"You sound strange."

"A bad connection," she said. "When're you coming out?"

"After I'm through in Warm Springs."

Of course. He'd told her he would be presenting an award on behalf of the Templar Poliomyelitis Rehabilitation Facility in Warm Springs, Georgia. The recipient was Dr. Jonas Salk, who had just completed testing his vaccine on hundreds of thousands of school children with no ill effects and no cases of polio. *If only this serum had been on the market last summer,* Ann thought, sighing. *If only Michael could have been vaccinated.* . . .

After a moment, Quent said, "I should be in California on Friday."

The following morning, after walking Janey to school, she felt lazy. Instead of starting to work with the horrible nylon—despite her arguments, Mr. Sever had remained convinced that with the right cut and trim, he would have a winner—she reheated the coffee.

She was sipping dreamily when the front door, which she never locked in the daytime, opened.

"Quent! What're you doing here? Why aren't you in Georgia?"

"What did you really want to tell me yesterday?"

"I . . . uh . . ."

He stared at her, a tall pillar blocking her from the sunlight streaming through the window. "Come on, Ann. I knew something was on your mind. At least tell me to my face if you're going back to him."

"To Larry?"

"Aren't you?"

"Why would I do that?"

"He's your husband, he's Janey's father."

"I called you because . . ." She watched his face carefully. "Because, well, this is all tentative, I haven't checked with a doctor, but the symptoms are there. I, well, I'm sort of pregnant."

"Pregnant?"

"I'm pretty sure."

He walked to the window, his back to her. She knew that she could never bring herself to get an abortion. Staring at the broad shoulders and back, she held her breath.

When he turned, the blue eyes glinted with tears. Taking her hand, he kissed the palm. "Hey, Ann. . . . I'm sorry we're not married, I wish more than anything on earth that we were. But it's a good thing I skipped Georgia. Who needs to wait for such terrific news?"

75

On April 4, Gilberte attended the eighty-seven-year-old Toscanini's farewell performance with his NBC Symphony Orchestra, an all-Wagner program. The repeated leitmotifs so admired by the Nazis generally gave her the willies, but since Quent had invited her to the concert this afternoon the Wagnerian orchestral turbulences brought her to her feet with enthusiastic applause.

During the intermission, Gilberte wound her way through the crowded, smoky lobby holding her husband's arm, her bearing that of a queen on her coronation day. Face anointed with pleasure and self-confidence, she inclined her Lilly Daché hat in regal recognition of acquaintances. When greeted by part of their fashionable circle, she halted Quent, laughing and chatting for a minute or so. After the Dejongs moved on, heads moved closer together in buzzing speculation. Were the couple back together again? The lights blinked on and off. Returning to their seats, she hugged Quent's arm closer.

After the performance, as they made their way down the poster-adorned steps into the cold twilight, Quent asked, "Mind if we walk a bit?"

"Perfect."

They started down 57th Street with Jordan in the car trailing them. The surging, exultant theme from *The Valkyrie* still resounded in Gilberte's head, and in this mood of triumph, it seemed to her that her husband was about to tell her that he'd made a monumental blunder, that he was sick of living in a hotel, that he missed the amenities of a well-run household—that he'd missed *her*.

"What a performance! I can't thank you enough, darling."

A flamboyantly dressed old woman shoved between them, crowding into the Russian Tea Room with other concertgoers.

When they stepped back together, Quent said, "Gilberte, there's something you have to know."

She turned expectantly. "Yes?"

"Ann's coming back to New York."

With her anticipation of a radically different remark, all she could do was gape at him. "What?"

"Ann's moving back here."

"So that's on again."

"It's never been off since the day I met her. I've taken a place for her."

Gilberte pulled her coat tighter around her. "Where?"

"The Village. It's not likely I'll bump into people you and I know there."

"Shall I award you a *croix de guerre* for heroism above and beyond the call of normal adultery?"

"Ann likes the area," he said. "Gilberte, I didn't want you hearing this from somebody else."

"Such consideration." She glimpsed their reflections in a shop window, a tall, handsome couple. "For some reason, darling, I don't see you as a Village type."

"I won't be living there."

"Oh, you *do* deserve a medal. Tell me, how's the noted flack barfly taking the news?"

"Larry's leaving for Vegas tomorrow."

"A Nevada divorce." Gilberte disguised her tremor with a laugh. "How much is that little jaunt costing you?"

"Enough so you'll get what he owes you. He's met a Texas widow. From everything he says, she sounds like a thoroughly nice woman. Quite well-to-do. They've set a wedding date."

"A pity for you two turtledoves that I'm not so amenable."

"Gilberte, just tell me what you want, and it's yours."

"What I want has always been on the table, darling. You. And it's a bit chillier than I thought. I'll drive the rest of the way."

He raised his hand, and Jordan braked beside them.

As Quent opened the car door for her, she said lightly, "Give Ann my best." She waited until the car turned left on Fifth Avenue before she slumped in the corner. She had believed that his moving out had immunized her to further pain and humiliation, yet her muscles were unglued by that old sense of ineptitude. *La p'tite bâtarde* couldn't keep her husband. At home, unable to climb the stairs, she went into the drawing room. The new decor, stark white enlivened by her Impressionist paintings, had been much admired. Today, however, Gilberte decided that all the room lacked was a velvet rope to be an exhibit at one of those dreary suburban tours of decorated houses put on for charity. She stood at the window gazing across the lights of Fifth Avenue to the darkness of Central Park. Quent's departure to the Pierre had almost killed her, and the job would be finished by this. For years she had been the envy of every married woman in her wide acquaintanceship, and now they would all hear that her "dream of a husband" had taken up with a nobody little divorcée. Quent, the stainless spouse, the paragon, keeping a mistress! Oh, how the laughter would reverberate!

The idea of bolting came to her full-blown.

I'll go to Paris, she thought.

Paris, her birthplace, her girlhood home.

Paris . . .

Gilberte was always a careful planner, yet in that moment, her breath misting the window, she decided to leave as soon as she feasibly could.

Having a course of action worked on her like both a sedative and a stimulant. She hurried to the library telephone, calling two widowed Dejongs, notorious gossips both, inviting them to a "pickup supper" that same Sunday night. Over the veal cordon bleu, her expression animated, she told them that she needed to regenerate her creativity, and where better than in the fashion center of the world?

After that her days blurred by. She was scratching corrections on

Yves Roland's meticulous watercolor sketches for the fall collection. She was flying to Bermuda to oversee a shoot for the summer ads—she could scarcely bring herself to look at the Gilberte de Permont Girl, Marjan. She was arguing with fabric and trimming suppliers. She was training Moe Sbicca, her sales chief, how to take over her black walnut desk. Moe's regency was limited. For any agreement above two thousand dollars, he would have to confer with her via transatlantic telephone. Though her business had been denuded of its original purpose, she could not relinquish her grasp: Gilberte de Permont, Incorporated, had become as inextricably part of her as the red corpuscles in her bloodstream. Jack Convy sent her a three-page report that Mr. Dejong had subleased an apartment on Washington Square and a Mrs. Porter with her daughter, aged six, had moved in. Gilberte worked yet more hours a day.

And then, suddenly one dusk she was tilting toward the lights of Paris.

Gérard, one half of their Paris couple, was on hand with the new Jaguar to speed her to a smartly refurbished nineteenth-century house fronted with boxhedge. Several years ago when this building on the curve of the avenue Gabriel had been renovated into luxury apartments, she and Quent had bought an entire floor as their Paris pied-à-terre. Gérard's wife emerged to help him lug five suitcases up the service stairs—Yvonne, flying in early tomorrow, would bring the remainder of Gilberte's baggage.

Though Gilberte was exhausted, her insomnia prevailed. She lay on the wide bed, her mind fluttering with methods of destruction —revolvers, daggers, arsenic, the *baignoire,* strangling ropes. These thoughts of violence persisted even though Gilberte was convinced that the cruelest punishment she could inflict on Horace Blakely's daughter was the course she had already embarked upon: an endless back street (or, more accurately, Greenwich Village) affair without hope of marriage or a child. Grimacing with painful irony into the darkness, she thought: *Maman had a child.*

A church bell chimed eleven strokes and Gilberte pulled on her robe. Unlocking her briefcase, she extracted the Gestapo reports. She handled the tattered wartime paper more tenderly than an acolyte entrusted with a sacred relic. Returning to bed, she fell asleep.

She awoke before six in a mood of despairing nihilism.

Why had she come to Paris? At least in New York she was perceived to be a highly successful businesswoman and (by most people, anyway) as the cosseted wife of a powerful and wealthy man. Here, she was a blight on two fine old family trees.

Sighing heavily, she tugged on the tapestry bellpull for her breakfast tray.

Her depression remained but the café au lait stirred her metabolism. Maybe she could order a few outfits from Dior: Yves Roland lacked every trace of inspiration, but at least she could spur him on to top-notch copies. And also she should see what Balenciaga was doing with his sack-back silhouette.

It wasn't yet seven. No couturier house would be open for hours. Gilberte decided to check the working Parisiennes—on occasion it was the young without much to spend who started fashion trends.

This time when she rang the bell, Yvonne responded.

"So you arrived," Gilberte said. "I'll be going out. Have you unpacked my navy and white?"

"*Oui,* Madame," Yvonne retorted. She surveyed Gilberte with concern. Her employer, understandably, had appeared frazzled since Monsieur moved out, but now there was a frantic glint in the topaz eyes. "But perhaps Madame should rest?"

Yvonne, by dint of her unobtrusive loyalty, had escaped Gilberte's generic dislike of servants, nevertheless, she snapped, "You may sleep if you need, but as for me, I have a business to run! Tell Gérard to have the car brought around. I'll drive myself."

It was drizzling. Gilberte, who seldom took the wheel, jerked forward on the wet street.

Crazily jockeying Citroëns crowded the Champs-Elysées, and Gilberte could only dart glances at the women hurrying along under their umbrellas. In their raincoats, they displayed no obvious trends. After several near accidents, she shifted to the broad, empty avenues of the *seizième arrondissement, le beau quartier,* the purlieus of the upper class. The car was drawn down the avenue Foch as if the springing-jaguar hood ornament were attached by a sturdy chain to the boulevard Suchet.

Gilberte had been vigilant about avoiding her girlhood home, where had dwelt mortification, loneliness, loss and grief. Yet the pull was irresistible. As she came into sight of the tall, graceful house with its fresh paint and gleaming mansard roof, memories burned like acid. Little Gilberte, sitting erect and proud next to her father in his bullet-shaped car as he bore her off to some pleasure-smeared outing, Gilberte under that shell-shaped canopy, a naked, shorn collaborator. Gilberte, an exultant bride, opening the cartons that were her elderly Prussian lover's legacy to her—

The dossiers!

Had she relocked them in her briefcase? She could not recall.

Her hands slipped on the wheel. The car swerved. She heard the violent honking of a horn, the squeal of tires on wet pavement. She jolted forward. Her head clanged into the windshield.

Galaxies whirled and danced then died behind her eyeballs.

Quent, she thought. And the darkness closed around her.

76

Ann stood on a stepladder hammering a nail in the fresh white paint above the fireplace to hold the last of the black pottery plates from Acoma. The apartment on Washington Square was old, with fifteen-foot ceilings. The living room was made yet more spacious by its two eccentric ells: the larger held Quent's elaborate record-player that turned the stack, his library of record albums and a Bösendorfer piano on which he performed with astonishing skill, the other held Janey's toys. The room proper swallowed up the only furniture, Ann's old couch, freshly slipcovered in a ferny pattern, and her easel set up in the bay window. The two weeks since she'd given up designing for Mr. Sever had been hectic, and yesterday Quent had insisted she take off a few hours: accordingly she had tried her hand at a watercolor of the budding trees in the square below.

As Ann descended the ladder to retrieve the final plate she wore a vaguely penitent expression. Early this morning when Quent had left—unwillingly—for a conference in Calcutta that had been set up the previous year, he had extracted a promise from her that she would let Coriana do all the physical work. But Coriana was picking Janey up from a nearby private school.

When Ann had phoned Coriana about their return to New York, the Jamaican woman had promised to give the Newcombes her notice: it was her heart's desire, she said, to be reunited with her lamb. Janey was equally delighted, and from time to time would prop her soft little chin in her hand to peer at the maid, then shift closer until she was nudging the familiar rotund, cinnamon-odored presence.

The child had lost her innocent acceptance of the universe, but her hereditary winsomeness remained intact. She had been the rallying point at what might have been an ulcer-invoking lunch at the Pierre: the first get-together of the two couples who held sway over her, Ann and Quent, Larry and Maisie Wentkus.

Maisie spoke in a high-pitched Texas accent and wore a large, bird-shaped brooch glittering with carats of diamonds. The mother of three teenage sons in military school, she had gazed adoringly at Larry each time he spoke, and Ann had decided that once she got over the embarrassment of being an admitted three years older than her betrothed (from appearances, more like a decade) she would gather him to her capacious, maternal bosom and spoil him like an errant fourth son. As the main course was being served, Larry had signaled for another martini. Maisie had slapped his arm playfully. "Now, honey, don't you reckon you've had enough?" and he'd canceled his order with a grin: he had acquired a firm if doting mother figure.

"After you're married, are you going to be a dad to Mrs. Wentkus's kids?" Janey had inquired of Larry, adding, "And play Wiffle Ball with them like you did with Michael?"

Larry's mouth had quivered, and Ann had reached over to rest her hand on his.

"I'll always be *your* daddy, baby," he had said. "You're going to be a bridesmaid at the wedding, so as soon as I get back from Nevada, Auntie Maisie, you and me'll go shopping for a beauteous pink dress. And when you visit the ranch you'll have your own pony. And she and I'll fly to New York a lot of times to be with you. How does that sound?"

"Fine," Janey had replied in a small, flat voice.

Ann empathized wholeheartedly with Janey's problems in adjustment. She was having her own difficulties. Her handwriting wavered unevenly on the checks she wrote on the account that Quent had opened for her. He never left her in any doubt that he was crazy about her and exultant about the baby. Yet also he seldom ventured with her beyond the thick old front door with its incised laurel crown. Though Ann understood that he didn't wish to demean Gilberte, his circumspection made her feel yet more like the kept heroine in Fannie Hurst's *Back Street*. Her parents, were they living, would be horrified at her life and would consider the baby a sin. Despite these impediments, Ann was unabashedly happy. She had regained some of the weight she'd lost and her collarbones no longer stood out, her skin glowed, her brown eyes were luminous.

She was on top of the ladder hanging the plate when the telephone rang. Pulling a face, she put out a hand, smudging fresh white paint with newsprint as she climbed down carefully. She ran into the kitchen—though her waist remained slim, her stomach flat, she was already moving a little clumsily.

"Yes?" she said.

"Western Union," a woman's voice droned. "I have a telegram for Mr. Quentin Dejong."

Ann frowned. Who would know he might be here? She was about to refer the wire to Templar Enterprises then decided that Quent himself must have given the number to somebody.

"Yes, go ahead."

" 'Mrs. Dejong injured in automobile accident. Stop. Condition grave. Stop. Come immediately. Stop. Yvonne Latrielle, forty-four avenue Gabriel, Paris.' "

Who's Yvonne Latrielle? Quent's being so ultradiscreet, why would he tell her about this apartment?

"Would you like me to repeat that?"

"Please."

This time Ann scribbled the message. As she hung up, the phrase *condition grave* jumped out at her.

Quent, who never flew the corporate plane on intercontinental jaunts, would be incommunicado until his arrival in Calcutta three days hence, and after that it would take him several more days to make the connecting flights to Paris. Ann bit her lip then picked up the telephone again.

Four different operators, two American, two French, put her through to Paris with remarkable swiftness, but it was a terrible connection. Sonar noises rolled in waves over Yvonne Latrielle's faraway voice explaining her connection to Madame Dejong; however, Ann deduced that she was Gilberte's personal maid. Then the static cleared and Yvonne's rapid French came through clearly.

". . . I found Monsieur's address in Madame's book."

For a moment Ann's forehead creased—she was quite positive that Quent had not given Gilberte the Washington Square number. "How is she?"

Again the response was garbled. Ann repeated her question.

"Automobile . . . her head . . . Hasn't regained consciousness." There was a sound that might or might not have been weeping. ". . . critical . . . family member should be here . . ."

"Let me see what I can arrange," Ann said.

She hung up, her hand remaining on the telephone. The doctors in Paris had asked for a family member. Ann could always call Quent's father, whom she did not know, however, Gilberte had never disguised her scorn for that overage Don Juan.

Within five seconds of hanging up, Ann had come to a decision. She herself would go to Paris.

On the surface, a ridiculous impulse: the husband's girlfriend (kept woman? bimbo? whore?) does not rush off to nurture and sustain the wife. Gilberte, however, was the friend of her youth, and for Ann the bonds of mortal love and friendship were more permanent and irrevocable than life itself. With no consideration to the paragraph in her obstetrician's pamphlet that warned against long journeys, she dialed Quent's office. Miss LaRosa, whom Quent had alerted to help Mrs. Porter in all manners possible, promised to relay the telegram message to Calcutta. Ann then asked the crisp-voiced executive secretary to please book her a seat on the soonest flight, immediately amending that to three seats. Janey couldn't be left parentless in New York (Larry was in Las Vegas obtaining his Nevada residency) nor could she be entrusted to strangers in Paris, so child and maid would have to come along. Miss LaRosa didn't reply that she would see what she could manage: in her efficient manner, she assured Ann that three first-class tickets on tonight's Air France flight would be sent by messenger over to Washington Square. And if there were any passport difficulties, please give her a buzz: Mr. Dejong had connections at the State Department.

Retrieving her scuffed suitcases from the enormous walk-in hall closet, Ann reflected that though wealth can neither buy happiness nor prevent physical and mental anguish, it can sure oil away the squeaks and rattles of everyday existence.

77

Ann had not returned to Paris since the war ended, and as the taxi drove in from Orly she was ambushed by memories: her mother, dear and irrevocably middle-American, altered not one whit by Paris, her father with his loving hugs and weak-chinned, handsome face . . . young, innocent Gilberte with her pseudosophisticated little smile . . . the witty baron and his elegant baronne . . . Quent's Jacques Tinel sweater, which smelled of cheap, adulterated wartime tobacco . . . Larry in his officer's pinks . . . Michael, slippery as a fish in his convulsions. Holding Janey in her lap, she responded automatically to Coriana's lilting Jamaican excitement about the Eiffel Tower, the Arc de Triomphe.

At the avenue Gabriel flat, they were met by Yvonne Latrielle. With profuse, slightly tinny gratitude for Ann's prompt arrival, the lady's maid showed them to adjoining guest rooms. Janey, who would share with Coriana, predictably chose the pink room.

The paneling in Ann's room was quilted with opaline blue silk that matched the blue in the floral needlepoint carpet. A scent of potpourri emanated from the blue satin *plumeau*. Ann, light-headed with fatigue, touched the turned-down linen regretfully, knowing she wouldn't relax until she'd seen Gilberte. She bolstered herself with a quick bath and freshly brewed coffee, pushing away the thought that she couldn't organize one home this effi-

ciently, much less seven—or was it eight?—and therefore Gilberte
was infinitely more qualified for the role of Mrs. Quentin Dejong.

Gilberte had been taken to a private hospital on the avenue Paul
Doumer just off the Trocadero. It had originally been the home of
a titled family, and a coat of arms was chiseled in the black marble
fireplace of the front hall. At an outsize gilded desk sat a sharp-
faced nurse.

When Ann asked to see Madame Dejong, the nurse's thin shoulders went back, a seneschal guarding the privacy of sufferers within
these walls.

"Is Madame perhaps a relative?"

"A very good friend."

"Ah, a pity. Madame Dejong's condition is grave and only her
family may visit her."

"But I flew from New York especially."

The patients in this hospital bore well-known names, many preceded by titles. Americans, of course, had no lineage, so their
power was more difficult to assess. The nurse's thin lips disappeared entirely as she studied this Madame Porter. Hatless, wearing a handsomely cut, belted green coat, the pretty, weary-faced,
auburn-haired young woman had the right casual look, yet there
was a softness in her flawless French, a lack of innate arrogance.

"The doctor was most explicit. Family only."

Ann raised her chin, striving for the bearing and tone with which
Gilberte had gained admittance to Mount Sinai's polio unit. "Then
you will have to make an exception."

"Permit me to find out her condition for you," the nurse said
with less assurance.

"That won't be necessary. Direct me to her room."

Glancing down at her chart, the nurse capitulated. Ann climbed
a staircase, hurried down a broad corridor whose handsome wain-
scoting was at odds with the utilitarian brown linoleum and hospital equipment, ascended three shallow steps.

Though Gilberte's room was handsomely proportioned, the furnishings were spartan—many of the patients ordered their own
furniture and paintings brought here. On the dresser stood a water
glass with a bunch of violets. Briefly, Ann contrasted the wilted
little bouquet with the exotic flowers that had crowded every avail-

able surface in Gilberte's room at Dr. Kreiger's gynecological facility. Then her attention focused on the patient. One arm, in a cast to the shoulder, was suspended by a trapeze. Bandaging like a nun's cowl hid the circumference of her face, and bandages crisscrossed her nose. For a heartbeat Ann halted in the doorway, wondering if the cruel-lipped nurse had dispatched her to the wrong room. But that unmistakable black hair flowed in glossy luxuriance from beneath the bandages.

She took two steps forward. "Gilberte?"

Gilberte didn't stir.

"It's me, Ann."

Gilberte's chest continued to rise and fall lightly.

The nurse by the bed had looked up from her book with a smile that gave her face the pleasant contours of a brioche.

"Is Madame Dejong sedated or in a coma?"

"The doctor, he will explain her condition when he comes. Possibly a half hour or so. Madame, if you'll take a seat."

The free chair, apparently designed by a corrupt chiropractor, had legs too high, a seat too shallow and a back that sloped forward at an awkward angle: to keep from sliding off the slick Leatherette, Ann had to keep her muscles braced. Because of either her discomfort or her exhaustion, her thoughts seemed to be crisscrossing at different levels, like one of those futuristic Los Angeles freeway intersections.

On one level she was aware that this gravely, perhaps mortally injured woman was her oldest friend, her sole link with the misplaced yet unassailable happiness of those hungry wartime schooldays. This was Gilberte, with whom she had pretended sophistication, Gilberte, with whom she had giggled about boys and shared her unexamined thoughts and fantasies, Gilberte, her fellow player in the dippy paper doll game that had later sanctioned their careers.

On another level, she was brooding about Gilberte who had sung her Lorelei songs of luxury to lure the susceptible Larry into the maelstrom of debt. Gilberte had lied to Quent about her miscarriages. Gilberte had never shown Michael a tinge of affection from the moment Ann had carried him down that dingy staircase in

Saint-Ouen—in fact, had appeared to forget his existence until the final days of his life.

On the bottommost, subterranean level were her own ambiguities. She loved Gilberte's husband and was carrying his child, she had no intention of nobly stepping aside, and even if because of his own quirks of conscience he never obtained a divorce, she would be his until death did them part. On this level she was aware of the immense benefit to her—and the baby—if the bandaged figure slipped from her comatose state into the column of Paris traffic fatalities.

Yet Ann sat there willing Gilberte not to die. For whatever the rancors and rivalries of their Siamese-twin lives, she was no more capable of willing Gilberte's death than of aiming a loaded Mauser at the bandaged head.

An hour and a half later, at one-thirty, when a young aide in a striped uniform came to relieve Gilberte's nurse for lunch, Ann, who hadn't eaten breakfast and knew that food would cure her mild nausea, couldn't force herself to leave. What if she missed the doctor?

It was after four when he finally hurried through the hand-hewn door. Although tall and big-bellied, his narrow mustache and pointed little goatee gave him an unmistakable resemblance to that legendary dwarf, Toulouse-Lautrec. Ann identified herself as Madame Dejong's closest friend, the emissary of Monsieur Dejong, who was en route to India and therefore unable to reach Paris for days. The doctor identified *himself* as a neurologist who had been summoned when it was realized that in addition to the multiple fracture of the arm, the broken nose, the facial lacerations, Madame Dejong had also suffered cranial injury.

"The skull is cracked on the right side, and there is some indication of subdural bleeding."

"Does she have brain damage?" Ann's mouth was dry.

"There is no injury to the spinal nerves," the doctor said guardedly.

"Will she be able to function normally?"

"Madame, one thing at a time. First we must keep her alive."

"But . . . what if she's like this?"

He looked Ann up and down, his brown eyes sharp, as if he could somehow discern the tiny embryo floating in her uterus. "Madame, I suggest you return to your hotel and rest. There is nothing you can do here."

"I'm staying at Madame Dejong's. Will you call me if her condition . . . changes?"

"Assuredly."

The next forty-eight hours buffeted Ann until she felt as if she were sailing on choppy seas. She forced down the meals set in front of her. She slept heavily, but never longer than four hours. She was passively grateful to the chauffeur, Gérard, for renting a replacement for the wrecked Jaguar and giving Janey and Coriana the grand tour of Paris, just as she felt an irritation at Yvonne's veiled hostility, but the major investment of her emotional energy was at the hospital. A medical ukase had been handed down that she could stay no longer than ten minutes of each hour in the sickroom. Sitting in the waiting room, a charming, oval boudoir that had been the retreat of a duchess, she imagined herself trapped like an unquiet spirit in an endless purgatory of hospital waiting rooms. When at the bedside, she couldn't take her eyes from the terrifyingly blank face.

On Ann's second evening in Paris, during her final allotted visit, she saw a faint quiver of the bruised flesh above the left eye. She jerked forward, not daring to blink lest she miss another movement. But Gilberte's slow, regular breath came and went while her flesh remained lax. Ann asked herself whether the quiver had been a figment of her hopeful imagination. She stared, waiting, waiting. Then, when her time was almost up, there was another minuscule creasing of maroon-streaked skin.

"She's trying to open her eyes," Ann murmured in hushed awe.

The pleasant-faced nurse, folding towels into a bureau drawer, turned. "Eh?"

"Madame Dejong," Ann whispered. "She's waking up."

The nurse hurried to the bed, peering, lifting Gilberte's free wrist to take a pulse, then raising a lid to look into the expressionless eye. She shook her head.

"But I saw her move," Ann insisted.

The nurse glanced upward at the ugly, dangling fixture that defaced the molding. "The electricity, sometimes it wavers."

Nevertheless, by the time Ann was back in the avenue Gabriel apartment, she had regained a trace of her usual optimism. She slept six hours, awaking at three filled with Lourdes-like faith that if Gilberte touched a familiar object, she would regain consciousness. Pulling on a robe, she moved through the dark, silent flat to the master bedroom. On the escritoire stood Gilberte's briefcase. Hoping to find the shagreen date book that Gilberte had referred to constantly at work, she pressed the gold catch.

As the lid sprang up, she saw the finger-smudged envelopes stamped with swastika and death's-head. The Gestapo's insignia. On one envelope was typed in German:

Section IV, Geheimdienst
Terrorist acts at Gare de l'Est, October 6, 1941
André de Permont, closed case

The other envelope bore a similar inscription with the name Vivienne Cagny. Though Yves Roland had whispered the ancient scandal, a bitchy snip of gossip that Ann had respected Quent for never repeating, she took a moment to adjust to the baronne's true name. Then questions rushed at her. What was Gilberte doing with Gestapo dossiers? Had she brought them to Paris with her? Had she just uncovered them? Ann picked up the baron's report, fumbling as she drew out the four tattered pages.

Amid Teutonic words, the name *Horace Blakely* jumped out. Ann bleated, a soft little sound. Her mind tightened like a fist as she summoned her German.

She translated laboriously, her full mouth forming a downward curve as if she were about to weep, but her eyes remained dry. She took over a half hour to finish. *Body returned to family March 25, 1942.*

The clock ticked, a faraway dog howled. Looking at papers in her lap, but not seeing them, Ann recalled that day when her parents had been held by the French police. After she had sought information at the commissariat and become a game for a dirty-minded, pimply *agent de police*, she had relinquished the search to Baron de Permont, obeying his orders to attend school. That afternoon, Dorothy had been at home, ready with logical tales of passport checks, of being permitted to sleep in somebody's office after curfew. A fiction. Ann knew now that her parents had been at the avenue Foch Gestapo headquarters. *Oh, poor, terrified Daddy* . . . A month later, Gilberte and her parents had disappeared. . . .

Ann was jarred from the past by the beeping ring of a French phone. She reached hastily before the sound could awaken the household.

A local operator told her Calcutta was on the line for Madame Porter. The connection was tenuous. She needed to shout every sentence several times. Gilberte was in a coma. *A coma.* The doctors were being cagey. *They don't seem to know her condition.* No, they weren't planning an operation. *There had been no mention of surgery.* When would he get to Paris? *What was that? How long?* Her throat was raw when she hung up.

She replaced the two reports in Gilberte's briefcase, padding back to the silk-paneled guest room. Her muscles ached as if she'd been at some unaccustomed exercise for hours.

The past mornings she had been dressed by the time the cook brought her breakfast tray. Today she was still in bed. The burden of false guilt that Gilberte had knowingly placed on Quent was as heavy and lethal as the rocks loaded onto his shoulders at the Mauthausen quarry.

Ann could not force herself back to the hospital room.

78

She was in an endless, curving corridor, a tubular white labyrinth that swayed and dipped so that balance was impossible, forcing her to drag herself on hands and knees. At some point, she accepted that she was winding through Time itself. No sun or moon divided the days and months so she had no way of knowing how long her journey had lasted, nor was there any means of knowing how much farther she must travel, there was only this weary crawl through the white, elastic tunnel of eternity. . . . Then, without comprehending why or how, she was hauling herself onto a stable resting place. Now, however, she could no longer see where she was. She decided she must be a peregrine falcon with eyelids sewn together in training for the hunt. Laboriously she puzzled out this supposition, and decided it was impossible. Falcons belonged on a dark brown, mold-ruined canvas. This thought conjured up a fiercely proud bird perched on the gloved fist of an early de Permont.

My name, she thought, *is Gilberte de Permont Dejong.*

She forced her eyes open. A blazing yellow, the light of a thousand suns, blinding as the incandescent flash of an H-bomb. She shut her eyes in terror. Fear now seemed her oldest comrade. Why? She recalled being prodded and poked, stabbed in the arm, helplessly suffering things thrust up her nose and urethra. Where was she? Prison? Was she coming to after torture?

Her skin prickled everywhere with benumbed pins and needles. One arm sent out pain signals yet was assuredly paralyzed. Her face was covered, but she dared not move her free hand to explore the covering. She heard an echoing sound. Not attempting to open her eyes, she became a surveillant eavesdropper. A man and woman began speaking. Though the conversation resounded, blurring against her eardrums, she sensed it was being conducted in normally pitched French. She made out a word: *the patient.*

I'm in hospital, Gilberte thought.

The wadding in her brain cleared briefly. The man was a doctor, the woman a nurse, and they were discussing her.

"The left eyelid moved last night," the nurse said.

"Why didn't you telephone me? I could have had good news when I spoke to Monsieur Dejong."

"Is he still in Calcutta?"

"He's chartered an airplane—these rich Americans, money is their magic carpet. He'll be here in a day or so."

The left side of Gilberte's head throbbed as though she were being struck with a burning steel paddle. Her thought processes were becoming less labored, though. *Quent's coming. I've been unconscious. How long? What happened to me?*

Then she remembered being on the boulevard Suchet, and a violent lurch of the car.

She opened her eyes.

The eerie brilliance was not so blinding, and she was able to make out a black smudge at the foot of the bed. The smudge separated into two silhouettes.

"Mon dieu!" The woman's voice. "Look!"

Gilberte closed her eyes, surrendering to the reverberations of footsteps.

"Madame Dejong?"

A head hung above her. She saw, blurrily, as if superimposed on the light, a mustache and little goatee. "Madame Dejong. You're awake."

"How long have I been here?" With enormous effort she squeezed out a webby tissue of sound.

"Yes, yes, you're in hospital."

She repeated the question.

"You want to know why? A nasty accident. But you've had a fine rest."

"Head . . . hurts . . ."

"Yes, he'll be here soon. And your friend, Mrs. Porter, has come from the States."

Ann.

Gilberte vaguely recalled something calamitous connected with Ann, then the memory drifted away and she accepted that her friend had come to her.

"She's been here constantly," the doctor said. "I have no doubt you'll see her today."

Slowly the small muscles under the bandaging tugged Gilberte's bruised and swollen lips into a smile of gratitude.

The remainder of the day she drowsed much of the time. Awakening, she would think of Ann, and if by chance remembrance whispered, she refused to hear its malevolent voice. Her friend had been to the hospital. Her friend had flown to Paris to be with her.

The next morning that mucilage, that mental sluggishness, no longer protected Gilberte and she couldn't evade the knowledge that Ann was her bitterest rival, her inherited enemy. Her thoughts took a natural path to the dossiers. *For my eyes only,* she thought. *They must never be seen by anyone else.* She remembered her doubts just before the accident. *Did I lock them back in my briefcase?*

She pulled away from the nurse's ministrations, demanding coffee. Sipping sweetened, tepid *café au lait* through a glass straw, she continued to fret. *I'll have Ann bring me my briefcase,* she decided.

Ann didn't come that morning. In the early afternoon, when the doctor visited, he attributed his patient's ceaseless fidgeting to discomfort from the tractioned arm and ordered a sedative. She dozed on and off: each time she awoke now, however, her mind was alive with questions. Ann had flown the Atlantic to her side, Ann had been a constant visitor. Why wasn't she here now? Why wasn't there so much as a telephone inquiry? Gilberte's conviction that Ann had stumbled on those dossiers rose. By nightfall her anxiety had eclipsed her pain, the benumbing sedatives and her swirl of lesser emotions.

* * *

In the morning, a gray, desolate wind thrashed at the linden tree outside the window. Gilberte was staring at the whipping, newly leafed branches when Ann arrived.

Ann's greeting was muted. She did not sit down.

Gilberte said, "They told me you'd been here."

"Several times."

"Your next visit, would you stop at the apartment first?"

"I'm staying there."

"Oh?" Gilberte said. "I'd like my briefcase."

"Why? You're not well enough to work."

"You've seen the reports." It was an accusation.

"I was looking for something familiar, I figured it might bring you out of your coma," Ann said. "I never intended to snoop."

"Well, how does your dear father appear to you now?"

"Gilberte, now's not the right time to—"

" 'A more than willing informant,' the Gestapo called him."

"He was terrified. He was frightened for my mother, can't you understand that?"

"Don't you think my father had a few minor qualms about letting *my* mother be beaten to death, and me raped and tortured?"

"I've often wondered about that."

"You'd understand perfectly if you came from a background with any kind of honor. A friend doesn't betray a friend. He was a fawning, groveling creature."

Ann's full, soft mouth stiffened in resentment and anger. "He was an ordinary human being who was caught in a trap."

"I'll build a monument in his name, shall I? Do you know how I've hated myself for giving over Papa's grandson to Horace Blakely's daughter?"

"I'm sorry, Gilberte," Ann said emotionlessly.

"Being sorry will never bring back my parents, will it? At least with the Nazis, one knew where one stood. He was a worm."

"All right, Gilberte. That's enough."

"Nothing I say would ever be enough. A miserable little worm without so much as a shred of honor—"

"How can you, of all people, keep talking about honor!" Ann had moved to the windows and the angry linden branches clashed behind her. "Why have you let Quent go on believing that *he* gave your parents away? Why have you *encouraged* him to believe it?"

"There's no need for me to answer that," Gilberte said, her voice cold, as if she remained in charge of the situation, but inwardly she trembled.

"No, why should you? It's obvious. Every time you wanted something from him, every time he seemed on the point of leaving you because of something rotten you'd done, you'd drag in the guilt factor."

Gilberte's heart was beating very fast, despite the dulling morphine. "That's between me and my husband, not his little trollop."

"For God's sake, Gilberte, how could you have done it to him?"

How could she indeed? If she had to pick one regret out of the thousands that cluttered her life, this unfair, unjust means of subjugating Quent would be it. Yet how else could she have kept him for so many years? "And now, I suppose," she said, "you're about to tell me the way to atone for my deadly sins is to give him over to you?"

"Give him over? He's a human being, not a piece of furniture. But then you've never considered people's feelings, have you? Even at Madame Bernard's. I admit the girls were rough on you, but you saw them as obstacles to be climbed over. All you wanted from them was an admission of your superiority. You're pitiable, Gilberte. You've missed out on everything that's worthwhile because you've never been able to give love of any kind."

I have, I have. . . . I loved my father, I loved Michel, I loved Quent, and they've all been taken from me. "My, my, now we move on to your ritual analysis of my character."

Ann studied her a moment, then picked up her purse and umbrella. "It'd take somebody much more up on abnormal psychology than me to figure out why you're so twisted."

79

The press didn't get wind of the accident until a week after it occurred, but from then on they made up for it. Though Gilberte de Permont was not accorded the status of a Hollywood star, she was a highly publicized fashion designer whose life contained all the elements that the public found endlessly fascinating: beauty, aristocratic birth, hints of scandal, vast wealth from her marriage to a man eminently identifiable as the grandson—and sole heir—of Jason Templar. The early mentions on American radio and television announced that her injuries were probably fatal, a cliff-hanger approach copied around the world. Even the French press, preoccupied as it was with the fall of the Dien Bien Phu garrison to Communist forces, gave the automobile crash substantial coverage. The staid *New York Times* ran a front-page box that spilled into a column on the fifth page detailing her meteoric rise to fame, likening her to Christian Dior with those innovative fashion contributions of hers, the use of vivid Thai silks, last year's peasant silhouette and the recent Santa Fe Look, a laudatory career summation that resembled a premature obituary. The Hearst chain managed to hint at sexual peccadilloes by playing up the conflicting tales of her years in occupied France—had she been the collaborative mistress of a high-ranking Nazi war criminal or, like her martyred parents, a Résistance fighter brutalized for her patriotism? The marital split became public knowledge when Earl Wilson wondered in print whether the veddy, veddy posh couple would kiss and make up in the sickroom? A dozen or so stringers lounged smoking on the avenue Paul Doumer. The London *Daily Mirror* man ingeniously borrowed a florist's delivery van, almost reaching Gilberte's room with a bouquet of spring flowers. After that, the hospital chief of staff, accustomed to shaking off the fleas who gather around political figures and splashy minor royalty, hired guards to check anyone entering the gate.

It was the AP man who recognized the black-haired man rolling down the window of an American car to speak to the guard. Cameras were aimed at Quent.

With the unexpected entrance of Monsieur Dejong, the round-faced nurse abandoned her task of straightening the monogrammed blanket cover (Gilberte had ordered her own linens brought from the apartment) and scuttled into the corridor.

Quent had seen Ann before he came and spoken on the phone to Gilberte's doctors. Their warnings, though, hadn't prepared him. He halted, gazing with horrified concern at his wife's upraised arm, the bandaging swathed around her head, face and chest.

"I call it my Nefertiti look," she said.

He chuckled and went to the bed. "Sorry it took me so long. I didn't find out until I got to Calcutta, and then there was rotten flying weather."

"Better late than never," she said.

Sitting in the bedside chair, he took her unbandaged hand. Warmed by his firm grip, she felt hopeful for the first time since her set-to with Ann. (She had told the nurse she wanted no contact with Madame Porter, an unneccessary command since Ann had neither phoned nor visited.)

"What happened?" he asked. "Can you remember?"

"All I know is something slammed into the Jaguar—a small lorry, they said."

"But Gil, why were you in front of your old house? You normally went miles out of your way to avoid the boulevard Suchet."

"I don't understand it myself," she said, adding softly, "Quent, it means everything to me that you're here."

He let go of her hand.

"Shouldn't I have said that?" she asked.

Not replying, he went to the window. The midday sun slanting through the linden branches shifted dots of light and shade across his bowed shoulders.

After what seemed a long silence, she said, "I went there because I was thinking what my life would have been if Papa and Maman had lived. There would have been no torture, no rapes, no Hocherer, no Michel. I would have given you children."

"We would never have been married," he said quietly.

"What makes you say that?"

"I've had some thoughts too."

"So she showed you the files," Gilberte said bitterly.

"Ann and I don't keep any more secrets from each other."

"Some heroic father your beloved had."

"A lot of people caved in to the Gestapo."

"You didn't, my parents didn't."

His brows drew together and his voice was cold. "You've lied to me about everything, including them."

"What did you expect, marrying a woman with snakes for hair?"

Quent drew a breath. "Later," he said. "Let's hash it out later."

"But I'm interested in how you feel now." The bandages compressed Gilberte's skull until there seemed far too much blood within the curve. "What do you think about your dear little Mrs. Blakely Porter now."

"This mess had nothing to do with Ann."

"The sins of the fathers," Gilberte said.

Quent was silent for more than a minute. "You know, it's funny," he said slowly. "Ann told me that Larry was positive you had it in for him all along. It sounded typical, nothing's his fault. Now it seems I owe him an apology. You were punishing Ann through him, weren't you?"

"Do you remember our ancestor's oath? The last time I saw Papa, he reminded me of the noble Guy. He told me to avenge him in the same way. Through the generations."

"Come on, Gilberte. André never in a million years would have asked you to do that."

"But he did."

"I don't believe it. He would never, never condemn you to a life of meaningless revenge."

The visible parts of Gilberte's face were white as the bandaging. "Meaningless? What's meaningless about settling one's obligations?"

"So you deliberately tried to ruin Ann's life." His eyes had a dangerous sheen.

Fear vibrated through Gilberte's recumbent, helpless body, yet she retorted challengingly, "The daughter of the man who betrayed *your* family and ruined *my* life."

He stared at her a moment longer, then shook his head. "You're certifiable."

"Am I?" she asked.

She was laughing as he closed the door. In the silent room, her peals of laughter rang shrilly.

80

Gilberte elected to return to New York for her convalescence.

In the Fifth Avenue house, she kept to her rooms, refusing to see visitors, who soon ceased to show up. The facial lacerations healed, and the few, near invisible scars were chemically peeled away by a cosmetic surgeon. Her arm regained its full function. But still she didn't go out. Not only that, but she began refusing to take her business calls. Moe Sbicca, sitting behind her desk at Gilberte de Permont, Incorporated, finally dispatched a telegram inquiring how to finance the winter collection. Previously she had acted as her own factor, lending the corporation what was necessary, shifting money from one pocket to the other as it were. When she didn't respond to the wire, Moe took his gray fedora in hand to trudge to the Dejong Bank on Seventh Avenue, where the company paid the same interest rate as everyone else in the rag trade.

Gilberte shored up the levees of her isolation with books she couldn't remember afterward, with old movies that blurred in front of her eyes as though the tubes of her Zenith were going on the blink.

Then, suddenly, it was autumn.

On October 1, Gilberte stood at her window. It was early afternoon and the sun had risen high above the tall buildings of mid-

Manhattan to dapple through the crimson and gold trees in Central Park. Nurses wheeled baby carriages, mothers watched toddlers at play, old people in overcoats chatted on the benches and the cleanup men carried portable radios to listen to the World Series. A couple of horse-drawn carriages moved sedately amid the cars. Gilberte paid no attention to the Impressionist charm spread below her.

She was sunk in the preoccupation that had shaped her summer. How to carry out her father's command. (A bounden duty that she had long ago accepted must eventually extend to Horace Blakely's dimple-chinned little granddaughter.) As she brooded on the punitive, the dark, lunar side of her old friendship, her feelings were jumbled and confused. It was as if she were harnessed to a tyrannical engine that pulled her, willy-nilly. She despised herself, yet was unable to avoid her covenant with the dead. So she pursued each cunning scheme in her mind. As she would near her injurious goal, she would inevitably meet the large, protective form of Quent. Quent, forewarned, would always make certain that there was no hanky-panky. The sole reliable maneuver she had come up with to harm Ann in all these months was her base tactic, delaying the divorce as many years—decades—as possible.

The vacuum was roaring in the hall, an intensely irritating noise. She frowned. When the vrooming ceased she heard two of the servants talking.

"They're in New Mexico," said Mrs. Kalinska, the cook. "It's a crying shame that he can't marry her. She's a darling, that Mrs. Porter. Imagine! While her boy was dying with the polio, she remembered to keep thanking me for taking care of dear little Janey. She just sent me a lovely picture of the desert, painted it herself she did, her name's signed in the corner. I'll show you later, it's in my room."

"I'll say a rosary for her. Will she have the baby there, then?"
"Who knows?"
"When's it due?"
"Any day now."
"Poor little thing, a bastard."
The vacuum started again.

Gilberte—*la p'tite bâtarde*—pressed her knuckles against her teeth to stifle the terrible howl.

A child . . .

A child? *If I hadn't locked myself up for so many months, I'd have heard.*

Gilberte tottered across the room and dropped into the chaise longue. Ann was doing what she could not do, what she had twice pretended to do. Considering her barren state, Gilberte was convulsed by those gasping sobs that had shaken her at Michel's funeral.

She took all afternoon to integrate the shock with the many other violations to her spirit. It was dark before she realized that the news had trapped her in an untenable position. This unborn child, her father's kin, her own cousin, was Horace Blakely's grandchild, her sworn adversary.

She shifted uneasily, recalling Quent's words in the Paris hospital. *André never in a million years would have asked that. . . . He would never, never condemn you to a life of meaningless revenge.*

But Quent hadn't been in the Santé basement with them, Quent hadn't heard that last conversation.

Gilberte pressed both hands against her skull, reconstructing the nightmare.

Bruised, naked and bleeding under her school clothes, she had said, *He—or she—ought to suffer as much as you have.*

When I find out who it was, I plan to arrange that. Her father bound in the sturdy chair.

And the family, too, they should be in as much pain as yours has been. It will be like the oath Guy de Permont swore with his son.

Gilberte—

There was a pulsing at the back of her neck as though her brain were expanding then contracting. According to her gospel of the past at this point, her father had extracted her sacred vow. But instead she heard him say only her name.

The conversation had been cut off by Knecht, who with crumbs on his black tunic had come in to tell Wissman to take her back upstairs.

For as long as I live, Papa, she had said at the doorway, her voice high and racing, *the betrayer's family will suffer.*

Gilberte's eyes opened wide in horror, then squeezed shut.

There was a tap on the door.

"Madame, your dinner tray," Yvonne called.

"I'm not hungry."

Undressing with swift, jerky movements, Gilberte got into her bed.

All night swift and evil dreams rode her between baleful bouts of self-honesty, self-revelation, self-recrimination.

Why did I believe Papa asked me to promise?

Maybe on a level below consciousness she had yearned to be a true de Permont, a legally born descendant of the gallant Guy, maybe she had wanted to hang on for dear life to a tangible tie with her parents. What did it matter why? Below all explanations lay a solid bedrock of truth. In her anguish after the gang rapes, she had misheard her father.

And since then she had woven through the years in an ecstasy of vindictive ingenuity.

She awoke from the last of the nightmares at dawn. Getting up from her bed, she went without hesitation to the wall safe.

Removing the reports, she arranged them atop their manila envelopes on the brass grate. Flicking her thumb on the silver lighter, she drew a deep breath, then held the flame steadily to yellowing paper. As the pages burned, rising like black and orange birds, she experienced a catharsis, as if a poison were leaving her. Using the poker, she prodded until all traces of paper were consumed by fire.

She stared at the ashes of her vendetta with the generations of Horace Blakely. All that remained was a puddle of wax and her jealousy of her rival.

At her command, battalions of lawyers would joust until long after the as yet unborn child had reached maturity. But for those years Quent would be living with Ann, and from her own experience Gilberte knew that a family is a family is a family even on the far side of wedlock.

As a de Permont surely she had enough honor and pride not to mold the future according to the dictates of petty personal jealousy.

Her face white and coldly beautiful, she sat at her desk. She wrote steadily for over a half hour, then folded the sheets into a cream-colored envelope.

Dressing, she went downstairs. For a full minute she halted on the top step, succumbing to her past months' agoraphobia. A few cushiony white clouds pranced across the bright blue sky. The bright sunlight bounced against the cars moving up and down Fifth Avenue, windows shone like diamonds, and the massive gray block of the Metropolitan Museum was etched with gold. In the park, a slight breeze flirted with branches, teasing the turning leaves. As she watched, a flurry of copper beech leaves scooted through the iron-spike fence. The weather was fair, the weather was safe. Hugging her elbows to her sides, she forced herself down the steps.

She walked only as far as the mailbox.

Juan drove the pickup into Santa Fe early, and soon after Miss Keely, the youngish, quiet English governess, took Janey and Coriana in the new Cadillac to visit the potters in the nearby village of Tesuque. Ann and Quent finished their coffee then went for their walk (the obstetrician had prescribed two miles daily) along the unpaved road that led toward the Sangre de Cristo mountains.

Ann was enormous now, and Quent slowed his pace to hers, keeping an arm around her shoulders. His New York associates would have had a hard time recognizing him in his battered cowboy hat, old plaid shirt and Levi's. The main difference, however, showed in his face. The remoteness was gone, and he looked like his own younger, more sunny-natured brother.

When they got back to the house, the mail was spread on the refectory table. Ann gathered up the letter embossed *Mrs. Lawrence J. Porter*: Maisie, because Larry was a lousy correspondent, kept in touch about her stepdaughter's welfare, often sending Janey gift-wrapped packages from Neiman-Marcus.

Quent picked up his mail. "Something from my wife," he said, hefting a fat cream-colored envelope.

Ann looked down with the same trepidation she would show if a rattlesnake had materialized in his hands. To read about vendettas in a novel is a far different proposition from learning that a friend has dedicated her life to penalizing you.

"I'll go heat the coffee while you read it," she said.

"Who'll hold up the crucifix to ward her off?"

Their laughter was forced. No matter how well deserved their bitterness, they both felt as if they were ganging up on Gilberte when they joked about her. Quent waited to slit the envelope until Ann returned with the coffee, then they sat side by side on the *banco*, shoulders touching as they read at the same time.

Dearest Quent,

While recovering from the accident, I've been going through one of my hermit phases—yes, I know as you read this that you're dying to remind me that I dragged you out eight nights a week, as you put it. But honestly, I have gone into hiding several times before, and once again I've been an anchorite.

The unhappiness that I have caused you, the misery, is so unforgivable that I refuse to ask your pardon. And certainly I can't beg forgiveness for the lies I fed you about my parents' capture and my so-called pregnancies. You have to believe me that I never set out to be your nemesis. My admittedly flimsy excuse is that I've always loved you not too wisely, but well. I used whatever desperate means I could in my attempts to keep you.

Quent, again this is not to excuse myself, but you surely know that I am one of the walking wounded. The war has reverberated through my life, and the echoes refuse to fade away. Self-contempt is a weak word for how I feel about myself and my actions.

Enough of the confessional merde. *The point of this letter is to tell you that I agree to a divorce.*

I will be the guilty or innocent party, whichever you prefer. You set the terms of the settlement. (Frankly, I'm asking you to do this for my own good —I'll end up with considerably more than my lawyers and I would dare request.)

In return for my cooperation, I ask for one thing, which may at this point in time be extremely difficult if not impossible for you to grant.

Give me the same affection you did in Ile de France. Be my cousin, be my friend.

I don't trust myself to read over this sticky letter, so look at it as a cri de coeur *from your once and future*

Gilberte

Gilberte, Quent and Ann
Paris, 1964

81

In 1964, seven years after Gilberte Dejong obtained her divorce on grounds of desertion, the André de Permont and Vivienne Cagny Museum of French Costume Art was opened in Paris. Gilberte had plowed her business profits (these had increased annually since she had replaced Yves Roland with a plump and talented young woman from Patou) into buying and renovating the eighteenth-century house behind ancient paulownia trees on the place Furstemburg. Initially she had flinched from having the unmatched names of her parents—the running sore of her early years—incised in four-foot lettering on the marble portico. Time, however, had faded the old scandal, and the couple were emerging as Tristan and Iseult, the legendary lovers, in the spate of books that were now being published about the Résistance. Her agents had scoured the country estates for the finest antique garments that came on the market. To obtain the twentieth-century collection, she had coaxed and arrogantly bullied the couturiers as well as their clients.

And now everything was in place for the opening gala.

President de Gaulle would be the host, and the guest list included Princess Margaret and Lady Byrd Johnson as well as the pantheon of the fashion world from both sides of the Atlantic. Chanel, Vionnet, Schiaparelli, poor Molyneux, whose sight was failing, Balenciaga and young Saint Laurent, who had recently taken over the House of Dior. Charles James and Hardy Amies were coming from England. The American contingent included Mainbocher, who had designed the Duchess of Windsor's wedding dress and trousseau—the Windsors would be there too. Since many of the guests were invited at the behest of the Elysée Palace, protocol was involved and Gilberte had no part in the *placement*.

Still, the habits of a hostess die hard. She arrived at the museum before the party began, moving amid the voluble, last-minute rush of caterers and florists to check the place cards. Her knee-length claret silk evening gown was sewn all over with iridescent paillettes and appeared the *dernier cri*. In actuality it was her mother's, resurrected from the basement of the boulevard Suchet house by frog-faced Jean-Jacques de Permont. The de Permonts—including Jean-Jacques—and the proud if impoverished de Mascarets had acknowledged her as one of their own. This long-delayed familial acceptance was a source of great comfort as well as self-esteem to Gilberte.

As she reached the cards, M. Dejong, Mme. Dejong, her expression showed a secretive sadness so deep that it could not be probed.

She still loved Quent. She saw him and Ann often enough to have learned to hide the melancholy fact. These reunions, however, were always *en famille*, and tonight they would be surrounded by the brightest wits in a city famed for its malicious humor. It wouldn't matter how circumspect she was: the gladiatorial circus of the ex-wife facing the current wife would be scrutinized with relish.

To hell with them all! she told herself with a shrug of her glittering shoulders. Tonight was for her parents, and her father's cousin belonged here.

Since the apartment on the avenue Gabriel was one small part of Gilberte's record-shattering divorce settlement and since Quent had never bought another pied-à-terre in Paris, the Dejongs were staying at the George V. He was on the bedroom phone and she on the living room one, both listening to the loud sobs of a child three thousand miles away.

"Give me that again, Billy," Quent said. "I can't figure out what you're saying."

Billy gave a weeping account of the twins ganging up on him. The twins, aged ten, were Jason and Jessamyn, born out of wedlock, both redheads and both, in the fond description of their mother, absolute fiends. But whatever their faults, the twins did not gang up on Billy, as the legally born, seven-year-old heir to the Templar Trust always insisted they did.

The twins got on the line, laughingly explaining that Billy was crying because he'd just lost at Parcheesi.

Then it was Janey's turn. Janey, as exquisitely fragile as a Pre-Raphaelite maiden with her long, fair hair parted in the middle, was a true denizen of the sixties and her talk of going to a Beatles rock and roll concert with some friends from Foxcroft brought worried arguments from her stepfather.

When Quent hung up, he returned to the sitting room.

"Sometimes I feel like there's four dozen of them, not four," he said.

Ann smiled, but her eyes were mournful: for her there would always be one child missing. *He'd be twenty*, she thought. *He'd have come to Paris with us for the opening of his grandparents' museum.*

The procession of long black cars crowded the rue de l'Abbaye and the rue Jacob, edging slowly toward the place Furstemberg and the museum. As Ann and Quent emerged, the bulbs of the intricate lampposts shone down on her anxious face and his composed calm. Though he had recaptured a portion of his cousinly warmth toward Gilberte, before he saw her warnings would toll within him. Ann, whose nature let past wrongs drift away, had a far less psychological concern. Tonight everybody would be conjecturing why Quent had left Gilberte for her, a small, ordinary divorcée. What in God's name had made her decide to wear this short chiffon, which she had designed herself? (Ann still got a kick from designing, but her passion was watercolor landscapes: she'd had four one-woman showings whose success she attributed, wrongly, to Quent's circle, who had taken her to their collective bosom: even that old reprobate, his father, confided that she looked so

much like his sweet, lost Jessamyn that had he seen her first, Quent
wouldn't have stood a chance.)

It was very noisy in the high foyer. Laughter trilled above multi-
lingual conversations and the arpeggios of a string orchestra filled
in the chinks. Through the haze of cigarette smoke drifted perfumes and the rich fragrance that accompanies recent barbering.
The guests were shedding their elegantly labeled wraps and coats
before moving slowly up the sweeping double staircase. On the
first landing hung a spotlit portrait of Vivienne Cagny—the
baronne, as Ann still termed her. The artist, by misplacing eyebrows, shifting the nose and darkening the blond hair, had managed to capture her unique and malicious charm as well as the
indefinable something that had marked ViVi de Mascaret Cagny as
one of the *haute noblesse*.

Directly below the portrait stood the sternly erect, six-foot-six
figure of Charles de Gaulle, whom Ann had met several times
previously. At his side, Gilberte was a glowing flame.

When Ann reached the landing, there was a lull in the voices and
all heads swiveled in concordance. Gilberte reached out with both
hands—which were icy. "Be of good cheer," she murmured in
French. "The lions are forbidden to eat the Christians."

Ann confounded *le tout Paris* by laughing out loud and hugging
Gilberte.

After the eight superlative courses and the inevitable canticles of
praise to Gilberte and to French couture, charming, socially correct young women paraded in antique clothes.

Then the guests rose to stroll through the *musée*, inspecting each
other and the elegant tableaux set up to display the collection:
Quent was netted by an imperious and deaf dowager de Permont
who shouted stories of his maternal grandmother.

Gilberte's glittering paillette fringes danced as she moved to the
window embrasure where Ann was stifling a yawn.

"If you have a few minutes, we're close to the rue Daguerre."

"Go there *now*? Gilberte, this is your night," Ann said, and in the
same breath added, "I haven't been back since the war."

"Neither have I," said Gilberte. "But can you think of a more appropriate way to top off this extravaganza than the two of us going there?"

Gilberte told the chauffeur to stop on the rue Delambre, and their evening slippers clicked along the dark street that had been their old shortcut to and from Madame Bernard's. But where there had once been an alley that connected with the rue Daguerre now stood a new shop: *Pompes Funèbres, B. Maigne.* They were forced to go around the long way, on the boulevard Edgar Quinet.

A couple stood in a tight clinch outside the iron gates of the Montparnasse Cemetery.

"Love hath no fear of ghosts," Ann said.

"That's exactly the tone," Gilberte laughed, "that you would have used then."

"Oh, God, Gilberte! Twenty-five years . . ."

"Almost a quarter of a century, dear heart."

There was something about the rue Daguerre that seemed wrong to Ann. It took her several steps to realize it was the occasional glowing window or the gray flicker of a television: in her memory, the street observed blackout regulations.

Nearing number 74, Ann slowed. Memories of the final time she'd seen her parents swooped around her. . . . She felt the soft, dry paper of Dorothy's thin cheek in their last embrace, smelled the mustiness of Horace's tears, heard their repeated exhortations that she give up the reckless idea of fleeing Paris and play it safe. Shivering, she pulled her silk evening coat tighter around her.

Gilberte had reached the building. Her bead-embroidered shoe traced a line on the granite steps. "They've never repaired the crack," she called. "It's still here."

Ann walked slowly to her side. "Gilberte . . . Daddy never meant to harm them . . ."

Gilberte stiffened. "What a dreary place this is." Her voice rang jarringly in the moon-silvered silence. Though she had come to terms with Ann, the coefficient of her old grief could not—would never—forgive that cowardly vermin, Horace Blakely. "What could I have had in mind, dragging us over here."

She strode rapidly toward the car, and Ann followed. Neither spoke on the return through empty streets to the place Furstemberg.

Cars were leaving, and Quent stood at the bottom of the steps. Gilberte remained in her car. Ann went to hug her husband. As she pressed against him, the curtains on the past parted again. She felt the warmth of the radiant electric logs, she smelled the rare perfume of American tobacco, heard the small click as Quent, tall and infuriatingly assured, leaned forward to light Gilberte's cigarette, she recalled the exact arch of Gilberte's narrow black eyebrow as she inhaled. She heard Larry's easy laughter, felt the flush in her own cheeks as she tried to smooth out the rain-damp pleats of her uniform skirt. *How young we all were, how heartbreakingly young.* She longed with all her strength to arrest that moment, to re-create all future time from then.

Quent's chest moved and his voice reverberated against her. "Bad memories at the old stamping ground?"

"A lot of ghosts."

And she was back in the present. Linking her arm in her husband's, she pressed close to his side as they watched Gilberte's car pull away.